Her Privates We

The Middle Parts of Fortune: Somme and Ancre, 1916

Frederic Manning

To Peter Davies who made me write it

Prefatory Note

While the following pages are a record of experience on the Somme and Ancre fronts –with an interval behind the lines– during the latter half of the year 1916, and the events described in it actually happened, the characters are fictitious. It is true that in recording the conversations of the men I seemed at times to hear the voices of ghosts. Their judgments were necessarily partial and prejudiced; but prejudices and partialities provide most of the driving power of life. It is better to allow them to cancel each other, than attempt to strike an average between them. Averages are too colourless, indeed too abstract in every way, to represent concrete experience. I have drawn no portraits; and my concern has been mainly with the anonymous ranks whose opinion, often mere surmise and ill-informed but real and true for them, I have tried to represent faithfully.

War is waged by men; not by beasts, or by gods. It is a peculiarly human activity. To call it a crime against mankind is to miss at least half its significance; it is also the punishment of a crime. That raises a moral question, the kind of problem with which the present age is disinclined to deal. Perhaps some future attempt to provide a solution for it may prove to be even more astonishing than the last.

VOLUME I

On fortune's cap we are not the very button ...Then you live about her waist, or in the middle of her favours?...Faith, her privates we.

SHAKESPEARE

Chapter I

By my troth, I care not; a man can die but once; we owe God a
death ... and let it go which way it will, he that dies this year
is quit for the next. – SHAKESPEARE

The darkness was increasing rapidly, as the whole sky had clouded,
and threatened thunder. There was still some desultory shelling. When
the relief had taken over from them, they set off to return to their original
line as best they could. Bourne, who was beaten to the wide, gradually
dropped behind, and in trying to keep the others in sight missed his
footing and fell into a shell hole.

By the time he had picked himself up again, the rest of the party had
vanished and, uncertain of his direction, he stumbled on alone. He
neither hurried nor slackened his pace; he was light-headed, almost
exalted, and driven only by the desire to find an end. Somewhere,
eventually, he would sleep. He almost fell into the wrecked trench, and
after a moment's hesitation turned left, caring little where it led him.

The world seemed extraordinarily empty of men, though he knew the
ground was alive with them. He was breathing with difficulty, his mouth
and throat seemed to be cracking with dryness, and his water bottle was
empty. Coming to a dugout, he groped his way down, feeling for the
steps with his feet; a piece of Wilson canvas, hung across the passage but
twisted aside, rasped his cheek; and a few steps lower his face was
enveloped suddenly in the musty folds of a blanket. The dugout was
empty. For the moment he collapsed there, indifferent to everything.
Then, with shaking hands, he felt for his cigarettes and, putting one
between his lips, struck a match. The light revealed a candle-end stuck
by its own grease to the oval lid of a tobacco-tin, and he lit it; it was
scarcely thicker than a shilling, but it would last his time. He would
finish his cigarette, and then move on to find his company.

There was a kind of bank or seat excavated in the wall of the dugout,
and he noticed first the tattered remains of a blanket lying on it, and then,
gleaming faintly in its folds, a small metal disc reflecting the light. It was

the cap on the cork of a water bottle. Sprawling sideways, he reached it; the feel of the bottle told him it was full, and uncorking it, he put it to his lips and took a great gulp before discovering that he was swallowing neat whisky. The fiery spirit almost choked him for the moment, in his surprise he even spat some of it out; then recovering, he drank again, discreetly but sufficiently, and was meditating a more prolonged appreciation when he heard men groping their way down the steps. He re-corked the bottle, hid it quickly under the blanket, and removed himself to what might seem an innocent distance from temptation.

Three Scotsmen came in; they were almost as spent and broken as he was, that he knew by their uneven voices; but they put up a show of indifference, and were able to tell him that some of his mob were on the left, in a dugout about fifty yards away. They, too, had lost their way, and asked him questions in their turn; but he could not help them, and they developed among themselves an incoherent debate, on the question of what was the best thing for them to do in the circumstances. Their dialect only allowed him to follow their arguments imperfectly, but under the talk it was easy enough to see the irresolution of weary men seeking in their difficulties some reasonable pretext for doing nothing. It touched his own conscience, and throwing away the butt of his cigarette he decided to go. The candle was flickering feebly on the verge of extinction, and presently the dugout would be in darkness again. Prudence stifled in him an impulse to tell them of the whisky; perhaps they would find it for themselves; it was a matter which might be left for providence or chance to decide. He was moving towards the stairs, when a voice, muffled by the blanket, came from outside.

"Who are down there?"

There was no mistaking the note of authority and Bourne answered promptly. There was a pause, and then the blanket was waved aside, and an officer entered. He was Mr Clinton, with whom Bourne had fired his course at Tregelly.

"Hullo, Bourne," he began, and then seeing the other men he turned and questioned them in his soft kindly voice. His face had the greenish pallor of crude beeswax, his eyes were red and tired, his hands were as nervous as theirs, and his voice had the same note of overexcitement, but he listened to them without a sign of impatience. "Well, I don't want to hurry you men off," he said at last, "but your battalion will be moving out before we do. The best thing you can do is to cut along to it. The only about a hundred yards further down the trench. You don't want struggle back to camp by yourselves; it doesn't look well either. So you had better get moving right away. What you really want is twelve hours solid sleep, and I am only telling you the shortest road to it."

They accepted his view of the matter quietly, they were willing enough; but, like all tired men in similar conditions, they were glad to have their action determined for them; so they thanked him and wished him goodnight, if not cheerfully, at least with the air of being reasonable men, who appreciated his kindliness. Bourne made as though to follow them out, but Mr Clinton stopped him.

"Wait a minute, Bourne, and we shall go together," he said as the last Scotsman groped his way up the steeply pitched stairs. "It is indecent to follow a kilted Highlander too closely out of a dugout. Besides, I left something here."

He looked about him, went straight to the blanket, and took up the water bottle. It must have seemed lighter than he expected, for he shook it a little suspiciously before uncorking it. He took a long steady drink and paused.

"I left this bottle full of whisky," he said, "but those bloody Jocks must have smelt it. You know, Bourne, I don't go over with a skinful, as some of them do; but, by God, when I come back I want it. Here, take a pull yourself; you look as though you could do with one."

Bourne took the bottle without any hesitation; his case was much the same. One had lived instantaneously during that timeless interval, for in the shock and violence of the attack, the perilous instant, on which he stood perched so precariously, was all that the half-stunned consciousness of man could grasp; and, if he lost his grip on it, he fell back among the grotesque terrors and nightmare creatures of his own mind. Afterwards, when the strain had been finally released, in the physical exhaustion which followed, there was a collapse, in which one's emotional nature was no longer under control.

"We're in the next dugout, those who are left of us," Mr Clinton continued. "I am glad you came through all right, Bourne. You were in the last show, weren't you? It seems to me the old Hun has brought up a lot more stuff, and doesn't mean to shift, if he can help it. Anyway we should get a spell out of the line now. I don't believe there are more than a hundred of us left."

A quickening in his speech showed that the whisky was beginning to play on frayed nerves: it had steadied Bourne for the time being. The flame of the candle gave one leap and went out. Mr Clinton switched on his torch, and shoved the water bottle into the pocket of his raincoat.

"Come on," he said, making for the steps, "you and I are two of the lucky ones, Bourne; we've come through without a scratch; and if our luck holds we'll keep moving out of one bloody misery into another, until we break, see, until we break."

Bourne felt a kind of suffocation in his throat: there was nothing weak or complaining in Mr Clinton's voice, it was full of angry soreness. He switched off the light as he came to the Wilson canvas.

"Don't talk so bloody wet," Bourne said to him through the darkness. "You'll never break."

The officer gave no sign of having heard the sympathetic but indecorous rebuke. They moved along the battered trench silently. The sky flickered with the flash of guns, and an occasional star-shell flooded their path with light. As one fell slowly, Bourne saw a dead man in field grey propped up in a corner of a traverse; probably he had surrendered, wounded, and reached the trench only to die there. He looked indifferently at this piece of wreckage. The grey face was senseless and empty. As they turned the corner they were challenged by a sentry over the dugout.

"Goodnight, Bourne," said Mr Clinton quietly.

"Goodnight, sir," said Bourne, saluting; and he exchanged a few words with the sentry.

"Wish to Christ they'd get a move on," said the sentry, as Bourne turned to go down.

The dugout was full of men, and all the drawn, pitiless faces turned to see who it was as he entered, and after that flicker of interest relapsed into apathy and stupor again. The air was thick with smoke and the reek of guttering candles. He saw Shem lift a hand to attract his attention, and he managed to squeeze in beside him. They didn't speak after each had asked the other if he were all right; some kind of oppression weighed on them all, they sat like men condemned to death.

"Wonder if they'll keep us up in support?" whispered Shem. Probably that was the question they were all asking, as they sat there in their bitter resignation, with brooding enigmatic faces, hopeless, but undefeated; even the faces of boys seeming curiously old; and then it changed suddenly: there were quick hurried movements, belts were buckled, rifles taken up, and stooping, they crawled up into the air. Shem and Bourne were among the first out. They moved off at once.

Shells travelled overhead; they heard one or two bump fairly close, but they saw nothing except the sides of the trench, whitish with chalk in places, and the steel helmet and lifting swaying shoulders of the man in front, or the frantic uplifted arms of shattered trees, and the sky with the clouds broken in places, through which opened the inaccessible peace of the stars. They seemed to hurry, as though the sense of escape filled them. The walls of the communication trench became gradually lower, the track sloping upward to the surface of the ground, and at last they emerged, the officer standing aside, to watch what was left of his men file out, and form up in two ranks before him. There was little light, but under the brims of the helmets one could see living eyes moving restlessly in blank faces. His face, too, was a blank from weariness, but he stood erect, an ash-stick under his arm, as the dun-coloured shadows shuffled into some sort of order. The words of command that came from him were no more than whispers, his voice was cracked and not quite under control, though there was still some harshness in it. Then they moved off in fours, away from the crest of the ridge, towards the place they called Happy Valley.

They had not far to go. As they were approaching the tents, a crump dropped by the mule-lines, and that set them swaying a little, but not much. Captain Malet called them to attention a little later; and from the tents, camp-details, cooks, snobs, and a few unfit men, gathered in groups to watch them, with a sympathy genuine enough, but tactfully aloof; for there is a gulf between men just returned from action, and those who have not been in the show, as unbridgeable as that between the sober and the drunk. Captain Malet halted his men by the orderly-room tent. There was even a pretence to dress ranks. Then he looked at them, and they at him for a few seconds which seemed long. They were only shadows in the darkness.

"Dismiss!"

His voice was still pitched low, but they turned almost with the precision of troops on the square, each rifle was struck smartly, the officer saluting; and then the will which bound them together dissolved, the enervated muscles relaxed, and they lurched off to their tents as silent and as dispirited as beaten men. One of the tailors took his pipe out of his mouth and spat on the ground.

"They can say what they bloody well like," he said appreciatively, "but we're a fuckin' fine mob."

Once during the night Bourne started up in an access of inexplicable horror, and after a moment of bewildered recollection, turned over and tried to sleep again. He remembered nothing of the nightmare which had roused him, if it were a nightmare, but gradually his awakened sense felt a vague restlessness troubling equally the other men. He noticed it first in Shem, whose body, almost touching his own, gave a quick, convulsive jump, and continued twitching for a moment, while he muttered unintelligibly, and worked his lips as though he were trying to moisten them. The obscure disquiet passed fitfully from one to another, lips parted with the sound of a bubble bursting, teeth met grinding as the jaws worked. There were little whimperings which quickened into sobs, passed into long shuddering moans, or culminated in angry, half-articulate obscenities and then relapsed, with fretful, uneasy movements and heavy breathing, into a more profound sleep.

Even though Bourne tried to persuade himself that these convulsive agonies were merely reflex actions, part of an unconscious physical process, through which the disordered nerves sought to readjust themselves, or to perform belatedly some instinctive movement which an over-riding will had thwarted at its original inception, his own conscious mind now filled itself with the passions, of which the mutterings and twitchings heard in the darkness were only the unconscious mimicry. The senses certainly have, in some measure, an independent activity of their own, and remain vigilant even in the mind's eclipse. The darkness seemed to him to be filled with the shudderings of tormented flesh, as though something diabolically evil probed curiously to find a quick sensitive nerve and wring from it a reluctant cry of pain.

At last, unable to ignore the sense of misery which filled him, he sat up and lit the inevitable cigarette. The formless terrors haunting their sleep took shape for him. His mind reached back into past day, groping among obscure and broken memories, for it seemed to him now that for the greater part of the time he had been stunned and blinded, and that what he had seen, he had seen in sudden, vivid flashes, instantaneously: he felt again the tension of waiting, that became impatience, and then the immense effort to move, and the momentary relief which came with movement, the sense of unreality and dread which descended on one, and some restoration of balance as one saw other men moving forward in a way that seemed commonplace, mechanical, as though at some moment of ordinary routine; the restraint, and the haste that fought against it with every voice in one's being crying out to hurry. Hurry? One cannot hurry, alone, into nowhere, into nothing. Every impulse created immediately its own violent contradiction. The confusion and tumult in his own mind was inseparable from the senseless fury about him, each reinforcing the other.

He saw great chunks of the German line blown up, as the artillery blasted a way for them; clouds of dust and smoke screened their advance, but the Hun searched for them scrupulously; the air was alive with the rush and flutter of wings; it was ripped by screaming shells, hissing like tons of molten metal plunging suddenly into water, there was the blast and concussion of their explosion, men smashed, obliterated in sudden eruptions of earth, rent and strewn in bloody fragments, shells that were like hellcats humped and spitting, little sounds, unpleasantly close, like the plucking of tense strings, and something tangling his feet, tearing at his trousers and puttees as he stumbled over it, and then a face suddenly, an inconceivably distorted face, which raved and sobbed at him as he fell with it into a shellhole.

He saw with astonishment the bare arse of a Scotsman who had gone into action wearing only a kilt-apron; and then they righted themselves and looked at each other, bewildered and humiliated. There followed a moment of perfect lucidity, while they took a breather; and he found himself, though unwounded, wondering with an insane prudence where the nearest dressing-station was.

Other men came up; two more Gordons joined them, and then Mr Halliday, who flung himself on top of them and, keeping his head well down, called them a lot of bloody skulkers. He had a slight wound in the forearm. They made a rush forward again, the dust and smoke clearing a little, and they heard the elastic twang of Mills bombs as they reached an empty trench, very narrow where shelling had not wrecked or levelled it. Mr Halliday was hit again, in the knee, before they reached the trench, and Bourne felt something pluck the front of his tunic at the same time. They pulled Mr Halliday into the trench, and left him with one of the Gordons who had also been hit. Men were converging there, and he went forward with some of his own company again.

From the moment he had thrown himself into the shellhole with the Scotsman, something had changed in him; the conflict of tumult of his mind had gone, his mind itself seemed to have gone, to have contracted and hardened within him; fear remained, an implacable and restless fear, but that, too, seemed to have been beaten and forged into a point of exquisite sensibility and to have become indistinguishable from hate. Only the instincts of the beast survived in him, every sense was alert and in that tension was some poignancy. He neither knew where he was, nor whither he was going, he could have no plan because he could foresee nothing, everything happening was inevitable and unexpected, he was an act in a whole chain of acts; and, though his movements had to conform to those of others, spontaneously, as part of some infinitely flexible plan, which he could not comprehend very clearly even in regard to its immediate object, he could rely on no one but himself.

They worked round a point still held by machine-guns, through a rather intricate system of trenches linking up shell-craters. The trenches were little more than boltholes, through which the machine gunners, after they had held up the advancing infantry as long as possible, might hope to escape to some other appointed position further back, and resume their work, thus gaining time for the troops behind to recover from the effect of the bombardment, and emerge from their hiding places. They were singularly brave men, these Prussian machine-gunners, but the extreme of heroism, alike in foe or friend, is indistinguishable from despair.

Bourne found himself playing again a game of his childhood, though not now among rocks from which reverberated heat quivered in wavy films, but in made fissures too chalky and unweathered for adequate concealment. One has not, perhaps, at thirty years the same zest in the game as one had at thirteen, but the sense of danger brought into play a latent experience which had become a kind of instinct with him, and he moved in those tortuous ways with the furtive cunning of a stoat or weasel. Stooping low at an angle in the trench, he saw the next comparatively straight length empty and, when the man behind was close to him, ran forward still stooping. The advancing line, hung up at one point, inevitably tended to surround it, and it was suddenly abandoned by the few men holding it.

Bourne, running, checked as a running Hun rounded the further angle precipitately, saw him prop, shrink back into a defensive posture, and fired without lifting the butt of his rifle quite level with his right breast. The man fell, shot in the face, and someone screamed at Bourne to go on; the body choked the narrow angle, and when he put his foot on it squirmed or moved, making him check again, fortunately, as a bomb exploded a couple of yards round the corner. He turned, dismayed, on the man behind him, but behind the bomber he saw the grim bulk of Captain Malet, and his strangely exultant face; and Bourne, incapable of articulate speech, could only wave a hand to indicate the way he divined the Huns to have gone.

Captain Malet swung himself above ground, and the men, following, overflowed the narrow channel of the trench; but the two waves, which had swept round the machine-gun post, were now on the point of meeting; men bunched together, and there were some casualties among them before they went to ground again. Captain Malet gave him a word in passing, and Bourne, looking at him with dull uncomprehending eyes, lagged a little to let others intervene between them. He had found himself immediately afterwards next to Company-Sergeant-Major Glasspool, who nodded to him swiftly and appreciatively; and then Bourne understood. He was doing the right thing. In that last rush he had gone on and got into the lead, somehow, for a brief moment; but he realised himself that he had only gone on because he had been unable to stand still. The sense of being one in a crowd did not give him the same confidence as at the start, the present stage seemed to call for a little more personal freedom. Presently, just because they were together, they would rush something in a hurry instead of stalking it. Two men of another regiment, who had presumably got lost, broke back momentarily demoralised, and Sergeant-Major Glasspool confronted them.

"Where the bloody hell do you reckon you're going?"

He rapped out the question with the staccato of a machine-gun; facing their hysterical disorder, he was the living embodiment of a threat.

"We were ordered back," one said, shamefaced and fearful.

"Yes. You take your fuckin' orders from Fritz," Glasspool, white-lipped and with heaving chest, shot sneeringly at them. They came to heel quietly enough, but all the rage and hatred in their hearts found an object in him, now. He forgot them as soon as he found them in hand.

"You're all right, chum," whispered Bourne, to the one who had spoken. "Get among your own mob again as soon as there's a chance." The man only looked at him stonily. In the next rush forward something struck Bourne's helmet, knocking it back over the nape of his neck so that the chinstrap tore his ears. For the moment he thought he had been knocked out, he had bitten his tongue, too, and his mouth was salt with blood. The blow had left a deep dent in the helmet, just fracturing the steel. He was still dazed and shaken when they reached some building ruins, which he seemed to remember. They were near the railway station.

He wished he could sleep, he was heavy with it; but his restless memory made sleep seem something to be resisted as too like death. He closed his eyes and had a vision of men advancing under a rain of shells. They had seemed so toy-like, so trivial and ineffective when opposed to that overwhelming wrath, and yet they had moved forward mechanically as though they were hypnotised or fascinated by some superior will. That had been one of Bourne's most vivid impressions in action, a man close to him moving forward with the jerky motion a clockwork toy has when it is running down; and it had been vivid to him because of the relief with which he had turned to it and away from the confusion and tumult of his own mind. It had seemed impossible to relate that petty, commonplace, unheroic figure, in ill-fitting khaki and a helmet like the barber's basin with which Don Quixote made shift on his adventures, to the moral and spiritual conflict, almost superhuman in its agony, within him.

Power is measured by the amount of resistance which it overcomes, and, in the last resort, the moral power of men was greater than any purely material force which could be brought to bear on it. It took the chance of death, as one of the chances it was bound to take; though, paradoxically enough, the function of our moral nature consists solely in the assertion of one's own individual will against anything which may be opposed to it, and death, therefore, would imply its extinction in the particular and individual case. The true inwardness of tragedy lies in the fact that its failure is only apparent, and as in the case of the martyr also, the moral conscience of man has made its own deliberate choice, and asserted the freedom of its being. The sense of wasted effort is only true for meaner and more material natures. It took the more horrible chance of mutilation. But as far as Bourne himself, and probably also, since the moral impulse is not necessarily an intellectual act, as far as the majority of his comrades were concerned, its strength and its weakness were inseparably entangled in each other.

Whether a man be killed by a rifle bullet through the brain, or blown into fragments by a high-explosive shell, may seem a matter of indifference to the conscientious objector, or to any other equally well-placed observer, who in point of fact is probably right; but to the poor fool who is a candidate for posthumous honours, and necessarily takes a more directly interested view, it is a question of importance. He is, perhaps, the victim of an illusion, like all who, in the words of Paul, are fools for Christ's sake; but he has seen one man shot cleanly in his tracks and left face downwards, dead, and he has seen another torn into bloody tatters as by some invisible beast, and these experiences had nothing illusory about them: they were actual facts. Death, of course, like chastity, admits of no degree; a man is dead or not dead, and a man is just as dead by one means as by another; but it is infinitely more horrible and revolting to see a man shattered and eviscerated, than to see him shot. And one sees such things; and one suffers vicariously, with the inalienable sympathy of man for man. One forgets quickly. The mind is averted as well as the eyes. It reassures itself after that first despairing cry: "It is I!"

"No, it is not I. I shall not be like that."

And one moves on, leaving the mauled and bloody thing behind: gambling, in fact, on that implicit assurance each one of us has of his own immortality. One forgets, but he will remember again later, if only in his sleep.

After all, the dead are quiet. Nothing in the world is more still than a dead man. One sees men living, living, as it were, desperately, and then suddenly emptied of life. A man dies and stiffens into something like a wooden dummy, at which one glances for a second with a furtive curiosity. Suddenly he remembered the dead in Trones Wood, the unburied dead with whom one lived, he might say, cheek by jowl, Briton and Hun impartially confounded, festering, fly-blown corruption, the pasture of rats, blackening in the heat, swollen with distended bellies, or shrivelling away within their mouldering rags; and even when night covered them, one vented in the wind the stench of death. Out of one bloody misery into another, until we break. One must not break. He took in his breath suddenly in a shaken sob, and the mind relinquished its hopeless business. The warm smelly darkness of the tent seemed almost luxurious ease. He drowsed heavily; dreaming of womanly softness, sweetness; but their faces slipped away from him like the reflections in water when the wind shakes it, and his soul sank deeply and more deeply into the healing of oblivion.

Chapter II

But I had not so much of man in me
And all my mother came into mine eyes
And gave me up to tears. – SHAKESPEARE

It was late when they woke, but they were reluctant to move. Their tent gave them the only privacy they knew, and they wanted to lie hidden until they had recovered their nerve. Among themselves they were unselfish, even gentle; instinctively helping each other, for, having shared the same experience, there was a tacit understanding between them. They knew each other, and their rival egoisms had already established among them a balance and discipline of their own. They kept their feelings very much to themselves. No one troubled them, and they might have lain there for hours, preoccupied with their own formless and intangible reveries, or merely brooding vacantly; but whatever remote and inaccessible world the mind may elect to inhabit, the body has its own inexorable routine. It drove them out in the end to the open, unscreened trench which served as a latrine. This is furnished with a pole, closer to one side than to the other, and resting at either end on piled-up sods, and on this insecure perch they sat, and while they sat there they hunted and killed the lice on their bodies.

There was something insolent even in the way they tightened their belts, hawked, and spat in the dust. They had been through it, and having been through it, they had lapsed a little lower than savages, into the mere brute. Life for them held nothing new in the matter of humiliation. Men of the new drafts wondered foolishly at their haggard and filthy appearance. Even the details kept a little aloof from them, as from men with whom it might be dangerous to meddle, and perhaps there was something in their sad, pitiless faces to evoke in others a kind of primitive awe. They for their part went silently about the camp, carrying themselves, in their stained and tattered uniforms, with scornful indifference. They may have glanced casually at the newcomers, still trim and neat from the bullring at Rouen, who were to fill the place of the

lying out in all weathers on the downland between Delville
...es and Guillemont, but if one of the new men spoke to them,
with unrecognising eyes and curt monosyllables.

Outside the tents two or three men would come together and ask after
their friends.

"Where's Dixon?"

"Gone west. Blown to fuckin' bits as soon as we got out of the trench,
poor bugger. Young Williams was 'it same time, 'ad most of an arm
blown off, but 'e got back into the trench. Same shell, I think. Anyway, it
were the first thing I see."

They spoke with anxious, low voices, still unsteady and inclined to
break; but control was gradually returning; and all that pity carried with
it a sense of relief that the speaker, somehow, but quite incredibly, had
himself managed to survive.

When breakfast came they seemed at first to have no appetite, but once
they had started, they ate like famishing wolves, mopping up the last
smear of bacon fat and charred fragments from the bottom of the pan
with their bread. When they returned to camp on the previous night, there
had been tea waiting for them, a rum issue left very largely to the
indiscretion of the storekeeper, and sandwiches of cold boiled bacon.
Bourne had drunk all he could get; but on biting into a sandwich it had
seemed to chew up into so much dry putty in his mouth, and he had
stuffed the rest of his ration away in his haversack. The other men had
been much the same, none of them had had any stomach for food then,
though the sandwiches were freshly cut with liberal mustard on them;
now, though they had turned dry and hard and the bread had soured, they
were disinterred from dirty haversacks and eaten ravenously.

Gradually their apathy cleared and lifted, as first their bodily functions,
and then their habits of life asserted themselves. One after another they
started shaving. Bourne and Shem had an arrangement by which they
fetched and carried for each other alternately, and it was Bourne's job
today. There was a shortage of water, and rather stringent regulations
concerning its use. Bourne had long ago come to the conclusion that
there was too much bloody discipline in the British Army, and he
managed to procure, on loan, a large tin, which had been converted into a
bucket by the addition of a wire handle. He got this more than half full of
water, as well as a mess-tin full of hot water from one of the cooks, and

going and coming he worked round behind the officers' tents, so as to avoid other companies' lines, and sergeants or sergeant-majors, who, zealous in the matter of discipline, might have hypothecated both the bucket and water for their own personal use. Then, out of sight behind their own tent, he and Shem washed and shaved. They had not had a bath for five weeks, but curiously enough, their skins, under their shirts, were like satin, supple and lustrous; the sweat washed out the dirt, and was absorbed with it into their clothing which had a sour, stale, and rather saline smell. They were not very lousy.

They had achieved more of the semblance than the reality of cleanliness and were drying themselves when Corporal Tozer, who knew their value, came round to the back of the tent and looked at the water, already grey and curdled with dirt and soap.

"You two are the champion bloody scroungers in the battalion," he said; and it was impossible to know whether he were more moved by admiration or by disgust. Shem, whose eyes were like the fish pools of Heshbon, turned on him an expression of mingled innocence and apprehension; but Bourne only looked on indifferently as the corporal, making a cup of his hand, skimmed off the curdled scum before dashing the dirty water over his own head and neck. Bourne had no modesty in the demands he made on his friends, and he had got the water from Abbot, the company cook, by asking for it casually, while discussing the possibility of procuring, illegally, a grilled steak for his dinner, preferably with fried onions, which for the time being proved unobtainable.

"Tell me when you've finished with the bucket, will you, corporal?" he said quietly as he turned to go back to the tent with Shem. Before putting on his tunic, after taking it outside to brush rather perfunctorily, he looked at the pockets which the machine gun bullet had torn. The pull of his belt had caused them to project a little, and the bullet had entered one pocket and passed out through the other, after denting the metal case of his shaving-stick, which he had forgotten to put into his pack, but had pocketed at the last moment. His haversack had been hit too, probably by a spent fragment of a shell; but the most impressive damage was the dent, with a ragged fissure in it, in his tin hat. His pulse quickened slightly as he considered it, for it had been a pretty near thing for him.

Then he heard Pritchard talking to little Martlow on the other side of the tent.

"...both 'is legs 'ad bin blown off, pore bugger; an' 'e were dyin' so quick you could see it. But 'e tried to stand up on 'is feet. `'elp me up,' 'e sez, `'elp me up.'--`You lie still, chum,' I sez to 'im, `you'll be all right presently.' An 'e jes give me one look, like 'e were puzzled, an' 'e died."

Bourne felt all his muscles tighten. Tears were running down Pritchard's inflexible face, like raindrops down a window pane; but there was not a quiver in his voice, only that high unnatural note which a boy's has when it is breaking; and then for the first time Bourne noticed that Swale, Pritchard's bed-chum, was not there; he had not missed him before. He could only stare at Pritchard, while his own sight blurred in sympathy.

"Well, anyway," said Martlow, desperately comforting; "'e couldn't 'ave felt much, could 'e, if 'e said that?"

"I don't know what 'e felt," said Pritchard with slowly filling bitterness, "I know what I felt."

"Bourne, you can take that bloody bucket back to where you pinched it from," said Corporal Tozer, as he came into the tent, wiping the soap out of his ears with a wet and dirty towel, and Bourne slipped out as inconspicuously as a cat. Still rubbing his neck and ears, Corporal Tozer caught sight of Pritchard's face, and noticed the constraint of the others. Then he remembered Swale.

"Get those blankets folded and put the tent to rights," he said quietly. "You'd better open it up all round and let some air in; it stinks a bit in here."

He picked up his tunic, put it on, and buttoned it slowly. "Swale was a townie of yours, wasn't he, Pritchard?" he said suddenly. "A bloody plucky chap, an' only a kid, too. I'm damned sorry about him."

"That's all right, corporal," answered Pritchard evenly. "Bein' sorry ain't goin' to do us'ns no manner o' good. We've all the sorrow we can bear on our own, wi'out troublin' ourselves wi' that o' other folk. We 'elp each other all we can, an' when we can't 'elp the other man no more, we must jes 'elp ourselves. But I tell thee, corporal, if I thought life was never goin' to be no different, I'd as lief be bloody well dead myself."

He folded up his blanket neatly, as though he were folding up something he had finished with and would never use again. Then he looked up.

"I took 'is pay book an' some letters out o' 'is tunic pocket, but I left 'is identity disc for them as finds 'im. If our chaps hang onto what we got, there'll be some buryin' parties out. There's 'is pack, next mine. I suppose I'd better 'and them letters in at th' orderly-room. There were a couple o' smutty French photographs, which I tore up. 'E were a decent enough lad, but boys are curious about such things; don't mean no 'arm, but think 'em funny. 'Tis all in human nature. An' I'll write a letter to 'is mother. Swales is decent folk, farmin' a bit o' land, an' I'm only a labourin' man, but they always treated me fair when I worked for 'em."

"I suppose Captain Malet will write to her," said Corporal Tozer.

"Cap'n 'll write, surely," said Pritchard. "E's a gentleman is Cap'n Malet an' not one to neglect any little duties. We all knew Cap'n Malet before the war started, an' before 'e were a cap'n. But I'll write Mrs Swale a letter myself. Cap'n Malet, 'e mus' write 'undreds o' them letters, all the same way; 'cause there ain't no difference really, 'cept tha' know'st the mother, same as I do."

"Have you a wife and children of your own?" Corporal Tozer inquired, breaking away a little.

"Ad a little girl. She died when she were four, th' year before th' war. The wife can look after 'erself," he added vindictively. "I'm not worryin' about 'er. Th' bugger were never any bloody good to me."

He lapsed into a resentful silence, and the corporal was satisfied that his emotion had been diverted into other channels. The other men grinned a little as they shook the dried grass-stems and dust off the groundsheets. When they had finished tidying the tent, they sat about smoking, without their tunics, for the day was hot and airless. The corporal stood outside with his eye on the officers' tents watching for the appearance of Captain Malet. Then by chance he saw Bourne talking to Evans, who had been the colonel's servant, had been taken over in that capacity by the officer commanding them temporarily, who was a major from another regiment. Evans, who never in private referred to his new master otherwise than as "that Scotch bastard', though he had nothing Scots about him but a kilt, was now idly swinging the bucket, into which

Bourne, Shem and the corporal himself, had washed more than the dust of battle.

"E 'as some bloody 'ide, pinchin' the commandin' officer's bucket," was the corporal's only comment, turning his gaze towards the officers' tents again. Presently Bourne stood beside him.

"We're on the move, corporal," he announced.

"Who says we're on the move? Evans?" He added the name as an afterthought so that Bourne might guess he knew where the bucket came from, and not underrate either his powers of observation and inference, or his more valuable quality of discretion.

"Evans!" explained Bourne indifferently; "Oh, no! I was only giving him back his bucket. Evans never hears anything except the dirty stories the doctor tells the major in the mess. Abbot told me. He said the cookers were to be ready to move on to sand-pits at two o'clock. We're on the move all right."

"Them bloody cooks know what we're doing before the orderly-room does," said Corporal Tozer drily. "Well, if it's goodbye to the fuckin' Somme, I won't 'arf' ave a time puttin' the wind up some o' these bloody conscripts. Seen 'em yet? Buggered-up by a joy-ride in the train from Rouen to Mericourt, so they kept 'em fuckin' about the camp, while they sent us over the bloody top; you an' I, old son; in it up to the fuckin' neck, we was! When they've 'ad me at 'em for a fortnight, they'll be anxious to meet Fritz, they will. They'll be just about ready to kiss 'im."

Suddenly, he shed his confidence as Captain Malet emerged from one of the tents on the other side of the extemporised road, looking up at the sky as though he were chiefly concerned in estimating the weather prospects for the day. Then, rapidly surveying his company lines, he saw Sergeant Robinson and Corporal Tozer and waved them to him with a lift of his stick. Bourne turned, and going into the tent sat down beside Shem. When he told them what he had heard from Abbot, there was a flicker of interest; though they were not surprised, for the fighting strength of the whole battalion was by now little more than that of a single company. They were to be taken out of the line, fed with new drafts, and then thrown in again, that was all, except that whenever the new drafts were mentioned, a certain amount of feeling was shown against them.

Bourne began to be a little sorry for the new men, though some malicious imp in his mind was amused by the resentment they aroused. A draft had arrived the night before the attack, consisting of men enlisted under the Derby scheme, the first of that class to join the battalion; and there was some uncertainty concerning their temper and quality. The question had been, whether it were better to distribute the men among the different companies immediately on the eve of the attack; or to leave them out, and absorb them more slowly afterwards. Probably the commanding officer had preferred to rely entirely on men already experienced in battle, even though their numbers were rather depleted, and it might be argued very reasonably that his decision was right. At the same time, the new men suffered by it. They were friendless among strangers, without having been long enough together to form a coherent unit to themselves; being rather soft, thirty hours in a troop train tightly packed in sweltering heat and then a longish march from Mericourt, the railhead, had left them dead-beat; not being borne on the ration strength, they had at first to make shift for their provisions as best they could and, because there was nothing for them to do, all sorts of futile and unnecessary fatigues were invented by those in authority for their especial benefit. They were bullied even by the details, and stood at the beck of any storekeeper. All this, of course, was in the best tradition of the British Army; but after swanking in a service company at some training camp in Blighty, cheek by jowl with some of the slightly obsolete heroes from Mons, it was a little disheartening to find themselves suddenly precipitated again to the level of a recruit. After all, Bourne reflected, when he had come as one of a draft, he had been made to suffer similarly: but he had gone immediately into a show and that had made some difference. Presently these men would be indistinguishable from the others, and share their common experience.

Corporal Tozer reappeared in the tent.

"Parade for rollcall at eleven o'clock: fatigue order."

There was just a trace more importance than usual in his manner, and though it was barely discernible Bourne noticed it, and looked up with his incorrigible smile.

"Got an extra stripe, corporal?" he inquired.

"Don't you worry about what I've got," said the corporal. "You be bloody careful what you get."

Chapter III

Is your Englishman so expert in his drinking?
Why, he drinks you with facility your Dane dead drunk; he sweats
not to overthrow your Almain; he gives your Hollander a vomit ere
the next pottle can be filled. – SHAKESPEARE

After dinner, they moved back about two miles to another camp at Sand-pits. The invaluable and long-suffering draft had preceded them there, to make straight the ways; but the men who composed it were ill-regarded, as there was not enough tent-room for their own shelter, and they paired off, each pair trying to make a bivvy out of a couple of groundsheets fastened together by string passed through the eyelets, and then slung on a horizontal pole suspended between two uprights. Their efforts might have been more successful if it had not been for a shortage of string and wood. There was more bustle and life in the new camp, and the men who had been in action moved about more freely. After roll call a change had worked in them; the parade had brought them together again, and, somehow, in talking of their common experience they had mastered it. It ceased to be an obsession; it was something they realised as past and irrevocable, and the move to sand-pits marked a new beginning.

They were still on a shoulder of the downs, and beneath them they could see Albert, and the gilt Virgin, head downwards, poised imminent above the shattered city, like an avenging wrath. Clouds, apparently of hewn marble, piled up for a storm, and already, over the distant flats, there were skirts of rain drifting across the sunlight. An observation balloon, sausage-shaped and thickened at one end by small subsidiary ballonets, lifted itself, almost as though it was being hoisted by a series of pulls out of one of the hollows beneath them, and then hung swaying in the air, much as a buoy heaves in a tide-way. High above it some silvery gleams circled, seen fugitively and lost again, and occasionally one of these gleams would detach itself from the group and make off, leaving a little trail of vapour behind it. The men watched the balloon idly, since there were interesting possibilities in that direction: it might be shelled, or attacked by hostile aircraft and set alight, in which case the occupants would have to jump for it; then perhaps their parachutes would not open. They were rather disappointed as it continued to swing there undisturbed. Now and again, however, an aeroplane would become too inquisitive concerning other people's business, and then, suddenly, miraculously it seemed, puff after puff of white smoke appeared in its immediate neighbourhood; it would ignore these attentions contemptuously for a time, and then turn away, apparently satisfied with the result of its inquiries. There was very little excitement to be found in that quarter either, unless it was by the pilot and his observer.

"Them bloody chaps 'ave a cushy job," said little Martlow with resentful envy. "Just fly over the line, take a peek at ol' Fritz, and as soon as a bit o' shrapnel comes their way, fuck off 'ome jildy, toot sweet."

He was sprawling beside Shem and Bourne, to whom he had attached himself for the moment. Having no particular chum, he was everybody's friend; and being full of pluck, cheekiness and gaiety, he made his way very cheerfully in a somewhat hazardous world. Shem was talking to him, but Bourne was occupied with other matters and seemed to be interested in the movements of Regimental-Sergeant-Major Hope, who was at the other end of the camp.

He was interested for many reasons. At roll-call it was found that there were thirty-three men left in the company, but probably many of those absent were not severely wounded. Bourne only knew a few of the men outside his own section by name, and the only two men belonging to it whom he had actually seen wounded were Caswell and Orgee, during the last stage of the attack near the station, when they had been brought down by a machine-gun. They had crawled into shelter, and eventually a stretcher-bearer had helped them. Caswell had been hit in the upper part of the chest; and Orgee in the cheek, the bullet knocking out some teeth and breaking part of the lower jaw. Some men by him had been hurt by splinters before they went over the top. One of them, Bridgenorth, had only been slightly hurt, and had subsequently gone over the top with them, but later in the day, having been hit again, went back with some walking wounded.

It was a long business. They had gauged the extent of the losses suffered by the company as soon as they went on parade. Name after name was called, and in many cases no particulars were available. Then for a moment the general sense of loss would become focused on one individual name, while some meagre details would be given by witnesses of the man's fate; and after that he, too, faded into the past. Behind Bourne was a big stevedore from Liverpool, though he was of Cockney origin, a man called Pike, a rough, hard-bitten character, with a good heart.

"Redmain" was the name called out; and as at first there was no reply, it was repeated. "Has anyone seen anything of Redmain?" "Yes, sir," cried Pike, with sullen anger in his voice. "The poor bastard's dead, sir."

"Are you sure of that, Pike?" Captain Malet asked him quietly, ignoring everything but the question of fact. "I mean are you sure the man you saw was Redmain?"

"I saw 'im, sir; 'e were just blown to buggery," said Pike, with a feeling that was almost brutal in its directness. "E were a chum o' mine, sir, an' I seen 'im blown into fuckin' bits. 'E got it; just before we got to their first line, sir."

After a few more questions, Sergeant Robinson, calling the roll in place of Sergeant-Major Glasspool, who had been rather seriously wounded soon after Bourne had seen him in the German front line, passed to another name.

"Rideout."

Even though they could not always hear what he said, the other men would crane their heads out to watch any man giving information, and the officers questioning him. Officers and men alike seemed anxious to restrain their feelings. The bare details in themselves were impressive enough. But under that restraint one could feel the emotional stress, as when Pritchard told of Swale's end. It was only after the roll of the men had been called that the men were asked if they could give any information about Mr Watkins, or Mr Halliday.

Of those on parade, Bourne, apparently, was the only one to have seen Mr Halliday after he had been wounded, and Captain Malet had questioned him very closely. Bourne, like every man who came in touch with Captain Malet, had a great admiration for him. He was about twenty-four years of age, with a sanguine complexion, blue eyes, and fair, rather curly hair. He stood about six feet four, and was proportionately bulky, so that his mere physical presence was remarkable; at the same time, the impression he left on the mind was not one of mass, but of force, and speed.

It was his expression, his manner, something in the way he moved and spoke, which made one feel that only an enormous effort enabled him to bridle the insubordinate and destructive energy within him. Perhaps in battle it broke loose and gratified its indomitable appetites. This is not to say that he was fearless; no man is fearless, fear is one of the necessary springs of human action, but he took pleasure in daring, and the pleasures of men are probably incomplete unless some poignancy accompanies them. Just before the attack was launched, he had climbed out of the trench and walked along the parapet, less as though he were encouraging the men, than as though he were taunting them, and after they were back in their original position that night, he had found that he had forgotten his ash-stick, and had returned to the captured trenches to get it. There was nothing deliberate in either of these actions, they were purely spontaneous. He would not have gone into an attack with a hunting-horn, or dribbled a football across no-man's-land; probably he would have thought anything of the kind a piece of sentimental levity. All that he did was improvised, and perhaps he had more than his fair share of luck.

Evidently he was very much troubled about Mr Halliday, and whenever he was troubled, he became impatient and angry, not with any particular individual, but with the nature of things, and the order of the universe. Mr Watkins had been killed outright, and there was no more to be said on that point, except that he was one of many good fellows. There was nothing perfunctory in that summary regret; it was keen and deep, but one could not pause on it. The case of Mr Halliday was different. Bourne had seen him first with a slight wound in the arm, and had then seen him wounded again in the knee. Probably the bone was broken. That was in the German outpost line, and he had been left there in comparative shelter with other wounded who were helping each other. After that moment, nothing further was known of him, as they had no information of him having passed through any dressing-station. Moreover, the medical officer, after working all day, had taken the first opportunity to explore a great part of the ground, and to make sure, as far as that were possible, that no wounded had been left uncollected. Of course night and the shellholes may not have yielded up all their secrets. The problem of Mr Halliday's fate seemed insoluble. At last, Captain

Malet ceased to probe the mystery. He dropped it abruptly, and asked Bourne about himself, with a half humorous kindliness. Then, the men having been dismissed, he walked off towards the orderly-room looking preoccupied and tired.

Shortly afterwards, Captain Malet saw Corporal Tozer and asked him a good many questions about Bourne; and then a little later the corporal met the regimental, who also asked about Bourne, and added that he wished to see him when they had moved to Sand-pits. Corporal Tozer, finding that two separate lines of inquiry were converging on Bourne's somewhat insignificant person, concluded that he was to be given a stripe and told him so, as they sat smoking together after dinner, giving him besides a full account of everything that had been said. Bourne had no ambition to become an acting lance-corporal, unpaid. He preferred the anonymity of the ranks. He wished that he had not taken down his crossed guns on coming overseas, for if Mr Manson had seen them on his sleeve, he would have been put in the snipers' section, and whatever the trials and perils of a sniper's life might be, it was solitary and, up to a point, inconspicuous. Bourne's preferences were irrelevant to Corporal Tozer, who gave him good advice, which Bourne hoped was premature.

The conversation flagged for a moment, and then Corporal Tozer took it up again.

"Captain Malet's not in a very good skin today," he said; "'e 'as to take over as adjutant, temp'ry; and there ain't no bloody love lost between 'im an' the O. C., I can tell you. An' then, there's another thing: that bloody old colour-sergeant in the orderly-room, if 'e got 'arf a chance o' puttin' a knife into the regimental 'e'd take it, dam' quick, see? Well, you know what Captain Malet's like. Oh, I'm not sayin' anything against 'im; 'e knows a good man from a bad un, an' you couldn't wish for a better officer. But 'e doesn't know 'ow bloody bad some o' the bad uns can be. When you come to think of it in that way, Captain Malet ain't got no more sense than a kid at school."

"He's all right," said Bourne dispassionately; "anyway, he will always take his own line."

"Would 'e take 'is own line wi' the O. C.? Yes, 'e would too; an' a nice bloody mess 'e'd make of it. The major's only temp'ry 'imself. An' what's a man like who's only temp'ry, an' wants 'is job pukka? Why a bloody guardsman couldn't please the bugger. You take a corp'ral comin' from the first battalion, or from the second, same as I did, an' what's 'e think o' this fuckin' mob, eh? Well, it's a dam' sight worse when you get an officer from another regiment takin' command o' the battalion. E's been cribbin' everything. 'E's asked Brigade already to send 'im an officer competent to take over the duties of adjutant. Captain Malet don't want the adjutant's job; but 'e don't want Brigade to think he'll never make anything better'n a good company officer, does 'e? The colour-sergeant's just goin' to sit back, an' let 'im get on with it. 'E's due for 'is pension, an' 'e's tryin' to work 'is ticket. Then there's the regimental.'

"Well, nobody can teach the regimental his job," said Bourne, decisively.

"I'm not sayin' anything against 'im," said the corporal. "E's a friend o' yours, though I can't say I'm sweet on 'im myself. I don't mind a man bein' regimental, but 'e gives 'imself too many bloody airs, thinks 'imself more class than most of us, an' tries to talk familiar to officers as don't know enough to keep 'im in 'is place. I'm not worryin' about 'im. But what's goin' to 'appen if 'e an' the colour-sergeant start scrappin' in the orderly-room?"

The thought of a scrap in the orderly-room gladdened Bourne's jaded soul, and he had laughed softly to himself. The corporal got up, dusted bits of dead grass from his trousers, and they put their kit together for the move.

Now, listening a little distractedly to Shem and Martlow while watching the approach of the regimental-sergeant-major, Bourne turned over these matters in his mind. He did not doubt for a moment that Tozer had told him all this so that he could drop a hint to the regimental if he thought fit; and Tozer was a decent man, who wasn't trying to work off a grudge, or make mischief. The position of affairs was very much as the corporal had described it, but Bourne saw it from a slightly different angle. He had had it on the tip of his tongue, more than once in the course of the conversation, to tell the corporal that Major Blessington was a gentleman, and, whatever his private feelings for Captain Malet might be, would do nothing that was not honourable, but he had wisely refrained, for fear of seeming to imply that the corporal's standard of conduct in these matters was necessarily inferior because it was different. After all, honour, in that connection, is only an elaborate refinement of what are the decent instincts of the average man, and in the process of its refinement, perhaps there is a corresponding finesse thrown into the other scale as an off-set.

War, which tested and had wrecked already so many conventions, tested not so much the general truth of a proposition as its truth in relation to each and every individual case, and Bourne thought of many men, even men of rank, with military antecedents, whose honour, as the war increased its scope, had become a fugitive and cloistered virtue, though it would probably renew its lustre again in more costermonger times.

He did not blame them; only, after considering all possible grounds for their absence, it left him perplexed. What he did blame in them was their readiness to judge others who had at least submitted to the test. It was rather as though they wished to make some vicarious atonement for their own lapse, but a man who has forgotten the obligations of loyalty should not set up as a judge. If this conventional notion of honour would not fit into the corporal's scheme of things, he himself could safely discard it. It may have been very well so long as it had been possible to consider the army as a class or a profession, but the war had made it a world. It was full of a diversity of God's creatures: honour, with some, might be a grace, and with others duty an obligation, but self-interest, perhaps in varying measure, was common to them all. Even in the actual ecstasy of battle, when a man's soul might be torn suddenly from its scabbard to flash in an instant's brightness, it was absent not for long. When one returned to the routine of camp and billets, one had to take the practical and more selfish view, and if a nice sense of honour were unable to restrain the antipathy which the major and Captain Malet felt for each other, their own interests might be expected to provide an efficient check. It operated equally, where there were none of these niceties, with the regimental and the colour-sergeant, but here the interests did not follow the same direction.

As the colour-sergeant was quite openly working his ticket, incompetence, if calculated, might even help to procure his end, and would be charitably condoned as only another symptom of his pensionable years. If he were out to satisfy some old grudge, he had his opportunity in the present condition of affairs, and the corporal was right; but, after all, it was none of Bourne's business, apart from the fact that the regimental, when a sergeant-instructor at a training camp, had been decent to him. Anyway, he had to go and see him now; and telling Shem he would be back in a minute, he moved off to intercept his man before he should reach the sergeant-majors' tent.

"Corporal Tozer told me you wished to see me, sir."

"Hullo, Bourne, your bloody luck has brought you through again, has it? Captain Malet has been talking to me about you. I think he means to tackle you about going in for a commission when we get behind the line. We are going back for a rest. It won't be any bloody rest for me, though. I have to do the work of the whole battalion. I thought you might come along to my tent tonight, though as a matter of fact I haven't a tent to myself, in this bloody camp. Have to muck in with the company-sergeant-majors. However, you come along about nine o'clock. There's some buckshee rum. There'll be a rum ration in any case at nine o'clock, so perhaps you had better come a bit later."

"I rather wanted to see you alone, sir. I don't like butting in, where there are a lot of sergeant-majors. They probably won't like it either, and to tell you the truth I don't much care about leaving Corporal Tozer sitting in the tent. After all, I shall have to tell him where I'm going."

"Oh, that's all rot. I'll make it right with the sergeant-majors; after all I'm running this show, and I don't see why I shouldn't please myself once in a bloody while. You weren't so particular at Tregelly, when you pinched a sergeant's greatcoat and came into the sergeant's mess of the fifth-sixth with us that Sunday. Where's the difference? Bring Tozer along with you, he's in orders for an extra stripe, and we can make the excuse that he has only come along to wet it. Sergeant Robinson is to be company-sergeant-major. Poor Glasspool was pretty badly damaged, I hear. Tell Sergeant Tozer I told you to bring him."

"You tell him, sir, and tell him to bring me. It will look much better that way; and he's an awfully decent chap. I don't want a commission. But I wanted to give you a tip on the quiet. I don't know yet whether it is worth bothering about, but has that old colour-sergeant in the orderly-room got any grudge against you?'

"My good bloody man, every incompetent ass in the battalion has got a grudge against me. What's his trouble?"

"Oh. I don't know enough to say; I have just put one or two things together. Probably I hear a good many things you don't; but if he hasn't any motive, then it is not worthwhile giving a thought to the matter."

"You leave the motive to me. What's the game?"

"Well, they say that with the colonel and the adjutant both gone, and with the Major not entirely pleased with Captain Malet as adjutant, he may be able to find or make an opportunity. If I were in your place..."

"Well, I don't mind hearing your advice, even if I shouldn't take it."

"Don't anticipate him, and don't try to get in first. Let the orderly-room do its own work, instead of trying to run the whole show yourself. And if you must quarrel with him, quarrel on a point of your own choosing, not on one of his. He's pretty cunning, and he has got you weighed up."

"So have you, apparently. I thought the bugger was being a little more oily than usual. Anyway, thanks for the tip. I shall tell Sergeant Tozer to bring you along with him."

He walked off, and Bourne went back to Shem and Martlow. Several of the company-sergeant-majors and quartermaster-sergeants were with the regimental when Sergeant Tozer, whose new rank sat a little stiffly on him as yet, came up on some routine duty; and the regimental used the opportunity to make them consenting parties to his invitation.

"I'm damned glad your promotion has gone through, sergeant. Come along to us after the rum issue tonight and wet the stripe for luck. Bring Bourne with you, if you like. None of you fellows mind if Sergeant Tozer brings Bourne along, do you? He's quite a decent chap. Plays the game you know, so it won't matter for once in a way. That's all right, then; bring him along, sergeant. Bourne and I became rather pally at Tregelly; of course at a musketry camp you all muck in together more or less. I was his instructor, and when he came out here and found I was regimental, you might have thought he'd never seen me before in his life. You may tell him privately, if you like, sergeant, that Captain Malet wants him to go for a commission. Said he was a damned useful man."

A little to his surprise, Sergeant-Major Robinson indirectly supported him.

"I was goin' to ask you about Bourne, major," he said. "Thought there might be a chance to shift 'im into the signals section, where 'e'd find things a bit easier. 'E's pretty well buggered-up, an' it's not as though 'e were a slacker. 'Owever, if 'e's goin' for a commission..."

"That's just the bloody difficulty,' said the regimental. "I'd bet a level dollar that, when the captain asks him, Bourne will say he would rather stay as he is. Of course if he did, one could shove him into sigs whether he liked it or not; that's if we don't get enough trained signallers in the new drafts. You can't put an untrained man in, if there are trained men waiting. After all, we don't get much chance of training men ourselves."

"Well, if I'd my way," said Sergeant-Major Robinson obstinately, "I'd let them bloody conscripts sweat a bit first."

"It's no damned good talking," answered the regimental. "We've got to make the best of 'em. Once they're here you can't make any difference between them and the older men. They've got to shake down together, and you know it as well as I do. A good many of them are boys, too, who couldn't have come sooner."

Considering little Martlow and Evans, neither of whom were seventeen, the sergeant-major remained unconvinced; but he recognised the expediency of the argument, and no more was said. Sergeant Tozer walked off, surprised and flattered, both by the invitation and the manner of it. His importance showed a definite increase.

"I don't want to go and butt in among a lot of sergeant-majors," said Bourne petulantly, and his manner by no means implied that he considered sergeant-majors to be the salt of the earth. Then, with apparent reluctance, he allowed himself to be persuaded, Shem intervening effectively.

"Take your cooker," said that astute counsellor. "It'll do as a mug; and then if you can scrounge any buckshee rum for tea in the morning, the cover will keep it good. See, it fits quite tight."

Army rum is potent stuff, especially when the supplies of tea and water have run out, and one drinks it neat out of a dixie. They had just settled down comfortably, and the regimental was telling them some of his experiences with Bourne at Tregelly, when Major Blessington returned from visiting friends in the neighbourhood and was heard shouting outside the tent. The regimental buttoned himself into his tunic hurriedly, shoved on a cap, and went out. The others in the tent heard the commanding officer say:

"Sergeant-major, don't you think there's rather a lot of light showing from the camp? Oh, I don't mean from your tent."

ey heard the regimental, full of zeal, and bursting with
l blasphemy.

at light out! Put that light out!" His voice showed he was
moving bout the camp. "Put that bloody light out!"

"Put two o' them fuckin' candles out, Thompson, and please the
bugger," said Hales, quartermaster-sergeant of B Company, who was one
of the party in the sergeant-majors' tent, to the storekeeper. "E's as fussy
as five folks, now 'e's out o' the bloody line again. 'E don't stir up there
no more'n a mouse. It don't make no differ to us; we can find the way to
our mouths in the dark. 'Ave you got a bit o' cheese there 'andy? I could
fancy a bit o' cheese."

Major Blessington had retired to his tent, determined in his mind that
now they were going behind the line he would lick this sloppy mob into
something like shape.

"That bugger takes me for a bloody lance-jack," said the regimental,
hot and indignant, on his return. "Who put out those candles?" "I told
Thompson to put two of 'em out," said Hales, "just to please the bastard.
'E can light 'em again now, if you like."

"He expects me to go to kip in the fuckin' dark, I suppose? Give me
some more of that bloody rum, Thompson. I've been shouting myself
hoarse. What was I saying? Oh, yes! About how Bourne and I palled up
at Tregelly. Well, there were these two bloody great Lancashire laddies
firing their course there, and they were so thick you could never separate
the buggers, but on the Saturday they went into Sandby for a spree, and
got properly pissed-up there. They picked up with some woman or other,
and she walked part of the way back with them over the golf links.

"I don't know exactly what happened, but when they came back into
camp they started out to call each other everything they could get their
bloody tongues round, and things went from bad to worse until one of
'em fetched the other an almighty clout on the jaw, which toppled the
bugger over. When he got on his feet again, he went absobloody-lutely
fanti; picked up a bayonet, and wounded his best pal in the arse. Of
course he bled all over the fuckin' hut, and that sobered him up a bit, but
by that time every bugger there was trying to get the bayonet away from
the other artist. Old Teddy Coombes got it. Do you remember old
Teddy? Well, when the wounded man saw his best pal in the centre of
what looked like a Rugby scrum--you know how all Lancashire men

fight with their feet, it comes o' wearing clogs, I suppose--he sailed in again from behind shouting out, 'I'm comin' Bill; give the buggers hell.' Bill was biting one of the recruits in the calf of the leg at that particular moment, so he didn't really need any bloody encouragement."

"Just at that moment I got back from the sergeants' mess, so I began to take a lively interest in the proceedings myself, and the next minute there were two bloody scrums where there'd only been one before. However, at the end of the discussion, and it was a first-class scrap I can tell you, there was Teddy Coombes with about ten recruits sitting on one of the fuckin' heroes, and there was I with another ten sitting on the other; and when you couldn't hear anything else but loud breathing, two of the military police came in and wanted to know in a superior way what the fuckin' hell all the noise was about. Would you credit it? Those two buggers had been at the door the whole time, and had been in too big a bloody funk to come in, until it was all over and they knew they weren't wanted. Of course it was all up then; but it took a small army to march those two Lancashire laddies down to the clink all the same. They were a bonny pair all right. When I'd wiped the sweat from my face, and was taking stock of the situation, the first thing I noticed was Bourne, sitting up in his bed quite quietly, smoking a fag; and looking as though he thought the whole thing in very poor taste.'

"I wasn't taking any fortresses that night," said Bourne contentedly. He was drinking rum out of an enamelled mug; and the cooker with cover complete had passed, quite openly, so as to escape remark, into the hands of the storekeeper.

"It made me bloody wild to see him sitting there like that. It didn't seem to me that there was any esprit de corps about it. All right, you bugger, I said to myself, meaning him of course, I'll get you yet. I didn't know him then. Do you know Sergeant Trent? A first battalion man. I had been up at the mess with him, but he didn't know anything about the scrap, as he'd gone straight down to the big barrack-room. He was going to put in for a pass until midnight on Monday, and make an excuse that he wanted to see his wife. Well, our two sportsmen from Lancashire, one of whom was suffering from what the M. O. described as a superficial flesh wound, though it would have been a damned sight more serious if he'd had it himself; they spent all Sunday recovering in the clink, and on

Monday, after we got back from the range, they were up before the camp commandant.

"Bourne was escort; and you never, in all your life, saw anything so bloody funny as Bourne leading in my two Lancashire lads, either of whom could have put him in one of their pockets and kept him there. They'd nothing to say, very wisely, except that they really loved each other like brothers, and that the whole episode had been a pure accident. The commandant was unsympathetic, and asked them whether they would take his punishment or go before a court-martial; and again very wisely they left it to him. You couldn't have met a nicer pair of lads on the whole, except for their bad habits. He gave them all he could give them, which was a hundred and sixty-eight hours' cells.

"Well, they had to have an escort to Milharbour, and I arranged with the officer that Bourne and I should be the escort, the general idea being, of course, that if there were any more bloody trouble lying about he could help himself to all he wanted and a bit more as well; or if the lambs went quietly, then Bourne and Sergeant Trent and myself could have a merry party in Milharbour after we had handed them over, Bourne to be in the chair. We tried to put wind up him by telling him they were pretty hard-bitten offenders, and he seemed to mop it up. We got to the station, and then Sergeant Trent and I saw two pushers we knew from Sandby on the train, and Trent was pretty keen on one of them..."

"Thought you said 'e 'ad a wife in Milharbour?' interrupted Company-Quartermaster-Sergeant Hales, with the solemnity of a man who is a little drunk but still unsatisfied.

"Well, she was no fuckin' use to him when he was at Tregelly, was she? She didn't live at Milharbour, either; and he wasn't going to see her anyway. He was very fond of her really, and wouldn't have done anything to hurt her feelings for a lot. Would he, Bourne?"

"They were a most devoted couple, sir," said Bourne tersely.

"Well, Sergeant Trent and I got in with the two pushers, and left Bourne with the two prisoners. How did you get on with them, Bourne?"

"Oh, we hit it off all right, sir,' said Bourne indifferently. "Of course, you had given me orders to treat them strictly. They were two able-bodied six-footers, accustomed to chucking tons of coal about, and I stood a pretty poor chance if they chose to make a rough house of it. Besides they had their kitbags with them, as well as their rifles: and they could have brained me with either. Of course, I may have looked pretty in belt and bayonet, but I was not exactly filled with confide. My business was to establish a moral superiority over two members of the criminal classes. One of them turned to me as soon as the train started, and said: "Can we smoke, chum?" I said no, like a fool; and they turned away quietly and looked out of the windows at the sea. Well, I was sorry for them and I wanted to smoke myself; and if they couldn't smoke because they were prisoners, I couldn't either, because I was on duty. You had told me I was to treat them strictly, but after all, sir, you had deserted from duty..."

"I like your blasted cheek," exclaimed the regimental, surprised; but there was a general appreciation of the point, and Bourne continued tranquilly.

"...so I had to take such practical measures as I thought best, and I took out my cigarette case, and handed it to them. The man who had been wounded was not too well. I expect his behind was sore. I carried his kitbag for him when we changed trains at Pembroke; and then again up the hill to the gate. You and Sergeant Trent didn't come on the scene again until I had landed my prisoners in the guardroom, and the sergeant wouldn't take them over from me because you had the ticket. In the interval the prisoners and I had all become quite friendly."

"I wonder you didn't tell them to cut and run for it," said the regimental ironically. "After I handed over the prisoners, Sergeant Trent and I went into the mess and had a bottle of Bass each, and gave Bourne one at the back door. Then the three of us went up to Sergeant Willis's bunk; we had some tea there and passed the time until the boozers had opened. We thought we had got Bourne weighed up, and he was only a bloody fool. He was a bloody masterpiece.

"As soon as we got into a boozer, we started mopping up the beer, and he had drink for drink with us, beer or stout, but then he said he was tired of long drinks, and suggested that we had better have some gin and bitters. We improved quite a lot on that, but it didn't seem to make any difference to Bourne, who said we ought to have a meal. We were down in the Hare and Hounds then, in the back parlour. He ordered some steak and onions, but we couldn't eat much, though he seemed pretty hungry, and when we sat down to the table he said we had better make a party of it, and he ordered some champagne. Oh, he took charge all right, and did the thing properly; said he wanted a sweet, and as they didn't have anything but tinned peaches, ordered those, and told us liqueur brandy was the proper stuff to drink with tinned peaches. There were two girls there, Sergeant Trent was a bit sweet on..."

"Sergeant Trent be blowed, sir," interrupted Bourne. "I don't know anything about the two girls in the train, but the girl at the pub was your affair; only you didn't want it known because your affections were ostensibly engaged in another part of the town. After all, Sergeant Trent was a good friend of mine, and I can't..."

"Have it your own way, then; it didn't matter a damn anyway; because as soon as they heard Bourne had been standing us gin and bitters, and champagne, and liqueur brandy, they were all over him. One sat on one arm of his chair, and one on the other, and he fed them bits of peaches stuck on the end of a fork, treating them just as though they were a pair of pet dogs or two bloody parrots; and then he said in an absent-minded way that he didn't want to break up the party, but the last train went at eight-thirty, and it was a quarter past already, so that there was just time for a stirrup-cup, as he called it, before we left.

"If any of you chaps go on the piss with Bourne, and he offers you a stirrup-cup, you can take it from me he has got you beat. He ordered brandy and soda for five, and that made the girls lively too, as they had had a few before they came in. And now, he says, we really must say goodbye. It was bloody easy to say goodbye, but Sergeant Trent tried to get up, and then he sat down again, laughing in a silly way. We were both just silly drunk, and there was Bourne as smart and quick as Sergeant Chorley on parade, except that his cap was off and one of the girls had ruffled his hair a bit. We heard the bloody engine whistle and the train go, and there we were, with ten or eleven bloody miles to walk back to Tregelly before rouse parade. Bourne was quite philosophic about it; said it would sober us all up, there was nothing like a good long walk to sweat it out of you, only we ought to allow plenty of time. Whenever I thought of it I got wind up, and then I'd pretend it was a joke and laugh like hell. Sergeant Trent was the same: we were both just silly drunk.

"Well, Bourne said he must get a little air, he would go out for ten minutes, and in the meantime we were not to have anything to drink. Those two bitches didn't pay any attention to us, said we'd insulted them, and were no gentlemen, but Bourne could do anything he liked with them, and he was just as polite as he could be. Well, he went out after whispering something to the two girls who stayed with us, and in about ten minutes or a quarter of an hour he was back again.

"We had a few more drinks, but he didn't press us; only he drank drink for drink with us, that I'll swear. I seemed to see him sitting there, looking as though he doubted our ability to walk, and the next thing I knew was that I woke up, in bed with my boots on, in the big barrack-room at Tregelly; and there was Sergeant Trent looking bloody awful in the next bed. We had moved down out of the hut on Monday morning before leaving for Milharbour, as another party left the camp that day. I didn't know how we had got back; but Corporal Burns told me that at about half-past twelve Bourne had come in, and asked him to come down to the wall and help carry us up. When the corporal came down he saw, on the other side of the wall, a car, and the driver, and the two girls. They had butted us over the wall, because one of the other regiments furnished the guard that night, so Bourne had stopped the car and made the driver switch off the lights some way back. Corporal Burns told me that he sat by the fire talking to him a bit, and then got into kip much as usual."

"Corporal Burns was an odd chap," said Bourne in a disinterested way. "Sometimes he would sit up most of the night, looking into the fire and brooding. I never knew why, but somebody said that he had deserted from another regiment because of some trouble, and that the authorities knew about it, but sympathised with him, and wouldn't take action. He had a proper guardsman's word of command. He was a nice chap. I remember he was sitting over the fire when I came in; and after we had put you on your bed I said to him that he looked as though he could do with a drink. He had some sugar, so we boiled some water and had a glass of hot rum before we turned in."

"Yes," said the regimental, "there was this bugger recommending plenty of hot tea in the morning, to flush out our kidneys, and he and the greater part of a bottle of rum hidden in his kit. Sergeant Trent and I both drank tea, and we were both bloody sick; but about ten minutes before rouse parade he gave us each a bottle of beer, which he had brought back from Milharbour, and that just got us through. He told us sweetly he was orderly-man, and was not going on rouse parade. Mr Clinton took us out for a run, and when we came back we were sick again. Bourne always knew someone likely to be useful in emergencies, and we asked him to go up to the canteen manager and try and scrounge some more beer; but he said we must eat something first; he would see what could be done after breakfast. Well, we went across to the cookhouse, and tried to ram food down, but it didn't do, and then Bourne, he always came into the cookhouse instead of the mess-room too, appeared behind us suddenly, with a medicine bottle, and poured a good double tot of rum into our tea. I couldn't speak; but Trent looked up at him with tears of gratitude and said under his breath: 'You're a bloody miracle.' He didn't have any himself."

"I was firing at four hundred, five hundred, and six hundred yards that morning," Bourne explained. "I took the same bottle down to the range with me, and when the detail before mine was firing I got behind a sandhill to take a small swig to steady myself. Just as I got the bottle out, Mr Clinton came round, and saw it; he was firing too, you remember. 'Bourne, what have you got in that bottle?' he said. 'Oil, sir,' I replied. 'That's the very thing I want,' he said. 'Well, sir," I said, 'here's a piece of four by two ready, and, wait a bit, sir, here's a clean piece, as well.' 'Thanks awfully, Bourne," he said, and when he had sauntered off I drank that rum so quickly I nearly swallowed the bottle with it. I fired quite well: got seventeen at four hundred, eighteen at five hundred, and seventeen at six, Top scores at each range, and I got my crossed guns with a couple of points to spare. Well, sir, I think I had better go to kip."

"We had all better go to kip, but you can have another tot of rum before you go. Now you all know what I think about Bourne. He has never asked a favour of me, and when Sergeant Trent and I took him out meaning to get him canned up and generally make a fool of him, he drank us both to a standstill. You didn't leave us there, Bourne, to get out of the mess we had made for ourselves as best we could, while you went back by train. You got us back with considerable difficulty, and you put us safely into kip, and you had the laugh on us, and you forgot it. Well, I think you are a bloody good sport. Goodnight, Bourne, goodnight, sergeant."

"Thanks awfully, sir," said the embarrassed Bourne. "Goodnight, Sir. Goodnight, all."

As he was going, the storekeeper handed him his cooker casually. "Thanks, goodnight, Thompson, see you tomorrow at Meaulte. Mind that tent rope, sergeant. Here, give me your arm."

"You know, Bourne, old chap," said the sergeant, who was a little unsteady in speech as well as in gait, but very solemn. "That wash a lie you tol' that offisher."

"I'm afraid it was, sergeant. It touches my conscience sometimes; and I pinched some of his whisky, too, up the line the other night."

"I wouldn't 'a' believed it of you, Bourne. I really wouldn't 'a' believed it o' you if you 'adn't tol' me yo'sel'."

Bourne managed to deposit the sergeant in his place without making any undue disturbance in the tent. Then he undressed, pulled up his blanket, and smoked another cigarette. It was a lie, he admitted cynically to himself; but not being exactly a free agent in the army, he wondered how far the moral problem was involved. Every man had a minimum of self-will, and when an external discipline encroached on it, there was no saying what might happen as a result. When he had finished his cigarette he turned over and slept without a dream.

Chapter IV

And now their pride and mettle is asleep. – SHAKESPEARE

The next day they moved back to the sordid squalor of Meaulte, where they spent two nights housed in stables, and the draft ceased to have a separate existence, being absorbed by the various companies. There was a kit inspection, at which Bourne's tin hat was condemned, the fact being entered in a notebook by Sergeant-Major Robinson; and that piece of ritual concluded the matter for the time being, the company-quartermaster-sergeant having no surplus tin hats at his disposal. At Meaulte they were still within the battle area, and there was nothing for them to do. Shem, Bourne and Martlow idled about, looking at the interminable train of motor lorries, which passed through, day and night, without ceasing, and so densely packed that it was difficult to cross the narrow street between them. Little Martlow had a grievance. In the attack, he had annexed the field glasses of two German officers, who, being dead, had no further use for them. At Happy Valley, seeing him needlessly decorated with the loot of battle, the commanding officer had said to him peremptorily: "Hand over those glasses to me, my boy. I shall see that they are forwarded to the proper quarter." His action may have been correct, from the official point of view, but to little Martlow it was an unjustifiable interference with the rights of private ownership.

"And now the bastard's wearin' the bes' pair slung round 'is own bloody neck. Wouldn't you've thought the cunt would 'a' give me vingt frong for 'em anyway?"

"Your language is deplorable, Martlow," said Bourne in ironical reproof; "quite apart from the fact that you are speaking of your commanding officer. Did you learn all these choice phrases in the army?"

"Not much," said little Martlow derisively; "all I learnt in the army was me drill an' care o' bloody arms. I knew all the fuckin' patter before I joined."

Shem grinned maliciously at Bourne, who could never offer any serious resistance to Martlow's rosy-cheeked impudence. Bourne had seen the boy blubbering like the child he really was as they went over the top a couple of days earlier, but unaware that he was blubbering, and possessed at the same time by a more primitive fury than filled the souls of grown men. It was unsafe to give oneself the airs of riper experience with a boy of Martlow's breed. Probably life to him had always been a kind of warfare; and his precocity at times could be disconcerting.

"Voulez-vous m'embrasser, mademoiselle?" he cried provocatively to a bovine female who replied only with a look of virtuous indignation. "Well, thank Gawd we're going back to decent billets where there'll be some chance of a bon time."

They marched from Meaulte to Mericourt, and on the way an enemy plane swooped out of the blue and dropped two bombs, which, exploding on the hard macadam, sent gravel and road metal flying in all directions. In spite of their casualties, the men were very steady, and though there was no cover, they moved quietly off the unenclosed road on to soft wet turf, which would stifle to some extent the effect of any more bombs. Some of their own planes at once attacked the Hun, and drove him off; a running fight ensued, but it was apparently indecisive. Evidently the enemy was challenging the temporary supremacy in the air with a new type of machine, for in the earlier stages of the battle, he had not been very troublesome.

Bourne had been set to pulling a Lewis-gun cart, a job which he liked because it enabled him to get rid of his pack, which was carried on the cart itself. There were a couple of men behind, to hold the cart back with a length of rope when going downhill. Passing through Ville, the men behind, in fooling with the rope, let the cart run forward, and one of the iron rests in front tore open the back of Bourne's left boot, and the flesh of his heel as well. It was a trivial thing, but painful, though he did not trouble about it. They had dinner just outside Mericourt, and then entrained, but the van in which Bourne found himself had nearer fifty than the forty men it was supposed to hold packed into it. He contrived to keep by the door, sitting there with his feet on the footboard outside, so that he got the air, though he had no shade and the sun was fierce. The men at the back suffered considerably: they were both stifled and cramped: and, unable to sit, in standing with nothing to steady them, when the train swayed and jolted they fell and jostled against each other. A kind of impersonal bad temper, which could not find any very definite object, developed among them; there was some abuse, there were even threats and counter-threats, but no actual quarrelling. The general effect was one of a recalcitrant acquiescence in the dispensations of an inscrutable providence.

In the last couple of days, their whole psychological condition had changed: they had behind them no longer the moral impetus which thrust them into action, which carried them forward on a wave of emotional excitement, transfiguring all the circumstances of their life so that these could only be expressed in the terms of heroic tragedy, of some superhuman or even divine conflict with the powers of evil; all that tempest of excitement was spent, and they were now mere derelicts in a wrecked and dilapidated world, with sore and angry nerves sharpening their tempers, or shutting them up in a morose and sullen humour from which it was difficult to move them.

Bourne often found himself looking at his companions as it were from a remote distance, and then it sometimes seemed to him that they had very little reason or sense of responsibility, apart from that which the business imposed on them. He was not supercilious in this; he was merely wondering how far what he felt himself was similar or equivalent to what they felt. It is a little curious to reflect that while each man is a mystery to himself, he is an open book to others; the reason being, perhaps, that he sees in himself the perplexities and torment of the mental processes out of which action issues, and they see in him only the simple and indivisible act itself. While he imagined that the other men were probably a little less reflective and less reasonable than he was himself, he frankly envied them the wanton and violent instincts, which seemed to guide them, or at least carry them, so successfully through this hazardous adventure. It was a piece of naivety on his part. They had accepted him, and he had mucked in with them quite satisfactorily. But there was a question which every man put to another at their first acquaintance: What did you do in civil life?

It was a question full of significance, not only because it recognised implicitly the endless variety of types to which military discipline had given an apparent uniformity; but because it implied also that, for the time being, civil life had been obliterated, at least as far as they were concerned: it existed only precariously, and in a very attenuated form somewhere in the rear of the embattled armies, but for all practical purposes it was not worth a moment's consideration. Men had reverted to a more primitive stage in their development, and had become nocturnal beasts of prey, hunting each other in packs: this was the uniformity, quite distinct from the effect of military discipline, which their own nature had imposed on them.

There is an extraordinary veracity in war, which strips man of every conventional covering he has, and leaves him to face a fact as naked and as inexorable as himself. But when a battalion has been so thinned that it becomes negligible as a fighting unit, and it is withdrawn from the line to refit, there is a tendency for individual characteristics to reassert themselves; the pressure of the opposed force is removed, and discipline, until the establishment has been reorganised, is necessarily relaxed. The bad temper which steamed or exploded ineffectively among this van-load of angry men, childish as it was, was symptomatic. Bourne, who had scored in so far as he had air and could sit on the floor, nursed his sore heel and was as hot and as angry as the rest of them.

It was already dusk when they detrained, and Bourne did not notice the name of the station, though he imagined they were somewhere in the neighbourhood of St Pol. They had a march of nine or ten miles in front of them; another man having taken his place with the Lewis-gun cart, Bourne fell in between Shem and Martlow, and marched with his company again, but he was now quite lame, and tired easily. He was pretty well dead-beat before they came to the end, otherwise the march through the cool dusk was pleasant; a few scurrying rainstorms crossed their line, and evidently, from the state of the road, it had rained heavily there, but now the sky was mainly clear, with stars and a half-moon, which looked up at them again from the puddles, and there were long, straight lines of poplars which stood on either side of them, erect, like notes of exclamation. Bourne was a little indignant when Shem, a tough, sturdy and generous person, seeing him limping, offered to take his rifle. It was after eleven o'clock when they came to Beaumetz. As soon as they entered the village the battalion split itself up into several detachments, and Mr Sothern, in charge of the party in which Bourne was included, was not quite sure whether he had found the right billets; but he told the men to fall out while he went in search of information, and they sat in the kennel of the muddy street. Except for lights in one or two windows, there was not a sign of life. The men sat there quietly, tired enough, but with not a trace of bad temper left in them; a kind of contentment seemed to soak into them from the stillness of the place.

When they had found their stables for the night, Bourne took his boot off and examined his heel; his sock was hard with dried blood, and the wound itself looked dirty, so as there was a light showing in the house, he thought he would try for some hot water to bathe it, and he knocked persuasively at the door. It was opened by an old man with a patient, inquiring expression on his face. When Bourne, speaking lamentable French, explained his need, he was invited to enter, and then made to sit on a chair, while his host brought some hot water in a basin and insisted on bathing the wound himself. When it was clean, he went to a sideboard—the room was a kind of kitchen-parlour—and brought out a bottle of brandy, pouring some into a cup so that Bourne's heart rejoiced in him, but the old man only took a strip of clean linen, which he folded into a pad, and after saturating it with brandy, he once again took up Bourne's foot in his capable hand, and squeezed the linen, so that the brandy fell drop by drop onto the broken flesh. It stung a little, and Bourne, rather sceptical of its healing power, would have preferred to take it internally; but against the old man's voluble assurances that it was bon, tres bon pour les plaies, he could find nothing to say. Finally, his host took up what was left on the linen pad and placed it on the wound, and Bourne drew a clean sock over it. He always carried an extra pair in his kit, but it was a mere chance that they were clean. Like most of the men, he had dumped everything that was not necessary, even his spare shirt and underpants; for when a man has to carry nearly three stone of kit and equipment on the march, he becomes disinclined to take much heed for the morrow, and prefers to rely on the clean change provided at the divisional baths, in spite of the uncertain interval.

By the time the treatment was complete, Bourne's gratitude had almost left him bankrupt in the French language; but the old man increased his obligations by giving him a cup of steaming coffee, well laced with that sovereign remedy for a torn and swollen heel, and they talked a little while. He could not persuade his host to take any payment, but he accepted a few cigarettes, which he broke up and smoked in his pipe. He was alone in the house, Bourne gathered, and he had a son who was at the front. His only other relation was a brother who was a professor of English at a provincial university. These two facts seemed to establish a degree of kindred and affinity between them, and when Bourne left to sleep in his stable, he was invited to come in again in the morning.

He woke early, and not knowing where the cookers were, he took advantage of the invitation, so that he could beg some hot water for shaving. He was surprised by the effect of the brandy on his heel, as all the swelling had disappeared and the pain was no more than a slight discomfort when he flexed his foot. He found the old man ill, and brewing himself some tea, which he took only as a kind of physic, somewhat reluctantly. Bourne looked at his newspaper, in the hope of learning something about the war, but apart from a few colourless details from the French front there was nothing; no one knew anything about it; it was like one of the blind forces of nature; one could not control it, one could not comprehend it, and one could not predict its course from hour to hour. The spirit of the troops was excellent, the possibility of defeat was incredible; but to calculate the duration of the conflict was quite beyond the resources of the human mind: it was necessary to look at these matters from a scientific standpoint, and the scientific method was that of trial and error. Bourne only glanced hastily at all the solemn empty phrases, and was wondering whether he could get a new pair of boots from the shoemakers, unofficially to save time, before they paraded; and when the old man had at last brewed his tea, he got a little hot water and departed to shave. The snobs were also kind to him, and gave him a pair of boots which they assured him were of a type and quality reserved entirely for officers, being of the best Indian roan, a kind of leather of which Bourne had never heard.

"Strictly speakin'," said his friend Snobby Hines, "it's an officer's boot, but it's a very small size, so you may 'ave that pair, as they fit you. 'Ope we stay 'ere a bit. It's quite a bon place, two decent estaminets an' some mad'moiselles, not that I see anything much in these French girls, you know: my ol' curiosity at 'ome would make most of 'em look silly. Well, you can't 'ave everythink, so you've got to be content with what you git."

Bourne did not trouble about the cryptic significance of these words, he agreed with everything unreservedly, this being one of the secrets of a happy life. He liked his new boots because the leather was strong but soft and pliable, and if they were a bit oily, well, that would keep the wet out, and one did not have to polish boots on active service. They paraded at ten o'clock, for a little extended order drill; but when they had fallen in Sergeant Tozer asked if there was any man capable of working a typewriter. There was no reply from the ranks, though Bourne had played about a little with a Blick. They moved out into the fields to drill. But at eleven o'clock the regimental appeared on the scene; and once again a typist was demanded, and as there was no reply, the regimental singled out Bourne, and cross-questioned him. He knew very well that Bourne was the most likely man, and when the latter admitted under pressure that he could use the machine, he was told to report at the orderly-room at one o'clock. He was very unwilling to take the job. He was by no means an expert with a typewriter, but that did not trouble him; what he disliked was the fact that he would be sitting, for the greater part of the day, under the eyes of authority. He had no personal experience of the orderly-room staff but, from hearsay alone, he had a very definite prejudice against the men composing it, and it was almost a relief to him to find from the very first moment that there were good grounds for it, because he was spared the trouble of attempting to adjust himself to these new conditions. His job was a temporary one, and it was his object to see that it didn't become permanent; with which end in view, obedience, and a certain amount of innocent stupidity, seemed the proper tactics to adopt. He had made his own place in the company, and he was quite willing to go back to it, that very night if they should think fit; and to find an ample compensation for the apparent setback in the rowdy good humour of his comrades.

The lance-corporal received him, with a suspicious air, and passed him on to the corporal, who wore a more truculent expression, and presented him to the colour-sergeant. He was a cat-like individual, who showed all his false teeth in a deprecating smile, and seemed to consider Bourne as only the latest of those many tribulations with which God, in his inscrutable wisdom, had chosen to afflict a faithful servant. While this little ceremony was in progress, Captain Malet, upon whom the adjutant's duties had temporarily devolved, entered the orderly-room; and as they stood to attention, he acknowledged their existence coldly with a brusque salute; but when he sat at his table and turned over some papers, Bourne caught his eye, and a quick ripple of impish schoolboy humour flickered for an instant on the officer's face. He seemed always to find in Bourne some stimulus to mirth. Of course the others noticed it, with the air of not noticing it, with an almost ostentatious indifference, and wondered what this indecorous recognition might imply.

"Show Bourne what he is supposed to do," said the colour-sergeant to the lance-corporal with an almost ingratiating benevolence, but with a slight stress on the word "supposed" that gave a sub-acid flavour to his oiliness; and Bourne sat down before a small Corona to learn his way about on it. It did not occupy his whole attention; he was aware that the others were scrutinising him carefully, and his own rather delicate sensibility put out little groping feelers in an attempt to apprehend some of the realities of the situation. The colour-sergeant was of course the dominating factor, and the other two did not count, though in the rude phrase of better men, they should have chalked their bloody boots.

When Captain Malet, who spent as little time as possible in that uncongenial atmosphere, went out again, they talked among themselves; and if the matter of their conversation was difficult for an outsider to follow, its manner was sufficiently illuminating. Bourne saw at once that his own particular job was a myth: even the lance-corporal, Johnson, was not overburdened with work, and all the typing done in the course of a day would not have taken up twenty minutes of his time. What these luxurious creatures really wanted was a man to skivvy for them; and, though Bourne as a rule avoided the use of coarse language, he knew precisely what he would be before he acted as a kind of general batman to the orderly-room; so when teatime came, he did not enter into any unseemly competition with the lance-corporal for the honour of fetching the colour-sergeant's; but, taking his mess-tin, went off and sat with his own friends for half an hour.

"Ow do you like it?" inquired Sergeant Tozer.

"Oh, it's cushy enough," Bourne answered indifferently. "I don't mind it for a week or so; but it is not a job I want for keeps. I would rather be with the company."

"Some people don't know their bloody luck," said the sergeant tersely.

"I don't know. Your section were always fairly contented, except when Fritz strafed them unnecessarily."

"Sergeant-Major Robinson wanted to know whether you would pinch 'im some notebooks from the orderly-room, an' a few pencils? 'e an' the quarter-bloke can't get anything out o' them buggers."

"I'll pinch anything the sergeant-major wants," said Bourne recklessly; "only he will have to give me time to learn my way about." He went back to the orderly-room, and was released from his arduous labours a little after half-past five; then, picking up Shem and Martlow, he went off to an estaminet, determined to have as bon a time as the place and their purses afforded. The battalion had been paid out at twelve o'clock, and the place was crowded with uproarious men, stamping time with their feet on the floor as they sang at the top of their voices:

Mademoiselle, she bought a cow, Parley-voo,

To milk the brute, she didn't know how, Parley-voo,

She pulled the tail instead of the tit,

And covered herself all over with—MILK...

A storm of loud cheers and laughter at the unwonted delicacy of phrase drowned the concluding gibberish of the chorus. Bourne ordered a bottle of some poison concocted out of apples and potatoes labelled champagne, which had a little more kick in it than the vin rouge or French beer. Then the three of them crowded in among the men playing "crown and anchor", with Snobby Hines rattling the dice-box.

"Oo's goin' to 'ave somethin' on the old mud'ook? Come on, me lucky lads, if yer don't speckyerlate yer can't accumyerlate. Somethin' on the of mud'ook jest to try yer luck. Y'all finished, then? Right! There y'are. It's the sergeant-major. I tol' yer so. An' off we go again, an' off we go again."

Bourne struck a vein of luck, and as he had crushed in next to Thompson, the storekeeper, he gave him ten francs for services rendered at Sand-pits. He lost that in a few minutes, and Bourne gave him another ten, which went the same way. As Bourne's generosity seemed to dry up, Thompson asked him for the loan of five, and that vanished with an equal rapidity. Shem won a little, and Martlow lost, but lost cannily, buttoning up his purse when he found the dice running against him. But Bourne had a bit more than his share of luck, and as the disconsolate Thompson still hung about the altars of fortune, on which he had sacrificed already more than double his pay, Bourne gave him five francs, and told him to go and try his luck with wine or women, as he might do better at another game. Thompson took his advice, and turned away disillusioned from an unsympathetic world; and then, oddly enough, for a little while Bourne lost; but he played on, and his luck turned again. He got up having won about seventy-five francs, and they had another bottle of champagne before setting off through the darkness to their billets.

The old man still had a light in his kitchen, and Bourne decided to pay him a visit and inquire after his health. Bourne had a briar pipe in a leather purse, which a friend in England had sent him, though he never smoked a pipe; and he took it with him, and presented it to his host as a tribute of gratitude. The old man was surprised and delighted. He was quite well again, and offered Bourne some cafe-cognac; but Bourne refused, explaining that they would march away in the morning; though, if monsieur were agreeable, he would come in early and have some coffee. Monsieur professed himself enchanted.

Chapter V

I begin to find an idle and fond bondage in the oppression of aged
tyranny, who sways not as it hath power but as it is suffered. –
SHAKESPEARE

For the next few days they were continually on the move, and Bourne
did nothing for the orderly-room but help to stow and unstow a few tin
deed-boxes, eating, marching and sleeping with his company. Captain
Malet had gone on leave unexpectedly, and Captain Havelock became
adjutant in his place. The roads were dusty, a lot of the route pave, hot
and unyielding to the feet, and the flat stones worn or shifted to an
uneven surface while the sycamores or poplars bordering the sides were
not close enough to give much shelter from a pitiless sun.

At the end of the second day's march after leaving Beaumetz, they
halted under a stone wall which must have been about fifteen feet high,
with a single arched gateway opening in it. On the other side of the road,
pollarded willows leaned away from them to overhang a quick-flowing
little river, full of bright water. Several of the new men had fallen out,
and would be on the mat for it in the morning, and they were all tired
enough, the sweat having soaked through their shirts and tunics to show
in dark patches on the khaki where the equipment pressed on it.

On the other side of the archway was a wide courtyard, with the usual
midden in the centre of it; at the back, a large house, half-farm, half-
chateau, with a huge stone-built barn on one side, flanking the yard, and
on the other almost equally substantial stables and outbuildings. It was
conventual in appearance, with a prosperous air. When they pushed open
the great doors of the barn, and entered into that cool empty space, which
would have held two companies at a pinch, it had seemed to offer them
the pleasantest lodging they had known for months: it was as lofty as a
church, the roof upheld by unwrought beams and rafters, the walls
pierced with narrow slits for light and air, and the floor thick-littered
with fine, dry straw. Some panicky fowls flew up into their faces, and
then fled precipitately as they took possession. They slipped off their

equipment and wet tunics, and unrolled their puttees before sprawling at ease.

"Cushy place, this," said Shem contentedly. "Wonder what the village is like; it would be all right if we were billeted here for a week; that is, unless we're going on to some decent town."

"Some bloody thing's bitin' my legs," said Martlow after a few minutes.

"Mine, too," said Bourne. "What the hell...?"

"I'm alive with the buggers," said Pritchard angrily.

Men were scratching and cursing furiously, for the straw swarmed with hen-fleas, which seemed to bite them in a hundred different places at one and the same time. Compared with these minute black insects of a lively and vindictive disposition, lice were merely caressing in their attentions; and the amount of profane blasphemy which broke from the surprised and discomfited men was of an unusual fervour. For the moment they were routed, scratching themselves savagely with dirty fingernails; and then gradually the bites decreased, and they seemed, with the exception of an occasional nip, to have become immune, hen-fleas apparently preferring a more delicate pasture. They caught one or two with considerable difficulty, and examined them curiously: after all, they were not so repulsive as the crawling, white, crab-like lice, which lived and bred, hatching in swarms, on the hairy parts of one's body. These were mere raiding pleasure-seekers, and when the first onset had spent its force, the fitful skirmishes which succeeded it were endurable.

Old soldiers say that one should never take off boots and socks, after a march, until one has cooled down, and the swelling in legs and feet has vanished; bathing hot swollen feet only makes them tender. They rested until tea was ready, and in the distribution of rations they were lucky; a loaf of bread among four, and a tin of butter and a pot of jam among six. Shem, Bourne and Martlow ate, smoked and then, taking towels and soap, followed the river until they found some seclusion, and there they stripped and bathed. They did not know that bathing had been forbidden, and even after they had dressed themselves partly again they sat on the bank with their feet on the gravel bottom, letting the water ripple over them. One of the regimental police found them there, and rapped out an adjectival comment on their personal characters, antecedents and future prospects, which left nothing for the imagination to complete. As they showed an admirable restraint under the point and emphasis of his remarks, he contented himself with heading them back to billets, with a warning that the village was out of bounds, and then took his own way along the forbidden road in search of pleasure, like a man privileged above his kind.

"They don't care a fuck 'ow us'ns live," said little Martlow bitterly. "We're just 'umped an' bumped an' buggered about all over fuckin' France, while them as made the war sit at 'ome waggin' their bloody chins, an' sayin' what they'd 'ave done if they was twenty years younger. Wish to Christ they was, an' us'ns might get some leaf an' go 'ome an' see our own folk once in a while.'

"Too bloody true," Shem agreed. "Five bloody weeks on the Somme without a bath, and thirteen men to a loaf; and when they take you back for a rest you can't wash your feet in a river, or go into a village to buy bread. They like rubbing it in all right.'

"What are you chewing the fat about?" asked Bourne. "You've had a bathe, and you're not paying for it. Can't you take an ordinary telling-off without starting to grouse about it? You don't want to drink someone else's bathwater in your morning tea, do you? I'm going over to the house to inspect the inhabitants. There's a mad'moiselle there, Martlow; just about your mark."

"You please yourself," said Martlow. "I'm not goin'; I don't like the look of the fam'ly."

Bourne found the womenfolk hospitable enough, and pleased himself enormously. He bought a couple of glasses of wine from madame, who asked him not to tell the other men, as there were too many of them. Snatches of soldiers' choruses came from the barn across the yard, and madame was full of praise of the English, their courage, their contentment. She asked Bourne if he sang, and he laughed, lifting up his voice:

Dans le jardin de mon pere, lilas sont fleuris....

She seemed astonished by that, and beamed at him, her red face bright with sweat.

Aupres de ma blonde, qu'il fait bon, fait bon, fait bon,
Aupres de ma blonde, qu'il fait bon dormir....

But he knew no more than a few lines of it. She knew it well enough, and told him it was not proper, at which he cocked his head aside and looked at her knowingly, and then, satisfied that he had turned that flank, gave his attention to the girl, who ignored it discreetly. She was not really pretty, but she had all the bloom and venusty of youth, with those hazel eyes which seem almost golden when they take the light under dark lashes. Two oldish men came in, and looked at Bourne with grave suspicion, while madame and the girl bustled to get their evening meal. Every time either of these ladies approached him, Bourne, with an excessive politeness, rose from his chair, and this seemed to increase the suspicion of the younger man.

"Asseyez-vous, monsieur," he said with a tranquil sarcasm. "Elles ne sont pas immortelles."

"C'est dommage, monsieur," Bourne replied, apt enough for all his clumsy French, and madame beamed at him again; but the discouragement the men offered to his presence there was too strong for him, and he took up his cap, thanking her for her kindness, bowing respectfully to mademoiselle, and finally saluting the two hobereaux so punctiliously that they were constrained to rise and acknowledge his elaborate courtesy. As he crossed the courtyard in the half-dark he laughed softly to himself, and then whistled the air of "Aupres de Ma Blonde" loudly enough for them to hear in the lighted room.

No one could tell what luck tomorrow might bring.

The girl had moved him a little. She had awakened in him that sense of privation, which affected more or less consciously all these segregated males, so that they swung between the extremes of a sticky sentimentalism and a rank obscenity, the same mind warping as it were both ways in the attempt to throw off the obsession, which was less desire than a sheer physical hunger, and could not feed itself on dreams.

In the shuddering revulsion from death one turns instinctively to love as an act which seems to affirm the completeness of being. In the trenches, the sense of this privation vanished; but it pressed on men whenever they moved back again to the borders of civilised life, which is after all only the organisation of man's appetites, for food or for women, the two fundamental necessities of his nature. In the trenches his efforts were directed to securing an end, which perhaps has a poor claim on his attention, for in comparison with the business of keeping himself alive, the pursuit of women, or even of food, may seem to rank only as the rather trivial diversion of a man's leisure moments; and in the actual agony of battle, these lesser cupidities have no place at all, and women cease to exist so completely that they are not even irrelevant. Afterwards, yes. Afterwards all the insubordinate passions released by battle, and that assertion of the supremacy of one's own particular and individual will, though these may be momentarily quiescent from exhaustion, renew themselves and find no adequate object, unless in the physical ecstasy of love, which is less poignant.

Unfortunately, they moved off again next morning, and the girl, standing with her own people in the yard, watched them go, as though she regretted vaguely the waste of good men. About the middle of the day something in the character of the countryside seemed familiar, and the reminiscence teased their memory to make it more definite, until they came upon a signpost which told them they were marching in the direction of Noeux-les-Mines, and reminiscence became anticipation. The thought of a town where decent conditions still prevailed, and where they might have a bon time, put new heart into them, and the marching column broke into cheerful song. They had put, at least partially, their own words to the air of song sufficiently sentimental:

Oh, they've called them up from Weschurch,
And they've called them up from Wen,
And they'll call up all the women,
When they've fucked up all the men.

After which the adjuration to keep the home fires burning seemed rather banal. Entering Noeux-les-Mines they were exuberant, but after they had passed the lane leading from the main street to the camp, the chorus of song became less confident. When the great slagheap and the level crossing had been left behind them, they reconciled themselves to the less joyful, but still tolerable prospect of Mazingarbe. Then Mazingarbe, with its brick-built brewery, fell behind them too.

"We're goin' into the bloody line again," shouted Minton, who was marching just ahead of Bourne.

"Well, it's cushy enough up this part o' the line now," said Pritchard resignedly.

"Cushy be buggered," said Minton angrily.

They continued a little way along the road to Vermelles, and halted finally in Philosophe, a mining village, brick-built and grimy, from which the inhabitants had been evacuated. There they fell out and went to billets in sullen silence. Almost immediately, Shem and Martlow were posted with field glasses and whistles to give warning of the approach of enemy aircraft. The troops were ordered to keep close in to the houses when moving about the village, and to take cover when the whistles were blown.

Bourne went off to the orderly-room. The main street of Philosophe was at right angles to the road from Mazingarbe to Vermelles, and at the end of it was another street, roughly parallel to the road, the orderly-room being in the third house down on the left. The village was practically undamaged by shellfire, but it was a dour, unlovely place. One or two families remained there, and children either belonging to them, or to Mazingarbe, which was not far away, passed up and down the street with large baskets on their arms at intervals through the day, shouting, 'Engleesh pancakes, Engleesh pancakes', with a curious note of melancholy or boredom in their high-pitched voices.

Bourne, quite inadvertently, had improved his position in the orderly-room. The colour-sergeant, with his usual irony, had referred to the possibility of making him a permanent member of the orderly room staff, and Bourne had replied with great firmness that he would prefer to go back to his company. As they saw at once that he really meant it, they became more friendly. While he and the lance-corporal unpacked the boxes, he asked for the notebooks and pencils which Sergeant-Major Robinson wanted, and got them without any difficulty. When he and the lance-corporal went for their dinners, he took them to the sergeant-major, with whom were Sergeant Tozer and the quarter-bloke.

"You're bloody lucky to be in the orderly-room for a spell," the sergeant-major told him. "The C. O. thinks the men have got slack, and says that all time available must be spent in drill. Company guards as well as headquarter guard are to parade outside the orderly-room for inspection at eleven o'clock every morning; an' I suppose there'll be working parties up the line every bloody night. How do you like Captain Havelock in th' orderly-room? The men call him Janey. Saw him walking over to Brigade with the C. O. a few minutes ago. Brigade's at Le Brebis. Captain Malet's coming back to the company in a few days.

We're going to spend most of our time carrying bloody gas cylinders up Potsdam Alley: that's what I heard anyway."

The prospect of carrying gas cylinders, which weighed about a hundred and eighty pounds apiece, and were slung on a pole carried on the shoulders of two men, proved conclusively to Bourne that the orderly-room had its uses. The work was made more difficult by the fact that the men had to wear their P. H. gas helmets, which were hot and suffocating. He went back to the orderly-room in a somewhat chastened frame of mind.

The next day, each company in turn marched back to the brewery in Mazingarbe for baths. They stripped to the buff in one room, handing over towel, socks, shirt and underpants to the men in charge, who gave them clean things in exchange: these were rolled up in a bundle, ready, and a man took what he was given without question, except in the case of an impossible misfit or a garment utterly useless, in which case he might ask his sergeant-major to intervene, though even his intervention was not always effective. It was invariably the same at casualty-clearing-stations or divisional baths, the leadswingers in charge and their chums took the best of the stuff they handled, and the fighting men had to make shift as best they could with their leavings. The men left their clean change with their boots and khaki, and passed naked into one large room in which casks, sawn in two and standing in rows, did duty for baths. There were a few improvised showers. Here they splashed and soaped themselves, with a riotous noisiness and a good deal of indecent horseplay.

"Dost turn thysen to t' wall, lad, so's us'ns sha'n't see tha dick?" one man shouted at a shy young newcomer; and when the boy turned a red and indignant face over his shoulder, he was met with derision, and another man pulled him out of the tub, and wrestled with him; slippery as they both were with soap. They were distinctly fresh. Rude and brutal as it was, there was a boisterous good humour about it; and laughing at his show of temper and humiliation, some other men intervened, and they let him slip out of their hands back to his tub, where he continued the washing of himself as modestly as he could. Finally, after fighting for the showers, they dried, dressed themselves and marched away, another company taking their place.

In the orderly-room Bourne sat next to the signaller, at a long table which was pushed in to the wall under two windows. He sat with his back to the room, looking out into the street, down which a few soldiers passed occasionally. During the few days they had been at Philosophe he had sunk into a fit of depression, which was not usual with him. He did not understand the reason for it himself. He told himself he was only one of thousands whose life, when they were out of the line, was blank emptiness: men who were moved about France and saw nothing but the roads they travelled and the byres in which they slept. They were mere automatons, whose only conscious life was still in England. He felt curiously isolated even from them. He was not of their county, he was not even of their country, or their religion, and he was only partially of their race. When they spoke of their remote villages and hamlets, or sleepy market-towns in which nothing happened except the church clock chiming the hour, he felt like an alien among them, and in the vague kind of homesickness which troubled him he did not seek company, but solitude.

The day after they went to the baths, he was entering orders in the book, when the commanding officer came in, and asked brusquely for a sheet of foolscap and a pencil. Bourne got what was wanted and returned to his place, completing the entry and closing the book softly. He never did any typewriting while the commanding officer was in the room or during orders-hour. So he looked out of the window as the various guards fell in for inspection.

The orderly officer, Mr Sothern and the regimental were on parade and made a preliminary inspection of the men. Then the regimental came over to the orderly-room, entered it, and saluted. The adjutant put on his cap, and went out of the room, and the regimental followed him. They were in the passage leading to the front door, when Bourne, looking out of the window, saw a blinding flash followed instantly by an explosion, and a shower of glass fell on the table in front of him. For an instant the street was a blur; but he saw the regimental rush out, evidently shouting orders to the men, who took cover. Nine were left lying on the paving stones. Then there was a second explosion, evidently in the other street. Bourne's first instinct was to rush out and try to help. He flung a foot over the form on which he sat and, turning, saw the commanding officer shrinking in his chair, eyes staring out of a blank face, and teeth bared in a curious snarl, the old colour- sergeant with his fingertips on the floor in the posture of an ape walking, and Johnson cowering against the wall. Reynolds was standing up to it, cool, still, as though he listened.

"Sit still," whispered the signaller to Bourne warningly; but as the corporal went to the door, Bourne followed him.

"Can we help?" he said quietly.

"No," said the corporal sternly. "The stretcher-bearers are there already. You shouldn't have left your place. Come outside with me, now."

They went into the street, and the adjutant and orderly-officer brushed by them into the orderly-room. It was extraordinarily still again, and the last of the wounded was being carried away by the stretcher-bearers. The C. O., with Captain Havelock and the orderly-officer, came out again and disappeared round the corner into the main street, so that Bourne and the corporal were the only two left on the scene. They looked at the blood on the paved roadway, and then up to the sky, where a few puffs of white smoke showed still against the blue, but, as they watched them, drifted and faded gradually from sight.

"So much for their bloody parades," said Bourne bitterly to the corporal.

"I suppose its war," answered Reynolds with a touch of fatalism.

"War," exclaimed Bourne. "They post men with field glasses and whistles to give warning of enemy aircraft; the troops are ordered to show themselves as little as possible in the streets, and to keep close to the houses, and the police are told to make themselves a nuisance to any thoughtless kid who forgets; and then, having taken all these precautions, fifty men are paraded in the middle of the street opposite the orderly-room, as a target, I suppose, and are kept standing there for twenty minutes or half an hour. It's a bloody nice kind of war."

"What's the use of talking about it? If Jerry hadn't taken all his stuff down to the Somme, we'd be shelled to shit in half an hour. Come inside and get on with it."

The colour-sergeant glanced at them enigmatically as they came into the room, and Bourne, without speaking, began to clear away the litter of broken glass from the table and floor, stacking the larger pieces in a heap. The lance-corporal came to his help, and when they had taken up all they could manage with their hands, Bourne swept up the splinters. Then he sat down to his typing. Every now and again the instrument in front of the signaller would tick out a message in Morse, and the signaller would take it down on a slip, which he passed to Johnson, who handed it to the colour-sergeant. Bourne, typing orders, heard broken fragments of conversation behind him, and sometimes the signaller speaking softly with a hand up to his mouth into the transmitter. It was meaningless to him, for he was not thinking of it.

"...surprise...quiet place, not a sound...artillery on the Somme...all so quiet and still...swank, that's what it is... I'm too old for this...not a bomb...anti-aircraft battery...it was a bomb all right...says two shells didn't explode...major...what...yes... thought he'd get under the table...does put wind up...quite a cushy part...aeroplanes..."

It was all so much senseless babble to him. When he had finished typing orders, he put in a clean sheet, and typed whatever came into his head, to practise speed; odd bits of verse, Latin tags, Aequam memento rebus in arduis Servare mentem. He had a text of Horace with Conington's translation in his pocket. "And richer spilth the pavement stain," that was pavimentum mero; why did that come into his head now? "Richer spilth" was ill-sounding anyway, and "stain" on top of it made an ugly line. Well, it didn't matter, it was all experience, and gave him some mechanical occupation to fill in time. He kept on striking the keys: "Than e'er at pontiffs supper ran." What he needed was to go on a big drunk somewhere, and break this bloody monotony. When he had filled up the sheet he took it out to turn, so that he could use the other side; but first he looked at it, to see how many mistakes he had made, and then through the window he saw two men swilling and sweeping the street. Yes; Fritz is mighty careless where he drops a dixie. He rested his chin on clasped hands and watched them in a kind of reverie.

Men were cheap in these days, that is to say men who were not coalminers or ship's rivetters, to whom war only meant higher wages. Officers were scarce, but they might be scarcer by one or two, without much harm being done. They had a good lot of officers on the whole. Major Shadwell and Captain Malet, who took the last ounce out of you, but anyway pulled their own weight as well and poor Mr Clinton, who was plucky but played out, and Mr Sothern, who was a bit of an ass, but a very decent chap. There was that old brigadier, who had spoken to him in Trones Wood: he must have been sixty, but he wasn't too old to come

65

and do his bit, and stuck it too. But there were some who could be quite easily spared. It would soon be time for dinner.

"Bourne," said the colour-sergeant, suddenly; "Lance-Corporal Johnson is taking some books to the quartermaster in Noeux-les-Mines. You will help him carry them in; and I dare say he will find you useful while he's there. You will stay there tonight and come back tomorrow afternoon. Be ready to start at three o'clock. You had better bring your pack here after dinner, and go straight away."

"Very good, sir," said Bourne quietly, with none of the surprise he felt. He didn't anticipate any particular liveliness in the company; of Lance-Corporal Johnson, but he might come upon some unpremeditated pleasure. Putting his things together, and covering up his typewriter, he considered his financial position; and though it was satisfactory, he wondered whether he could get a cheque cashed through the chaplain, or Mr White, the transport officer, who would probably be seeing the field-cashier shortly, as another payday was approaching. He had to look ahead, and either of them would manage a fiver for him. At last the colour-sergeant told him he might go; he took up his mess-tin and haversack, in which he carried a knife and fork and a notebook and pencils, so that he could put his equipment together after he had eaten, and started off with the lance-corporal, but they went to different cookers. Sergeant Tozer was getting his own dinner at the cooker, and he and Abbot looked at him, but Bourne only nodded to them and went over to where Lance-Corporal Jakes was superintending the dishing out of dinners.

"Was you in the orderly-room when that bloody bomb dropped?" inquired Corporal Jakes.

"Yes. I was looking out of the window."

"Knock some of the swank out of that bloody regimental you're so pally with," said one of the men angrily, and Bourne looked at him quietly: he was a pretty tough proposition from Lancashire, called Chapman.

"I expect he will carry out his orders as usual," Bourne said, stooping to get his food. "What the hell has it got to do with you who my pals are?"

"Well, that one will get a bit of extra weight if 'e's not careful."

"When you talk silly, you ought to talk under your breath," said Bourne, leaning forward a little, so that his face was about a foot away from Chapman's. "Anyone who didn't know you as well as I do might think you meant it."

"We don't want any of that talk 'ere," said Jakes, positive and solemn. "Not when there are two poor buggers dead, and five more not much better."

"Well, we don't want any more talk about it. It don't do no good; an' you've got no call to butt in; nobody said anythink to you. If you can't talk reas'nable you can keep your bloody mouth shut."

"What did they think about it in th' orderly-room?" Martlow asked him.

"What does everybody think about it?" replied Bourne. "They think it was damned silly to have a parade there. You can't think anything else. What they are saying now is that it was not a bomb at all, but a shell, or rather two shells from one of our own anti-aircraft batteries. Were you on aeroplane guard, Martlow?"

"No bloody fear," said Martlow hastily. "I 'ad enough t'day before yesterday. You can't see nowt, an' you get a crick in your bloody neck; an' them field glasses is not 'arf as good as what the C. O. pinched off me."

"I didn't hear any whistles, not till t'bomb burst," said Chapman, somewhat mollified by food. "You ask Bill. 'E was on airyplane guard."

"First thing I see was a shell burstin', an' then another," said Bill Bates nervously, "an' I blew me whistle as soon as I see the first shell. T' sun was in me eyes. What d'you want to bring me into 't for?"

"You've got no call to worry, kid," said Jakes. "You was on the other side o' the town."

"Well, then, what's 'e want to bring me into 't for?" asked Bates, with indignation.

The sight of Bourne putting his equipment together created a diversion, and when he explained the reason they looked at him as though he were one of those who had all the luck.

"I think we must be going to move somewhere else," said Bourne to Shem, "or Lance-Corporal Johnson wouldn't go in full pack. We shall have to carry a lot of stuff. Do you or Martlow want me to bring anything back?"

"Bring what you like," said Shem smiling. "Martlow and I have mucked in together, since you've been in the orderly-room."

"Well, the three of us can muck in together now," said Bourne.

"When you come back to the company, you mean," said Martlow.

Bourne showed no curiosity concerning the business which had brought them into Noeux-les-Mines. He was glad to dump the box which he and Lance-Corporal Johnson had carried the three miles from Philosophe on the floor of the quartermaster's office. They had carried it between them. It had those handles which hang down when not in use, but turn over and force one's knuckles against the ends of the box when it is lifted. By reversing the grip, one may save one's knuckles, but only at the expense of twisting one's elbow, and the muscles of the forearm. Having tried both ways, they passed their handkerchiefs through the handles, and knotted the corners, so that it was slung between them, but the handkerchiefs being of different sizes, the weight was not equally distributed. The quartermaster's store was a large shed of galvanised iron, which may have been a garage originally. He was not there, but the carpenter, who was making wooden crosses, of which a pile stood in one corner, thought he might be at the transport lines; on the other hand, he might be back at any moment, so they waited for as long as it took to smoke a cigarette, watching the carpenter, who, having finished putting a cross together, was painting it with a cheap-looking white paint.

"That's the motto of the regiment," said the carpenter, taking up one on which their badge and motto had been painted carefully. "It's in Latin, but it means 'Where glory leads.'"

Bourne looked at it with a sardonic grin.

"You're a bit of an artist with the paintbrush, Hemmings," he said, to cover up his thought.

"Well, I take a bit o' pride in me work. It don't last, o'course, the paint's poor stuff, and that wood's too soft; but you might just as well try to make a good job of it."

"What about going down to the transport lines?" asked Johnson.

"I'm ready, corporal," said Bourne, and they left Hemmings to his work.

"Not very cheerful, sitting there with a lot of wooden crosses," said Johnson, as they turned into the street.

"Why not?" Bourne asked him callously. "Would you like stone any better?"

"As soon as we see the quartermaster, we shall be able to look for our billets," said Johnson, not wishing to pursue the subject. "Then we can dump our packs and look round the town. He won't want me until the morning.'

"I hope we find some place where we can get a decent drink," said Bourne. "Why don't we get a rum issue every night, or a bottle of beer with dinner? The French get their wine. Did you see that shop as we came through Mazingarbe, with bottles of Clicquot and Perrier Jouet in the window, and a label on them, Reservee pour les officiers? Bloody cheek. Half of them don't know whether they are drinking champagne or cider. And we have to be content with that filthy stuff they sell us in the estaminets."

"I don't know anything about wine," said Johnson primly. "Sometimes when I took my girl out in Blighty we would go into a hotel, a respectable house, you know, and have a glass of port wine and a biscuit. And port wine and brandy is good for colic, it's binding. I've got a photo of my girl in my pocketbook. Here it is. It's only snap, of course, not very good; and the sun was in her eyes. Do you think she's nice looking?"

"Awfully pretty," said Bourne, who could be a fluent liar on occasion. He really thought that she looked rather binding, too; but they were turning into the transport lines, and Johnson buttoned the photograph into his pocket again. The quartermaster was not there, nor was the transport officer, so they inspected the houses, and Bourne stroked the nose of the old grey mare, who drew the Maltese cart for the officers' mess. His conscience was a little sensitive on her account. The officers' mess-cart generally preceded the Lewis-gun cart which Bourne helped to pull on the march; and whenever they came to a hill, if the officer were preoccupied with other matters, Bourne would hitch his rope to the mess-cart and leave it to the mare. She bore no malice, the old lady, as though she knew they had a pretty thin time. The mules did not move him to any sentiment; to him they seemed symbolical of modern war, grotesque, stubborn, vindictive animals. There was nothing for it but to trudge back to the quartermaster's stores again; and they found him this time. He talked to the lance-corporal and gave them a chit for the town-major, so they went off to look for him; he was out too, but a corporal in the office took matters into his own hands, and showed them to some billets in a back street, on the way to get his own tea. They would have to go to the town-major's office again, to make sure that it was all right. A thin woman of about forty, with a long- suffering expression on her face, was the only occupant of the house; and she left her work in the kitchen to show them into an empty room. Bourne noticed that the floorboards were clean.

"Mais c'est tout ce qu'il y a de plus commode, madame," said Bourne, and he began to tackle her at once on the prospect of getting a more or less civilised meal.

"Mais, monsieur, l'encherissement est tel..."

But he would not be denied, insinuating himself into her good graces with the flexibility of an eel in a bundle of grass; but after making a number of suggestions, he had to leave it to her, only he insisted on her getting him a bottle of good wine, Barsac for choice; and he gave her some notes with which to do her marketing.

"O, la, la!" she cried amusedly.

"What does she say?" inquired Johnson.

"That's the French for 'Good God,'" said Bourne, laughing. They followed her out into the kitchen, where she collected her shawl and basket, her sleek head needing no hat, while they went on into the yard, and surveyed the vegetables which she grew in a little garden at the end of it. Then they heard a familiar sound, though it seemed strange there: the long whine of a shell through the air, and its explosion on the outskirts of the town. She had come out with her basket, and looked up at the sky very much as though she were wondering whether it would rain. Then again came the whining sound.

"Ah, des obus!" she said in a tranquil tone, and set off on her errands.

"You'd think these Frenchies had lived in a war for years, and years, and years," said Johnson.

"Well, you do get accustomed to it, don't you?" replied Bourne. "It seems to me sometimes as though we had never known anything different. It doesn't seem real, somehow; and yet it has wiped out everything that came before it. We sit here and think of England, as a lot of men might sit and think of their childhood. It is all past and irrecoverable, but we sit and think of it to forget the present. There were

nine of us practically wiped out by a bomb this morning, just outsid
window, and we have already forgotten it."

"It wasn't a bomb, it was an anti-aircraft shell."

"Was it?" Bourne asked indifferently. "What really happened?'

"An anti-aircraft battery reported in answer to inquiries by Brigade that they had fired nine rounds on an enemy plane, and the fifth and sixth failed to explode."

That would give an accidental colour to the incident. One might anticipate an attack by enemy aircraft and avoid unreasonable exposure to it; but one could not anticipate a defective shell, which failed of its object and then exploded on striking the hard pavement of a street. Bourne kept what he thought to himself; but the men had said that no whistles were blown until after the first explosion, and the men on aeroplane guard had said that they did not actually see the plane, but blew their whistles when puffs of smoke appeared from the first couple of shells. If they were right, the official version was untrue, for the explosion which had killed two men in the street must have occurred before the shelling began. The practical futility of an aeroplane guard chosen at random from among the men was not a relevant consideration: they had not been trained to do that particular work. It was also irrelevant to say that the bomb found its target by the merest chance. Bourne took the men's point of view that these parades were silly and useless; then he reflected, with a certain acidity of thought, that there was a war on, and that men were liable to be killed rather cursorily in a war.

They waited until madame returned from her shopping; and she exhibited a bottle of Barsac in triumph to Bourne. She was giving them an omelette, a fillet of beef, and what Johnson called "chips", with a salad and cream cheese, and Bourne became eloquent in the appreciation of her zeal. They left her to prepare it, and went off to the town-major's office, when the same corporal whom they had seen in the afternoon told them that they might have the billets they were in for that night. They asked him to meet them at an estaminet and have a drink, and he told them of one at which he might look in later. Then they went for half an hour to sit in a room full of noise and smoke, where they drank vin blanc.

Back at their billets they had a satisfactory wash in a bucket with plenty of clean water; and then madame gave them their meal. Bourne tried to persuade her to eat with them; she declined firmly but amiably, only relenting so far as to drink a glass of wine. She didn't give very much attention to the lance-corporal, but she talked readily enough to Bourne. Her husband was at the front, and her daughter, who was to marry a man also with the colours, had gone to some relations to be out of the battle zone. She would marry when the war finished. When the war finished! When would it finish? She gave a low, curious laugh that expressed the significance of the tragedy more closely than any tears could do. She was extraordinarily tranquil in her pessimism: it was not so much as though she despaired, but as though she suppressed hope in herself for fear it would cheat her in the end. But all this pessimism was apparently for the course which the war was taking: she was perfectly clear that the Hun had to be defeated.

The world for her was ruined, and that was irreparable; but justice must be done; and for her justice was apparently some divine law, working slowly and inexorably through all the confused bickerings of men. She interested him, because though she was a comparatively uneducated woman, her thought was clear, logical, and hard.

He tried to speak hopefully to her, wondering whether he were not on trying to speak hopefully to himself. She admitted that the Hun was stopped; and England's strength was increasing: "Maintenantelle est tres bien montee," as she put it: though perhaps her manner implied that it was a tardy atonement for years of culpable negligence. There was in her some trace of that spirit which he had noticed among the older men in the ranks, a spirit which had ceased to hope for itself and yet was undefeated.

He finished the wine, of which Johnson had only drunk a couple of glasses, while she cleared away the plates and dishes. Then she called him into the room in which he and the lance-corporal were to sleep; and he found she had left there a pile of eight blankets, which were legally, perhaps, the property of the French republic, as they were all horizon blue in colour. One apiece was enough to cover them, and by folding three for each bed they could sleep on softness.

Bourne had long ago ceased to trouble about where or when he slept; but her kindness touched him, and he thanked her so warmly that perhaps she was touched too. A little thing meant a lot in these days. He no longer wanted to go out on the spree; he had had a decent meal and some good wine, and he would have been quite content to sit where he was until it were time to sleep; but Johnson had arranged to meet the corporal, and he had better go; after all there was little chance of any indecorous behaviour with Johnson.

They found the estaminet full of troops, and the corporal, who had been talking to a few men, came across to them. He was evidently at home in the place, for as soon as they had taken possession of a table, one of the two girls who were serving drinks came for their order, and he pulled her towards him familiarly, seating her on his knee, slipping his hand round her waist upwards under her arm so that he could feel her left breast, caressing it with inquisitive fingers, while she squealed and wriggled to make him more adventurous.

Bourne felt the contagion of the place take hold of him and course in his veins like a subtle flame; it was as though there were some enormous carnal appetite loose among them, feeding on them as fire on its fuel; from all sides came the noise of loud unsteady talk, senseless arguments suddenly uplifted to the pitch of quarrelling and swept aside again by a torrent of hard, almost mirthless laughter, while through it all drifted irrelevantly the sound of raucous voices, with the quality of a hand-saw, singing:

And the old folks at home,
They will sit all night and listen,
In the evening,
By the moonlight,
By the moonlight.

There was just that waft of nostalgia through the riot of beastly noise, which rose to drown it; and Bourne found the girl looking at him, as the corporal fondled her, with her insolent and furtive eyes. She exasperated him, so that he almost felt the lust of cruelty which such women provoke in some men, and she saw it.

"What the hell are we going to drink?" he asked with abrupt impatience; and the corporal shifting in his chair, the girl rose, straightened her skirts, and then, lifting both arms to smooth her hair with her hands, came round the table, and stood beside Bourne, purring, with the composed perversity of a cat. He did not want the bloody woman, he said angrily to himself, and ignoring her, he discussed drinks with the corporal, who had no ideas beyond the cheap champagne which Bourne only drank when he could get nothing else. They would not give

ny cafe-cognac there, but she suggested the privacy of an adjoining
ment.

"Very well. You drink the champagne, if you like it," said Bourne,
sending the girl away with the order. He got up and pushed his way over
to the bar, from where madame, hot and tightly buttoned, and monsieur
surveyed their barbaric customers as from a position of legal, if not
moral superiority. Bourne tackled monsieur, and after some hesitation
the man left the bar and returned with a half-bottle of white wine and the
assurance that it was good. He paid for it, they drew the cork for him,
gave him a clean glass; and he took it back to the table with him.

"I don't want to go into any back parlours for the sake of some cognac
in my coffee. If you would rather have some of this, corporal...?"

But the corporal preferred the champagne which the girl brought, and
Bourne paid for it, throwing in a small tip. He did not drink much of his
wine, though it was tolerable; he did not want to drink; and he knew that
the place would soon close for the night. Johnson and the corporal had
plenty to say to each other, and he only needed to join in the
conversation out of civility now and again. So he sat there quietly
smoking, and drinking a little wine, until it was time to leave. The girl
looked at him sulkily when they said goodnight.

Chapter VI

So! in the name of Cheshu Christ speak lower. It is the greatest
admiration in the universal world when the true and aunchent
prerogatifes and laws of the wars is not kept...there is no
tiddle-taddle nor pibble-pabble in Pompey's camp. I warrant you,
you shall find the ceremonies of the wars, and the cares of it,
and the forms of it, and the sobriety of it, and the modesty of it,
to be otherwise. – SHAKESPEARE

Lance-corporal Johnson went off to the quartermaster by himself next
morning, telling Bourne that there was no need for him to come; but to
be ready to start for battalion headquarters at noon. Bourne went out to
buy some food to take back to Shem and Martlow. He found a decent-
looking shop in the main street, but the first thing to take his eye in the
window was a notice in English saying that the sale of bread to troops
was prohibited until after midday. He went in, and was allowed to buy a
small cake, a couple of tins of sardines, and a jar of cherry jam. The
difficulty was to find something which would make a change for them,
and was easily carried. He couldn't very well buy a ham, or a tin of
biscuits. Since leaving the Somme even fresh meat was scarce, and their
dinner was almost invariably a stew composed of bully-beef, some patent
soup powders, dried or tinned vegetables, and potatoes. There were some
pastries in the shop, but these could not be stowed in his pack like the
cake and the cherry jam.

The tins of sardines he could carry in the side pockets of his tunic.

Johnson returned a few minutes before twelve with the news that the
battalion had been moved back to Mazingarbe, and were in huts by the
cemetery; and that there was a big working party going up the line that
night. He and Bourne would pick up the box at the quartermaster's
stores. They would get back to Mazingarbe too late for any dinner; but
madame had given them a good bowl of café au lait, with about a foot of
bread each, fresh butter and boiled eggs for breakfast. As she went off to
work early, Bourne had paid her, and said goodbye, in case they should

have left before she returned at midday. For all that look of long suffering on her face, she was a bracing and indomitable soul. He folded her blankets up and left them neatly in a pile, as they had received them; and then they left the empty house, closing the door behind them.

They had the same trouble as before with the box, and though they had not so far to go, it was heavier. Bourne was relieved when it was placed finally in a corner of the hut which was now the orderly room. He looked about him, and the first thing he saw was a notice, printed in large capitals; MIND WHAT YOU SAY, THE HUN HAS LISTENING APPARATUS, AND CAN HEAR YOU. It was a disturbing statement, and he concluded that it was intended only for the signaller; but he saw it later posted up on the outside of some huts. The colour-sergeant, greeting him affably, administered a more serious shock. "Bourne, you will sleep in the orderly-room in future."

"Yes, sir," he said, amazed, but with the mechanical obedience required of him. He didn't want them to see and covet the food he had brought back with him, so after a pause he said:

"I shall go for my blankets, sir; and for some things I left with one of my chums."

The colour-sergeant nodded, and he went out with his pack still on his shoulders, and talked to Shem and Martlow for a little while before they went on parade.

"You'll never come back," said Shem in a matter-of-fact way. "You've got a cushy job; an' if they didn't want you, they'd have sent you back before now. You'd better keep one tin o' sardines, an' take half the cake with you."

"I don't want it. I had a good feed in the town."

The division of the food proposed by Shem's practical mind seemed to him too like a formal act dissolving their partnership. He went back to the orderly-room in a mood of apathy, and copied orders into the book. The adjutant had complained that his handwriting was too small; and he tried to write large, with the result that his script became uneven and stiff, like that of a child, who is thinking in letters, instead of in words or in phrases. It seemed to him, somehow, symbolical of the loss of balance which he had detected in himself in the last few days. He heard the colour-sergeant speaking in his usual tone of affected diffidence, the sharp, business-like whisper of the corporal, and Johnson's, an empty echo. Occasionally Reynolds or Johnson would give him a paper to type, and for the moment he was busy with the clicking keys. The thing finished, he would sink again into apathy, thinking, with a singular intensity, about nothing, his consciousness not submerged or inhibited, but so dilated that it became too tenuous to hold any reality.

The adjutant came in, and after sitting at his table for a little while with his accustomed air of patient perplexity, went to the field telephone. To overhear one half of a conversation is always a little mystifying, but the adjutant's part of it seemed idiotic. Yes, he was pepper; and apparently he received, and in some cases repeated, instructions concerning a rat-hunt, and these were all about rats, and poles, which would be found at Potsdam Dump, and salt. Bourne came back from the emptiness of his interior conscience to take a little interest in the matter. Pepper and salt were code words for two battalions in the Brigade, and when the adjutant went back to his place, Bourne scribbled on a scrap of paper the question, "What are rats?" and passed it to the signaller, who wrote underneath, "gas cylinders", and pushed it back to him. If the Hun continued to develop his inventive faculty at this alarming rate, they would soon all be using the deaf and dumb language.

Then a pugnacious little officer with two pips up, called Wirral, who was a newcomer unknown to Bourne, entered, and politely but firmly asked the adjutant whether he, Wirral, was expected to do not only all the work of his own company, but apparently also the combined work of every other company in the battalion. The adjutant seemed to be impressed, or at least embarrassed, by the magnitude of the issues involved in these questions; but having a pathetic faith in the fallacy that man is a reasonable animal, he pointed out to Mr Wirral all the difficulties in which he found himself owing to the momentary shortage of officers, Captain Malet being on leave, Mr Clinton being in the hands of the dentist, and a few other officers being absent on one pretext or another. Mr Wirral was not at all moved by the difficulties of the adjutant; in fact he seemed disposed to increase them by every means available to him, unless he were treated with a minimum of consideration; if Mr Clinton happened to be suffering from a decayed tooth, he himself was at present a martyr to an ingrowing toenail. The adjutant held that these rival disabilities fell within different categories, the care of the feet, with all ranks, being an entirely personal responsibility. Mr Wirral's sense of injustice only became more acute at this complete lack of sympathy, while the adjutant stiffened in his chair.

The malicious imp in Bourne's heart laughed again for a moment. If Captain Malet had been in the adjutant's place, the interview might have lasted a minute, but scarcely longer, and under the gaze of his intolerant eyes, Mr Wirral would not have proceeded to argument, for with Captain Malet the immediate necessity was all that counted, and if he were ever driven to repeat an order, his voice and expression almost converted it into a threat of personal violence. Bourne had no feeling against the adjutant, he rather admired the conscientious and painstaking way in which he stuck to his work; but his manner was more likely to gain the approval of his superiors, than to command the obedience of those who worked under him. Mr Wirral was told in the end that as he had but lately returned from England to the front, it was only right that he should take some of the burden from the shoulders of officers who had been overworked for months. That closed the discussion and he retired after saluting the adjutant with an air of marked hostility. Then the colour-sergeant went over to the adjutant's table, and bending down had a few minutes' whispered conversation with him. Scenes of this kind always interested Bourne, the tension excited him; but he thought it rather humiliating that they should occur in the presence of the orderly-room staff. Old Tomlinson, Reynolds, and even Lance-Corporal Johnson knew all that there was to know about every officer in the battalion. He and the signaller knew too much. Except on one or two occasions, Bourne always left the room during orders-hour, but the others remained, and after the delinquencies of the men had been dealt with, an officer was occasionally sent for and asked to explain his conduct in certain circumstances. This should have been done quite privately. If an officer wished to complain to the adjutant, as in the case of Mr Wirral, there was no reason why the orderly-room staff should have witnessed the incident.

The army organisation is supposed to work with the impersonal and remorseless action of a machine, but this action is not single and indivisible, a human agency is always intervening, so that sometimes what is only the inexorable functioning of the machine takes on the character of a duel between opposed personalities, and while the mechanical action, having attained its object, ends, the other is more lasting. Under all this monotonous routine of duty, which made war seem a dull and sordid business, there was the sense of encompassing danger, a sense which perhaps grew stronger under the efforts of the will to subdue it.

Men acting together in constant peril of their lives demand at least that the chances shall be evenly divided among them. They could be generous and accept additional burdens without complaint, if there were real need; but in moments of bitterness it seemed to them that duty and honour were merely the pretexts on which they were being deprived of their most elementary rights. Even on carrying parties and in the mere routine work of ordinary trench life in quiet sectors, men were killed in rather a casual and indiscriminate way. Though he was by no means inclined to help carry a gas cylinder on a pole, while watching the working party fall in on the road that night, Bourne felt rather out of it; he felt as though he were swinging the lead.

For his breakfast now he went straight to the cookers, and unless it were raining, he ate it there, talking to Abbot, while sitting in the shelter of a thin straggling hedge. He had in his pocket a small tin of toffee which had come in a parcel from England. He offered some to Abbot.

"Thank 'ee," said Abbot, "but I ain't very partial to sweet stuff. There's Williams there. 'E's always hungry for toffees. 'E don't drink, an' 'e don't smoke, an' unless 'e goes after the women I don't know what 'e does do. You might give 'im a few. 'Ere, Williams, 'ere's some toffee for you."

Williams was a little Welshman, Headquarter-company cook, with a face like a Phoenician, etched all over with fine lines, but with none of the deeper wrinkles, a curiously impassive face, which had aged early, as he could not have been fifty. He came at once, in his greasy smoke-blackened suit, wiping his hands on a cloth.

"It's a long time since I 'ad any decent toffee," he said, with a curious hunger in his black eyes.

"I believe 'e'd sell 'imself for a tin o' toffee," said Abbot with a grin.

"Here you are, then; take the lot," said Bourne. "I have some more inside, and I don't care about them, but some friends of mine are always sending out a tin. I shall bring you out some."

"I'd be glad of them," said Williams simply; he was a man of few words, a rare quality in a Welshman.

"How did the carrying party get on last night?" Bourne inquired. "You know, as each party get back the officer in charge comes into the orderly-room, with a slip of paper, I think. I was half-asleep and didn't pay much attention. And sometimes a runner comes in, too, and leaves a paper on the table; and the old colour-sergeant is cribbing like hell this morning about it. They disturb the sleep of a hard-working man."

"'E were a colour-sergeant when 'e went on reserve," said Abbot. "You knew 'im, didn't you, Williams? The men were pretty tired when they got back at about two this morning, after the move, an' parades an' one thing an' another, an' wearin' them bloody gas 'elmets the 'ole time. Parade again at ten today, an' another big carryin' party tonight. No sense workin' men day an' night."

"Well, they'll 'ave to send us back into the trenches for a rest soon, I suppose," said Bourne, and asked Abbot for some hot water to rinse out his mess-tin, polished his knife and fork by rubbing them in the earth, and went back to the orderly-room. He arrived at the crisis of a scene; the adjutant, Captain Havelock, was at his table, looking irritable and rather nervous; at one side was the colour-sergeant, shaking with fury as he spoke, and opposite the adjutant was the regimental, perfectly cool and with slightly supercilious smile on his face. Corporal Reynolds impatiently waved Bourne out of the room again. He didn't hear what the adjutant said, but he heard the regimental's voice, rather cool, almost insolent, in reply:

"Of course, sir, if you will not support your regimental sergeant-major there is nothing more to be said." Bourne went right down the steps into the road, so as to be out of earshot; and he remembered Tozer's words about the regimental and the colour-sergeant scrapping in the orderly-room. The regimental came out almost immediately after him, smiling superciliously and carrying his head high as he walked way. He didn't see Bourne, whom decided to wait a few minutes, and give things time to settle down again, before going back to his work.

The row seemed to have been quite unpremeditated, and anyway Captain Malet was out of it. He was due back today, but he was going to carry on as company commander. Major Blessington seemed to like Captain Havelock; it was true he treated him in rather a casual way, but it was all to the good that he should like him. It was a pity Major Shadwell and Captain Malet could not run the battalion between them. Bourne had never seen much of Major Shadwell, but he was the same type as Captain Malet, only older, quieter, with more of iron and less of fire in his nature. Men said that he had changed a lot since coming out to France; he had been lively and full of humour, now he was rather taciturn, with a severe and inflexible expression. The men liked him: Captain Malet appealed more to the imagination, but they had more trust in Major Shadwell. He knew it too, apparently, because Bourne remembered talking to the padre, who told him how the major had said to him immediately after a show on the Somme, with a great effort to restrain himself; "It's bloody murder, padre, but by God there's nothing like commanding men."

That was after Colonel Woodcote had been wounded; since he had gone, and the old adjutant, Captain Everall, things had not been the same. The old lot had all kept together, and the men knew them, or knew of them, even before the war; but Major Shadwell and Captain Malet were the only two left of the old lot. Regular officers as a rule didn't understand the new armies, they had the model of the old professional army always in their mind's eye, and they talked of the fire discipline of the old army, and the rate of fire they were able to maintain in repelling counterattacks, saying that reliance on bombs had ruined musketry. They forgot how the war had changed since 1915, ignoring artillery developments; and it never occurred to them that if one Lewis-gun could do the work of ten men, it was rather foolish not to prefer it, since it offered a smaller target. The majority of them, though there were brilliant exceptions, did not understand that the kind of discipline they wished to apply to these improvised armies was only a brake on their impetus. Then again, as a rule the regular officers did not get on with the temporary officers of the new army; but the regular army, perfect as it was, was a very small affair; things were now on a different scale, and in these new conditions the regular officer was as much an amateur as his temporary comrades. After a few minutes, Bourne went back to his place, and the orderly-room was calm again.

Captain Malet returned to duty that afternoon, and on the following day he was one of the principals in another scene. When Brigade ordered the battalion to provide a working party for that night, it was discovered that in the state supplied to Brigade by the orderly-room, the strength of companies returned was not the fighting strength but the ration strength, and the demands made by Brigade, on the basis of the figures supplied, could only be met by taking every available man, even to the companies' cooks. The M. O. was one of the first to complain, with regard to his orderlies, and various specialist officers followed him. One of the penalties of infallibility is that it cannot remedy its mistakes, because it cannot admit having made them; and Captain Havelock was embarrassed but inflexible. Then Captain Malet arrived on the scene, quite ready to fight anything and principle be damned.

"Do you intend, sir, to take my cooks?" The adjutant saw no other way.

"I am not going to allow my men to suffer because of some damned incompetence in the orderly-room. Do you understand that if the cooks go up the line on this working party, the men will not even have any hot tea when they come back, at about three in the morning, exhausted?"

The adjutant tried to assert himself, but the angry officer would not let him speak.

"You haven't got the moral courage to stand up for your own men, or to admit your silly blunder. Well, I shall tell you what I shall do. I shall order my horse, and take two orderlies and go up to inspect trenches. I shall see you are two men short anyway, and fuck Brigade!" He brought his fist down on the table, turned on his heel without saluting and went out. The adjutant and the colour-sergeant looked at each other, as though they thought this kind of behaviour was not quite nice, and then there was a hurried consultation. There was never any doubt that Captain Malet would be as good as his word, and the outcome of this incident was that two cooks were left behind to make tea for the whole battalion. On the following day the M. O. saw the commanding officer in the orderly-room, and said the men did not have enough rest; they should not be expected to parade all day and to work all night as well. He put the matter very quietly, but Major Blessington treated him in an offhand way.

"Very well, sir, if any man reports sick to me I shall excuse him duty," said the M. O.; and he saluted, leaving Major Blessington to the contemplation of his fingernails.

Nobody had much sympathy for the adjutant, but he was bound by the nature of his office to be the mere reflection and echo of the commanding officer, and with all his faults and defects of manner he was doing his best to master his job. His duties were often unpleasant. A couple of days later he sent for Mr Clinton, who so far had not gone up the line once since they had been in this sector. The adjutant had to tell him that he would not accept any further excuses, and that he had been detailed to take up a party that night. Mr Clinton took what amounted to a telling-off very well, and the adjutant had said what he had to say, quite definitely, but in a friendly and reasonable way. There was nothing in the interview at all, it was a mere matter of routine; but as Mr Clinton went out, Bourne noticed an acid smile on the colour-sergeant's face, and he experienced a feeling of humiliation in himself. Clinton was such a good fellow; he had been through some of the worst shows on the Somme, and he had never spared himself; and there was that swine grinning at him.

He heard the working party come back in the small hours of the morning, and as usual there were slips to be left on the table, people came in and went out again, and the only light was from the moon shining through the windows. They woke the lance-corporal, and eventually he sat up, as another man entered, and Bourne heard a whispered conversation.

"They got Mr Clinton all right. One of them sausages came over and blew most of 'is guts out. No, 'e's not dead, they gave 'im morphia, and took 'im away on a stretcher. Well, if 'e's not dead yet, 'e pretty soon will be."

"Who's that?" said Corporal Reynolds, sitting up.

"Mr Clinton, corporal; 'is number's up all right. It fair made me sick to see 'im. 'E was conscious, too. 'E said 'e knew 'e was goin' to get it up 'ere. 'E knew it."

Bourne did not move, he lay absolutely still in his blankets, with an emotion so tense that he thought something would snap in him.

Chapter VII

'Tis no matter if I do halt; I have the wars for my colour,
and my pension shall seem the more reasonable. – SHAKESPEARE

The colour-sergeant had succeeded in working his ticket, it had gone through, as they phrased it, and he was leaving for home that night. He enhanced his own pleasure by expatiating on the many years of usefulness which still lay in front of his subordinates, a prospect which did not move them in the same way; and his purring satisfaction seemed to make it more difficult for them to find suitable words in which to express their regret at his departure. Congratulations on his release came more readily from their tongues. Bourne said nothing at all; as far as he was concerned in the matter, he was glad the old hypocrite was going; but he couldn't think of anything except the fate of poor Clinton, who had always been so decent to him. He wanted to see Sergeant Tozer and hear what had happened.

"I hoped that before I left," said the colour-sergeant, dripping with the unction of benevolence, "I should see Johnson a corporal, and Bourne with a stripe." Bourne, who never believed a word the old man said, looked up at him with startled surprise, which the other probably mistook for credulity, as he continued to purr pleasantly while lacing up his boots. Bourne, having made up his own bed and swept the floor, went outside to wash and shave, and after coming back for his tunic, crossed the road and found Sergeant Tozer.

"I'm damned sorry about it myself," said the sergeant. "It was one o' them sausages; they put wind up me, them things do. You can see the buggers in the air, but you can't always know where they're going to land. All our stuff 'ad to be carried up to the fire-trench, you see, and put in position there, ready. After each pair o' men 'ad dumped their load, they turned down a short bit of slit trench an' waited in the trench behind where I was. Well, the 'un isn't much more'n fifty yards away just there, an' 'e can 'ear a good deal of what's goin' on in our trenches, same as we can 'ear a good deal of what's goin' on in 'is. We 'eard this bloody

84

thing go up. Two o' our chaps 'ad just dumped their load an' turned into the slit, an' the officer who was takin' over the stuff went into a small dugout then to get a chit. We could see the dam' thing comin'. Mr Clinton an' a couple o' their sentries were the only people in the bay, an' 'e got it proper, 'e did. Fair made me sick when we was puttin' 'im on a stretcher; an' all 'e said before they gave 'im morphia an' took 'im away was; "I knew I'd get it 'ere, I knew." 'E kep' on sayin' it. One o' the men on the fire-step was 'urt too, but they said it was only a nice blighty one. Funny thing, don't you think, 'im sayin' 'e knew 'e'd get it 'ere?"

"I don't know," answered Bourne; "most of us have premonitions of the kind now and again, but they don't always prove right."

"I've got a kind of fancy I'm goin' to come through it all,' said the sergeant. "D'you know what I couldn't 'elp thinkin' about Mr Clinton? Well, 'e looked as though, now 'e knew, it didn't matter, it was all right. Of course, you could see 'e was in pain, until they gave 'im the morphia; an' 'e moaned a bit, an' you could see 'e was tryin' not to moan. I don't know what it was, but 'is face 'ad changed some'ow; it didn't 'ave that kind of sulky worried look any more. 'E knew 'is number was up all right."

"It was rotten bad luck, after coming through the Somme without a scratch," said Bourne. "I'm awfully sorry about him. Every time I was with him something funny would happen, and he was such a good sort. And he was always decent to the men, didn't lose his temper because he had got wind up or was beaten to the wide; he seemed to humour them and master them at the same time. He had such a clear, low voice, did you ever notice it? He didn't have to shout to make himself heard."

"Oh, the men all liked 'im," agreed the sergeant. "You can't fool the men. You will get an officer sometimes full of shout an' swank, an' 'e'll put 'em through it, an' strafe 'em, an' the walk off parade feelin' that 'e 'as put the fear o' God into 'em. Well, 'e 'asn't. 'E thinks they respect 'im, an' all they think is that 'e wears a Sam Browne belt, and they wear one waist, web, ditto. Men don't mind a bit o' chatter. 'E were a nice chap, were Mr Clinton, an' we all liked 'im.

"You know, to my way o' thinkin' some of us'ns 'ave a dam' sight more religion than some o' the parsons who preach at us. We're willin' to take a chance, we are. 'Uman nature's 'uman nature, an' you may be right or you may be wrong, but if you bloody well think you're right, you may as well get on with it. What does it matter if y'are killed? You've got to die some day. You've got to chance your arm in this life, an' a dam' sight more 'n your arm too sometimes.

"Some folk talk a lot about war bein' such a bloody waste; but I'm not so sure it's such a bloody waste after all. They think it's all about nothin', I suppose. Take some o' the men comin' out now. I don't mean the kids, but some o' the older men, who wouldn't join up till they was pushed. Those are the kind o' chaps who talk about what a bloody waste of life war is. They say there oughtn't to be no war, as though that 'elped matters.

"But when you send 'em over the top with a rifle, an' a bayonet, an' a few bombs, an' they find a big buck 'un in front o' them, they don't care a fuck about wastin' the other bugger's life, do they? Not a bit of it, it's their own bloody skins they think about, then. That's what they call their principle. 'Arf o' them snivellin' conshies at 'ome 'd fight like rats if they was cornered. It's 'uman nature. You can make nearly any bloody coward fight if you tease 'im into the right 'umour. But what about us? Who 'as the better principle? Do they think we came out for seven bloody bob a week? I'm not troublin' about my bloody conscience. I've got some self-respect, I 'ave."

Bourne appreciated Sergeant Tozer's point of view, because he understood the implications his words were intended to convey, even when he seemed to wander from the point. Life was a hazard enveloped in mystery, and war quickened the sense of both in men: the soldier also, as well as the saint, might write his tractate de contemptu mundi, and differ from him only in the angle and spirit from which he surveyed the same bleak reality.

He could not stay any longer, but went back to the orderly-room until within a few minutes of commanding officer's orders, when as usual he went out, and finding a cool place sat by himself and smoked. He spoke scarcely a word to anyone except the signaller, who would whisper occasionally or scribble something on a piece of paper, and push it along the table for him to read. The only person in whom he took any interest was the adjutant. When he had come in for the first time that day, Bourne had been going out with forms for one of the company offices, and they had met in the doorway. Bourne stood to attention on one side of the door, as he passed in, and he noticed the look of weariness and anxiety on the officer's face. He felt a great deal of sympathy for him. Now and again through the day he glanced in his direction, to find him sitting there in his place, doing nothing, his chin in his left hand, his eyes fixed, and his young, rather handsome face filled with the trouble and perplexity of his thoughts. They all knew what his thoughts were. The colour-sergeant would interrupt him occasionally, on some matter of routine; and he would turn to it with a look of wearied resignation, and having settled it, fall to fidgeting with his papers for a few moments, and then relapse again into his melancholy brooding. It is so easy to settle these questions of routine. He was even oblivious of the fact that the colour-sergeant had made a separate peace with the enemy, and when reminded with modest delicacy of the fact, he had only looked at him with some embarrassment and said:

"Oh, yes, sergeant-major"--for that was Tomlinson's present rank, the old 'colour-sergeant' being merely reminiscent of the rank, abolished earlier, with which he had retired from the pre-war army'--"what time do you leave?"

"I relinquish my duties at six o'clock tonight, sir."

"Well," said the adjutant desperately, "you will be glad to have a rest, won't you?"

Bourne, typing orders, was just ticking off on the typewriter the statement "18075 Cpl. T. S. Reynolds to be sergeant", and the date; and then a little later the notice of Sergeant Reynolds' appointment as orderly-room sergeant. He felt the hurt which the adjutant's preoccupation had given to the old man's vanity. Presently the chaplain came in, and immediately Captain Havelock got up and went out with him. Bourne remembered he wanted to ask the padre to cash a cheque. And then quite suddenly he heard that curiously tinny old voice, which always reminded him of an emasculated tomcat, behind him.

"Bourne, you will cease from duty here tonight at six o'clock."

"Very good, sergeant-major," said Bourne briefly; though the dismissal, which he had expected, took him by surprise at that particular moment. Evidently the sergeant-major thought there was some disappointment in his voice, and it roused in him the appetite to rub it in.

"You are not quite the man for the job," he said, with satisfaction.

"No, sergeant-major," said Bourne indifferently, and then added, simply as a matter of casual interest; "I shall be glad to go back to soldiering again."

Nothing could have flicked them more acutely on the raw, than the implied distinction between their job and his; and, satisfied with the effect of this counterthrust, he continued his typing. He had become almost an expert. A moment later the signaller looked up at him, and solemnly winked.

"'Ow d'you feel?" said Sergeant-Major Robinson when he presented himself at a few minutes after six, pack, rifle and bedding complete.

"Fat and idle, sergeant-major," replied Bourne, smiling.

"We can cure that. You may go to Sergeant Tozer's 'ut; dare say 'e can make room for you."

"Eard you was coming back, at tea-time," said little Martlow, as Bourne dumped all his stuff on the ground beside him. "We're not goin' up the line tonight. First night off we've 'ad since we've been in this fuckin' 'ole. What are we goin' to do about it?'

"Where's Shem?" Bourne asked him.

"Washin' 'isself. Let's go into bloody Mazingarbe an' 'ave a bon time, the three on us. I've got vingt frong an' a ten-bob note me mother sent me."

Shem appeared in the doorway.

"Do you know where the padre is billeted, Shem? Come and show me the way, and then I want to find Evans. You had better come along, too, Martlow, and we shall make a night of it."

"What d'you want Evans for?' asked Martlow jealously.

"I want him to buy me some of that champagne which is 'reserve pour les officiers;' as he is the commanding officer's servant, they'll sell it to him without fuss."

"Ask Sergeant Tozer to come," said Shem. "He has been pretty well fed up lately."

"All right, but I must find the padre first. We shall have plenty of time to look for the sergeant later; or you may go and look for him, while I'm waiting for the padre."

They took a short cut behind Headquarter Company's huts and the orderly-room, coming out in a side street, or rather lane, in which some of the better houses had secluded themselves. Bourne knocked at a door, and Shem and Martlow, having told him they would meet him at an estaminet in the main street a couple of doors away from the corner, went off to look for Sergeant Tozer. No one answered his knock. Then an old woman crossing the yard told him the chaplain was not in, but he would be back later; she was vague when asked how much later. Bourne idled up and down the street, waiting. Presently out of one of the houses came the adjutant. He looked at Bourne as he acknowledged the salute.

"Are you waiting for anyone?" he asked.

"I am waiting to see the chaplain, sir."

"He is with the commanding officer. I do not think he will be long."

That was encouraging. At last, the tall lean figure of the padre came out. He did not notice Bourne coming down the street, but turned away to go to his own billet, and Bourne followed him, overtaking him before he got to the door. He was surprised when Bourne told him that he was no longer in the orderly-room. There was no difficulty about the cheque, as he had plenty of money, which he needed for the use of the mess, and he was going into Noeux-les-Mines in the morning.

"Mr Clinton died of wounds this afternoon. Do you know, he told me some days ago he had a feeling that he would be killed if he went into the line here? I think he told me, because in a way he was rather ashamed of it; when he did go up, he went quite cheerfully, as though he had put it out of his mind."

Bourne shrank from talking about the incident with the padre, even though the padre was one of the best. He could only say, in some confusion, how sorry he was; it was odd to think he could speak more frankly about the matter with Sergeant Tozer.

"I don't know how you can go on as you are, Bourne," said the chaplain, abruptly changing the subject. "I suppose even the luckiest of us have a pretty rough time of it out here; but if you were an officer, you might at least have what comfort there is to be found, and you would have a little privacy, and friends of your own kind. I wonder how you stick it. You haven't anyone whom you could call a friend among these men, have you?"

Bourne paused for quite an appreciable time.

"No," he said, finally. "I don't suppose I have anyone whom I can call a friend. I like the men, on the whole, and I think they like me. They're a very decent generous lot, and they have helped me a great deal. I have one or two particular chums, of course; and in some ways, you know, good comradeship takes the place of friendship. It is different; it has its own loyalties and affections; and I am not so sure that it does not rise on occasion to an intensity of feeling which friendship never touches.

"It may be less in itself, I don't know, but its opportunity is greater. Friendship implies rather more stable conditions, don't you think? You have time to choose. Here you can't choose, or only to a very limited extent. I didn't think heroism was such a common thing. Oh, it has its degrees, of course. When young Evans heard the colonel had been left on the wire, he ran back to do what he could for him. Of course he owed a good deal to the colonel, who thought it a shame to send out a mere boy, and took him on as servant to try and give him a chance. That is rather a special case, but I have seen a man risking himself for another more than once; I don't say that they would all do it. It seems to be a spontaneous and irreflective action, like the kind of start forward you make instinctively when you see a child playing in a street turn and run suddenly almost under a car. At one moment a particular man may be nothing at all to you, and the next minute you will go through hell for him. No, it is not friendship. The man doesn't matter so much, it's a kind of impersonal emotion, a kind of enthusiasm, in the old sense of the word. Of course one is keyed up, a bit overwrought. We help each other. What is one man's fate today, may be another's tomorrow. We are all in it up to the neck together, and we know it."

"Yes, but you know, Bourne, you get the same feeling between officers, and between officers and men. Look at Captain Malet and the men, for instance."

"I don't know about officers, sir," said Bourne, suddenly reticent. "The men think a great deal of Captain Malet. I am only talking about my own experience in the ranks. It is a hard life, but it has its compensations, the other men have been awfully decent to me; as they say, we all muck in together. You know, padre, I am becoming demoralised. I begin to look on all officers, N.C.O.'s, the military police, and brass hats, as the natural enemies of deserving men like myself. Captain Malet is not an exception, he comes down on us occasionally, and disturbs the even tenor of our existence."

"I don't doubt you deserve it. Were you fired from the orderly-room?'

"Yes. I should think that is the right term to use, sir. I was taken into the orderly-room on the understanding that I should be there for ten days, while Grace was undergoing medical treatment. I have completed my ten days, and Grace is still swinging the lead. The post is now vacant. It was not really my milieu. Between ourselves, padre, there's not enough work in the orderly-room for three men, let alone four. Three are necessary when we are in the line; but they are now doing the sensible thing, and running it with two, until they can pick up a properly qualified clerk."

"Well, I don't think you ought to stay as you are. I don't think it is the right place for you. You might be more useful in some other way. However, I have got to do some work now. Come in and see me again some night, though I think we shall be on the move again very soon. Do you know that man Miller?"

"Miller, who deserted just before the July show, sir? I don't know him. I know of him."

"Well, he has been arrested down at Rouen. How he ever got so far I can't imagine. He found a woman there who sheltered him until his money was finished and then handed him over to the police. I can't help wishing either that he had got clean away, or that something had happened to him. It's a beastly business. Goodnight."

"I am awfully sorry that you should be troubled about it, sir; it won't be very pleasant for any of us. I hope I haven't kept you, and I am really very much obliged about the cheque. Goodnight, sir."

"Goodnight, Bourne; and look me up again sometime. Goodnight."

As he hurried down the twilit street, Bourne thought it certainly seemed more than likely that a firing party would be detailed for the purpose of ending the career of Lance-Corporal Miller, and on the whole he was more sorry for the firing party than for the prisoner. He had always thought that Miller should have spelt his name Muller, because he had a high square head like a Hun. It was a beastly business all right. When Miller disappeared just before the attack, many of the men said he must have gone over to the Hun lines and given himself up to the enemy. They were bitter and summary in their judgment on him. The fact that he had deserted his commanding officer, which would be the phrase used to describe-his offence on the charge-sheet, was as nothing compared to the fact that he had deserted them. They were to go through it while he saved his skin. It was about as bad as it could be, and if one were to ask any man who had been through that spell of fighting what ought to be done in the case of Miller, there could only have been one answer. Shoot the bugger. But if that same man were detailed as one of the firing party, his feelings would be modified considerably.

Suddenly Bourne wondered what he himself would do if he were detailed for the job. He tried to put that involuntary question he had asked himself aside, and he found it was impossible; he was one of those men who must try to cross a bridge before coming to it. It would be his duty; his conscience would not be too nice when there was a collective responsibility, but these justifications seemed unreal.

The interval between the actual cowardice of Miller and the suppressed fear which even brave men felt before a battle, seemed rather a short one, at first sight, but after all, the others went into action; if they broke down under the test, at least they had tried, and one might have some sympathy for them; others broke momentarily and recovered again, like the two men whom Sergeant-Major Glasspool had brought to their senses. It might even be necessary to shoot fugitives for the sake of preventing panic. All these cases were in a different class, and might be considered with sympathy. If he were on the firing party he would have to make the best of it; he took the same chance as the rest of them, none of whom would care for the job of an executioner.

He had forgotten to see Evans; but it would have been too late even if he had remembered, for Evans would be occupied in attending to the wants of the major. He found Shem and Martlow at the corner, but no Sergeant Tozer, they had not been able to find him; so he told them to wait where they were, while he went into a small restaurant, where he had eaten once before. Presently he emerged again with a girl of about seventeen; and, to the astonishment of Shem and Martlow, turned with her away from them, up the street. He was walking quite affectionately, his hand on her arm.

"It's a bugger, ain't it?" exclaimed Martlow. "Wish I knew some bloody French.'

"Well, I'm not going to wait here for him," said Shem a little sulkily. "Let's go into the estaminet and get a drink."

They waited until he was out of sight round the bend in the street, and noticed that an older woman came to the restaurant door, and looked after the couple a little anxiously.

"E 'asn't been the same, not since 'e 'as been in the orderly-room," said Martlow. "All right, let's go in an' get a drink."

They went into the estaminet and drank some vin rouge and grenadine, while they told each other what they really thought about Bourne, and the defects in his character, defects which had recently become more marked. In about twenty minutes Bourne reappeared, smiling, and asked if they were ready.

"Where 'ave you been?" they both asked him in one indignant breath.

"What is the matter with you?" said Bourne, surprised. "I have been to get Sergeant Tozer, of course. He is waiting in the restaurant."

"We thought you had cleared off with the girl," said Shem, a little awkwardly; "and left us on our own."

"Evidently your ideas want bucking up again," said Bourne. "It was about time I came back. I didn't think you would become softwitted in ten days."

He was not offended by their sulkiness; if he were a little hurt at first, he put it aside and ragged them into a good humour. Sergeant Tozer was glad he was back again, and liked the quiet little eating house, one could scarcely call it a restaurant, better than the big noisy room in the estaminet. They could only get an omelette and pommes frites in the way of food; but presently madame and her daughter, who both waited on them, crowned the table with a couple of bottles of Clicquot. Madame went straight back to her kitchen, but Bourne started to protest to the girl. She tried to reason with him, apparently, but he would not listen to her, and at length, a little reluctantly, she went to a drawer in a dresser and brought out a card with a piece of faded green cord, by which he suspended it on the corks of the two bottles. On it was printed boldly, in letters all the same size, "Reservee pour les officiers". Madame, returning with the food, promptly removed it; someone might see it, she protested. The military police were very troublesome. At last, to pacify her, Bourne put the card in his pocket, saying he would keep it as a souvenir of the war.

They ate and drank in great good humour after that, and little Martlow followed the movements of the girl who waited on them with round eyes of admiration. No one else came in that night, they had the room to themselves, and they finished their wine at their leisure. Then Bourne crossed to the kitchen door and asked for the bill, which brought forth madame and the daughter to him; he laughed as he went into their minute and detailed statements, and gave them money. Then quite impudently he kissed them both, the old woman first, and the daughter afterwards.

"What did you want to kiss the old woman for?" said Martlow as soon as they were in the street.

"So that I could kiss the girl afterwards," said Bourne, laughing in the darkness.

They turned the corner and came again to the huts. As Sergeant Tozer wanted to go into the company office for a minute, Bourne waited for him outside, and the other two went on by themselves.

"Don't let us go back to kip yet, sergeant," said Bourne when the other returned. "Let us go a little way behind the huts, and sit down, and smoke and talk. It is such a ripping night. Look at that slagheap over there, cutting the skyline like the rock of Gibraltar. There's another towards Sains. The wine has enlivened without exciting me..."

"It 'as gone a bit to my 'ead, too," said the sergeant.

"To say it has gone to my head would be incorrect," observed Bourne. "It has set my blood alight, it has warmed all my five senses simultaneously. I feel like a human being again. To tell you the plain, honest truth, sergeant, though I didn't want to stay in the orderly-room, when old Tomlinson came up to me in his cat-like way and told me to go back to my company, I felt a bit hipped by it. My vanity was hurt, and he seemed to get a kind of satisfaction out of it. But as you would put it, I have been in a bad skin ever since we left Sand-pits."

"You could 'ave worked it so that they'd 'ave let you stay in the orderly-room, if you 'ad wanted to stay there," said the sergeant.

"I didn't want to stay there," answered Bourne impatiently. "It bored me stiff, and I would rather be dog-tired than bored. I like being with the company. I like the swank of it, even if it's as empty as a drum. I like the swank of a drum. But if I had stayed in the orderly-room much longer, I should have become a lead-swinger too. I might have asked the colour-sergeant or the adjutant to send me back; but I didn't, because I wanted to dodge carrying gas cylinders. I was swinging the lead as it was. Of course, I don't mind swinging the lead a bit in the company, especially when I think I have earned a bit of a rest. It's a game, as they say."

"Well, don't you come any o' those games on me," said the sergeant with a note of warning in his voice. "That young Shem is the most artful bugger I know. 'E got on a workin' party 'ere, when we wanted every man we could get. 'E got off with 'is boots, I think. They was worn out, an' we didn't 'ave another pair to fit the bugger, 'e 'as got such short broad feet."

"He got off with his eyes," said Bourne laughing. "When an officer looks up and meets Shem's eyes, he always thinks he may conceivably be telling the truth. I can't work it like Shem. Anyway that is all in the game, so long as you don't overdo it. Do you think I'm windy?"

"You're not any more windy than the next man," said the sergeant with a judicial air in answer to the abrupt question. "Sergeant-Major Glasspool said you were all right, an' you've always been all right with me. Besides, if 'e thought you was shirkin' it, the cap'n would be down on you. What do you want to ask me for; don't you know yourself?"

"I wanted another opinion," said Bourne. "I don't think I'm windy. I am in the hell of a bloody funk, sometimes, but then everybody is. At first it seems to push me right over. I get a bit dazed; but when that has passed, funk only makes me think a damned sight quicker than usual. When I went to see the padre tonight, he asked me why I wanted to stay with the company, and I said I liked the men. Well, you and I know that there are all sorts among the men. You know more than I do, because you have got to keep them together, and push them into it sometimes.

"What I said to him sounded rather silly after I had said it, but I suppose it was true all the same. I like the life better when I'm with the men. When I was in the orderly-room, and saw the men fall in on the road to go up the line, I felt out of it. Now that I'm back again I feel better."

"Well, we'd better go to kip," said the sergeant. "I'm glad you're back, if that's what you want. All the same you was dam' lucky. I 'aven't 'ad enough sleep for a week. It's cloudin' over now. We'll get some rain before mornin'."

Chapter VIII

...ambition,
The soldier's virtue, rather makes choice of loss
Than gain which darkens him. – SHAKESPEARE

Captain Malet watched Sergeant Tozer drilling his section on some of the wasteland beyond the huts. It had rained a little in the night, and there was no dust. They had been doing some rapid wiring with screw-pickets, but there was not enough material for the work done to provide any test of efficiency. Afterwards, to wake them up, the sergeant gave them a little extended order drill, and Bourne being the last man on the right, the sergeant amused himself by giving the order left wheel repeatedly, so that Bourne sweated at the double for the greater part of that hour. Almost as soon as he dropped into quick march, on coming into line with the pivotal man again, there would be a shrill whistle from the sergeant, who, standing very erect, would sweep his outstretched arm round a quarter of the horizon, and Bourne was at the double again, saying, under his breath and while he had any breath, things that were more sincere than complimentary.

Captain Malet completely misunderstood the sergeant's motives. He had believed him to be a strict, efficient, but kindly instructor, and yet this looked very much like a kind of punishment drill. He struck at a few clods of earth irritably with his great ash-stick. He did not like this kind of thing. He waved to the innocent sergeant to halt his men, and advanced on him.

"The men don't seem to be working very well this morning, sergeant," he said with ominous amiability. "They don't keep a proper interval, and they don't wheel round evenly. I shall take them myself for a few minutes. You get on the left flank, will you, and let us see if we can't improve matters a bit."

Sergeant Tozer was disturbed. He was not quite sure from the start that Captain Malet's method was the right one, and he became convinced before two minutes had elapsed that it was entirely wrong. Captain Malet gave the order right wheel repeatedly, and Sergeant Tozer was doubling over clods and stubble for all he was worth, while Bourne merely made a right turn, and continued at a leisurely pace in the direction indicated. Bourne realised the significance of the matter immediately, and could with difficulty restrain his laughter. He wished he were on the other flank, and next to the sergeant; it would be worthwhile doubling if he could only hear what the sergeant must be saying to the circumambient air. The sergeant would see the point, too, and was certainly bursting with a sense of injustice. Probably the men thought nothing more about the matter than that it was rather good fun to see Sergeant Tozer taking quite a lot of unnecessary exercise. At last Captain Malet signalled to retire, thus bringing the men back towards himself; and having halted them, he called up a hot and indignant sergeant to listen to his views on the performance.

"Sergeant, these men all seem inclined to slow down to an infantryman's pace, and I think that on parade, at any rate, they might keep to our own quick, short step. Of course, one can't expect to get quite the same pace out of them under these conditions; they carry a bit more weight out here than they do at home. And it's very hot today, isn't it? That man on the right there; no, he's on the left now, he seems to be a bit slow. He shouldn't think about the other men. He seemed inclined to check his pace a little, as though to give 'em time to swing round into the new alignment."

He spoke slowly, giving the sergeant time to recover from his exertions.

"That man 'as been in the orderly-room the last ten days, sir. 'E may be a bit slack, an' out o' condition for the moment; but as a rule 'e's not bad at 'is drill. I thought 'e wanted a bit of extra work to get fit, sir, that's why I put 'im out on a flank."

"Oh, that was it, was it?" said Captain Malet, enlightened. "What do you think of your men, sergeant? Let me have your own opinion."

"I don't think they're a bad lot o' men, sir," replied Sergeant Tozer, secretly indignant that there could be any question on the subject.

"No. I don't think they're a bad lot at all," Captain Malet agreed. "When I come along with a few criticisms, I don't want you to think I am dissatisfied. I think you always keep to a high standard, and that gives me the impression that you handle your men well. Get 'em into extended order again, and double 'em down the field and back again. Then they may fall out for ten minutes and smoke."

Sergeant Tozer struck his rifle in salute, and turned to the men. Calling them to attention, standing them at ease again, and then calling them up with a bark, he told them off with considerable vigour and snap. He not only, by this means, did something to restore his prestige; but he also managed to convey the impression that his own contempt for their utter lack of all soldierly qualities was only an ineffectual echo of Captain Malet's opinion; and, in that way, he got home as well on his company officer, who quite appreciated the fact. Then, as he had been ordered, he extended the men, and sent them about a hundred and fifty yards and back again at the double. When he halted them they looked at him indignantly, panting like blown cattle. He considered them for a little while with an air of patient disparagement, and telling them to fall out for ten minutes, returned to Captain Malet.

"Fuckin' slave drivers, that's what they are!" said Minton, flinging himself on the ground. "What's the cunt want to come down 'ere buggerin' us about for, 'aven't we done enough bloody work in th' week?"

Captain Malet talked to the sergeant for a few minutes on matters of casual interest, glancing occasionally in the direction of the resting men.

"Sergeant, I want to speak to Bourne. Not yet, let him cool off and finish his cigarette. I think he might go for a commission. There's a great wastage in officers, and they seem to be running short. They are always pressing us to recommend likely men. I think he might do, don't you? What's your own opinion of him?"

"I don't know what to think of 'im, sir. 'E's a queer chap. When 'e first came to us, we all took 'im for a dud, but after a few days 'e seemed quite able to take care of 'imself; fact I thought 'e was gettin' a little too much of 'is own way; thought 'e might be gettin' a bit fresh, an' decided to keep an eye on 'im. I couldn't find any fault with 'im, 'e could take a tellin' off without showin' temper. 'E was a well-disciplined man. 'E didn't try to make friends with anyone, but 'e was quite friendly if anyone wanted to talk to 'im. 'E wouldn't be put upon, either. All the men got to like 'im. 'E's a gentleman all right, an' better educated than we are, but 'e never talks of 'imself. 'E seems out o' place in the ranks some'ow."

"You seem rather doubtful about him," Captain Malet observed.

"It isn't that, sir," said the sergeant. "I think 'e might make a very good officer. 'E's not quite the build of a soldier; bit light, sir; but he's pretty smart. Only 'e says 'e don't want to leave the comp'ny, sir."

"Well, a man can't shirk his responsibilities in that way. He might have stayed in the orderly-room if he had liked. I was rather interested to see what he would do, and I was rather glad he didn't stay there. Did he say anything to you about it?"

"Well, only between ourselves, sir," said the sergeant, discreetly.

"Not for the use of the young, eh? I see. Well, bring him up to me, and I shall have a talk with him."

The sergeant saluted, took a few steps towards the men, and then shouted Bourne's name. Captain Malet saw his man get up, after the momentary hesitation of surprise, dust the grass and dry earth from his trousers, pick up his rifle and double towards them. Yes, he was a bit light; pity he hadn't a bit more stamina; it counts for such a lot; and he acknowledged Bourne's salute.

"So you've given up the crown and the glory, Bourne," he said, humouring him with an easy smile.

"I don't know about the crown and the glory, sir. I was dumped."

"I am under the impression that you probably asked for it. You didn't go out of your way to make friends, did you? Why did you stay there so long, if you didn't like it?"

"I wanted to dodge work for a bit, sir."

"I don't think that is a very creditable proceeding," said Captain Malet, and noticed the uneasy resentment flickering in Bourne's face. "I like to get out of a man all he is worth. I work 'em until they drop, isn't that what they say? Then if the medical officer thinks they're past work, they can get a slacker's job among the details; it's usually rather a dirty, greasy, lousy kind of job, but I suppose they do some necessary work. Anyway they have done some by the time I have finished with them, if they never do any more. Of course, I do my best to find out in what way a man can be most useful, but it's often a case of hit or miss, one hasn't time."

He paused and looked at Bourne, who remained quite impassive under his gaze.

"As a matter of fact," continued Captain Malet, "I thought you deserved a bit of a rest. I think you do pretty well as a rule; as far as your work with the company is concerned, I haven't any fault to find with you. You're not windy, at least you keep your head. But you haven't the build."

"Sir, after all I am a good deal heftier than some of the boys..."

"Now, you know I'm right," said Captain Malet firmly. "These boys, as you call them, train on, most of them will fill out and make two of you. You are as fit as you ever will be, and you're quite fit now, in the pink, I should say. But all these men are hardened to all kinds of manual labour, which you can't do. I bet you were never in proper training until you joined the army. You won't train on, you're much more likely to train off. If you crock up, you will only be a damned nuisance. You are out of place where you are. I believe you have a certain amount of influence over the men about you; I don't mean that you try to influence them, but quite naturally they think you know a bit more than they do, and they are likely to be swayed by your opinion. Well, that's all wrong; you've no business in your position to have any influence over the men. Oh, yes, you get some stout fellow with bags of courage, and the other men look up to him. That is different. I don't say they don't admire your pluck, in fact I believe they do, but that isn't what influences them. It is something else. You ought to go in for a commission."

"I would much rather stay with the company, sir."

"It isn't a question of what you would much rather do," said Captain Malet, a little irritably. "It is a question of what you ought to do. You have no right to shirk your responsibilities in the matter. I said that to Sergeant Tozer, when he said he thought you would rather stay with the company. Well, I say it to you, too, and I mean it."

"Well, sir," said Bourne, firmly, "may I say what I think?"

"What is it?" asked Captain Malet, looking at his boot, and hitting it impatiently with his ash-stick.

"I was asked if I would take a commission when I first enlisted; that was at Milharbour, sir; and when the adjutant spoke to me I told him that I had absolutely no experience of men, not even the kind of experience that a public-school boy gets from being one of a large community. I didn't want to shirk my responsibilities, but I told him I thought it would be better if I got a little experience of men and of soldiering before trying for a commission. He hadn't thought of it in that way, but he agreed immediately he saw the point. Well, now, I think we were both wrong. Experience in the ranks doesn't help one a bit. I have only taken on the colour of the ranks. It would be very difficult for me now to look at war or to consider the men from the point of view which an officer is bound to take."

"Oh, you can forget all that," said Captain Malet cheerfully. "If you take my advice, I shall get the matter under way at once, but I won't press you for an answer today, in case you want time to think things over. I am sure it is the wisest thing you can do in the circumstances."

"There's only one other thing, sir. I don't want to be a trouble to you, but it looks as though they were getting us ready for another show. I don't want to slip away before the show. I would rather take my chance and go afterwards."

"Very well, Bourne," said Captain Malet after hesitating, perplexed, for a second or two. "Have it your own way. Only I can't promise you that you will remain in the company the whole time. It won't make much difference; you won't miss the show. You may go now."

He looked after him curiously as he went back to the men, and then he turned to Sergeant Tozer.

"You're right, sergeant, he's a queer chap. You can carry on with some drill now; but I shouldn't bustle the men any more. They have had a fairly hard time the last few days, and we move away tomorrow. You needn't make things easy for Bourne, you know; in fact it would be better if you put him through it a bit. He looks at a question upside down and inside out, and then in the long run he does just what an ordinary sensible man would do. Keep him at it."

The other men were rather curious to know why Bourne had been sent for, and Martlow, with his irrepressible curiosity, asked him, but Bourne refused to say anything, and the sergeant's order to fall in again prevented further questions. They had an easy hour. When they went back to the huts, for their midday meal, he was still silent and preoccupied. The men took it that he had been told off for something, very likely for his failure to give satisfaction in the orderly-room; and a martyr to authority always moved their profounder sympathies, though when he was out of hearing they agreed, that if a man tried to be too clever he was bound to come a mucker. Shem, who knew him, after a suspicious and furtive scrutiny, left him alone. Sergeant Tozer also held aloof, somewhat reluctantly, as the interview at which he had assisted in the morning had embarrassed him a little. However, he was quite clear in his own mind on one point; he wasn't going to bustle Bourne about just to please the company commander, so long as he went on quietly with his work. If a man thought he were being treated unjustly, it made him restive, then he became really troublesome and ended on the mat. There was no sense in it.

Bourne ate very little, and then went off to smoke alone. He had the faculty of withdrawing right into himself, his consciousness shrinking into its inmost recesses, contracting to a mere point, while the bodily part of him followed its ordinary train of habit unconsciously, like an automaton. He did not resent anything that Captain Malet had said to him. He felt a kind of vague impersonal resentment against enveloping circumstances, that was all. When one was in the ranks, one lived in a world of men, full of flexible movement and human interest; when one became an officer, one became part of an inflexible and inhuman machine; and though he thought that the war as a moral effort was magnificent, he felt that as a mechanical operation it left a great deal to be desired.

They paraded again at two, and at three there was a kit inspection, during which Bourne's tin-hat was condemned for the second time. Mr Marsden, who had come back to them after having been slightly wounded on the Somme, was the first to examine the hat, and then Mr Sothern remembered that it had been condemned at Meaulte. He reminded the sergeant-major of the fact, and turned to Bourne again.

"Did you see the quartermaster-sergeant about it?" he asked Bourne.

Bourne had a very vivid recollection of his interview with the quartermaster-sergeant, a bad old devil like the colour-sergeant, only violent as well because he drank. He had gone, too, pensioned off, and had reached by this time the summit of his ambition in the proprietorship of a pub.

"Yes, sir," Bourne replied mechanically.

"What did he say?" continued Mr Sothern inquisitively.

"He told me to go to buggery, sir," replied Bourne very quietly.

Sergeant-Major Robinson, and Sergeant Tozer as well, were scandalised that Bourne should divulge even part of a conversation so obviously intended to be confidential. The officers seemed to be only a little surprised by his candour.

"What d'you mean, talkin' like that?" said the sergeant-major severely. "'E only meant 'e didn't 'ave any."

Bourne thought that the quartermaster-sergeant's words might be interpreted in various ways; but in the face of the sergeant-major's righteous indignation, he didn't feel called on to supply any alternative glosses, so he stood to attention rigidly while he was told off by Mr Marsden, Mr Sothern, and the sergeant-major in succession. The sergeant-major thought it necessary to say to Mr Marsden that Quartermaster-Sergeant Leak had gone home.

"'E was no good, sir. 'E was too old, an' it made 'im irritable-like," he remarked with reasonable indulgence.

"See that this man has a new steel helmet by tonight," said Mr Marsden imperiously.

"There are none here, sir," protested the sergeant-major. "There may be a few at the quartermaster's stores in Noeux-les-Mines; but even there, they've probably got all their stuff packed ready for the move."

"Then see that he gets one at the first possible opportunity," said Mr Marsden, and with this indefinite extension of the original time limit he passed, somewhat hastily, to a detailed criticism of the next man's deficiencies.

All the men had pricked up their ears to hear Bourne being told off for the second time that day. Bloody shame, wasn't it? Once the buggers get their knives into you, you can't go right. No pleasin' 'em. Well, you've got to tell the truth, haven't you? But the sergeant-major's inadvertent reference to the prospect of a move effectively routed these desultory sympathies with a stronger interest, and as soon as they went for their tea they heard it was in orders; breakfast at eight, all huts to be cleaned up and ready for inspection by company officers at nine, and the battalion to be on parade, ready to move off, at nine-thirty. Bourne drank his tea alone, but Martlow invaded his solitude.

"Look 'ere, Bourne, you're comin' out wi' me, tonight, an' I'm goin' to pay, see? I've got plenty money; an' I'm not always goin' out with you, an' let you stan' treat. So you come along with Shem an' me, an' we'll 'ave a little bit of a beano on our own. An' you don't want to mind bloody officer says to you, see? You want to take it the right ...'t do no 'arm."

... the solemnity of Martlow's expression which overcame Bourne's already diminishing reserve. The notion that he couldn't take an ordinary telling-off made him inclined to laugh, but he restrained himself.

"All right, kid," he said gratefully. "We shall go out and have a beano together."

"An' I stan' treat,' said Martlow, immensely pleased, but then a sudden doubt clouded the youthful brow.

"I won't 'ave enough money to get real champagne," he said, facing the difficulty frankly; "but the other stuff's just as good, only it don't make you so drunk; an' after all we don't want to get pissed-up with a long day's march in front of us tomorrow, do we?"

"Oh, I only like champagne occasionally," said Bourne in a casual way, "as a rule I like beer or vin blanc better."

"Beer here's bloody," said Martlow. "All right, I'll go an' tell Shem, 'e's lyin' down outside."

Bourne wasn't alone for long in the hut; he was putting away his mess-tin and knife when Sergeant Tozer came in and noted the symptoms of recovery.

"Comin' down the village with me tonight?" he inquired briefly.

"Martlow has just asked me to go out with him, sergeant. Otherwise I should. I think he wants to return the compliment, you know; but thanks all the same."

"E's a decent kid," said the sergeant. "I was goin' to ask 'im an' Shem to come too. But I'll leave it to some other night. It might look as though I were buttin' in. 'Ave you told 'em anything about what Cap'n Malet said to you?"

"No, I'm not goin' to say anything about it, until it's more or less settled."

"Quite right. They think Cap'n Malet gave you a tellin' off."

"Well? How would you describe it?"

"E's a good officer, is Cap'n Malet; an' 'e's a nice gentleman too, but 'e may be wrong in a lot o' things. I thought there was a lot in what 'e said to you, because I've often thought like that about you myself. You've got a pull over us in some ways..."

104

"Well, you've got a pull over me in other ways."

"Yes, but that don't even things out, it makes 'em worse. I thought there was something in what you said to the cap'n. Only you didn't say all that you was thinkin'..."

"How the hell can you ever say all that you are thinking to an officer, without being bloody rude?" said Bourne indignantly.

The sergeant enjoyed the humour of it.

"You weren't polite about the quarter-bloke to Mr Marsden."

"That was a different thing. It's so damned silly. A private is ordered to complete some deficiency in his kit, and he goes to the quarter-bloke for it and gets nothing but abuse for his trouble. What can he say to the quarter-bloke? At the next kit inspection, he gets ticked off by the officer for not doing something that the officer knows bloody well he can't do. You have never heard me grouse about anything to the men, have you? Very well. I may tell you, that there are precious few mistakes made in the army that are not ultimately laid on the shoulders of the men. A fool of a clerk in the orderly-room sends in the wrong state to Brigade, and the men can do without their tea when they come back from a working party, wet and tired at four o'clock in the morning, having had nothing since five. Yes, Captain Malet put that right, and he was the only company officer I know with guts enough to do it.

"Some general streaks off in a car, at about forty miles an hour, to go on a binge in Amiens; an unfortunate sentry spots his pennon, just in time to turn out the guard to present arms to a cloud of dust. The general comes back with a fat head next morning, and reports them for slackness, with the result that there's a parade of guard-mounting, and Jerry comes over and bombs the lot. They're not exceptional cases, and you know as well as I do, the same sort of stupidities happen every day. I only hope to God Jerry salutes the swine some day with a 5.9 or something equally effective. The war might be a damned sight more tolerable if it weren't for the bloody army.

"I shall get another tin hat, when I can find one for myself in the trenches, I suppose, because I'm pretty sure I will not get one through the official channels. What do I do, when I want anything now? I go to the snobs for it. But they don't happen to have a tin hat, at the moment. I don't know whether Mr Marsden and Mr Sothern think they look impressive when they're ticking me off; but what I do know is, that a storekeeper, with a lance stripe up, has much more say in the matter of getting me a tin hat than either of them."

"Well, there's something in that," said Sergeant Tozer, feeling for his tobacco. "But it were silly to repeat what the quarter- bloke said. It didn't matter, as far as the officers were concerned; but it got up the sergeant-major's back. If Mr Marsden can't alter things, do you think you can?"

"I know perfectly well they can't be altered. They have got to run the machine more or less as it has been handed over to them; and because I know that, I have never groused to anyone until I started grousing to you a few minutes ago. If the sergeant-major has got his back up with me, I dare say I can stick it. The last time I heard from him was when he asked me to pinch him some notebooks and pencils out of the orderly-room. But don't worry, I shall forget it. I have given you a rough notion of my reason for not wanting to take a commission; but if it's up to me to take one, there's no option, is there? I mustn't shirk my responsibilities."

"You're all right," said Sergeant Tozer, and paused to light his pipe very deliberately. "Only you'll have to watch your step, you know. There are too many people interested in you, at present, for you to play the fool in safety."

Bourne said nothing but lit another cigarette, and they smoked in quiet. Then little Martlow came back and sat quietly beside them. He looked at the sergeant a little dubiously, and Bourne knew that he was telling himself that his money wouldn't run to the entertainment of three people beside himself. He could see Martlow determining firmly not to ask the sergeant; and then quite suddenly Corporal Greenstreet put his head in the hut.

"Bourne here?"

"Yes, corporal."

"Company guard tonight, six o'clock."

"Very good, corporal. Just gives me time to get ready. I'm sorry, Martlow, but we'll go on a binge together some other night. I dare say the sergeant-major thinks I have had too cushy a time lately."

"It's a bloody army!" said Martlow in disappointed tones, and he sat there looking at Bourne with his underlip thrust out in temper.

"Oh, I don't know," said Bourne cheerfully. "It's all right in peace time, as the old sweats say."

106

He looked at Sergeant Tozer with an almost laughing face, and the sergeant took his pipe out of his mouth.

"You an' Shem 'ad better come out with me tonight then, Martlow; it's about up to me. We can 'ave some eggs and chips, and then go and take a peek at a couple of estaminets. It'll pass the time. You might be able to bring Bourne back some vin blanc."

"That's a damned good plan, Martlow. Cut along and tell Shem."

"E don't seem keen on it," said the sergeant, as Martlow went reluctantly.

"He's disappointed about his own show, otherwise he would be bucked by it. It is awfully decent of you, sergeant."

Chapter IX

But thy speaking of my tongue, and I thine,
most truly-falsely, must needs be granted to be much at one.
— SHAKESPEARE

Bourne never slept much; as soon as he put out his cigarette and rolled himself up in his blankets, he would sleep like a log for an hour or two perhaps, and then so lightly that the least sound would wake him. It was a legend among the other men, that nobody ever woke during the night without finding Bourne sitting up and smoking a cigarette. Company guard didn't bother him in the least. It was a cushy guard, without formality; and he liked the solitude and emptiness of the night. One bathed one's soul in that silence, as in a deep, cold pool. Earth seemed to breathe, even if it were only with his own breathing, giving consciousness a kind of rhythm, which was neither of sound nor of motion, but might become either at any moment.

The slagheaps, huge against the luminous sky, might have been watchtowers in Babylon, or pyramids in Egypt; night with its enchantments, changing even this flat and unlovely land into a place haunted by fantastic imaginings. Morning gave again to life its sordid realities. He got himself some tea at the cooker, yarned to Abbot while he drank it, and was washed and shaved before the rest of his were fully awake.

The battalion fell in on the road at about twenty minutes past nine; and five minutes later the commanding officer, and the adjutant, rode down the line of men; perhaps less with the object of making a cursory inspection than for the purpose of advertising the fact that they had both been awarded the Military Cross, for their services on the Somme.

"Wonder they 'ave the front to put 'em up," said Martlow, unimpressed.

Major Shadwell and Captain Malet had no distinctions.

"I don't want no medals meself," added Martlow, disinterestedly.

108

Bourne was struck by the adjutant's horsemanship; when the grey he rode trotted, you saw plenty of daylight between his seat and the saddle; and the exaggerated action made it seem as if, instead of the horse carrying the adjutant, the adjutant were really propelling the horse. However, he brought to the business the same serious attention which he gave to less arduous duties at other times. The men were forbidden to drink from their water bottles on the march until permission were given. They moved on, and, by ten o'clock, were marching through Noeux-les-Mines again; and presently word was passed along that they were going to Bruay. There was no doubt about it this time; Captain Malet had told Sergeant-Major Robinson, and the men swung forward cheerfully, in spite of dust and heat, opening out a bit, so that the air could move freely between them. On the whole, their march discipline was pretty good. They arrived at their new billets at about one o'clock.

Bruay was built on two sides of a valley, and their billets were naturally in the poorer part of the town; in one of the uniform streets which always seem to lay stress on the monotony of modern industrial life. It was a quarter given up to miners. The street in which A Company had billets was only about a hundred yards long, led nowhere, and ended abruptly, as though the builders had suddenly tired of their senseless repetition. But it was all very clean; dull and dingy, but clean. Some of the houses were empty, and Bourne, Shem and Martlow, with the rest of their section, were in one of these empty houses. The town, however, was for the most part earlier than the days when towns came to be planned. You could see that the wisdom of cattle, which in such matters is greater than the wisdom of man, had determined the course of many of its sinuous streets, as they picked their way to and from their grazing, guided only by the feel of the ground beneath them, and the gradients with which they were confronted. So the town still possessed a little charm and character. It had its place, its sides all very unequal, and all of it on the slope. Even the direction of the slope was diagonally across it, and not merely from side to side or end to end. Perhaps the cattle had determined that too, for the poor fool man has long since lost his nature. Houses in the older parts of the town, though modest and discreet, still contrived to have a little air of distinction and individuality. They refused to be confounded with each other. They ignored that silly assumption that men are equal. They believed in private property.

It was obviously the intention of authority that the men should be given an opportunity to have a bon time. They were to be paid at two o'clock, and then were free to amuse themselves.

"You're comin' out with me tonight," said Martlow to Bourne decisively.

"Very well," said Bourne, dumping his pack on the floor of the room they occupied, and opening the window. They were upstairs; and he looked out and down, into the street. There were five or six corporals, and lance-corporals, standing just outside; and both Corporal Greenstreet and Lance-Corporal Jakes spotted him immediately, and shouted for him to come. He went, a little reluctantly, wondering what they wanted.

"You're the man we was lookin' for," said Corporal Greenstreet. "The sergeants are running a sergeants' mess for the couple of days we'll be 'ere; an' we don't see why we can't run a corporals' mess."

"Well, run one, corporal,' said Bourne disinterestedly. "There's nothing in King's Regs against it, so far as I know."

"Well, we can't run it ourselves. That's where you come in, you know the lingo a bit, an' you always seem able to get round the old women. A corporal don't get a sergeant's pay, you know, but we want to do it as well as we can. There'll be eight of us; Jakes, Evans an' Marshall are in billets 'ere, an' we could 'ave the mess 'ere, if she'd do the cookin'. You 'ave a talk to 'er."

"This is all very well," said Bourne reasonably, "but now we're in a decent town, I want to have a good time myself. I've just told Martlow I should go out with him tonight."

"Well, I've got 'im down for company guard tonight."

"Have you, corporal? Well, you just take him off company guard, or there's absolutely nothing doing. Every time we arrange to go out on a bit of a spree together, he or Shem or myself are put on company guard. I was on last night."

"Well, Sergeant-Major Robinson told me to put you on guard last night. 'E said it would do you good, you were gettin' a bit fresh."

"I guessed that," said Bourne. "He didn't want to be nasty, of course, but he thought he would give me a reminder. I don't mind taking my share of guards. But, if you put one of us on, you might just as well put us all on together, and make a family party of it. I don't mind helping you to run a mess, but I want to have a good time, too."

"Well, you muck in with us," said Corporal Greenstreet.

"An' you needn't put anythin' in the kitty," added Lance-Corpc
Jakes.

"Oh, thanks all the same, but I like to pay my own way," said Bourne
coolly. "I don't mind going in and asking madame what can be done in
the matter, and then, if we can come to some arrangement, I shall see
about buying the grub; but before things go any further, it has got to be
clearly understood that neither Shem nor Martlow is on any guard
tonight. We three are going out on a spree together. I shall muck in with
you tomorrow night."

"That's all right," said Corporal Greenstreet hastily. "I'll get some
other bugger for the bloody guard, if there is a guard. I've 'ad no orders
yet."

"It's just as well to take the possibility into consideration," said
Bourne; "but mind you, you would do it just as well on your own,
without me."

"Come on. You parlez-vous to the old woman," said Corporal
Greenstreet, and hurried him through the house into the forefront of the
battle, which was the kitchen. Madame was a very neat and competent-
looking woman, and she faced Bourne with her two daughters acting as
supports immediately behind her. Bourne got through the preliminary
politesses with a certain amount of credit. She had already understood
that the corporals required her assistance in some way, but they had
failed apparently to make matters clear.

"Qu'est-ce que ces messieurs desirent?' she inquired of Bourne,
coming to the point with admirable promptitude, and when he explained
matters they launched into a discussion on ways and means. Then
Bourne turned to Corporal Greenstreet.

"I suppose it is pukka that we stay here two nights, is it?"

"That's accordin' to present plans. Of course you can't be certain of
anything in the bloody army. Does it make any differ to 'er?"

"Not much," said Bourne. "You can have grilled fillet of steak with
fried onions, and chips and beans, or you can have a couple of chickens.
I am wondering what sort of sweet you can have."

"Could we 'ave a suet puddin' wi' treacle?"

"No, I don't think so," said Bourne reflectively. "I don't think the
French use suet much in cooking, and anyway I don't know the French

for suet, if they do. Suif is lard, I think. Could you pinch a tin of pozzy out of stores? Then you might have a sweet omelette with jam in it. Perhaps it would be better to buy some decent jam, you don't want plum and apple, do you? Only I want to make the money go as far as possible. I like those little red currants in syrup which used to come from Bar-le-Duc."

"Get 'em. I don't care a fuck where they come from. We don't want any bloody plum an' apple when we can get better. An' don't you worry about the money, not in reason anyway. They've only let us come 'ere for a couple of days to 'ave a bon time before they send us up into the shit again. Might just as well get all we can, while we can."

Bourne turned to madame again, and asked her if she would do the marketing for them, and the upshot of it was that they both agreed to go together. Bourne turned to Corporal Greenstreet and asked him about money.

"Will it do if we all put twenty francs into the kitty to start with?"

"I don't think I shall want so much; give me ten each, and if that isn't enough, then you can each give me up to another ten. I am going to let her buy the wine because she knows somebody in the trade, and says she can get us good sound wine, which you don't get in estaminets, fairly cheap."

"Dinner's up, corporal," said Corporal Marshall, putting his head in the door; and thanking madame, they left to get their meal rather hurriedly.

"Where've you bin?" said Martlow indignantly to Bourne, and Shem burst out laughing at the way in which the question was put.

"What the bloody 'ell is 'e laughin' at?' said Martlow, his face all in a pucker.

"I have been doing my best to get you off company guard tonight."

"Me!' exclaimed Martlow. "Me, on bloody company guard tonight, an' the only cushy town we've been in! It's a bugger, ain't it? D'you mean to say they 'ad me on bloody guard?"

"Well, I have taken on the job of rationing officer to the corporals' mess, on condition they find someone else in your place; that is if they should mount a guard tonight; they may give it a miss. It isn't a bad stew today, is it? Seems to me a long time since we had any fresh meat, except for a few weevils in the biscuits. As soon as I have had dinner, I shall go off with Corporal Greenstreet, and make the other corporals ante up.

Then I shall be back in time to get my pay, and afterwards I shall go out and do the marketing with madame. When we have had tea, the three of us had better hop it to the other side of the town right away, in case they come along and pinch us for any fatigues. There's a cinema, up there. And look here, Martlow, you're not going to pay for everything tonight, see? We shall have to make the most of our opportunity to have a bon time, as it may be our last chance. I hate the thought of dying young."

"Well, I'll stan' the supper," said Martlow reasonably. "I've got about three weeks' pay, an' me mother sent me a ten-bob note. I wish she wouldn't send me any money, as she wants all she gets, but there's no stoppin' 'er."

"Shem can pay for the drinks afterwards. Of course, he has got money. To be a Jew and not to have money would be an unmitigated misfortune. Enough to make one deny the existence of Providence. He never will offer to pay unless you make him. He wouldn't think it prudent. But all the same, if you are broke to the wide, Shem will come down quite handsomely; he doesn't mind making a big splash then, as it looks like a justification of his past thrift. Shem and I understand each other pretty well, only he thinks I'm a bloody fool."

"I don't think you're a bloody fool," said Shem indulgently; "but I think I could make a great deal more use of your brains than you do."

"Shem thinks he is a practical man," said Bourne, "and a cynic, and a materialist; and would you believe it, Martlow, he had a cushy job in the pay office, to which all his racial talent gave him every claim, and he was wearing khaki, and he had learnt how to present arms with a fountain pen; the most perfect funkhole in Blighty, and he chucks the whole bloody show to come soldiering! Here you are, clean out my dixie, like a good kid, and my knife and fork. I must chase after these corporals. I wouldn't trust any of them round the corner with a threepenny bit, not unless I were a sergeant."

He found Corporal Greenstreet ready, and they set off together; the corporal had collected all the money except from Corporal Farman and Lance-Corporal Eames.

"What about Corporal Whitfield?" Bourne asked him.

"'E's no bloody good," said Greenstreet. "'E never will join in with us in anything. Do you know, 'e gets at least one big parcel out from 'ome every week, an' I've never seen 'im give away a bite yet. In any case, 'e's no good to us. 'E's a Rechabite."

"What the hell is that?" inquired Bourne, somewhat startled.

"I don't know. It's some kind o' sex or other, I think. They don't drink, an' they don't smoke either; but you ought to see the bugger eat. 'E's no bloody good to us."

"I don't know anything about him," Bourne explained.

"No, an' you don't want to," said Greenstreet earnestly. "I'm in the same billets as I was last time, but I 'aven't 'ad time to look in on 'em yet. An old maid owns the 'ouse, an' she 'as an 'ousekeeper: cook-'ousekeeper, I should say. They're very decent to all of us. Respectable people, you know; I should say the old girl 'ad quite a bit o' rattle to 'er. Lives comfortable anyway. Likes you to be quiet an' wipe your feet on the mat. You know."

The house was in one of the streets leading off the place; and it had a gate at the side giving access to a small yard, with a garden, half flowers, half vegetables; there was a tree bright with early red apples, and a pollarded plane with marvellously contorted branches and leaves already yellowing. Corporal Farman was just coming out of the door, as they entered the gate, and he handed over his ten francs cheerfully. He and Corporal Greenstreet were perhaps the two best-looking men in the battalion, fair-haired, blue-eyed and gay-complexioned. The ménagère, recognising the latter, waved a welcome to him from the doorway.

"She's been askin' about you, corporal."

"Bonjour, Monsieur Greenstreet," she cried, rolling each "r' in her throat.

"Bongjour, madame, be there in 'arf a tick. I'll meet you up at the company office, corporal, and show you the billets. Bourne's runnin' the show."

Farman waved a hand, and departed on his own business. Corporal Greenstreet and Bourne went into the house, after using the doormat rather ostentatiously; but even so the ménagère looked a little suspiciously at Bourne.

"Vous n'avez pas un logement chez nous, monsieur," she said firmly.

"C'est vrai, madame; mais j'attends les ordres de monsieur le caporal."

He spoke deliberately, with a little coldness in his manner, de haut en bas, as it were, and after a further penetrating glance in his direction, she ignored him for the moment. Corporal Greenstreet left his pack in a room off the kitchen, but one step higher and with a wooden floor instead of tiled; then he returned, and the woman opened on him rapidly, expressing her pleasure at seeing him, and her further gratification at seeing him so obviously in good health. He did not understand one word of what she said, but the pleasure and recognition in her face flattered him agreeably.

"Ah, oui, madame," he said with a gallant effort.

"Mais vous n'avez pas compris, monsieur."

"Ah, oui, compris, madame. Glad to be back, compris? Cushy avec mademoiselle."

The expression on the face of the ménagère passed very rapidly from astonishment to indignation, and from indignation to wrath. Before Corporal Greenstreet realised what was about to happen, she had swung a muscular arm, and landed a terrific box on his ear, almost knocking him into a scuttle containing split wood and briquettes for the stove. Bourne, thinking with a rapidity only outstripped by her precipitate action, decided that the Hindustani "cushy" and French "coucher" must have been derived from the same root in Sanskrit. He interposed heroically between the fury and her victim, who without any hesitation had adopted the role of a non-combatant in trying circumstances.

"Mais madame, madame," he protested, struggling to overcome his mirth. "Vous vous meprenez. 'Cushy' est un mot d'argot militaire qui veut dire doux, confortable, tout ce qu'il y a de plus commode. Monsieur le caporal ne veut pas dire autre chose. Il veut vous faire un petit compliment. Calmez-vous. Rassurez-vous, madame. Je vous assure que monsieur a des manieres tres correctes, tres convenables. Il est un jeune homme bien eleve. Il n'a pour vous, ainsi que pour mademoiselle, que des sentiments tres respectueux."

Bourne's French was only sufficient, when circumstances allowed him an economical use of it; and these were enough to make him a bankrupt even in English. Madame was now moving about her kitchen with the fine frenzy of a prima donna in one of the more ecstatic moments of grand opera. Every emotion has its appropriate rhythm, and she achieved what was proper to her own spontaneously, through sheer natural genius. Perhaps she was too great an artist to allow Bourne's words to have their full effect at once. She could not plunge from this sublimity to an immediate bathos. Innocence in adversity was the expression patent on the corporal's face, and perhaps the sight of it brought into her mind some mitigating element of doubt; which she resisted at first as though it were a mere feminine weakness.

"Nous nous retirons, madame, pour vous donner le temps de calmer vos nerfs," said Bourne, with some severity. "Nous regrettons infiniment ce malentendu. Monsieur le caporal vous fera ses excuses quand vous serez plus a meme d'accepter ses explications. Permettez, madame. Je suis vraiment desole."

He swept the corporal out of the house, and into the street, and finding a secluded corner, collapsed.

"What the fuckin' 'ell is't all about?" the awed but exasperated corporal inquired. "I go into th' 'ouse, an' only get as far as 'ow d'you do, when she 'ands me out this bloody packet. You'll get a thick ear yourself, if you don't stop laffin'."

Bourne, when he had recovered sufficiently, explained that the housekeeper had understood him to express his intention of going to bed with her mistress.

"What! D'you mean it? Why, the old girl's about sixty!" Bourne whistled the air of "Mademoiselle from Armentieres", leaving the corporal to draw his own conclusions from it.

"Look 'ere," said Corporal Greenstreet, with sudden ferocity. "If you tell any o' them other buggers what 'as 'appened I'l..."

"Oh, don't be a bloody fool," said Bourne, suddenly firing up too. "If there's one thing that fills me with contempt, it is being asked not to tell. Do you think I have got no more sense than a kid or an old woman? You would look well with that tin can tied to your tail, wouldn't you? We had better get moving. They will have started to pay out by now."

"Wish to God I knew a bit o' French," said the corporal earnestly.

"I wish to God you wouldn't mix the little you do know with Hindustani," said Bourne.

The whole company were in the street, waiting to be paid; they formed in little groups, and men would pass from one group to another, or two groups would merge together, or one would suddenly split up completely, distributing its members among the others. Their movements were restless, impatient, and apparently without object. Corporal Greenstreet, finding Lance-Corporal Eames, collected his subscription to the mess, and then handed over the whole eighty francs to Bourne. Presently a couple of men brought a table and an army blanket out of one of the houses. The table was placed on the footpath parallel to the street, and the blanket was spread over it. One of the men went back into the house and returned with two chairs, followed by Quartermaster-Sergeant James, who detailed the same two men as witnesses. Almost immediately afterwards Captain Malet appeared with a new subaltern, a Mr Finch, who was not yet twenty, though he had already been in action with another battalion, and had been slightly wounded. The quartermaster-sergeant called the company, now grouped in a semicircle in front of the table, to attention, saluted, and Captain Malet, acknowledging the salute, told them to stand easy.

There was a moment's pause; and then one of the witnesses brought a third chair for the quartermaster-sergeant, who sat on Captain Malet's left. The three then proceeded to count the notes and arrange them in bundles, while the men in front shifted from one foot to another, and whispered to each other.

The sergeant-major, who had been to the orderly-room, returned and saluted Captain Malet. He was the first man to be paid, and then the quartermaster-sergeant, and Sergeant Gallion and Sergeant Tozer. The others were paid in alphabetical order; and as each man's name was called he came forward, saluted, and was ordered to take off his cap, so that the officer could see whether his hair had been properly cut. Men had a strong objection to their hair being cropped close. They had been inclined to compromise by having it machined at the back and sides, and leaving on the crown of the head a growth like Absalom's, concealing it under the cap. In the case of a head wound, this thick hair, matted with dried blood, which always became gluey, made the dressing of the wound much more difficult for the doctor and his orderlies, delaying other equally urgent cases. In consequence, all men were ordered to remove their caps before receiving their pay, and if a man's hair were not cropped it was only credited to him; and there were formal difficulties in the way of any attempt to recover arrears.

Bourne had always liked his hair very short. He objected to growing a moustache, which collected bits of carrot and meat from the eternal stew. He thought it inconsistent in the Army Council to make men grow hair one place and shave it in another, as though they were French poodles.

He had once, when they were discussing the matter in the tent, told the men that they should be made to shave all over, as then they would not provide so many nurseries for lice. They thought the suggestion indecent.

"Don't be a bloody fool," Minton had objected. "Fancy a man 'avin' to let 'is trousers down before 'e gets 'is pay!"

"But the commanding officer wants to put us all in kilts," Bourne had replied in a reasonable tone; and Major Blessington's avowed preference for a kilted regiment had always been a ground of resentment.

His name being early on the list, and his head almost shaven, he was soon free; and he left immediately to take madame marketing.

She had insisted that he should be present, so that he would know exactly how much everything cost. After Corporal Greenstreet's involuntary collision with the housekeeper, Bourne had become a little anxious as to the possibility of any misunderstanding with this other, more tractable but equally muscular, lady with whom he had to deal. However, when he presented himself in her kitchen, he found that she had changed her mind, and had decided that the elder of her two daughters should take her place. She explained that she had other work to do in the house.

The daughter was waiting, demurely clothed in black, which perhaps enhanced her complexion, but seemed in any case to be the uniform dress of nubile maidens in France. She carried a large basket, but wore no hat, content with the incomplete sleekness of her black hair, which was rolled up just above the nape of her neck. It was something about her neck, the back of her small head, and the way her little ears were set, flat against her bright hair, which attracted Bourne's appraising eyes. She knew, because she put up a hand, to smoothe or to caress it; and a question came into her eyes quickly, and was gone again, like a rabbit appearing and disappearing in the mouth of a burrow. Apart from the firm but delicate modelling of the back of her head and neck, and her rather large eyes, at once curious and timid, she had little beauty. Her forehead was low and rather narrow, her nose flattish, and her mouth too large, with broad lips, scarcely curving even when she smiled. She had good small teeth.

Bourne had always treated women with a little air of ceremony, whatever kind of women they might be. The case of the girl at Noeux-les-Mines was exceptional, but she was of the type who try to stimulate desire as by an irritant, and he had too sensitive a skin. All the same, he had reproached himself a little on her account, for after all it was her vocation in life. Now, he professed that he was entirely in the hands of madame; he did not think it necessary that he should go, but if she wished it, it would be a great pleasure to accompany mademoiselle. Madame was flattered by his confidence, but thought it right that he should go; perhaps she had less confidence in him than he in her; or was it only that she was interested where he was indifferent? He followed the girl out into the street. The greater part of the company were still waiting to draw their pay; and, as Bourne and the girl passed behind them, the men turned curiously to look at the pair.

"Ullo, Bourne! Goin' square-pushin'?" one of his acquaintances asked him with a grin.

Bourne only looked at him, and moved a little closer to the girl, a combative feeling rising in him. After all, if the girl were not beautiful, she had poise and character. She ignored all those eyes, which were filled with desire, and furtive innuendo, and provocative challenge; as though indifferent to the tribute which all men pay, one way or another, to the mystery she embodied. With women of her race, it was still a mystery. It gave her the air of saying that she could choose for herself as she pleased, her own will being all that mattered. Even Captain Malet, as Bourne passed on the other side of the street with a correct if perfunctory salute, glanced up at them with a fleeting interest.

"So that's the way he spends his money, is it?" he murmured, half to himself and half to the quartermaster-sergeant; though the two witnesses, all ears and attention, naturally overheard him.

As soon as they had turned the corner, she spoke to Bourne, opening out quite frankly. She had two brothers, who had been at the front, but were now working in a mine. They were apparently on a kind of indefinite leave, but were liable to be recalled at any moment to the colours. Then, others, who had also earned a rest from trench life, would take their place. C'est dure, la guerre. But all the same she felt about it as did so many of them, to whom war seemed as natural and as inevitable as a flood or an earthquake. Bourne had noticed very much the same feeling among peasants close to the line. They would plough, sow, and wait for their harvest, taking the chance that battle might flow like lava over their fields, very much as they took the chance of a wet season or of a drought.

If the worst happened, then the ruin of their crops might seem mere wanton mischief on the part of a few irresponsible generals, and whether it were a German or a British army which ravaged their fields and shattered their homesteads, did not affect their point of view very materially. On the whole, however, their pessimism was equal to the occasion.

"C'est la guerre," they would say, with resignation that was almost apathy; for all sensible people know that war is one of the blind forces of nature, which can neither be foreseen nor controlled. Their attitude, in all its simplicity, was sane. There is nothing in war which is not in human nature, but the violence and passions of men become, in the aggregate, an impersonal and incalculable force, a blind and irrational movement of the collective will, which one cannot control, which one cannot understand, which one can only endure as these peasants, in their bitterness and resignation, endured it. C'est la guerre.

The demure little person hurrying beside him with her basket realised that the war made life more precarious, chiefly because it resulted in a scarcity of provisions, and a rise, if only restricted rise, in prices. There was something always a little disconcerting to the soldier in the prudence, foresight and practical sense of the civilian mind. It is impossible to reconcile the point of view which argues that everything is so scarce, with that opposed point of view which argues that time is so short. She was amazed at his extravagance, as she bought under his supervision chickens and beef and eggs and potatoes and onions, and then four bottles of wine. Salad and beans her mother's garden could provide; but as an afterthought when buying the red currants in syrup, he bought some cream cheese. Then, their shopping completed, they turned back. She touched him lightly on the arm once, and asked him why he had no stripes on his sleeve.

"Je suis simple soldat, moi," he explained awkwardly.

"Mais pourquoi...?" And then, noticing his expression, she turned away from the subject with what was no more than the shadow of a shrug. Women must be always stimulating some man's ambition. He followed her movement, as she half turned away from him, almost with suffering in his eyes. He wanted to kiss that adorable neck, just where the black hair was lifted from it, leaving uncaught a frail mesh that was almost golden in the light. Then that pathetic face, almost monkey-like, with its lustrous velvet eyes, turned to him; and touching his sleeve again, she told him that he could, if he would, do her a great service, but it must be kept a profound secret. He asked her what it was, startled a little by her manner. She had a friend, an English soldier who had been billeted on them for ten days, not very long ago, and she gave the name of his regiment. He had written to her three letters, and she had written to him, but he knew no French, and she only knew a few words of English. She had promised him that she would learn, so that she might write to him in his own language. Would Bourne help her? The hand, a little red and shiny from work, fluttered on his sleeve. Would Bourne translate his letters to her, and help her to write him a letter in English? Bourne, amazed, tried to picture the man to himself, as though his mind were a kind of crystal in which he might expect to see visions, as a moment before he had been dreaming dreams. It baffled him.

"Restez, monsieur, restez un moment," she said, placing her basket on the footpath; and then, putting a hand into her blouse, and hunching her shoulders a little as she forced it slightly but perceptibly between her breasts and corset, she drew out a letter, an authentic letter stamped with the postmark of the field service post-office B.E.F., and with the name of the officer who had censored it scrawled across the lower left-hand corner of the envelope. She gave it to him.

"Lisez, monsieur. Je serai tres contente si vous voulez bien la lire. Vous etes si gentil, et je n'aime que lui."

It was a simple letter. There was no self-consciousness intervening between the writer and the emotion which he tried to put into words, though he had been conscious enough of the censorship, and perhaps of other things intervening between them.

Her hand fluttered again on Bourne's sleeve, as she coaxed him to translate it for her; and he did his best, his French halting more than ever, as he studied the handwriting, thinking it might give him some notion of the writer. The script was clear, rather large, commonplace enough; one might say that he was possibly a clerk. Everything was well, that went without saying; they were having a quiet spell; the village where they had their rest-billets had been evacuated by its inhabitants, except for a few old people; the war could not last much longer, for the Hun must know that he could not win now; and then came the three sentences which said all he could say; "I shall go back and find you some day. I wish we were together again so that I could smell your hair. I love you always, my dearest." There were signs of haste in the handwriting, as though he had found some difficulty at that point in opening his heart.

"C'est tout?"

"Je ne puis pas traduire ce qu'il y a de plus important, mademoiselle; les choses qu'il n'a pas voulu ecrire."

"Comme vous avez le coeur bon, monsieur! Mais vraiment, il etait comme ca. Il aimait flairer dans mes cheveux tout comme un petit chien."

She tucked the letter away into that place of secrets, and lifted her hand again, to caress the beloved hair. Suddenly he became acutely jealous of this other man. He stooped, and picked up her basket.

"Ah, mais non, monsieur!" she protested. "C'est pas permis qu'un soldat anglais porte un panier dans les rues. C'est absolument defendu. Je le sais bien. Il m'a dit toujours, que c'etait defendu.'

"Had he?" thought Bourne, and tightened his grip on the handle of it. "Je porterai le panier, mademoiselle," he said quietly.

"Mais pourquoi...?" she asked anxiously.

"Parce qu'apparemment, mademoiselle, Cest mon metier," he said with an ironic appreciation of the fact. She looked at him with troubled eyes.

"Vous voulez bien m'aider a ecrire cette petite lettre, monsieur?"

"Mademoiselle, je ferai tout ce que je puis pour vous servir."

She suddenly relapsed into anxious silence.

Chapter X

Do you pity him? No, he deserves no pity. Wilt thou love such
a woman? What, to make thee an instrument and play false strains
upon thee? Not to be endured! Well, go your way to her, for I
see love hath made thee a tame snake, and say this to her; that
if she love me, I charge her to love thee; if she will not, I will
never have her unless thou entreat for her. If you be a true
lover, hence, and not a word; for here comes more company.
– SHAKESPEARE

"Was I drunk last night?" Martlow inquired. He threw off his blanket
and, leaning on his left hand, drew up his naked legs so that he could rub
them with his right.

"Well, if you can't answer the question for yourself, you must have
been," said Shem, reasonably. "There's some tea there."

"I've got a bit of a fat 'ead," said Martlow, taking up the mess-tin; "an'
me mouth tastes of the bloody blanket. It's a bon place, this; I could stay
'ere for the duration. Where's ol' Bourne?

"He's outside, shaving."

"E were in a good skin last night. I like ol' Bourne when you get 'im
like that, spinnin' out all them little ditties. 'Ow did you like that one
about the young man courtin' 'is pusher upstairs with the window open,
and Sergeant Thomas knockin' at the front door o' the 'ouse in
Mil'arbour, at eleven o'clock one night an' askin' the old woman to take
'er grandchild off 'is new 'at? Beats me 'ow folk think o' some o' these
things."

"You couldn't have been very drunk if you can remember all that,"
said Shem.

"I felt a bit funny when we got into the street," Martlow admitted, and
he turned his head towards the doorway as Bourne came in. "Ere,
Bourne, was I bloody drunk last night?"

"No,' said Bourne, reviewing the matter in a judicial way. "No, I
shouldn't have said you were bloody drunk. You walked better going

uphill than going down; and you looked as though you were keeping your mouth shut tight for fear you might spill something; but I don't think you were bloody drunk, Martlow, you just looked as though you had got a comfortable skinful. You did us very well. I felt like enjoying life last night. It was awfully decent of you to take us out."

"That's all right," said Martlow. "I don't mind 'avin' a fat 'ead in the morning, if I've 'ad a real good do the night before; only I can't stan' the buggers who wake up grousin' about it.

"You know, me ol' dad at 'ome, 'e's a decent of sport, but when 'e gets a skinful sometimes 'e's that surly you wouldn't credit it. 'E's keeper to Mr Squele, 'e is; an' one day after a shoot me mother 'ad a good dinner for 'im, a real nice piece o' beef it were, an' 'e went into the Plough at Squelesby wi' some o' the other keepers, an' they all started moppin' up a few drinks there, an' chewin' the fat about what kind o' sport they'd 'ad, an' what bloody poor shots some o' the guns were. Well, me mother didn't want the beef spilin' in the oven; an' at last she cut 'im off some, an' put it on a plate wi' another plate over it, an' put it back in the oven, leavin' the door open, so as it would keep 'ot. An' we all 'ad our own dinners, me mother, an' me sister, who was in gentleman's service, she were with Mr Squele too, then, an' me two brothers, they're out in Salonika now wi' the Cheshires. An' after we'd all 'ad our dinner, an' it were real nice beef, wi' a bit o' Yorkshire puddin' an' cauliflower and taters, me sister's young man calls to walk back wi' er, and me elder brother, Dick, 'e goes off to meet 'is pusher, and then me brother Tom slips out. 'E didn't 'ave a girl then, but 'e used to follow 'em up, and 'ide be'ind a 'edge to 'ear 'em tellin' the tale. 'E got the 'ell of a leatherin' for it one night.

"Well, I stayed be'ind to 'elp me mother wash up, and put the things away, an' she were gettin' a bit up the pole then, an' she'd go to the oven, an' take the plate out an' look at it, an' put it back again, an' she'd give me a clout over the 'ead for summat I 'adn't done; an' at last she looked at the plate, an' the meat were all gettin' dried up, so she put it on the rack, an' said she wouldn't give a damn if 'e never came back. She left the cloth on the table, an' 'is knife an' fork, an' she got the lamp, an' sat down to darn stockin's by the fire. She 'ad one o' them china eggs for darnin', an' I used to think that if you tied it up in the toe of a stockin' what a bloody great crack on the 'ead you could give someone wi' it. She wouldn't let me go out, made me get a book an' sit opposite 'er. I only wanted to get out o' the way, I did.

"Then 'e comes in, an' chucks 'is 'at down on a chair, an' tries to stan' 'is stick up in a corner where it won't stan' up, an' then 'e 'as got to pick it up again, an' 'e starts blastin' an' buggerin' an' all, an' she says nowt. She goes on wi' 'er darnin', an' only cocks an eye at 'im over 'er specs, an' 'e goes out into the scullery an' washes 'isself, an' then, when 'e's sat down at the table, she gets up an' puts the plate in front of 'im, an' says nowt, but just sits down an' goes on darnin'; an' you 'ear 'im cuttin' up the meat, an' then suddenly 'e chucks 'is knife an' fork on the table an' says; 'This meat's neither 'ot nor cold.' An' then she gets up, an' goes roun' to 'im wi' 'er 'ands on 'er 'ips. 'If you 'ad come in sooner,' she says, 'it would 'a' bin 'ot; an' if you'd stayed out later, it would 'a' bin cold; an' such as it is, you can take it or leave it. I don't care if it's your last.' So 'e gets up then, 'e a'n't got no more to say; an' she goes back to 'er darnin'; and 'e goes outside to look at the new moon, from the corner o' the 'ouse, and see if it were goin' to be a wet month or a dry. 'E were wunnerful good really at foretellin' weather. Some folk 'ave a gif' that way."

Bourne was rolling his puttees on by this time.

"I should say, Martlow, that your father had been crossed in love," he said gently.

"Well, me mother were," said Martlow, grinning. "They get on well enough together, because they're accustomed to each other's ways. Me mother always says you've got to be patient wi' folk, an' folk ain't got no patience now. If any o' us said anything about me father she'd gi'e us a clout on the side o' the 'ead, quick too. But she 'ad to be father an' mother, both, to us. Keeperin's a funny sort o' game; but my dad's a good ol' sport. 'E'd give you anything 'e'd got. An' 'e's a lot better nor 'e were. That's because she wouldn't give in to 'im. 'Charlie,' she'd say to me, 'you do what's right, an' don't let no man get master on you.' That's my motter in life, an' another is if you've got a fat 'ead you've earned it. That's what I say."

"Quite a cheerful philosophy," said Bourne, who had a great admiration for the impartial candour with which Martlow looked back on family life. Probably he took after his mother; in any case he would seem to have been nurtured in a stern school.

"Some o' these buggers what come out 'ere now," observed Martlow, "ave never done anythin' they didn't want to do in their lives before, and now they're up against somethin' real nasty, they don't 'arf make a song about it. They think they're fuckin' 'eroes just because they're 'ere."

He had shifted his blue-grey shirt round to one side, and with his legs apart was searching the lower part of his belly for lice, when Corporal Marshall came into the room.

"Ere! Why don't you get dressed?" the corporal asked him. "Time you was up, me lad. You don't want to sit there showin' the 'ole bloody world all you've got."

"All right, corporal," said Martlow cheerfully. "I'm just 'untin' up a few o' me bosom friends, you know. Wish I could see all I've got, meself; they take a 'ell of a lot o' findin'. Wonder what all the buggers will do when peace comes?"

He rapidly assumed his trousers and socks, and then, after lacing up his boots, took up his towel and went out to wash, leaving even Shem laughing.

"That was a bloody good supper we 'ad las' night, Bourne," said the corporal. "Sergeant-Major Robinson came in in the middle of it, and you've never seen a man look more surprised in your natural. 'E was quite wild about it; said the bloody corporals did 'emselves better'n the officers' mess. 'E did, straight! An' it were true, too. We were real sorry you weren't there; if you 'ave all the trouble you might as well 'ave some o' the fun. You'll come in tonight, won't you?"

"Oh, that's all right, corporal," said Bourne. "I went into the house last night when I got back, just to ask madame how you had liked it. She's a nice woman, and she had all the trouble. I shall see if there's anything extra wanted for tonight, but I don't think I had better go in. I shall have a glass of wine with you after you have eaten. Madame had all the trouble; you might put a bit extra in the kitty for her just before we go. What time do we parade?"

"Nine o'clock. Just muck about a bit in the street to keep the men together. There's a rumour we may pack up again today, but I 'aven't rumbled anything yet. I've got a sort o' feelin' we shall stay 'ere tonight anyway; from what I 'eard, the officers are bein' told what the plans are about the next show. Then we go off to practise the attack, an' I suppose in a fortnight or so we'll all be for the 'igh jump again."

126

"What hopes we've got!" said Shem softly.

"We've got nothin' to grouse about," said the corporal evenly. "That bloody man Miller's to be court-martialled tomorrow or the nex' day, chap as 'opped it in July. I expect 'e's for the electric chair all right. Bloody, ain't it?"

A silence fell on them for a moment.

"Well, I must get a move on; the bloody orderly-corporal's always on the run. See you later."

"Corporal, you might take me off on an imaginary fatigue at about half-past eleven. That's if there's nothing much doing. You can work it with Sergeant Tozer. I thought I might go in about that time and see if madame wanted anything.'

"All right. I'll see if I can work it."

They heard him, heavy on the stairs, going down, and Shem looked up at Bourne with a curious grin.

"Seems to me you're getting a bit cunt-struck."

Bourne only turned away disdainfully, and Martlow coming back and putting on his tunic, the three of them went off for breakfast.

The morning wore on very slowly; parades should never be perfunctory, and these seemed to be merely devised to kill time in a back street. The bayonet fighting was useful; and they were doing arms drill when Corporal Marshall, passing down the street, stopped and spoke to Sergeant Tozer. It was about twenty past eleven. Ten minutes later the sergeant called out Bourne, and told him to go down to the corporals' billets. He found nobody in the house but the girl, who was in the kitchen; and he told her that now he was at her service, if she wished to write her letter.

She hesitated, embarrassed for a moment, and made her decision. He drew up a chair to the table, and bringing her pen, paper and ink, she came and sat beside him. He had his own fountain pen, into which, after filling it with water, he had only to drop a pellet of ink; and then he started to translate her phrases into English, writing them so that she could copy them in her own script. It was a somewhat mechanical business. There was nothing determinate in his mind, there was only the proximity of this girl, and some aching sensibilities.

He saw the man's name again; Lance-Corporal Hemmings, written with his address at the top of the paper. He might be anything, there were all sorts in the army; anyway he was in the line, and what were the odds against him ever coming back? She kept his letter tucked away in there between her breasts. What had he seen in her? She was not even pretty; and yet Bourne himself had found his curiosity awakening almost as soon as he had seen her. It had been no more, after all, than a casual interest, until she had brought in this unknown man, and it was he, curiously enough, who provided the focus for Bourne's own rather diffuse desires. He seemed to see the other man caressing her, and the girl yielding, no, not reluctantly, but with that passive acquiescence characteristic of her; and then, imaginatively, his own desires became involved with those of the other man, even as a sense of antagonism increased in him. She possessed herself of this other man so completely, and to Bourne he was only a shadow. The fact that he was only a shadow made an enormous difference; if he had been Corporal Greenstreet, or indeed anyone actually present there, then his value, and the value of their several relations to each other, and to her, would have dropped perceptibly in the scale.

These were not merely sentimental considerations; they corresponded to an actual reality which weighed in varying measure on all of them. He was in the line, and within another few days Bourne himself would be in the line too. Perhaps neither of them would ever come back. Bourne could realise completely the other man's present misery; could see him living, breathing, moving in that state of semi- somnambulism, which to each of them equally was their only refuge from the desolation and hopelessness of that lunatic world. In fact, the relation in which he stood to this unknown man was in some ways closer and more direct than that in which he stood to the girl beside him. She knew nothing of their subterranean, furtive, twilight life, the limbo through which, with their obliterated humanity, they moved as so many unhouseled ghosts, or the aching hunger in those hands that reached, groping tentatively out of their emptiness, to seek some hope or stay.

Yesterday or tomorrow might hold it for them, for men hope for things remembered, for a past irrevocably lost. Why did she talk to him of this other man? He knew; he knew so much better than she did; he realised him now so completely in his own mind, that they might be one and the same man. She spoke softly, without raising her voice; but the need she felt to make him understand, to find expression for her desire, gave it apparently an infinite flexibility, and from time to time he felt again on his sleeve the touch of that disturbing hand. The dead words there on the paper before him, those graven and rigid symbols, could never again kindle with the movement and persuasion of her living voice. They too, were the mere traces of something that had passed. Some kind of warmth seemed to come from her, and flow over the surface of his skin with little pricklings of fire, and to lay hold of his veins, glowing there, until the lit blood rose and sang in his head.

"Je t'aime, cheri! Je t'aime eperdument! Je n'aime que toi"; she almost chanted it; and suddenly his arm was round her shoulder, and his mouth was shut fast down there behind her ear, where the hair swept upwards from the firm white neck.

She collapsed astonishingly under his touch; neither towards him nor away from him; she seemed to go to nothing in her chair. She pushed him away with her right hand, firmly, quickly. He shifted, shifting his chair away, too, and then put up a hand to his brow. He was sweating lightly. The other hand went into his pocket. He stood up, feeling criminal, and looked at her.

"Vous m'aimez?" There was a kind of rage in his suffocated voice, and she turned her face to him, looking at him with eyes in which was neither anger nor fear, but only the surprise of recognition. It was as though she had not known him before, but now she remembered. He sat again, turned sideways towards her; and put his hands over her hands lying clasped in front of her on the table. They remained still, impassive.

"Vous m'aimez? C'est vrai?"

There were light steps in the hall; they heard someone heave a sigh of relief. Oh, la! la! And madame came from the passage into the kitchen. She put her basket on the dresser, and turned to them. "Bonjour, monsieur!" she said almost gaily.

"Bonjour, madame!"

She looked at the paper, pens and ink on the table, and a smile of amused comprehension came into her eyes. She lifted her hands and let them fall again with a gesture of despairing humour. "C'est fini, maintenant?"

"Oui, madame," said Bourne tranquilly; "l'est fini."

He did not rise from his chair immediately; a point of some delicacy restrained him.

"What's 'e want to go back an' 'ave a glass o' wine wi' the corporals for?" Martlow asked. "Why don't 'e stay an' 'ave another bon night with us? You can get all the bloody wine you want 'ere."

Shem laughed.

"You've got quite a lot o' sense for a kid, you know, Martlow, but a man wouldn't want to ask so many questions."

Martlow grunted resentfully.

"Some o' these mademoiselles are too bloody artful for anyone. You want to watch your step wi' 'em, I can tell you."

The battalion was to move from Bruay at two o'clock, and about midday Bourne went to find Corporal Greenstreet at his billet. He wanted the corporal to pay madame and the girl for their services. He had an absurd scruple about doing it himself. Altogether the corporals had given him a hundred and twenty francs, and their expenses, with some extra wine the night before, had been just under ninety.

"Give her the bloody lot," said the corporal; "she did us all well."

"You give it to her,' said Bourne; "give her twenty, and give the girl ten."

"It's all in the family," said the corporal.

"Yes, but some families like to be considered as a group of individuals," said Bourne, "and the individuals like to be distinguished separately."

He sent the corporal in by himself, and waited until he returned.

"That's all right," said Corporal Greenstreet, with the air of a man who has brought a difficult business to a successful issue. "I believe you're a bit sweet on that girl, Bourne."

"How did you get on with your cook-housekeeper?" Bourne asked him irrelevantly, and Greenstreet's ruddy face became scarlet. "She never said nothin' more," he stammered precipitately. "She give me a cup o' coffee that night, an' mademoiselle come out an' said a few kin' words. It were bloody funny, weren't it?"

"It's funnier when you look back on it than when you're in the middle of it," said Bourne dryly. "It's curious how events seem to change their character when one looks back on them.'

"E 'as gone potty," said the corporal to himself, as he walked away and Bourne turned to go into the house.

When Bourne entered the kitchen, the girl took up a basket, and went into the garden. Madame looked from her to Bourne a little anxiously.

"Je viens faire mes adieux, madame," he said, ignoring the girl's flight, and he thanked her warmly on behalf of himself and of the corporals. He hoped that they had not caused her any inconvenience. She was perfectly satisfied, but when he asked if he might go and say goodbye to mademoiselle, she looked at him again with that expression of droll despair which she had shown when interrupting them yesterday. Then she decided the question once and for all.

"Therese!" she called from the doorway, and when the girl came reluctantly, she added; "Monsieur veut faire ses adieux."

And they said goodbye, with that slight air of formality which madame's presence imposed on them, their eyes searching through it to try and read each other's thought, and each warding off the other. Madame might have her suspicions, but she evidently could restrain an unprofitable curiosity; and part of their secret was even a secret to themselves.

In all action a man seeks to realise himself, and the act once complete, it is no longer a part of him, it escapes from his control and has an independent objective existence. It is the fruit of his marriage to a moment, but it is not the divine moment itself, nor even the meaning which the moment held for him, for that too has flown feather-footed down the wind. Bourne had a positive hatred of the excuse that "it does not matter" being given as a reason for any action; if something did not matter, why do it? It does matter. It matters enormously, but not necessarily to others, and the reasons why it matters to you are probably inexplicable even to yourself. One need not confuse them with the consequences which one has to shoulder as a result, and one cannot shift the burden with a whimper for sympathy.

He fell in with his pack slung, and with Martlow and a couple of others helped to pull the Lewis-gun cart; as usual the old grey mare, Rosinante, as he called her, was just ahead, and they took the road towards Bethune. At about half-past four, clouds that had been piling up all day became leaden, and trees and fields stood out under them for a little while curiously transparent in a livid golden light; then that vanished, and it became almost dark. The storm burst on them, shattering the stillness with vivid lightning and crash upon crash of thunder; trees creaked and wailed, bending under a sudden onset of wind, lashing them with heavy rain and hail, and tossing away small branches and leaves not yet yellow. They were all drenched to the skin before they could get their overcoats out of their packs, and it was not until the storm had practically passed that they were given an opportunity. Then, being all wet, it was not worthwhile, and no order was given.

Before the storm had quite passed, they came to a ford, where a brook, swollen considerably by rain, crossed the road, and here Rosinante avenged herself for all the past injustice she had suffered at their hands. After hesitating for a moment, she suddenly charged across it, her nerves shattered by the storm. They couldn't see the ford until they were in it, and then they couldn't free the Lewis-gun cart from the mess-cart in time; Martlow and a man on the other side jumped clear, but Bourne and another man could not extricate themselves from the ropes, and while Rosinante, in her impetuous rush, carried the Lewis-gun cart with her, the water over their knees in the middle impeded them. They were both swept off their feet. Bourne, clutching the rope, was dragged through and out; the other man was knocked down and run over by the Lewis-gun cart, which represented a fairly heavy weight. His knees were cut and his legs bruised from the wheels.

"Serves you all bloody well right," cried an exultant chorus.

Bourne, whose face had expressed every kind of comic anxiety during his accelerated passage of the ford, had to laugh at himself.

"I've never seen anybody," said the delighted Martlow, "look 'arf so bloody funny as you looked, Bourne."

They freed the ropes rapidly, in case anyone having authority should come to inquire into the cause of the sensation. They had left Bethune on their left and were now heading for Noeux-les-Mines again, and marched to the huts there, rain still falling steadily. Before they were dismissed, they were ordered to strip to the buff immediately afterwards and take their clothes to the drying-room, keeping only their overcoats and their boots.

Overcoats are scarcely a sufficient covering for man's nakedness. The cloth caps had to be dried, though the cap badges were distrustfully removed by their owners first; and for a time one saw men wearing nothing but an overcoat, a tin hat and boots, moving about fetching wood and coal to make fires in the huts. They were given, perhaps as an additional aid to warmth, cocoa instead of tea. After an hour or so, their clothes were returned to them dry, and then, during a lull in the rain, Bourne, Shem and Martlow went to the nearest estaminet for a drink, but were only out for twenty minutes, returning glad to go to bed. The next day it rained, except for a slight intermission after their dinner, all day.

The rain cleared away that night, and they marched all the following day, and the day after, chasing skylines. There were occasional showers, but only enough to lay the dust a little. On the evening of the second day the company were billeted in a village apart from the rest of the battalion, which was at Reclinghem; Vincly, Bourne thought, was the name. He was at a farm on the outskirts of the village, where there were only two old men, a thin bent old woman whom life had long since ceased to surprise, and a boy. When they had settled in, Corporal Marshall came up to Bourne and said, anxiously, but unofficially, that he wanted his help.

"That Lance-Corporal Miller is my prisoner, an' I'm responsible for 'im. 'E's not to be shot anyway –Captain Malet an' the chaplain worked tooth an' nail to get him off– an' the sentence will be promulgated later, so they've given the bugger to me to mind. 'E ought to be wi' the police, but 'e's under a kind of open arrest, on parole you might say. I don't trust 'im."

Bourne gave the other man, standing a few yards away, a brief glance, and decided he didn't trust him either. He had a weak, mean and cunning face, but there was something so abject in his humiliation, that one felt for him the kind of pity which can scarcely tolerate its own object. It might be I, one felt involuntarily, and the thought made one almost merciless towards the man who carried with him the contagion of fear.

"What will you do if he tries to do a bunk again?" Bourne asked.

"Shoot the bugger," said Marshall, whitening to the lips. "By God, if he tries that game on me, I won't give 'im a dog's chance."

"All right," said Bourne, in a quiet matter-of-fact voice. "Don't get windy. I can't take any of your responsibility, but I shall see he doesn't let you down if I can help it, corporal. He had better sleep between us, because I wake easily. Only I shall have to explain to Shem and Martlow. I'll shift my corner, and then we shall not have to shift them."

"Jakes will be sleepin' 'ere too, but 'e sleeps like a log," said Marshall, partly reassured. "I'll be bloody glad when they sentence 'im, I can tell you. Why the 'ell can't they do the thing quick, instead of puttin' it all on us? You 'elp me, an' I won't forget it, see."

Probably the unfortunate man knew they were speaking of him, for Bourne, glancing once again in his direction, saw him looking at them narrowly, his mouth half-open with a foolish grin. After Bourne had recovered from that instant wave of pity and repulsion, he became more and more indifferent to him. Miller would have been completely irrelevant, but for the fact that he was a nuisance. He would be better dead, and then a man's riddling conscience could ask no more questions about him; one felt even a little impatient at the thought of a court-martial and a firing party, senseless parades clothed in the forms of law. To keep him like this, exhibiting him to the battalion, was not a warning or a deterrent to other men; it merely vexed them. He should have been killed cursorily; but as they evidently did not intend to kill him, he should have been sent away. He was no longer a man to them; he was a ghost who unfortunately hadn't died.

It might be true, as the men believed, that Captain Malet and the chaplain had been able to intervene in his favour; and that would seem to imply that there were some extenuating circumstances. There was no one who grudged him a reprieve, but naturally enough they were reserved about him. A man who had deserted on the Somme, and had got as far as Rouen, and had eluded the military police for six months, could not be entirely a fool; and after one glance at that weak mouth and the furtive cunning of those eyes, Bourne distrusted him. The men were right, too, about his physical characteristics; he had the look of a Hun. One turned away from the question. Bourne, lying next to him that night, and tired after the long day, fell asleep almost at once. When he woke a few hours later, the prisoner was sleeping quietly beside him, and then Bourne himself slept again. In the morning the prisoner was still there.

Bourne did not watch him the following night. At two o'clock, when they paraded in the open space in front of the village inn, Bourne, Shem and Martlow were told to fall out; and when the rest of the company moved off, Sergeant-Major Robinson told them that they were to go to the signals section for instruction. He talked to Bourne alone, sending the other two to get their equipment.

"I'm rather sorry you're goin', but they're short of signallers. You made me wild the other day, talkin' like that to an officer. I knew you couldn't 'elp not 'avin' a proper 'at; but you shouldn't 'ave said anything. You ought to put in for a commission, as Captain Malet told you."

"Well, I'm going to put in for one. Why do they want to send me to the sigs? It seems to be the principle of the army, to find out something you can't do, and make you do it."

"I 'eard the adjutant said you seemed to 'ave some sense. 'E mentioned you, an' as they wanted three men, I told the captain Shem were pretty quickwitted, an' Martlow young enough to learn."

"That was decent of you, sergeant-major. I'm sorry I made you wild the other day. I didn't have any intention of making you wild. I thought it time I kicked a bit."

"You ought to 'ave shown more sense. I know you don't want to leave the company."

"I don't mind now, sergeant-major. I'm sorry to go, for many reasons, but I don't feel the same way about it now. I decided the other day that I should take Captain Malet's advice. I haven't any wish to be an officer, but if I were to stay any longer in the ranks, I should become a slacker. He's quite right."

"Well, you had better buzz off an' get your pack," said the sergeant-major. "I suppose as soon as you put in for a commission you will come back for a bit as a lance-corporal. Did you know Major Blessington was leaving to go to his own battalion tonight? Major Shadwell will be in command until the new colonel comes tomorrow or the nex' day.'

"No, I didn't know."

"Well, goodbye for the present, Bourne."

"Goodbye, sergeant-major; and thank you."

But he did not go immediately, for the quartermaster-sergeant told him there were some letters and a parcel for him, and the parcel looked a promising one. He got them.

"Which is the way to Reclinghem, sergeant-major?"

"Up the 'ill past the church, an' then turn down 'ill to your right. It's a mile an' a 'arf. Just the other side o' the valley."

He went back to his billet for his pack, and then with Shem and Martlow set off on their new career.

VOLUME II

I have led my ragamuffins where they are peppered; there's not three of my hundred and fifty left alive, and they are for the town's end, to beg during life. – SHAKESPEARE

Chapter XI

Where is this straw, my fellow?
The art of our necessities is strange,
That can make vile things precious. – SHAKESPEARE

Sergeant-Major Corbet of Headquarter Company was a cheerful, alert and intelligent man; an excellent signaller himself, he looked on the eight men who had come from the various companies for instruction with a more or less favourable eye. He did not notice signs of a blazing intellect on any of their faces, which he glanced at cursorily; but he had not expected anything different, and he had a lively faith in the things which, under the educative influence of himself and of Corporal Hamley, were yet to come.

"Corporal Hamley has taken the section out, and it is not worthwhile sending you after him, as you wouldn't get there until it would be time to come back. The signals section is billeted just opposite that estaminet. You can wait there for him. He will tell you where your billets are."

So they found their way to a yard enclosed by barns and byres, where one of the orderly-runners, who were also billeted there, pointed out that part of the premises allotted to the signallers. Finding a place to themselves, Bourne, Shem and Martlow sat down in the straw to investigate the contents of Bourne's parcel. It was a large parcel from some well-known West End stores, securely packed in a box of that thin wood known as threeply, and Bourne, pulling out his jack-knife from the pocket of his tunic, and slipping from under his shoulder strap the lanyard by which it was secured, prised the box open with a steel spike probably intended for punching holes in leather, or for removing stones from a horse's hoof. The first sight of the contents was a little disappointing, as a great deal of room was taken up by a long loaf of bread, called by some a sandwich loaf because it cuts into square slices and is intended to be made into sandwiches.

"What do they want to send us out bread for?" Martlow exclaimed indignantly, as though the parcel had been addressed to them collectively.

A tin of chicken, a small but solid plum cake, a glass of small scarlet strawberry jam, and a tin of a hundred Russian cigarettes.

"Yes, I wonder why they sent the bread. He's a sensible chap, but perhaps the bread was his wife's idea. You know, Martlow, my friend is about fifty-five, but he is a very good sport, and married for love last year."

"Well, never mind 'im now,' said Martlow. "I'm feelin' a bit peckish. Let's eat the chicken, and then we shan't 'ave to carry it about."

"We can save the cake for tea," said Shem. "I suppose they only sent the bread to fill up the box, but it will come in useful with the chicken."

"Open the chicken, then," said Bourne; "and cut some bread, Martlow."

Martlow, however, was too interested in watching Shem opening the tin to turn to the loaf immediately. He waited until he saw the carved fowl, set in pale, quivering jelly.

"Looks all right," he said, and grabbed the loaf.

It was fast in the box, and needed a bit of effort to pull it out.

"Bloody fine packers!" said Martlow; "they don't care 'ow..."

He gave a wrench, and it came up by the end he grasped; the other end, as soon as it was released from the pressure of the box, fell off, and a bottle with a white capsule over the cork slid out and would have fallen to the floor, but that Shem caught it.

"Well, you can fuck me!' exclaimed the astonished Martlow.

"Here, hide it, hide it quick!" said the excited Shem. "There'd be no end of a bloody row if they got to know your friends were sending you bottles o' Scotch. Bloody fine packers! I should think they were! They've scooped out nearly all the crumb. We'll have to eat dry crust with the chicken. Here, open it quick; and let's all have a tot, and then put the rest away in your pack."

"Shem," said Bourne earnestly, "if I ever get a Victoria Cross I shall send it to Bartlett as a souvenir."

"You don't want to go lookin' for no Victoria Crosses," said Martlow in a didactic vein, "you want to be bloody careful you don't get a wooden cross instead."

They gave the bones of the chicken to a dog in the yard, so that nothing of it was wasted, and the empty tin they threw into a pit dug for the purpose in a bit of field behind the yard. Shem poured some more whisky into Bourne's cooker, the lid of which fitted quite tight. That would be good in their tea, he said, as he corked the bottle and, folding it in the skirt of Bourne's overcoat, concealed it in his pack. Then, each smoking a Russian cigarette, they awaited placidly the return of Corporal Hamley from his arduous duties.

Corporal Hamley was rather like Sergeant Tozer in build, a lean, raw-boned man, but of a dark complexion, where the other man was fair and ruddy; and of a softer nature, where the other, if reflective and sensible, was still hard and sharp. The corporal, too, just because he was a little weaker than Sergeant Tozer, was inclined to be influenced by what he may have heard of a man's character before he had sufficient experience to form an opinion about him for himself. Someone had evidently prejudiced him against Bourne and Shem.

When the new men fell in for his inspection outside the stable, he was inclined to single the two of them out from the rest, by looking at them fixedly, while he delivered to the squad a little homily on the whole duty of man. There being only billets for four men in the stables, he divided the parade arbitrarily into two, and Martlow, Shem and Bourne, with a big dark man called Humphreys, were sent off to other billets about a hundred and fifty yards away down a by-road, where there were some more orderlies and some snipers. It was inconvenient being so far away from the rest of their section. "Doesn't seem to like us much," said Shem, in a pleased voice. "No bloody love lost, then," said Martlow stoically.

"He's all right," said Bourne. "In fact, I think he's probably a nice chap, only he doesn't know us, and somebody has been telling him that we need watching. Did you hear what he said about the regimental? I don't think I have spoken to the regimental since we were at Beaumetz, except to say good morning, sir, if I passed him. The corporal will be all right in a couple of days, you'll see. Mr Rhys is a pretty difficult proposition, I believe; a nice chap, but liable to cut up rough any morning when he happens to have a fat head. He and Mr Pardew are boozing-chums, you know: when they get canned up they get canned up together; and when I was in the orderly-room I used to notice that whenever Mr Rhys was ratty with the signallers, Mr Pardew was ratty with the snipers. Isn't it nice to think we've got three-quarters of a bottle of good Scotch whisky?"

"We want to keep that, until we can have a quiet beano on our own. We'll have what I put in your cooker for tea, and we'll have another tot at tea-time tomorrow, then it will last three or four days. We can get something at the estaminet. Mind you don't pull it out with your overcoat. Put a sock round it, and then keep your towel on top of it."

"It'll look dam' funny 'im pullin' 'is coat out ev'ry time 'e wants 'is tow'l, won't it?" Martlow suggested. "It'll be all right in a sock."

Bourne proved to be right about the corporal, who may have watched them with a little suspicion for two or three days, but by that time had become more favourable towards them. They had to begin at the beginning; learning the Morse code, flag-wagging, a succession of acks, and practice on the buzzer. Martlow, whose whole wit lay in his quick, teachable senses, was easily the best pupil, and Bourne the least satisfactory of the three, Shem having considerably greater power of applying himself to the matter in hand. Madeley, one of the signallers usually on duty in the orderly-room, had become friendly with Bourne there, though they only saw each other casually. Perhaps he helped to correct Corporal Hamley's point of view. On their part, they liked their work and the men in their section.

Their first day the whole battalion paraded at nine o'clock in the main street at Reclinghem, and Major Shadwell made a brief inspection of them. It was really extraordinary, but one could not help being struck by the changed feeling among the men, as he passed along the ranks. It was not simply that they liked him, but he belonged to them, he belonged to their own earth. His rather stern and uncompromising manner did not matter a damn to them. It was the general opinion that here was a man who should be sent home on a senior officers' course, and then come back and command them for the duration. It was not that he was popular among them as other officers were; their feeling towards him was not without affection, but had more in it of appreciation and respect.

One might have thought that this feeling would tell against the new colonel, who arrived and took over command that night; but when Colonel Bardon inspected them in the morning, he moved along the ranks with an air of quiet efficiency, with a great deal of reserve, as though past experience had told him that, if he were inspecting these silent rigid men, they also were inspecting him, with a penetration and a power of judgment equal to his own. The severity of his clean-cut face was that of Major Shadwell's; he was shorter in stature, but compactly built, well-balanced and alert, with grey-blue eyes that were keen and quick in sizing up his men. That seemed to be his whole object, to find out the kind of men he had to command; and the answer to his question was for his own private mind.

There was nothing of the romantic swagger and arrogance to which, in the past couple of months, they had become accustomed and indifferent. Bourne always had the illusion that his own senses stretched right along the line of men on either side of him. When one is standing to attention, one is still, erect, with eyes looking straight in front of one, but as the footsteps of authority come closer and closer, one seems to apprehend something of the reality before it is visible; then into one's field of vision, at first vague and indeterminate, then suddenly in sharp definition, comes a face, cold and unrecognising but keen and searching in its scrutiny, and it blurs again and is gone. For those brief seconds one feels one's breath being drawn in through one's nostrils and filling the cavity of one's chest, and then its expiration, and once again the in-draught of air. One feels that one should either restrain one's breathing, as in aiming at a target, or else, as the only possible alternative, snort, as a dog or a horse might, at the apprehension of some possible danger. Those were Bourne's feelings, anyway, when he first met the scrutiny of those incisive eyes. Colonel Bardon passed, like some impersonal force, and the tension relaxed. Then Madeley, next to him in the ranks, whispered under his breath, and practically without moving his lips:

"Well, he looks like a bloody soldier, anyway."

After all, that was what mattered most to them; and since their duty and service implied some reciprocal obligations on his side, their opinion meant more to him than perhaps he knew. They were his men all right, if he handled them well, that was settled when once they had looked into the just, merciless face; and the companies marched off to their drills, and the specialists to their duties, well aware that presently there would be another big killing of men. They marched out of the village, past the stone calvary at the end of it, and men who had known all the sins of the world lifted, to the agony of the figure on the cross, eyes that had probed and understood the mystery of suffering.

Shem was the moving spirit in an episode which might have brought himself, Bourne and Martlow face to face with Colonel Bardon in a more unpleasant aspect. They were content with their work, and Corporal Hamley, and the section in general; but already the question had been raised as to what would be their duties when the battalion went into the line. Obviously they would be unable to act as signallers, except perhaps in the subsidiary duties, such as helping to repair or lay lines. Even Martlow, whose light touch and quick ear made him a very apt pupil on the buzzer, would scarcely be qualified for the duty. There being a shortage among the runners, they might be useful in that capacity.

Then it was arranged that for three consecutive days the whole battalion was to practise an attack, and once again this question emerged. They were told by the corporal that they were to report to their companies. Shem, who was quite a reliable person where all serious duties were concerned, but an inveterate lead-swinger with regard to any parades or fatigues which he considered unnecessary, promptly made a grievance of the matter.

"Well, we've got to go."

"We haven't got to go," said Shem. "I am willing to bet nobody in A Company knows anything about our going to them. We have only got to get into the loft here every morning, and we have a couple of days' rest. It's a gift."

"Please yourself," said Bourne reflectively, "but I would just as soon go out with the company."

"We'd be on the mat," said Martlow, dubiously.

"If one goes back to the company, the lot of us will have to go. There's no sense in our going, unless we are going over the top with the company. These bloody practices are no good anyway. A lot o' brass hats make the most elaborate plans, and they issue instructions to all concerned, and officers are taken to inspect a model of the position to be attacked, and then we're buggered about, and taken over miles o' ground, all marked out with tape to represent trenches, and then when everything is complete, and every man is supposed to know exactly what he has to do, the whole bloody thing is washed out, and we all go over the top knowing sweet fuck-all of what we are supposed to be doing."

Shem's simple and perspicuous account of staff methods reduced Bourne to compromise; he proposed to visit his friends in A Company, Sergeant-Major Robinson and Sergeant Tozer, and find out how the land lay. Shem was recalcitrant.

"You will only give the show away," he said obstinately. He refused to walk up to A Company's billets with Bourne, who went with Martlow eventually.

"I don't mind bein' on the mat, if it's wo'th it," said Martlow reflectively.

"It isn't," said Bourne. "However, old Shem wants it, and we have to hang together."

The sergeant-major and Quartermaster-Sergeant Deane were surprised when Bourne put his head in at the door, and asked if there were any parcels for him.

"Do you want a parcel every bloody day?" inquired the quarterbloke. "You got a good 'un two days ago, didn't you?"

"I expected a small parcel of cigarettes," said Bourne innocently. "I've got a few good ones left, but I'm running out of gaspers. Try one of these, sergeant-major. Mr Rhys forgot his cigarette case yesterday, we were about a mile and a half the other side of Reclinghem, flag-wagging, and when we had an easy he asked me for a cigarette, if, mind you if! It were a decent one. Like a fool, I gave him one of these, and he has forgotten his cigarette case all day today. I can't keep the officers in cigarettes. I want some gaspers; they're good enough for the troops."

"You've got a 'ide, you 'ave," said the sergeant-major, lighting one as Bourne offered the case to the quarter-bloke.

"'Ow d'you like the sigs?' inquired the latter, lighting his.

"Oh, it's cushy enough," said Bourne indifferently. "I was always content with the company. Apparently they don't know what they're going to do with us when we go into the line. I suppose we shall know more or less tomorrow, as when we go over the top we shall presumably go over with the section with which we practise. They say we may be used as orderlies.'

"You can't say, really," said Sergeant-Major Robinson, "because they generally muck everything up at the last minute. Seems to me all these practices are just so much eyewash for the staff; an' if anything goes wrong they can say it's not for want o' preparation. Anyway, whether you go with the runners or with the sigs tomorrow, you'll 'ave an easier time than we'll 'ave. I'm the bugger who has most of the work to do in these stunts. When you get your commission, Bourne, don't you ever let your sergeant-major down. Don't you ever forget that 'e does all the bloody work."

The reference to the possibility of a commission infuriated Bourne. The sergeant-major had forgotten the presence of Martlow, sitting quietly on a box by the doorway, and now looking at Bourne with the round eyes of astonishment.

"Why don't they send us back to the company for the attack?" he exclaimed, with an impatience which was impatience at the sergeant-major's blundering indiscretion, and an attempt to cover it.

"Oh, you're a bloody fool!" said the sergeant-major. "You've got a cushy job with the sigs until you go 'ome, an' you don't want to go askin' for trouble. When you 'ave the chance of an easy, you take it. You won't find bein' a second loot as cushy a job as you think; an' if you want to make a good officer, don't you be too ready to tick off your comp'ny sergeant-major when any little thing goes wrong. You just remember all the work 'e does, an' all 'is responsibilities, see?"

"Well, I have not put in for a commission yet, sergeant-major," said Bourne, trying to affect an indifference under Martlow's eyes. "What's in orders; may I have a look?"

He glanced at the couple of typewritten sheets as if to hide his embarrassment.

"Them's part two orders you're lookin' at. Part one's the first page."

He glanced through them quickly. The sergeant-major could not teach him anything about orders. Then he put them back on the table.

"Well, we shall have to move back. If a parcel should come for me, I suppose the post-corporal will bring it along. Goodnight, sergeant-major. Goodnight, sir."

He and Martlow went out into the twilight.

"Shall we get a drink here, or wait until we get back to Reclinghem?" he asked Martlow.

"Wait," said the other briefly.

They stepped out in silence for a little while, and then Martlow turned his face up sideways to him.

"Bourne, are you goin' to be an officer?"

144

The question itself seemed to divide them sharply from each other. There was something cool, remote, and even difficult in the tone in which it was asked. It was as though the boy had asked him if he were going over to surrender to the Hun.

"Yes," he answered a little harshly, accepting bitterly all the implications in the question.

They were approaching the church, and came suddenly through the shadows on the old cure, in his soutane and broad-brimmed hat. Bourne drew himself up a little and saluted him. The old man took his hat right off, and bowed, standing uncovered, in something like an attitude of prayer, while they passed; and even though he had noticed before the kind of reverence which some French priests put into their courtesy towards a soldier, the trivial incident filled Bourne with a sense of trouble. He thought he had heard somewhere that it was unlucky to meet a priest in the dusk, and as the thought flitted through his mind, he had the sensation of goose flesh all up his spine. He was a reticent and undemonstrative man, but after a few more steps through the silent shadows, he put his arm round Martlow's neck, his hand resting on his shoulder.

"I don't want it. I have got to go," he said.

"We're all right as we are, the three on us, aren't we?" said Martlow, with a curious bitterness like anger. "That's the worst o' the bloody army; as soon as you get a bit pally with a chap summat 'appens."

"Well, it has got to be," said Bourne. "I am not going before the show comes off, anyway. The three of us shall be together, and then...well, it's not much use looking ahead, is it?"

They did not say much more for the rest of the way, but picked up Shem, and then went into the estaminet in Reclinghem for a drink. Shem laughed scornfully when they told him that the company did not apparently expect them to report in the morning.

"What did I tell you?" he said, and Bourne, in a sulky way, told him he had better go and buy some provisions.

"We'll get our bread and cheese ration," he added.

In the morning they drew a bread and cheese ration with the rest of Headquarter Company, and then secreted themselves in a loft over their billets. Through some slats, in a ventilating window at the gable end, they could just see the front of the house; and presently the military policeman billeted there came out, with his stick in his hand, and proceeded briskly about his duty. They knew his times, more or less, but what they failed to appreciate for the moment was the fact that today's stunt rather disturbed the normal routine of duty, making his movements less definitely calculable.

Bourne had lost the schoolboy spirit of truancy, which was still predominant in Shem and Martlow, and he was rather bored. The whole joy of disobedience is in the sense that one has chosen freely for oneself, and Bourne had not chosen freely, he had fallen in with Shem's plan; on the other hand, though he was equally involved with them now, he was not primarily responsible for it, and was free to criticise it from an almost disinterested point of view. There was a certain amount of pleasure in that, as it brought him into opposition with Shem, and naturally enough he liked to maintain a kind of moral, or immoral, ascendancy over his ally. He was bound, of course, to do his best to secure the success of Shem's plan, and if it failed he was certain to suffer equally with its author, but among themselves he could always disclaim responsibility, except in so far as an amiable weakness of character, by vitiating his better judgment, had engaged him in it. These considerations were all that gave him a kind of zest in the exploit.

The military policeman had been gone for little more than half an hour, and they did not expect him back until about a quarter to twelve. They were, therefore, rather surprised to hear obviously military footsteps in the yard, and a certain amount of anxiety mingled with their surprise when the footsteps turned into the stables beneath them, passed by the ladder which gave access to the loft, and then moved down the length of the building from one partition to another. Someone was evidently inspecting their billets. He returned to the foot of the ladder, and then they held their breath, for the ladder was only secured in position by a hook fixed to a beam under the entrance to the loft and fastening to a staple in the ladder itself. The ladder moved, as a hand was placed on it, and someone was now ascending. Bourne, with the foolish mirth which sometimes overcomes one in the face of danger, could have laughed at the sight of Shem and Martlow couched on a pile of little sheaves, and watching the entrance like two animals prepared to defend their lair; and laughter came in an explosion when Humphreys' face suddenly appeared

146

above the floor level, its expression changing swiftly from guilt, surprised to disappointment as he recognised them.

"What the bloody 'ell do you want to come 'ere for?" Martlow shot at him in rage.

"I've got as much right 'ere as you 'ave," he replied, truculently.

"The question of right in this connection is of merely academic interest," said Bourne, delighted by the position of affairs, "but you would admit that we have a prior claim, and are therefore in a stronger position than you are. I am not going to conceal from you, Humphreys, the fact that your presence is unwelcome to us. If you're going to argue the toss with us, you will finish by being chucked out on your head. Yes, by the three of us if necessary. We haven't found you very companionable in the past few days, and an impartial consideration of your character and habits has reconciled us to the fact. However, you are here, and we have to make the best of your company, as of other inconveniences inherent in the situation, but if you become at all objectionable, we'll push you down the bloody ladder and take the consequences. Is that clear to your somewhat atrophied intellect?"

"Well, there's room for four on us," said Humphreys, with unexpected modesty.

"That's all right," said Bourne, whose main objects were to take charge of the situation, and forestall any unreasonable quarrelling on the part of Shem or Martlow. "This loft is a common refuge for the four of us; but don't you do anything to give the show away. I think I am the oldest soldier here, so that naturally I'm in charge. If we all end on the mat, I am the person who will bear the chief responsibility."

"Shoo," said Martlow, lifting a hand to warn them, and they heard more movement in the yard, a cackle of high female voices which invaded the stables, and then again the ladder moved, tilting a little as someone ascended.

"My God, we're holding a bloody reception," said Bourne, under his breath.

The face of madame, the proprietress of the farm, appeared above the floor, and turned from one to the other in a spirit of inquiry.

"Bonjour, madame!" said Bourne, with great self-possession. "J'espere que notre presence ici ne vous derange point. Nous nous trouvons un peu fatigues apres de marches longues, et des journees assez laborieuses. Or,

147

nous avons pris la resolution de nous reposer ici, pendant que le regiment fait des manoeuvres dans les champs. Ca n'a pas d'importance, je crois; ces exercices sont vraiment inutiles. Nous ne ferons pas de mal ici."

"Mais ce n'est pas tres regulier, monsieur," she replied dubiously, and some excited queries came from her two friends below. Bourne thought her objection incontrovertible but a little pedantic. Only half of her had risen through the floor, and there she paused in doubt, as though emerging, like a conjured spirit, from the shades.

"Montez, madame, je vous en prie"; he implored her. "Comme vous dites, ce n'est pas regulier, et ce sera vraiment dommage si nous sommes decouverts. Montez, madame, vous et vos amies; et puis nous causerons ensemble."

It took him some time to persuade her that they were not deserters, and that their escapade was without much significance except to themselves, but eventually he succeeded. She mounted the remaining rungs of the ladder; and, filled with curiosity, her two friends followed her, one fat and rubicund, the other one of those anaemic, childless women who haunt the sacristies of village churches. Shem and Martlow both looked as though they were half inclined to cut and run for it. Humphreys merely stared at the invasion with pugnacious resentment. Only Bourne seemed to grasp the essential fact that they were all in reality the prisoners of the three women, who had by now constituted themselves a jury of matrons for the purpose of trying the case. He had to play the part of advocate, not only in his own cause, but in that of these accomplices who from sheer stupidity did nothing to ingratiate themselves with their judges.

"For God's sake, smile!" he said, desperately, and Martlow at least responded by breaking into a broad grin, which gave them a less criminal appearance. Women are notoriously influenced by a man's facial expression and flatter themselves that their response to it is some subtle power of intuition. They have, in reality, about as much intuition as an egg. Bourne's too elaborate manner and Martlow's grinning humour were saving graces in the present situation, and the women discussed their right course of action, in what they thought was a reasonable spirit. They had to be humoured, and, considering their entire lack of charm, Bourne hoped that none of them might prove to have a romantic nature.

Madame, seated on the floor, took up a sheaf and stripped the ears from it, threshing off those which did not come away as she pulled it through her hand, into a cloth spread on the floor. Shem, Martlow and Bourne had been standing clear of the sheaves since she had arrived, but Humphreys was sitting on a pile. She made up her mind, after consultation with her sister Fates, and having finished her threshing, stood and delivered judgment.

They could not stay in the loft, it was "malsaine", she declared, as the grain stored there was her "vivres" for the winter. On the other hand, she would not betray them to the police. She thought they would be sufficiently safe from arrest in the further stable; and then, turning on Humphreys, she told him to get up. Bourne told him what she said, but he would not move, and he was rude. Even though she did not understand what he said, his manner was rude enough to be unmistakable, and reading in it a defiance of her authority, she advanced on him, and, before Bourne could interpose, had slapped him, first on one cheek, and then with the other hand on the other, while she told him what she thought of him. She did not raise her voice. She stood over him like a cat swearing at a dog, in a low hissing invective, and ready to claw him if he showed the least sign of fight.

Humphreys, of course, though he was a stupid, surly fellow, would not have retaliated against a woman; but he looked as though he were almost suffocated with anger. Bourne interposed again, as in the case of Corporal Greenstreet; but this time he did not try to soothe the angry woman, he turned on the angry man.

"You're the bloody fool who is going to get us all in the mush," he said, in a rage quite equal to their own. "I'm not going to tell you twice. You take up your kit, and get down that bloody ladder quick."

"What'd she want...?"

Madame advanced again with that purring hiss...

"Are you going?" said Bourne, the last strand of his control wearing thin. "There's your bloody pack."

He threw the pack down the ladder, and grumbling and arguing, Humphreys descended after it. They all had their hackles up by now, and Bourne told Shem and Martlow to get down with an air of curt authority. The women were flushed with triumph, but they were inclined to look on Bourne with a favourable eye, so he approached madame again, and

149

asked her if she had no other place where they might hide themselves for that day, and the next, perhaps even for the third. At last she led him across the yard, and showed him a small room with a cement floor. It may have been a dairy, or a storeroom of some kind, and it had two doors, one going out at the side of the house on to a narrow strip of grass bounded by an unkempt hedge with fields beyond; and the other into a passage, on the other side of which the military policeman had his lodging.

Bourne was satisfied. He made sure that madame intended no further move against Humphreys, and excused him as well as he could. She would not have Humphreys in the house, but said he might remain where he was. Then Bourne went back to the stables, and telling Humphreys that he would probably be all right where he was, that he could please himself whether he stayed there or not, but that if he went back to the loft madame would almost certainly inform the policeman who was billeted there, he took Shem and Martlow to the house with him. Then he asked madame to let them have some coffee, and paid her for it. With the coffee they drank a little of the fast-dwindling but carefully hoarded whisky. They heard the military policeman return at twelve o'clock. They could keep track of his movements more easily now, and aired themselves outside the house when he went out in the afternoon. They were glad when the battalion returned at four o'clock and they could slip out and mingle with the men.

The second day was pleasanter, as they took more chances, getting out into the field,; and Bourne, after stalking the policeman until he saw him well on the road to Vincly, turned back and bought a bottle of wine at one of the estaminets to eke out their whisky, of which they only had a tot each left. On that errand he ran into Evans, now servant to the new colonel.

"Lookin' for trouble?" Evans inquired, grinning. Bourne gave him a drink, and learned that the battalion would carry out the same practice the next day, unless it rained; as there were no facilities for drying the men's clothes, they wouldn't risk a wetting.

The next day, after the battalion had moved out, a storm broke, and the men were brought back. The three absentees had a certain amount of difficulty in getting back to the signals section unobserved; they had to get wet first; and Martlow became a little too wet by standing under a spout which took the water off the roof.

They had been absent from parade for three consecutive days, and had not found much pleasure in ill-doing. The same afternoon they were taken to some pit-head baths at a mine three miles away; and the next morning, the justice of fate, which is a little indiscriminating as to the pretexts on which it acts, descended on them. They were the last to fall in on parade, and Mr Rhys had a fat head. They were not really late, and other sections were still falling in; but the officer ordered Corporal Hamley to take their names, and they went before Captain Thompson at half-past eleven. Bourne merely pointed out that they occupied different billets from the rest of the section, and some distance away, but he did not attempt to justify himself. It was wisdom on his part. Captain Thompson, after cautioning them strictly, dismissed the charge. Martlow seemed aggrieved by the injustice of this disciplinary act, but Bourne laughed at him: "If we got twenty-eight days first field punishment for something we had not done we should still have deserved it," he said. "I suppose that kind of balance is always evened out in the end."

Immediately after dinner, a thrill of excitement passed rapidly from company to company; all parades were cancelled, billets were to be cleaned up, and the battalion was to be ready to march at half-past five. It was some time since they had marched by night. For once, too, they had some definite details; they were to march to St Pol, and entrain there for the front. It was very curious to see how the news affected them; friends grouped themselves together, and talked of it from their individual points of view, but the extraordinary thing was the common impulse moving them, which gathered in strength until any individual reluctances and anxieties were swept away by it. A kind of enthusiasm, quiet and restrained because aware of all it hazarded, swept over them like fire or flood. Even those who feared made the pretence of bravery, the mere act of mimicry opened the way for the contagion, and another will was substituted for their own, so that ultimately they too gave themselves to it. They might fail or break, they might shrink back at the last in an agony of fear, but this overpowering impulse for the time being swept them on towards its own indeterminate ends, as one common impulse might move in a swarm of angry bees.

The light was failing rapidly as they fell in, and they moved off in silence, marching to attention. A Company would join up with them at the crossroads, marching to meet them from Vincly. They noticed that their new colonel had a good word of command, which carried well without breaking in the effort. Shortly after A Company had joined them, they had the order to march at ease, and then to march easy. A few minutes later, Bourne again saw the old cure of Vincly. He was standing by the, roadside, watching them pass, his head uncovered and bowed, in his characteristic attitude of humility, which seemed at once beautiful and ominous.

Bourne felt a kind of melancholy, a kind of homesickness, stilling the excitement which had filled him a little while ago. He watched the colour draining out of earth, leaving all its contours vague and grey, except where the shadowy woods and downs took a sharper outline against a sky as luminous and green as water flowing over limestone. Some stars, pallid as yet, hung in it. He had the feeling that he had relinquished everything. It was not that silly feeling of sacrifice, the sense of being a vicarious atonement for the failure of others; the wind with which some men puff out an idle vanity. Memory drifted up on to the verge of his thought a phrase –la resignation, c'est la defaite, de l'ame– but it was not quite that, for there was no sense of defeat. He had ceased, in some curious way, to have any self-consciousness at all; it was as though his mind were brimmed up with peace, with a peace that still trembled a little on its surface, as though a breath would suffice to spill it; though he had the certainty in his heart that presently it would become still, and mirror only the emptiness of the night.

The rhythm of all those tramping feet, slurring the stresses slightly, held him in its curious hypnosis. He was aware of it all only as one might be aware of a dream. The men sang, sang to keep up cheerful hearts:

"'Ere we are, 'ere we are, 'ere we are, again,
Pat and Mac, and Tommy and Jack, and Joe!
Never mind the weather! Now then, all together!
Are we down'earted? NO! ('ave a banana!)
'Ere we are, 'ere we are..."

It might have gone on indefinitely, but the men suddenly switched on to "Cock Robin", into which some voices would interject "another poor mother 'as lost 'er son," as though to affront the sinister fate against which they were determined to march with a swagger. As they marched through one little village, at about ten o'clock, doors suddenly opened and light fell through the doorways, and voices asked them where they were going.

"Somme! Somme!" they shouted, as though it were a challenge. "Ah, no bon!" came the kindly pitying voices in reply; and even after the doors closed again, and they had left that village behind, the kindly voices seemed to drift across the darkness, like the voices of ghosts; "Somme! Ah, no bon!"

And that was an enemy to them, that little touch of gentleness and kindliness; it struck them with a hand harsher than death's, and they sang louder, seeing only the white road before them, and the vague shadows of the trees on either hand. At last the singing died away; there was nothing but the trampling of myriad feet; or they would halt for ten minutes, and the darkness along the roadside became alive as with fireflies from the glow of cigarettes through a low mist.

It must have been midnight when they reached St Pol, and there again their singing sent out a noisy challenge to the darkness, but now they sang one of their regimental marching songs, chronicling in parody their own deeds; it was the air of the Marseillaise:

At La Clytte, at La Clytte,
Where the Westshires got well beat,
And the bullets blew our buttons all away,
And we ran, yes, we ran,
From that fuckin' Alleman;
And now we are happy all the day!

Windows were thrown up, and recognising only the patriotic air, some of the virtuous townspeople joined in the singing; but after all there must be some misunderstanding in any alliance between two separate peoples. The men laughed with great delight, and then the order to march to attention imposed silence on them. They turned into a big camp, which Bourne was told was a hospital, and after waiting some little time restlessly in the dark, some huts were assigned to them.

"I like marching at night," said Martlow. "Don't you, Bourne?"

"Yes, I like it, kid. Are you tired?"

"A bit. Shem isn't. Shem never tires."

They laid themselves down, as they were to get a few hours' sleep; and Bourne, dropping off between the two of them, wondered what was the spiritual thing in them which lived and seemed even to grow stronger, in the midst of beastliness.

Chapter XII

Yes, in this present quality of war
Indeed the instant action, a cause on foot
Lives so in hope, as in an early spring
We see the appearing buds, which to prove fruit
Hope gives not so much warrant, as despair
That frosts will bite them. – SHAKESPEARE

Bourne roused himself, and, after a few minutes of dubious consciousness, sat up and looked round him, at his sleeping companions, and then at the rifles stacked round the tent-pole, and the ring of boots surrounding the riflebutts. His right hand finding the opening in his shirt front, he scratched pleasurably at his chest. He was dirty, and he was lousy, but at least, and he thanked God for it, he was not scabby.

Half a dozen men from Headquarter Company, including Shem as a matter of course, had been sent off yesterday to a casualty clearing station near Acheux, suffering or rejoicing, according to their diverse temperaments, with the itch. The day after their arrival at Mailly-Maillet, the medical officer had held what the men described irreverently as a prick-inspection. He was looking for definite symptoms of something he expected to find, and because his inquest had been narrowed down to a single question, it may have seemed a little cursory. The men stood in a line, their trousers and underpants having been dropped round their ankles, and as the doctor passed them, in the words of the regimental sergeant-major, they "lifted the curtain", that is to say the flap of the shirt, so as to expose their bellies.

Scratching his chest, Bourne considered the boots; if a sword were the symbol of battle, boots were certainly symbols of war, and because by his bedside at home there had always been a copy of the authorised version, he remembered now the verse about the warrior's boots that stamped in the tumult, and the mantle drenched with blood being all but for burning, and fuel for the fire. He lit a cigarette. It was, anyway, the method by which he intended to dispose of his own damned kit, if he should survive his present obligations, but the chance of survival seeming to his cooler judgment somewhat thin, he ceased spontaneously to be interested in it. His mind did not dismiss, it ignored, the imminent possibility of its own destruction.

He looked again with a little more sympathy on his prone companions, wondering that sleep should make their faces seem so enigmatic and remote; still scratching and rubbing his chest, he returned to his contemplation of the boots. Then, when he had smoked his cigarette down to his fingers, he rubbed out the glowing end in the earth, slipped out of the blanket, and reached for his trousers.

He moved as quickly as a cat in dressing, and now, taking his mess-tin, he opened the flap of the tent, and went out into the cool morning freshness. He could see between the sparse trees to the cookers, drawn up a little off the road. The wood in which they were encamped was just behind Mailly-Maillet in an angle formed by two roads, one rising over the slope to Mailly-Maillet, and the other skirting the foot of the hill towards Hedauville. It was on a rather steep reverse slope, which gave some protection from shellfire, and there were a few shelter-trenches, which had been hastily and rather inefficiently dug, as a further protection. It was well screened from observation. The trees were little more than saplings, young beech, birch and larch, with a few firs, poorly grown, but so far unshattered. Bourne strolled carelessly down to the cookers.

"Good morning, corporal. Any tea going?"

Williams stretched out his hand for the mess-tin, filled it to the brim, and then, after handing it back to Bourne, went on with his work, without a word. Bourne stayed there, sipping the scalding brew.

"Go up the line, last night?" Williams inquired at last.

"Carrying party," answered Bourne, who found his dixie so hot he could scarcely hold it, so he was protecting his hands with a dirty handkerchief. "I was out of luck. I was at the end, and when they had loaded me up with the last box of ammunition, they found there was a buckshee box of Verey lights to go, too. The officer said he thought I might carry those as well; and being a young man of rather tedious wit, he added that they were very light. I suppose I am damned clumsy, but one of those bloody boxes is enough for me, and I decided to dump one at the first opportunity. Then Mr Sothern came back along the top of the

156

communication trench, and, finding me weary and heavily laden, said all sorts of indiscreet things about everybody concerned. 'Dump them, you bloody fool, dump them!' he shouted. I rather deprecated any extreme measures. 'Give me that bloody box,' he insisted. As he seemed really angry about it, I handed him up the box of ammunition, as it was the heavier of the two. He streaked off into the darkness to get back to the head of the party, with his stick in one hand, and a box of ammo in the other. I like these conscientious young officers, corporal."

"E's a nice chap, Mr Sothern," observed Williams, with a face of immovable melancholy.

"Quite," Bourne agreed. "However, there's a big dugout in Legend Trench, and between that and the corner of Flag Alley I saw a box of ammunition that had been dumped. It was lying by the duck boards. It may have been the one I gave Mr Sothern: 'lost owing to the exigencies of active service.' That's what the court of enquiry said about Patsy Pope's false teeth."

Williams went on with his work.

"It won't be long before you lads are for it again," he said in his quiet way.

"No," said Bourne, reluctantly, for there was a note of furtive sympathy in Williams' voice which embarrassed him.

"The whole place is simply lousy with guns," continued the cook.

"Why the hell can't you talk of something else?' exclaimed Bourne, impatiently. "Jerry chased us all the way home last night. Mr Sothern, who knows no more about the bloody map than I do, tried a short cut, and wandered off in the direction of Colincamps, until we fetched up in front of one of our field batteries, and were challenged. Then an officer came up and remonstrated with him. After that, when we got on the road again and Fritz started sending a few across, you should have seen us! Leaning over like a field of corn in the wind.'

"A lot o' them are new to it, yet," said Williams, tolerantly. "You might take a drop o' tea up to the corporal, will you? 'E's a nice chap, Corporal 'amley. I gave 'im some o' your toffees last night, an' we was talkin' about you. I'll fill it, in case you feel like some more."

Bourne took it, thanking him, and lounged off. There was now a little more movement in the camp, and when he got back to his own tent he found all the occupants awake, enjoying a moment of indecision before they elected to dress. He poured some tea into Corporal Hamley's tin, and then gave some to Martlow, and there was about a third left.

"Who wants tea?" he said.

"I do," said Weeper Smart, and in his blue shirt with cuffs unbuttoned and white legs sprawled out behind him, he lunged awkwardly across the tent, holding out his dixie with one hand. Smart was an extraordinary individual, with the clumsy agility of one of the greater apes; though the carriage of his head rather suggested the vulture, for the neck projected from wide, sloping shoulders, rounded to a stoop; the narrow forehead, above arched eyebrows, and the chin, under loose pendulous lips, both receded abruptly, and the large, fleshy beak, jutting forward between protruding blue eyes, seemed to weigh down the whole face. His skin was an unhealthy white, except at the top of the nose and about the nostrils where it had a shiny redness, as though he suffered from an incurable cold; it was rather pimply. An almost complete beardlessness made the lack of pigmentation more marked, and even the fine, sandy hair of his head grew thinly.

It would have been the face of an imbecile, but for the expression of unmitigated misery in it, or it would have been a tragic face if it had possessed any element of nobility; but it was merely abject, a mask of passive suffering, at once pitiful and repulsive. It was inevitable that men living day by day with such a spectacle of woe should learn in self-defence to deride it, and it was this sheer necessity which had impelled some cruel wit of the camp to fling at him the name of Weeper, and make that forlorn and cadaverous figure the butt of an endless jest. He gulped his tea, and his watery eyes turned towards Bourne with a cunning malevolence.

"What I say is, that if any o' us'ns tried scrounging round the cookers, we'd be for it."

Bourne looked at him with a slightly contemptuous tolerance, gathered his shaving tackle together, flung his dirty towel over his shoulder, and set off again in the direction of the cookers to scrounge for some hot water. He could do without the necessaries of life more easily than without some small comforts.

Breakfast over, they cleaned up and aired the tent and almost immediately were told to fall in on parade with Headquarter Company. Captain Thompson, watching them fall in from the officers' tents, knocked his pipe out against his stick, shoved it in his tunic pocket, and came up the hill, carrying his head at a rather thoughtful angle. He had a rather short, stocky figure, and a round bullet head; his face was always imperturbable, and his eyes quiet but observant.

Sergeant-Major Corbet called the company to attention and Captain Thompson acknowledged the salute, and told the men to stand easy. Then he began to talk to them in a quiet unconventional way, as one whose authority was so unquestioned that the friendliness of his manner was not likely to be misunderstood. They had had a good rest, he said (as though he were talking to the same men who had fought their way, slowly and foot by foot, into Guillemont!), and now there was work in front of them--difficult and dangerous work--the business of killing as many superfluous Germans as possible. He would read out to them passages from the letter of instructions regarding the attack, which as fresh and reconditioned troops they would be called on soon to make. He read, and as he read his voice became rather monotonous, it lost the character of the man and seemed to come to them from a remote distance.

The plan was handled in too abstract a way for the men to follow it, and their attention, in spite of the gravity with which they listened, was inclined to wander; or perhaps they refused to think of it except from the point of view of their own concrete and individual experience. Above his monotonous voice one could hear, now and again, a little wind stray through the drying leaves of the trees. A leaf or two might flutter down, and scratch against the bark of trunk or boughs with a crackling papery rustle. Here and there he would stress a sentence ever so slightly, as though its significance would not be wasted on their minds, and their eyes would quicken, and lift towards him with a curious, almost an animal expression of patient wonder. It was strange to notice how a slight movement, even a break in the rhythm of their breathing, showed their feelings at certain passages.

"...men are strictly forbidden to stop for the purpose of assisting wounded..."

The slight stiffening of their muscles may have been imperceptible, for the monotonous inflection did not vary as the reader delivered a passage in which it was stated that the staff considered they had made all the arrangements necessary to effect this humanitarian, but somewhat irrelevant, object.

"...you may be interested to know," and this was slightly stressed, as though to overbear a doubt, "that it is estimated we shall have one big gun--I suppose that means hows and heavies--for every hundred square yards of ground we are attacking."

An attack delivered on a front of twenty miles, if completely successful, would mean penetrating to a depth of from six to seven miles, and the men seemed to be impressed by the weight of metal with which it was intended to support them. Then the officer came to the concluding paragraph of the instructional letter.

"It is not expected that the enemy will offer any very serious resistance at this point..."

There came a whisper scarcely louder than a sigh.

"What fuckin' 'opes we've got!"

The still small voice was that of Weeper Smart, clearly audible to the rest of the section, and its effect was immediate. The nervous tension, which had gripped every man, was suddenly snapped, and the swift relief brought with it an almost hysterical desire to laugh, which it was difficult to suppress. Whether Captain Thompson also heard the voice of the Weeper, and what construction he may have placed on the sudden access of emotion in the ranks, it was impossible to say. Abruptly, he called them to attention, and after a few seconds, during which he stared at them impersonally, but with great severity, the men were dismissed. As they moved off, Captain Thompson called Corporal Hamley to him.

"Where will some of us poor buggers be come next Thursday?" demanded Weeper of the crowded tent, as he collapsed into his place, and looking at that caricature of grief, their laughter, high-pitched and sardonic, which had been stifled on parade, found vent.

"Laugh, you silly fuckers!' he cried in vehement rage. "Yes, you laugh now! You'll be laughing the other side o' your bloody mouths when you 'ear all Krupp's fuckin' iron-foundry comin' over! Laugh! One big gun to every bloody 'undred yards, an' don't expect any serious resistance from the enemy! Take us for a lot o' bloody kids, they do! 'Aven't we been up the line and..."

"You shut your blasted mouth, see!" said the exasperated Corporal Hamley, stooping as he entered the tent, the lift of his head, with chin thrust forward as he stooped, giving him a more desperately aggressive appearance. "An' you let me 'ear you talkin' on parade again with an officer present and you'll be on the bloody mat, quick. See? You miserable bugger, you! A bloody cunt like you's sufficient to demoralise a whole fuckin' army corps. Got it? Get those buzzers out, and do some bloody work for a change."

Exhausted by this unaccustomed eloquence, Corporal Hamley, white-lipped, glared round the tent, on innocent and guilty alike. Weeper gave him one glance of deprecatory grief, and relapsed into a prudent silence. The rest of the squad, all learners, settled themselves with a more deliberate obedience. There was no sense in encouraging Corporal Hamley to throw his weight about, just because he had wind up. They took up their pencils and paper, and looked at him a little coolly; Weeper was one of them. With the corporal sending on the buzzer, the class laboriously spelt out his messages. Then he tried two men with two instruments, one sending, and the other answering and repeating, while the rest of the squad recorded. "You've been at this game before," he said to Weeper.

"I, corporal?" said Weeper, with an innocence one could see was affected, "I've never touched one o' these things before."

"No?" said the corporal. "Ever worked in a telegraph office? You needn't try to come that game on me. I can tell by your touch."

He was not in a humour to be satisfied, and the men, thinking of the show they were in for, did not work well. A sullen humour spread among them. Bourne was the least satisfactory of all.

"You're just swingin' the lead," said Corporal Hamley. "Those of you who can't use a buzzer will be sent out as linesmen, or to help carry the bloody flapper."

Things went from bad to worse among them. There was a light drizzle of rain outside, and this gradually increased to a steady downpour. Their sullen humour deepened into resentment, fretting hopelessly in their minds; and the corporal's disapproval was expressed now and again with savage brevity. Then the stolid but perfectly cheerful face of Corporal Woods appeared between the flaps of the tent.

"Kin I 'ave six men off you for a fatigue, corporal?" he asked pleasantly.

"You can take the whole fuckin' issue," said Corporal Hamley, with enthusiasm, throwing the buzzer down on his blankets with the air of a man who has renounced all hope.

Shem returned, wet and smelling of iodine, at dinner-time. All that day it rained, and they kept to the tents, but their exasperation wore off, and the spirit of pessimism which had filled them became quiet, reflective, even serene, but without ceasing to be pessimism.

Mr Rhys paid them a visit, and said that, taking into account the interruption of their training by other duties, their progress had been fairly satisfactory. He, too, picked out Weeper Smart as an expert telegraphist, and Martlow as the aptest pupil in the class; as for the other new men, it would be some time before they were fully qualified for their duties. At a quarter to three he told the corporal that they might pack up for the day. If the weather had cleared they would have gone out with flags, but they had been on the buzzer all the morning, and in the monotony of repeating the same practice, hour after hour, men lose interest and learn nothing.

From outside came the dense unbroken murmur of the rain, which sometimes dwindled to a whispering rustle, through which one could hear heavy drops falling at curiously regular intervals from the trees onto the tent, or a bough laden with wet would sag slowly downward, to spill all it held in a sudden shower, and then lift up for more. These lulls were only momentary, and then the rain would increase in volume again until it became a low roar in which all lesser sounds were drowned. There was little wind.

Mr Rhys told them they might smoke, and stayed to talk with them for a little while. They all liked him, in spite of the erratic and hasty temper which left them a little uncertain as to what to make of him. From time to time, without putting aside anything of his prestige and authority over them, he would try to get into touch with them, and learn what they were thinking. Only a very great man can talk on equal terms with those in the lower ranks of life. He was neither sufficiently imaginative, nor sufficiently flexible in character, to succeed. He would unpack a mind rich in a curious lumber of chivalrous commonplaces, and give an air of unreality to values which for him, and for them all in varying measure, had the strength, if not altogether the substance, of fact. They did not really pause to weigh the truth or falsity of his opinions, which were simply without meaning for them. They only reflected that gentlefolk lived in circumstances very different from their own, and could afford strange luxuries. Probably only one thing he said interested them, and that was a casual remark to the effect that, if the bad weather continued, the attack might have to be abandoned. At that, the face of Weeper Smart became suddenly illumined by an ecstasy of hope.

When at last Mr Rhys left them, they relaxed into ease with a sigh. Major Shadwell and Captain Malet they could understand, because each was what every private soldier is, a man in arms against a world, a man fighting desperately for himself, and conscious that, in the last resort, he stood alone; for such self-reliance lies at the very heart of comradeship. In so far as Mr Rhys had something of the same character, they respected him; but when he spoke to them of patriotism, sacrifice and duty, he merely clouded and confused their vision.

"Chaps," said Weeper, suddenly, "for Christ's sake let's pray for rain!'

"What good would that do?" said Pacey reasonably. "If they don't send us over the top here, they'll send us over somewhere else. It 'as got to be, an' if it 'as got to be, the sooner it's over an' done wi' the better. If we die, we die, an' it won't trouble nobody, leastways not for long it won't; an' if we don't die now, we'd 'ave to die some other time.'

"What d'you want to talk about dyin' for?" said Martlow, resentfully. "I'd rather kill some other fucker first. I want to have my fling before I die, I do."

"If you want to pray, you 'ad better pray for the war to stop," continued Pacey, "so as we can all go back to our own 'omes in peace. I'm a married man wi' two children, an' I don't say I'm any better'n the next man, but I've a bit o' religion in me still, an' I don't hold wi' sayin' such things in jest.'

"Aye," said Madeley, bitterly; "an' what good will all your prayin' do you? If there were any truth in religion, would there be a war, would God let it go on?"

"Some on us blame God for our own faults," said Pacey, coolly, "an' it were men what made the war. It's no manner o' use us sittin' 'ere pityin' ourselves, an' blamin' God for our own fault. I've got nowt to say again Mr Rhys. 'E talks about liberty, an' fightin' for your country, an' posterity, an' so on; but what I want to know is what all us'ns are fightin' for..."

163

"We're fightin' for all we've bloody got," said Madeley, bluntly.

"An' that's sweet fuck all," said Weeper Smart. "A tell thee, that all a want to do is to save me own bloody skin. An' the first thing a do, when a go into t' line, is to find out where t' bloody dressing-stations are; an' if a can get a nice blighty, chaps, when once me face is turned towards home, I'm laughing. You won't see me bloody arse for dust. A'm not proud. A tell thee straight. Them as thinks different can 'ave all the bloody war they want, and me own share of it, too."

"Well, what the 'ell did you come out for?" asked Madeley.

Weeper lifted up a large, spade-like hand with the solemnity of one making an affirmation.

"That's where th'ast got me beat, lad," he admitted. "When a saw all them as didn' know any better'n we did joinin' up, an' a went walkin' out wi' me girl on Sundays, as usual, a just felt ashamed. An' a put it away, an' a put it away, until in th' end it got me down. A knew what it'd be, but it got the better o' me, an' then, like a bloody fool, a went an' joined up too. A were ashamed to be seen walkin' in the streets, a were. But a tell thee, now, that if a were once out o' these togs an' in civvies again, a wouldn't mind all the shame in the world; no, not if I 'ad to slink through all the back streets, an' didn' dare put me nose in t'Old Vaults again. A've no pride left in me now, chaps, an' that's the plain truth a'm tellin'. Let them as made the war come an' fight it, that's what a say."

"That's what I say, too," said Glazier, a man of about Madeley's age, with an air of challenge. Short, stocky, and ruddy like Madeley, he was of coarser grain, with an air of brutality that the other lacked: the kind of man who, when he comes to grips, kills, and grunts with pleasure in killing. "Why should us'ns fight an' be killed for all them bloody slackers at 'ome? It ain't right. No matter what they say, it ain't right. We're doin' our duty, an' they ain't, an' they're coinin' money while we get ten bloody frong a week. They don't care a fuck about us. Once we're in the army, they've got us by the balls. Talk about discipline! They don't try disciplinin' any o' them fuckin' civvies, do they? We want to put some o' them bloody politicians in the front line, an' see 'em shelled to shit. That'd buck their ideas up."

"I'm not fightin' for a lot o' bloody civvies," said Madeley, reasonably. "I'm fightin' for myself an' me own folk. It's all bloody fine sayin' let them as made the war fight it. 'Twere Germany made the war."

"A tell thee," said Weeper, positively, "there are thousands o' poor buggers, over there in the German lines, as don' know, no more'n we do ourselves, what it's all about."

"Then what do the silly fuckers come an' fight for?" asked Madeley, indignantly. "Why didn' they stay't 'ome? Tha'lt be sayin' next that the Frenchies sent 'em an invite."

"What a say is, that it weren't none o' our business. We'd no call to mix ourselves up wi' other folks' quarrels," replied Weeper.

"Well, I don't hold wi' that,' said Glazier, judicially. "I'm not fightin' for them bloody slackers an' conchies at 'ome; but what I say is that the Fritzes 'ad to be stopped. If we 'adn't come in, an' they'd got the Frenchies beat, 'twould 'a' been our turn next."

"Too bloody true it would," said Madeley. "An' I'd rather come an' fight Fritz in France than 'ave im come over to Blighty an' start bashin' our 'ouses about, same as 'e's done 'ere.'

"E'd never 'ave come to England. The navy'd 'ave seen to that," said Pacey

"Don't you be too bloody sure about the navy," said Corporal Hamley, entering into the discussion at last. "The navy 'as got all it can bloody well do, as things are."

"Well, chaps," said Glazier, "maybe I'm right an' maybe I'm wrong, but that's neither here nor there; only I've sometimes thought it would be a bloody good thing for us'ns, if the 'un did land a few troops in England. Show 'em what war's like. Madeley an' I struck it lucky an' went 'ome on leaf together, an' you never see'd anything like it. Windy! Like a lot o' bloody kids they was, an' talkin' no more sense; 'pon me word, you'd be surprised at some o' the questions they'd ask, an' you couldn't answer sensible. They'd never believe it, if you did. We jes' kep' our mouths shut, and told 'em the war was all right, and we'd got it won, but not yet. 'Twas the only way to keep 'em quiet.

"The boozers in Wes'church was shut most of the day; but Madeley and I would go down to the Greyhound, at seven o'clock, an' it was always chock-a-block wi' chaps lappin' it up as fast as they could, before closin' time. There'd be some old sweats, and some men back from 'ospital into barracks, but not fit, an' a few new recruits; but most o' them were miners, the sort o' buggers who took our job to dodge gettin' into khaki. Bloody fine miners they was.

"Well, one Saturday night we was in there 'avin' a bit of a booze up, but peaceable like, when one of them bloody miners came in an' asked us to 'ave a drink in a loud voice. Well, we was peaceable enough, an' I dare say we might 'ave 'ad a drink with him, but the swine put 'is fist into 'is trousers' pocket, and pulls out a fistful of Bradburys an' 'arfcrowns, an' plunks 'em down on the bar counter. 'There,' he says, 'there's me bloody wages for a week, an' I ain't done more'n eight hours' work for it, either.

"I don't care if the bloody war lasts for ever,' 'e says. I looks up an' sees Madeley lookin' white an' dangerous. 'Was you talkin' to me?' says Madeley. 'Aye,' 'e says. 'Well, take that, you fuckin' bastard!' says Madeley, an' sloshes 'im one in the clock. Some of 'is friends interfered first, and then some of our friends interfered, an' in five seconds there was 'ell's delight in the bloody bar, wi' the old bitch be'ind the counter goin' into 'ysterics, an' 'ollerin' for the police.

"Then Madeley got 'old of 'is man, who was blubberin' an' swearin' summat awful, an' near twisted 'is arm off. I were busy keepin' some o' the other buggers off 'im, but 'e didn't pay no attention to nobody else, 'e just lugged 'is man out the back door an' into the yard, wi' the old girl 'ollerin' blue murder; and Madeley lugs 'im into the urinal, an' gets 'im down an' rubs 'is face in it. I'd got out the back door too, be that time, as I see'd some red-caps comin' into the bar; an' when 'e'd finished I saw Madeley stand up an' wipe 'is 'ands on the seat of 'is trousers. 'There, you bugger,' 'e says; 'now you go 'ome an' talk to yourself.' ''op it,' I says to 'im, 'there's the fuckin' picket outside'; an' we 'opped it over some palin's at the bottom o' the yard; one of 'em came away, an' I run a bloody great splinter into the palm o' me 'and. Then we just buggered off, by some back streets, to the Crown, an' 'ad a couple o' pints an' went 'ome peaceable."

"Look at ol' tear gas!" Martlow cried. "Thought you didn't like fightin', Weeper?"

Weeper's whole face was alight with excitement.

"A like a scrap as well as any man, so long as it don't go too far," said Weeper. "A'd 'ave given a lot to see thee go for that miner, Madeley. It's them chaps what are always on the make, an' don't care 'ow they makes it, as causes 'arf the wars. Them's the bloody cowards."

"Is it all true, Madeley?" asked Corporal Hamley.

"It were summat like, but I misremember," said Madeley, modestly. "But it's all true what 'e says about folks at 'ome, most on 'em. They don't care a fuck what 'appens to us'ns, so long as they can keep a 'ole skin. Say they be ready to make any sacrifice; but we're the bloody sacrifice. You never see'd such a windy lot; an' bloodthirsty ain't the word for it. They've all gone potty. You'd think your best friends wouldn't be satisfied 'til they'd see'd your name on the roll of honour. I tol' one of 'em 'e knew a bloody sight more'n I did about the war. The only person as 'ad any sense was me mother. She on'y fussed about what I wanted to eat. She didn't want to know anything about the war, an' it were on'y me she were afraid for. She didn't min' about aught else. 'Please God, you'll be home soon,' she'd say. An' please God, I will.'

"An' then they give you a bloody party," said Glazier. "Madeley an' I went to one. You should a see'd some o' the pushers. Girls o' seventeen painted worse nor any Gerties I'd ever knowed. One of 'em came on an' sang a lot o' songs wi' dirty meanings to 'em. I remember one she sang wi' another girl, "I Want a Rag". She did an' all, too. When this bloody war's over, you'll go back to England an' fin' nought there but a lot o' conchies and bloody prostitutes."

"There's good an' bad,' said Pacey, mildly, "an' if there's more bad than good, I don't know but the good don't wear better. But there's nought sure in this world, no more."

"No, an' never 'as been," said Madeley, pessimistically.

"There's nought sure for us'ns, anyway," said Weeper, relapsing. "Didst 'ear what Cap'n Thompson read out this mornin', about stoppin' to 'elp any poor bugger what was wounded? The bloody brass 'at what wrote that letter 'as never been in any big show 'isself, that a dare swear. 'E's one o' them buggers as is never nearer to the real thing than G.H.Q."

"You don't want to talk like that," said Corporal Hamley. "You've 'ad your orders."

"A don't mind tellin' thee, corporal," said Weeper, again lifting a large flat hand, as though by that gesture he stopped the mouths of all the world. "A don't mind tellin' thee, that if a see a chum o' mine down, an' a can do aught to 'elp 'im, all the brass 'ats in the British Army, an' there's a bloody sight too many o' 'em, aren't goin' to stop me. A'll do what's right, an' if a know aught about thee, tha'lt do as I do."

"You don't want to talk about it, anyway," said Corporal Hamley, quietly. "I'm not sayin' you're not right: I'd do what any other man'd do; but there's no need to make a song about it."

"What beats me," said Shem, sniggering; "is that the bloody fool who wrote that instructional letter doesn't seem to know what any ordinary man would do in the circumstances. We all know that there must be losses, you can't expect to take a trench without some casualties; but they seem to go on from saying that losses are unavoidable, to thinking that they're necessary, and from that, to thinking that they don't matter."

"They don't know what we've got to go through, that's the truth of it," said Weeper. "They measure the distance, an' they count the men, an' the guns, an' think a battle's no' but a sum you can do wi' a pencil an' a bit o' paper."

"I heard Mr Pardew talking to Mr Rhys about a course he'd been on, and he told him a brass hat had been lecturing them on the lessons of the Somme offensive, and gave them an estimate of the total German losses; and then an officer at the back of the room got up, and asked him, if he could give them any information about the British losses, and the brass hat said 'No', and looked at them as though they were a lot of criminals."

"It's a fact," said Glazier; "whether you're talkin' to a civvy or whether you're talkin' to a brass 'at, an' some o' the officers aren't no better, if you tell the truth, they think you're a bloody coward. They've not got our experience, an' they don't face it as us'ns do."

"Give them a chance,' said Bourne, reasonably; he hadn't spoken before, he usually sat back and listened quietly to these debates.

"Let 'em take my fuckin' chance!" shouted Weeper, vindictively.

"There's a good deal in what you say," said Bourne, who was a little embarrassed by the way they all looked at him suddenly. "I think there's a good deal of truth in it; but after all, what is a brass hat's job? He's not thinking of you or of me or of any individual man, or of any particular battalion or division. Men, to him, are only part of the material he has got to work with, and if he felt as you or I feel, he couldn't carry on with his job. It's not fair to think he's inhuman. He's got to draw up a plan, from rather scrappy information, and it is issued in the form of an order; but he knows very well something may happen at any moment to throw everything out of gear. The original plan is no more than a kind of map; you can't see the country by looking at a map, and you can't see the fighting by looking at a plan of attack. Once we go over the top it's the colonel's and the company commander's job. Once we meet a Hun it's our job..."

"Yes, an' our job's a bloody sight worse'n theirs," said Weeper.

"It's not worse than the colonel's, or the company commander's," said Bourne. "Anyway, they come over with us. They've got to lead us, or drive us. They may have to order us to do something, knowing damned well that they're spending us. I don't envy them. I think that bit in the letter, about not stopping to help the wounded, is silly. It's up to us, that is, but it's up to us not to make another man's agony our excuse. What's bloody silly in the letter is the last bit, where they say they don't anticipate any serious resistance from the enemy. That is the staff's job, and they ought to know it better."

"We started talking about what we were fighting for," said Shem, laughing. "It was Mr Rhys started it."

"Yes, an' you've been talkin' all over the bloody shop ever since," said Corporal Hamlety. "You all ought to be on the bloody staff, you ought. 'Oo are orderly-men? Shem and Martlow; well, tea's up."

Shem and Martlow looked at the straight rain, and then struggled into their greatcoats.

"All that a says is, if a man's dead it don't matter no more to 'im 'oo wins the bloody war," said Weeper. "We're 'ere, there's no gettin' away from that, corporal. 'Ere we are, an' since we're 'ere, we're just fightin' for ourselves; we're just fightin' for ourselves, an' for each other."

Bourne stared as though he were fascinated by this uncouth figure with huge, ape-like arms, and melancholy, half-imbecile face. Here was a man who, if he lost his temper with them, could have cleared the tent in ten seconds, and he sat with them, patient under daily mockery, suffering even the schoolboy cheek of little Martlow indifferently, and nursing always the bitterness and misery of his own heart.

Already dripping, Shem and Martlow dumped the dixie of tea in the opening of the tent, almost spilling it, as they slipped on the greasy mud, where many feet had made a slide by the doorway.

"I never knew such a miserable lot o' buggers as you all are," said Corporal Hamley. "And me over that pot o' pozzy."

"I'm not miserable, corporal," said little Martlow: "We're not dead yet. On'y I'm not fightin' for any fuckin' Beljums, see.

169

One o' them buggers wanted to charge me five frong for a loaf o' bread."

"Well, put a sock in it. We've 'ad enough bloody talk now." They ate, more or less in silence, and then smoked, contentedly enough. The rain was slackening, and there was more light. After they had smoked for a while, Glazier took his tunic and shirt off, and began to hunt for lice. One after another they all followed his example, stripping themselves of trousers, underpants and even socks, until the tent held nothing but naked men. They would take a candle, or a lighted match, and pass it along the seams of their trousers, hoping that the flame would destroy the eggs. A hurricane lamp hung by a nail on the tent-pole, and after it was lighted they still continued the scrupulous search, its light falling on white shoulders studiously rounded as they bent over the task. They were completely absorbed in it, when the air was ripped up with a wailing sigh, and there was a muffled explosion in the field behind them. They stopped, listening intently, and looking at each other. Another shell, whining precipitately, passed overhead to end with a louder explosion in some fields beyond the little wood, and well over the lower road. Then there was a silence. They sighed and moved.

"If Jerry starts shellin' proper," said the corporal, as they dressed themselves again, "you want to take shelter in them trenches."

"They're no' but rabbit-scrapes," said Weeper.

"Well, you get into 'em," said the corporal, "an' if they're not good enough for you, we can dig 'em deeper tomorrow."

Nothing more was said. They were bored a little, lounging there, and smoking again, but they took refuge with their own secret thoughts. Outside, the rain had stopped. They were all going up the line with a big carrying party that night. At about six o'clock they heard from the road below a heavy lumbering and clanking, and they listened with ears cocked. Then they heard hurrying movements outside.

"What is it?"

"Tanks! Tanks!"

They rushed out of their tent, and joined, apparently with the whole camp, in a wild stampede through the trees to the road below. None of them as yet had seen a tank. It was only a caterpillar tractor, which had come up to move a big gun to or from its lair. Officers hurried out to see what was the matter, and then returned disgusted to their tents. Sergeants and corporals cursed the men back to their own lines. As Bourne turned back with the others, he looked up to a clear patch of sky, and saw the sharp crescent of the moon, floating there like a boat. A bough threw a mesh of fine twigs over its silver, and at that loveliness he caught up his breath, almost in a sob.

The caterpillar continued its muffled clanking along the road, and the wood filled with low voices, as the men, laughing in the darkness, turned back up the slope to their dimly lighted tents. Bourne, who had lost Shem and Martlow in the downward rush, found himself beside Sergeant Morgan, the bombing sergeant, who for some little time past had nodded to him in a friendly way when they met, and then by degrees had come to know him better. He was a very decent, cheerful man. As they walked up the hill together, they came up with the regimental, to whom Bourne had scarcely spoken since they were at Beaumetz.

"Hullo, Bourne; it's a bloody long time since I've seen anything of you. How do you like sigs? Come along to my tent for a while, and have a yarn. I hear you are going in for a commission."

Sergeant Morgan, saying goodnight, disappeared into the darkness between the trees, and Bourne followed the regimental to his tent, which was at the top of the wood, a little apart from the others. A hurricane lamp burned low in it, and there was no one else there but Barton, the regimental's batman, whom Bourne liked, knowing as he did that, but for Barton's careful shepherding, the regimental might have been in serious trouble recently, on one or two occasions. They sat and talked of the prospects of the show for a few minutes, and the regimental told him that they were going out to practise it in the morning with the rest of the Brigade over some ground which had been taped out. A field day with the divisional general and most of his gilded staff. There would be a good deal of wind up before it was over.

"I'm laughing," said the regimental, "my job will be with the ammunition column."

"You may get it in the neck there, as well as anywhere else," said Bourne in a matter-of-fact way.

Barton went off on his own private affairs, and the other two talked in a desultory way, like men who have nothing much to say, but talk for the sake of company.

"You don't seem to be in a very good skin tonight," said Bourne at last. "What's the matter? Has the colonel been getting wind up about the practice tomorrow?"

"The colonel's a bloody soldier, an' don't you forget it," said the regimental, with an honest appreciation. "I don't know what's the matter with me. I'm bloody well fed up with it."

"You ought to take a pull on yourself," said Bourne, as though he were talking of the weather. "You have been inclined to run off the rails ever since we were at Mazingarbe."

"That's all a bloody tale..."

"I didn't suppose it was all true," said Bourne, quietly; "but you were canned-up, and you never know what you're doing when you're canned. You've been right enough since we left Noeux-les-Mines, and you ought to keep right now. I should be sorry if you made a mess of things. There are some who would be pleased, and you give them an opening..."

"You're all right, Bourne. I don't mind what you say, but pack it up now. I've got to travel my own bloody road, and I'm not asking for anyone's help. It's my own funeral. I know what a man's bloody friends are like when he makes a slip. Oh, I don't mean you. You're all right, but you can't be of any bloody use one way or the other."

"I know that," said Bourne, shortly. "The trouble with you is that you get things, get promotion for instance, too easily. You're too contemptuous. The only thing you do damned well you don't think worth doing."

They dropped again into idle question and answer, and after a little while Bourne left him, as presently he had to fall in with the carrying party.

They fell in under cover of the trees, just off the road, and Mr Marsden was in charge. The mere fact that they were moving about in the dark gave an air of stealth to the business. The words of command were given, and the men numbered off, with lowered voices; then they swung out of the wood, turning right, and right again as they struck the main road, which, in rising over the hill, curved round slightly towards the left.

There was starlight and a young moon, sharp as a sickle; and into the clear night great concrete standards, which had carried electric power, rose at regular intervals. On the reverse slope they were intact, broad at the base, pierced, so as not to offer too much resistance to the wind, and tapering as they rose, almost as obelisks; but the first to lift its peak above the crest of the hill had been damaged, and beyond that they had been all shattered by shellfire, only the truncated bases remaining.

Mailly-Maillet began at the top of the hill. There was a branch road to Auchonvillers; the main road, running straight through the town, was in the direction of Serre, which the Hun held, and a third road on the left went off to Colincamps. The town itself, though extensively damaged, had not been completely wrecked, but the few inhabitants who remained there were preparing reluctantly, under military compulsion, to leave.

Just after entering the town, Mr Marsden halted his men for a moment, and spoke to the military policeman in control. Then they continued straight through, keeping to the Serre road. Once through Mailly-Maillet, the ground fell away gradually, so gradually that the slope seemed almost flat. Most of the detail of the country, except for the shining road in front of them, was lost in darkness, or showed only as deeper shadow. They continued along the road a little way, and then turned off it to the left, across country now rough and derelict. A road running from Colincamps converged towards the road they had just left, to meet it at a point known as the sugar refinery, and, just before striking that road, they came to the large dump called Euston, and halted there, while Mr Marsden went to find the dump officer.

They were to carry up more ammunition. When Mr Marsden returned with the other officer, the boxes were checked, and even in the short interval of time which that business occupied, a couple of big shells had come whimpering overhead, searching for a battery, perhaps, and they heard, at no great distance, the eruption from the shells' explosion in the wet earth. Lower down the road Bourne could see a couple of ambulances drawn up, and from one very faint, very momentary gleam of light, he divined, rather than saw, the entrance to a dugout which would be the dressing-station. When the boxes were checked and each man loaded, they crossed the road, and Bourne, who had been over the same ground the night before, noticed a new feature a few yards away from the beginning of the communication-trench called Southern Avenue: a large shell-crater, the size of a good pond, but empty of water, except for a little seepage, which showed that it had only just been made.

The sound of the big shells and the sight of the crater quickened their apprehension of danger, without raising it to the point of fear. One's sensibility seemed to grow finer, more acute, while at the same time it became somewhat distorted. In the distance a star-shell would rise, and as its light dilated, wavered and failed, one saw against it the shattered trunks and boughs of trees, lunatic arms uplifted in imprecation, and as though petrified in a moment of shrieking agony. The communication-trench was deep, and one looked up out of it to a now tranquil sky, against which the same stark boughs were partly visible. Then on the right appeared the ruins of a shattered farm, an empty corpse of a building. There was for Bourne an inexplicable fascination in that melancholy landscape; it was so still, so peaceful, and so extraordinarily tense. One heard a shell travel overhead, or the distant rattle of a machine-gun, but these were merely interruptions of a silence which seemed to touch the heart with a finger of ice. It was only really broken when a man, stumbling on a defective or slippery duck-board, uttered under his breath a monosyllabic curse...

"Fuck..."

That reminder of man's proximity broke for a moment the dream, but otherwise, one seemed to be travelling through some sterile landscape in the moon, or some soulless region on the shadowy confines of hell. Coming out of the communication-trench, they turned to the right up Sackville Street, a breast-work only, giving one a sudden feeling of space and insecurity; and, continuing, they came on a more intricate system: Flag Alley, Flag Switch, Legend, and Blenau. In Legend there was a company in support, and they passed a sentry over a dugout and one or two men. Then again was a long lifeless stretch. Just before they reached the fire-trenches they stood aside to allow a stretcher party carrying down a man to pass. As he passed them they whispered encouragement.

"Good luck, chum. Don't you worry. You'll be back in Blighty soon."

He may not have heard them, he lay very still, but Bourne, whose ironical spirit was sometimes sardonic, felt with an irresistible conviction that their words were a ritual formula, devised to avert, somehow, a like fate from themselves. Even so, it showed how closely men were bound together, by some impalpable tie. They passed men on the fire-step, men as fixed as statues when that ghastly light fell tremblingly on them from the sky, and one or two sprawled on the step, their backs propped against the side of the bay, snatching a little fitful sleep, their tin hats tilted over their faces, and boots, puttees and trousers plastered thick with mud that caked like mortar. Sometimes their eyes met a face, blank from the weariness that is indifference; and perhaps, because at this point they only moved forward a few yards at a time, they would exchange a few whispers.

"What's it like?"

"Oh, 'e strafed a bit this afternoon, but it's cushy enough."

Bourne had never heard any other reply to that question, in all the hundreds of times he had heard it asked. A face of expressionless immobility, with hard inscrutable eyes, and that even monotonous whisper.

"Oh, it's cushy enough."

Presently Corporal Hamley motioned him forward into the next fire-bay. Shem followed him, and the others, for the moment, were barred. He saw Mr Marsden talking to an officer, and then he found that each man had to get out of the trench, and dump his stuff where a depression made an area of dead ground. He climbed out, and saw for a moment the rather loosely hung strands of wire, between the pickets, against the sky; there was a fairish depth of it. Almost as soon as he stood upright, a bullet sang by his head; it was as though something spat at him out of the darkness. In the deeper part of the hollow, an officer checked the boxes as they were dumped. As he returned to the trench, Shem got out with his box. Mr Marsden was still talking, in a low voice, to the other officer. There were only three or four more men behind, and then they would go back.

Bourne passed out of the fire-trench by a slit, running slantwise, to a trench in the rear, where the other men waited. Shem joined him, and another man. Then there was a loud elastic twang as a shell exploded fairly close to them; they heard stuff flying overhead, and another shell came, and another. One no sooner heard the hiss of the approaching shell than it exploded. The two last men, a little shaken, joined them. Shells continued to come over, bursting with that curious twang, and occasionally a blast of air fanned their faces. Weeper, who was standing by Shem and Martlow, leaned on the muzzle of his rifle. His face had an expression of enigmatic resignation. Mr Marsden did not come. The shelling was not very severe, but it seemed to increase slightly, and they wondered whether Jerry was going to start a real strafe. The range improved, too, and presently the word was passed along for stretcher-bearers. Their own stretcher-bearers, with Corporal Mellin, moved along to go to the fire-trench, but they were not wanted. Mr Marsden arrived and stopped them.

"It's all right. Their own bearers are there. We may want you ourselves later," he said, encouragingly.

They moved off, but even before they moved, the shelling slackened, and then ceased. Bourne had noticed that one or two of the new men had seemed a bit windy, that is, restless and impatient, not really in a funk. Weeper's passive acquiescence in whatever Fate might have in store impressed him more. He was a little surprised at himself. The zip of the bullet by his head had disconcerted him a little, and yet probably it was only a stray, and perhaps not so close as he imagined.

They had a rum issue with their tea when they got back, and then a final cigarette before turning to sleep.

Chapter XIII

He alone
Dealt on lieutenantry and no practice had
In the brave squares of war. – SHAKESPEARE

In the morning, the whole camp seethed with hot and angry men, as
was always the case when brass hats, and general officers, disturbed the
normal routine of their life. Preparations for the rehearsal of the attack
were complicated by the issue of orders, that blankets were to be handed
in, and the camp cleaned up, before the men paraded. They were to
parade in full kit with pack complete, and a bread-and-cheese ration was
issued to them. The unnecessary bad temper continued until they fell in
on the road, and the colonel came on parade, smiling slightly, as though
he were well satisfied, and looked forward to an amusing day. The high,
clear voice, which always seemed to carry without much effort, rang out,
and the battalion moved off in the direction of Bertrancourt.

After some miles, they turned off the road and continued over reaped
fields, finally mounting a ridge and taking up a position with other
battalions of their Brigade. There the men were allowed to fall out and
eat. They could see at once, more clearly than they had realised from the
instructions read out to them, the way they were to be disposed, and
started a general discussion on the rival advantages and disadvantages of
going over as the first or second wave, a discussion which had no other
effect than that of confirming each individual disputant in the opinion
with which he had originally started. It proved indirectly, however, that
there was a considerable fund of obstinacy, combativeness, and tenacity
of purpose among them, and these were clearly assets of military value.

The first excitement was provided by a hare. It was put up by some of
the troops in front, who chivvied it about in all directions, until, doubling
back, it came straight through their own H. Q. Company, almost running
over Bourne's foot. He didn't move, pitying the poor hunted thing. They
were in an angle of a field, along the boundaries of which ran a low fence
of rabbit wire, and as it was headed into the corner, Martlow flung

177

himself on it, caught it, and broke its neck scientifically with a blow from the edge of his hand.

"Why did you kill it?" exclaimed Bourne, as Martlow buttoned his tunic over the warm quivering body. Bourne thought hares uncanny creatures.

"It'll go into t' pot," said Martlow, surprised. Mr Sothern came up, and offered him ten francs for it, and after some hesitation Martlow sold it to him.

Presently arrived magnificent people on horseback, glancing superciliously at the less fortunate members of their species whom necessity compelled to walk. Bourne, who loved horses, had seen nothing for months but mules, Rosinante, some sorry hacks ridden by their officers, and a few lusty percherons threshing corn on akind of treadmill outside a French farm. The sight of these daintily stepping animals, with a sheen on their smooth hides, gave him a thrill of pleasure. He was less favourably impressed by some of the riders.

"That bugger will give his horse a sore back before the day is out," he said, as one of the great men cantered by importantly.

"You're learnin' a lot o' bad words from us'ns," said Martlow, grinning.

"Oh, you all swear like so many Eton boys," replied Bourne, indifferently. "Have you ever heard an Aussie swear?'

"No, 'n' I don't want," said Martlow. "Them buggers 'ave too much spare cash to know what soldierin' means."

They fell in, and there was another moment of suppressed bad temper. Most of the new signallers went with H. Q. runners, but Weeper Smart, though he was close to them, had to carry the flapper with H. Q. signallers. The flapper was a device by which it was intended to signal to aeroplanes. One could see by now that most of the men were keenly interested; they knew that the plan was intended to supply them with a kind of map, on the actual scale of the trenches they were to attack. Their interest did not fade out completely as they advanced, but they rapidly became aware of the unreality of it all. The files of men moved forward slowly, and, when they reached the tapes, followed the paths assigned to them with an admirable precision. Their formations were not broken up or depleted by any hostile barrage, the ground was not pitted by craters, their advance was not impeded by any uncut wire. Everything went according to plan. It was a triumph of staffwork, and these patient, rather unimaginative men tried to fathom the meaning of it all, with an anxiety which only made them more perplexed. They felt there was something incomplete about it. What they really needed was a map of the strange country through which their minds would travel on the day, with fear darkening earth and filling it with slaughter.

Bourne, Shem and Martlow, with the other orderlies, were following close behind the colonel, when the superb individual whose seat on a horse had seemed to Bourne to call for adverse comment, galloped up to them, and reined in his mount.

"What are all these men?' he asked the colonel, pointing almost at the embarrassed Bourne.

"These are my orderlies, sir," answered the colonel, and Bourne, from the angle at which he stood, saw his cheekbone as he turned to the rider with an amiable smile.

"You seem to have a great many of them," said god-like Agamemnon, with a supercilious coldness. They kept advancing slowly, and the horse was restive under his strange cargo.

"I don't think more than are usual, sir," hazarded the colonel with a bland diffidence.

Other important people on horseback, even the most important of them all, on a grey, arrived, and grouped themselves impressively, as though for a portrait. There followed some discussion, first apparently as to the number of the colonel's runners, and then as to why they were not within the imaginary trenches as marked out by the tapes. The colonel remained imperturbable, only saying, in a tone of mild protest, that they would be in the trenches on the day, though there were some advantages in separating them from the other men at the moment. They were all moving forward at a foot's pace, and apparently the Olympian masters of their fate were willing to admit the validity of the colonel's argument, when there was a sudden diversion.

They were passing a small cottage, little more than a hovel, where three cows were tethered to pasture on some rough grass, and the tapes passed diagonally across a square patch of sown clover, dark and green in comparison with the dryer herbage beside it. This was the track taken by a platoon of A Company under Mr Sothern; and as the first few men

179

were crossing the clover, the door of the hovel was flung open, and an infuriated woman appeared.

"Ces champs sont a moi!" she screamed, and this was the prelude to a withering fire of invective, which promised to be inexhaustible. It gave a slight tinge of reality, to operations which were degenerating into a series of co-ordinated drill movements. The men of destiny looked at her, and then at one another. It was a contingency which had not been foreseen by the staff, whose intention had been to represent, under ideal conditions, an attack on the village of Serre, several miles away, where this particular lady did not live. They felt, therefore, that they had been justified in ignoring her existence. She was evidently of a different opinion. She was a very stubborn piece of reality, as she stood there with her black skirt and red petticoat kilted up to her knees, her grey stockings and her ploughman's boots. She had a perfect genius for vituperation, which she directed against the men, the officers and the etat-major, with a fine impartiality. The barrage was effective, and the men, with a thoroughly English respect for the rights of property, hesitated to commit any further trespass.

"Send someone to speak to that woman," said the divisional general to a brigadier; and the brigadier passed on the order to the colonel, and the colonel to the adjutant; and the adjutant to Mr Sothern, who, remembering that Bourne had once interpreted his wishes to an old woman in Meaulte when he wanted a broom, now thrust him into the forefront of the battle. That is what is called, in the British Army, the chain of responsibility, which means that all responsibility for the errors of their superior officers is borne eventually by private soldiers in the ranks.

For a moment, she turned all her hostility on Bourne, prepared to defend her title at the cost of her life, if need should arise. He told her that she would be paid in full for any damage done by the troops; but she replied, very reasonably for all her heat, that her clover was all the feed she had for her cows through the winter, and that mere payment for the clover would be inadequate compensation for the loss of her cows. Bourne knew her difficulties; it was difficult enough, through lack of transport, for these unfortunate peasants to bring up provisions for themselves. He suggested, desperately, to Mr Sothern and the adjutant, that the men should leave the tapes and return to them on the other side of the clover. The adjutant was equal to the situation, and, as the rest of the men doubled round the patch to regain the tapes, and their correct position, on the other side, the general, with all his splendid satellites, moved discreetly away to another part of the field. One of the men shouted out something about "les Allemands" to the victorious lady, and she threw discretion to the winds.

"Les Allemands sont tres bons!" she shrieked at him.

An aeroplane suddenly appeared in the sky, and, circling over them, signalled with a klaxon horn. The men moved slowly away from her beloved fields, and the tired woman went back into the hovel, and slammed the door on a monstrous world.

When Bourne rejoined the runners he saw the colonel in front of him with shoulders still shaking, and they all proceeded, slowly and irresistibly, towards the capture of an imaginary Serre. When they had reached their final objective, there was a long pause, and the men, now thoroughly bored and disillusioned, leaned idly on their rifles, waiting. It was a victory for method. Presently there was another movement. Companies fell in on markers, the men seemed to wake out of a dream, and took a spontaneous interest in the proceedings, and the battalion moved off the field. The colonel had a horse waiting for him on the road, and about dusk they came to Bus-les-Artois.

Bourne ran into Sergeant Tozer in Bus, and with Shem and Martlow they made a reconnaissance of the town, visiting the Y.M.C.A., and then an estaminet, where they fell in with Sergeant Morgan, the bombing sergeant. They talked for a little while on the events of the day, and the splendours of the staff.

"Are them buggers coming over the top wi' us?" asked Martlow, innocently, and when the others laughed at him, he continued, indignantly. "Then what did they come out wi' us today for, swingin' their weight about? That bugger on the black 'orse spoke to the colonel just as tho' 'e took 'im for a lance-jack. Wunner the colonel stood it."

He and Shem went off to the cinema, so Bourne and the two sergeants found a little place where they could get rum and coffee; after which they went off to bed.

They were signalling with flags in the morning when their work was interrupted, and with others in the field they were fallen in, in two ranks. The adjutant came up from the orderly-room, which was a small hut on the other side of the road. He was followed by two military policemen, between whom was Miller, capless, and no longer with a stripe on his arm. He was white and haggard, but his mouth was half-open in an idiotic grin, and the small furtive eyes wandered restlessly along the line of men drawn up in front of him. Bourne felt a strange emotion rising in him which was not pity, but a revulsion from this degradation of a man, who was now only an abject outcast. In a clear, anxious voice, rather like that of a schoolboy reading a lesson, the adjutant read out a statement that Lance Corporal Miller had been found guilty of deserting his commanding officer, and had been sentenced to be shot, the sentence being afterwards commuted to one of penal servitude for twenty years. The parade was dismissed again, and the miserable man was marched away to be exhibited to another company. Miller would not, of course, go at once to gaol, the execution of the sentence would be deferred until the war ended. Men could not be allowed to choose gaol as an alternative to military service. That was where the absurdity arose, as Bourne understood the matter; because one could foresee that, when peace was restored, a general amnesty would be granted which would cover all cases of this kind, and the tragedy, but for the act of unspeakable humiliation which they had just witnessed, became a farce.

"We're goin' up to take over trenches tomorrow," said Corporal Hamley, "and this is just to encourage any other bugger who thinks o' desertin'."

"It don't make no differ whether th'art shot be thy own folk or be Germans, if th'art shot," said Weeper, pessimistically.

The corporal was right. The battalion paraded in fighting order at ten o'clock next morning, and moved up the line to take over trenches. They marched by the divisional artillery H. Q. at Bertrancourt, to Courcelles-aux-Bois, a village the greater part of which was already derelict. From there a road ran up to Colincamps, at the corner of which stood a military policeman as control, beside a red board, the kind of wooden standard used by road-menders as a danger signal, on which was painted in white letters: GAS ALERT ON. The reverse side was painted with the words GAS ALERT OFF; but it seemed a matter of indifference to everyone which way the board was turned.

After that point, a wide interval was left between the various platoons. Almost as soon as they left Courcelles, the road, mounting the hill to

Colincamps, was under direct observation of the enemy for about three hundred yards, so it had been camouflaged with netting like fishing nets, hung as a curtain between poles on the left side of the road. At the top of the hill was a bend, and, commanding the road, as well as another lesser road, was a more than usually substantial barn, a kind of bastion to the outskirts of Colincamps itself. Bourne thought what an ugly place it would be if it were in the hands of Fritz.

They were moving in dead silence now, not that the Hun could overhear them; and the interval between the various platoons must have been about one hundred yards. It implied a lively sense of favours to come. Passing the barn, there was a sharp bend first to the right then to the left, and they entered the long straight street of Colincamps. Jerry had registered on the church tower, which had a large hole in it, near the top; and the front of a house, on which still hung forlornly a sign, Cafe de la Jeunesse, had been stove in by another shell. There was not an undamaged house left, and some of the mud-built barns were collapsing, as an effect of repeated explosions in their neighbourhood. The street itself had suffered from heavy shelling, though some of the holes in the roadway had been filled in, when they did not allow of sufficient room for traffic to skirt them; the others had been converted into pools of very liquid mud. The same fine mud coated the whole surface of the roadway, and the mere pressure of one's foot was sufficient to set it oozing from the matrix in which the metalling was, now somewhat loosely, embedded.

The street ended, and the houses with it, on meeting a road linking it with Mailly-Maillet on the right, and on the left continuing to the sugar refinery, where it joined the main road from Mailly-Maillet to Serre. They turned left, downhill, the road curving into the valley, and there was another military control, with a dugout under the road where he could shelter. From that point the road, so long as it was on the slope of the hill, would be visible from the enemy lines. Visibility was poor today, there was a fine ground mist which made the distance vague. Even in the daylight, there was something beautiful and mysterious in that landscape. A line of woods, well away from the road, but gradually converging on it, though of no great depth, and shattered by shelling, curtained their movements once they were down the hill. Leaving the road, and picking their way between gun-pits and dugouts, they came again to Southern Avenue.

The shell-crater was now half-full of water, but there was a new one about twenty yards away.

Thence, onward, they followed the route they had taken on working parties, until they came to the big dugout in Legend Trench, which was battalion headquarters. There were two entrances, and about thirty steps to the bottom. Part of it was screened off with blankets for the officers, and the rest was allotted to the men. There was a small recess near the stairs, in which the sergeant-major or quartermaster-sergeant could sit at a table improvised from a box, and where a few stores were kept. Four or five candles stuck on tins lit it, and the air was foul and smoky.

Shem, Bourne and Martlow were sitting close to the door, three minutes after they had taken possession, when the sergeant-major, after the adjutant had spoken to him, turned to them.

"Ere, you three men. You go back to Colincamps, an' in one of the first 'ouses you come to, there's a runner's relay post; you'll find some Gordons there. You'll take over from them, see? Brigade messages will be 'anded to you, an' you'll bring 'em on 'ere; an' our runners will take you messages, which you'll carry on to Brigade at Courcelles. Got it? Well, get a move on."

They got up, and as they were pulling in their belts, Weeper, who had been sitting next to Shem, looked up at Bourne with a snarling grin, and said something about a cushy job, and some people being always lucky. Bourne did not trouble to reply, thinking, after what he had seen of the road, that headquarters dugout in the support trenches would have satisfied him. Martlow, however, had to say something.

"You 'ave a good sleep, ol' tear gas, an' then you'll feel better."

They climbed out of the dugout, and set off back to Colincamps. They had a bread-and-cheese ration in their haversacks. One of them would have to draw their full rations later.

"I wonder why Smart has got a set on me," said Bourne, reflectively.

"Cause you never take any notice of 'im when 'e starts grousin' at you," said Martlow.

"I believe you're right," said Shem, "but I'm a bit sorry for Weeper. He's always been an awfully good man up the line, at least they all say so in D Company. He hasn't got any friends, and he's so bloody miserable that he never will have any. You see, Bourne, you make friends with everybody, whether he's a cook, or a shoemaker, or a sergeant-major, or only Martlow and myself. Until you came along, well, I mucked in all right with the others, but I didn't have any particular chum, so I know what it feels--"

"Christ! Look out!' said Bourne, crouching, but his warning was unheard in the shrieking hiss and explosion which followed almost simultaneously. There was a huge eruption of mud, earth and stones a few yards behind the trench. They waited, tense and white, spattered with mud.

"Let's get out o' this place," said Martlow, in a shaken whisper, and, as he spoke, another came over. They held their breath as it exploded, further away than the first. Bourne was looking at Martlow, and saw that his underlip had fallen and was trembling a little. A third shell hissed for an appreciably longer time and exploded nearer to the dump. They waited motionless.

"It's bloody lucky that first shell wasn't closer, or we should have been buried," said Shem, with a rather lopsided grin, after an interval.

"Come on, kid," said Bourne to Martlow. "You never hear the one that gets you."

"I'm not worryin'," said Martlow, quietly.

"It must have been twenty yards off the trench," said Bourne, "but I'm not getting out to see. I think it would be better to use Railway Avenue. Fritz seems to have got Southern pretty well taped out; and I shouldn't like to be close to a big dixie like that in Sackville Street."

"You can't tell," said Shem, indifferently. "You've just got to chance it."

They were moving along at a fair pace, and were soon clear of trenches. The mud along the level by the dump was greasy, and slowed them down a bit; but on reaching the road it was easier going. Bourne asked the control where the relay post was, and they turned into the second yard on the right. There was not a sign of life there, and the houses on that side of the street had suffered more severely than on the other; little of them was left. Most of the buildings abutting on the street were byres and stables, at least at that end of the town. The houses stood farther back, just on the crest of the slope. Not seeing anyone, they shouted, and from a stable came a reply, and a great wooden door

185

They found three Gordons there, very far from gay. They were, ?, very decent civil men, and they looked as though they had ~~~~~ a rest. Their faces had forgotten, at least for the time being, how to smile. They looked at the colours sewn on their successors' haversacks and sleeves, which they knew meant business.

"We've come to take over from you," said Bourne.

"Thought you weren't comin'. Saw some o' oor chaps gae by..."

"Oh, the relief isn't complete yet," said Bourne, cheerfully. "They took us up the trenches and then sent us back. If they can do anything backwards in the army, they will, you know. It's the tradition of the service. What's it like here?"

"Oh, it's cushy enough," answered the Gordon, in a resigned voice.

"I had a bet with myself you would say that," said Bourne.

They looked at him curiously, perplexed by his manner, as they completed the business of putting their equipment together, fastening on their water bottles, haversacks, and entrenching tools. Their packs they carried slung, that is, without fastening them to their cross-straps, a practice which is irregular. On active service, however, the authorities allowed the men to use a little intelligence with regard to minor details, except on great occasions. At last, taking up their rifles, they moved to the door.

"Gude day t' ye, an' gude luck, chums," they said as they went out.

"Good luck," answered their successors, in more matter-of-fact tones. Bourne looked after them a little wistfully. He didn't grudge them the relief. He wondered when they would all be turning their backs on this desolation.

"I'm goin' to 'ave a peek round the village," said Martlow. "You won't want me, there'll be nothin' doin' yet awhile."

"All right," said Bourne. "Don't go far away, and don't be long."

He returned in about twenty minutes with all kinds of luxuries: tea mixed with sugar, four tins of bully-beef, a tin of Maconachie, and tins of pork and beans, the kind in which there was never any pork.

"I scrounged them from some R. E.'s," he said with a sober pride. "They're movin' out, an' 'ave a lot o' stuff they don't want to carry. I could 'ave got more if I'd wanted. They're that glad to be goin' they'd give you all they've got. So it don't matter if we don't get no rations 'til night."

"Good lad," said Bourne. "You are a champion scrounger, Martlow."

He was thinking that the anxiety of the R. E.'s to get away did not indicate that it was a particularly cushy place. Shem had also been reconnoitring the position, and announced that there was a decent cellar, with most of a house in ruins on top of it, only about twenty yards away. Martlow then decorated the door with a paper on which he had printed with an indelible pencil RELAY POST in block letters.

"Well, we may as well have some tea an' bully," said Shem.

It was after one o'clock, so they set to and had a good comforting meal and lounged about smoking until a little after two, when a message came from the trenches. One of the regular runners brought it, with Pacey. It was a regulation that two runners should take a message together, in case one might be wounded, but this was often disregarded owing to a shortage of runners: it was tacitly assumed that one of them would go at a time, so that in case of simultaneous messages both ways the post would not be without a man on duty. Shem and Martlow took the message to Brigade H .Q, just the other side of Courcelles, and Pacey and Hankin, the regular runner, sat and yarned with Bourne for a few minutes.

"You look all right 'ere, but Fritz 'as been bashin' the place about, 'asn't 'e?" said Pacey.

Part of the mud wall had come away, leaving only laths. After a cigarette, Pacey and Hankin set off back to the trenches. Bourne sat in a kind of reverie for about half an hour until Shem and Martlow returned, and idle talk continued for a time.

The whole air suddenly became alive, and crash after crash filled the town. They were stunned, and petrified, for a moment. More of the mud wall fell away, and there was a landslide of tiles. They cowered down, as though they wanted to shrink away to nothing. It was heavy stuff coming over. One shell struck the Cafe de la Jeunesse, and another corner of it went flying in all directions; loose tiles kept falling, and the walls rapidly became threadbare lath, merely from the effects of the concussion.

Bourne felt himself shaking, but they couldn't stay there.

"Get into that cellar!" he shouted to them, and grabbing their rifles and water bottles, which they had taken out, they moved out uncertainly. Bourne felt his breath coming heavily. Shells were bumping practically the whole length of the village. He didn't know what to do about the

187

relay post; and though he felt an awful fool, he decided. "I'll be after you," he shouted, and running as a man runs into a rainstorm, he disappeared into the street. He turned the corner and continued downhill to the control's dugout. On the hillside just beyond the control's dugout a man lay dead. His tin hat was blown some yards away, and the top of the head had been taken off, so that at a glance one saw some remnants of the scattered brains. Apparently the whole of Colincamps was going west, clouds of smoke and dust rose from it. Bourne fell down the steps of the dugout. He couldn't say why he was there at first.

"There's a man dead outside, sergeant," he said, dully.

"What the bloody hell are you doin' out in it? Are you sure 'e's dead?'

"Yes, sergeant; most of the head's gone. I'm at the relay post, runners. I thought I had better tell you that we had left the stable, and gone into the cellar of the house."

"I'm goin' out to see to that man."

They doubled out to him, and finding that he was really dead, shifted him off the road; and went into the dugout again.

"I'm going back now, sergeant."

"You 'ad better wait a bit," said the sergeant in a kindlier voice. "You know it's against regulations for you chaps to go alone. There ought to be a pair of you."

"I had better go back. I didn't know whether we ought to move, as I have not been on the job before. I'll go back to see how my chums are."

"All right," said the sergeant, in a curiously irritable way. "Write up on the door where you are."

The shelling was still violent, but seemed to be worse at the corner in the direction of Courcelles, and to have extended on this side farther along the Mailly-Maillet road. As Bourne came out, he could see shells exploding by the dump, with some shrapnel bursting, woolly-bears they called them, overhead. He couldn't say whether it was with a prayer or a curse that he made for the corner of Colincamps, doubling up the short rise with difficulty. Collapsing houses had spilt their bricks half across the street. One wall, about sixty yards away from him, suddenly crumpled and fell. He wouldn't look at things. He found himself saying over and over again in soldiers' language: "I've been out of the bloody shit too long": not uttering the words but thinking them with a curious intensity. His vision seemed narrowed to a point immediately in front of him. When he got to the stable, they had left, he went straight to Martlow's notice, and drawing a rough arrow underneath the words "RELAY POST', wrote in rough blocks the words "IN CELLAR'. Then he went to it, noticing as he descended that the entrance was turned the wrong way. Shem and Martlow looked at him, but he could scarcely see their faces in the gloom.

"What's it like now?" asked Martlow, with a very slight catch in his voice.

"Oh, it's cushy enough," said Bourne, with desperate humour.

Suddenly he felt inexpressibly tired. He bowed his head and sat gazing into nothing, emptied of all effort. The shells bumped for some time longer, slackened, and then ceased. Bourne had the sensation that the earth was left steaming.

A drizzle of rain began, and increasing by degrees filled the quiet with little trickling sounds. The cellar was comfortably furnished, as it had apparently been used as a funk-hole before, and by people of more importance than its present occupants. Its sole defect was that the entrance directly faced the Hun lines, and perhaps this inconvenience had prompted them to leave; but during their tenancy they had put in three beds, wooden frames standing about two feet off the floor, over which rabbit-netting had been stretched and nailed, as a substitute for spring mattresses. Some rather thin Wilson canvas curtained the entrance. Bourne remembered that there was some thicker sacking, in the stable which they had left, and he proposed to get it, and nail it over the outside of the doorway.

They went back, together, to their old quarters. Little of the stable was left except its frame, some laths, and a few tiles, still hanging precariously on the slats overhead, through which, now, the rain fell steadily. They wrenched some nails from the timbers, and Shem and Martlow fastened the extra sacking on the doorway of the cellar. Bourne wandered off by himself for a moment. He found that the premises included their own private latrine. He had been silent and preoccupied since coming back from the control, and had said nothing about the man killed on the hillside. He didn't want to talk.

"Bourne's getting windy," said Shem to Martlow.

"'E weren't windy goin' out in that lot," said Martlow, repelling the suggestion.

"Yes, he was," said Shem, chuckling; "that's just why he went."

"If it comes to that, we're all windy," grunted Martlow, loyally.

There was some truth in Shem's observation, all the same. Bourne came back in a few minutes, and, having inspected the curtain, he lit a small piece of candle. Martlow was going out, and was told to report if any light were visible from outside.

"There will be a message to take up the line, soon," said Bourne to Shem. "I might as well go by myself, I think. I want to try and scrounge a couple of candles from the quarter-bloke."

"Then I'll take the midnight message to Brigade," said Shem.

Martlow returned. The light did not show from outside, but it did, of course, when the curtains were twitched aside. They were too close together for them to hope that a man entering would lift first one and then the other. Bourne said they would have to cover or blow out the light on entering or leaving. Then, as the candle was all they had, they blew it out and talked in the dark; Fritz sent three shells over, a regular interval between them. Our own guns had been completely silent during the strafe. Now, however, after an appreciable pause, a trench-mortar battery sent three back to the Hun, and then, after an interval to give emphasis and point to their reply, added another for luck. Bourne looked at his wristwatch, and saw that it was a couple of minutes after six.

"That sounded like a regular stunt," he said.

A few minutes later they heard a couple of men shouting above-ground, and Martlow, going halfway up the steps, called to them. Two runners from Brigade came in, and when the sacking curtain had been put in place, Bourne lit the candle.

"Thought you'd all gone west," said one runner, "when I saw the bloody barn."

"I left a notice on the door," said Bourne, thoughtlessly.

"Well, I can't read it in the bloody dark, can I?" objected the runner. "Ere's the usual. We'll 'ave a fag, before we go back, chum. You chaps know 'ow to make yourselves comfortable."

"It's the first duty of a good soldier," said Bourne.

They talked about the strafe; now that it was over, none of them exaggerated its importance.

"Only a few shells came into Courcelles," said the runner, "but we knew Colincamps and the dump were getting it."

"I'm going now," said Bourne. "Don't show any light."

"You're getting wind-up," said Shem, laughing.

"Wind-up! 'E's talkin' bloody sense," said the runner. "You don't want to take any bloody chances up 'ere, I can tell you. It looks to me as though Jerry 'ad rumbled somethin' already."

That was Bourne's notion, but he did not pursue the subject.

"D'you go alone?" they asked him.

"Yes, we nearly always go alone," answered Bourne. "Goodnight."

Martlow covered the light with a can, as Bourne moved out into the dark. It was very dark, and the rain was fine, searching and cold. He would keep to the road as far as the dump, it was no use trying a short cut, and the wet surface of the road was at least visible, lots of little pools gleaming in it. The control was not there. Some instinctive scruple moved Bourne to avoid the side of the road where he had found the dead man, and, looking to where they had carried the body, he saw that it had been removed.

The dump was empty. In another couple of hours it would be alive with men and transport. He had a kind of talent for moving about sure-footedly in the dark. He did not mind the rain and he loved the quiet. There were fewer star-shells tonight, and the rain made their expanding and contracting haloes even more mysterious than usual.

He handed in the message, and then spoke to Corporal Hamley, who was with Sergeant-Major Corbet, about the strafe.

"Well, Captain Malet is out of it, now," said the sergeant-major.

"What happened to Captain Malet, sergeant-major?" he asked, anxiously.

"Dugout blown in; a beam fell on him, an' broke both his legs.

They were some time before they got him clear, they had to dig under the beam. They wanted to take a couple of rifles as splints for his legs, until they got him to the dressing-station; but he wouldn't have it. 'You may want 'em more than I do,' he said. 'You get me a couple of miles away from here and I'm laughing.' When they were getting him out he smoked a cigarette and didn't say a word, though they must have hurt him."

"Anyone else hurt?" asked Bourne.

"A boy called Bates was killed, and two others wounded or hurt. I haven't heard all the details. B Company had a few casualties. We had a sentry over the dugout wounded. Matheson. D'you know him? You came from A Company, didn't you? Thought so. Someone told me Captain Malet was going to get the colonel to recommend you for a commission, wasn't he? What are you going to do about it, now?"

While the sergeant-major was speaking of Bates having been killed, Bourne tried to remember who Bates was; and, at the effort of memory to recover him, he seemed to hear a high, excited voice suddenly cry out, as though actually audible to the whole dugout: "What's 'e want to drag me into 't for?"

And it was as though Bates were bodily present there; the sergeant-major's voice seemed less real. In the light of the unsteady candles, each haloed in the fog of smoke, Bourne saw all the quiet men, some half-asleep, some staring in front of them, thinking and waiting. He felt as though he were under some extraordinary hallucination, but he answered the sergeant- major reasonably enough, said he would have a talk to him when they went out of trenches again, suggested speaking to Mr Rhys, and all the time he heard his own voice saying things, which somehow did not seem to concern him, meaningless things which had to be taken very seriously. He knew no more of Bill Bates than that one phrase, passionately innocent: "What's 'e want to drag me into 't for?"

"Could I get our rations now, sergeant-major?" he said, evenly. "I have brought a mess-tin, for our rum ration; and I was going to ask if we could have some candles. We left the barn we were in, and moved into a cellar; and we need a bit of light."

"Who told you to leave the barn an' go into a cellar?"

"Oh, Fritz did. And the barn came unstuck. After the tiles had fallen off, and the walls began to tumble down, I thought we ought to go to ground. I told the sergeant on control duty where we would be, and I left a notice on the door. We're in the same yard, but in the cellar of the house. As all that is left of the house is a couple of thousand bricks, piled up in a heap on top of the cellar, we ought to be fairly safe there; only the entrance faces the line, and we have to be careful to screen the light."

"I can only let you have a couple of candles," said the quartermaster-sergeant.

"Oh, make it three, sir," said Bourne, in a tone of coaxing protest, and a little grudgingly the quarter-bloke dealt him out another, while Bourne talked to keep from thinking. "Just before I got to the control's dugout,

192

there was a man killed on the road. We lifted him to one side. He was a gunner, I think...I can take the rum ration in my mess-tin, sir...It made us all a bit windy, I think. There's not quite so much of Colincamps left as when you last saw it, sergeant-major."

"It's my belief Fritz has rumbled us," said the sergeant-major in a whisper.

"What can you expect?" said Bourne, pointing to the bright yellow material sewn on his haversack. "We are decked out in all the colours of the rainbow, and then marched over the whole countryside in order to advertise the show. Anyone can see we are in war paint. We are put into khaki, so as to be more or less invisible; and then rigged up in colours, so that we can be seen. It's genius."

"That's so as the artillery can spot us," said the sergeant-major soberly.

"Whose, sergeant-major?"

"You're a sarky devil, you are."

"There's your bag o' rations, and don't lose the bag, see?" said the quarter-bloke.

"All right, sir, thank you. I suppose I ought to be moving back. I am sorry about Captain Malet, but I suppose he's lucky. Do you think there's anything to go back, sir? I might save another man a walk."

"Go and wait inside for a few minutes," said the sergeant-major; they were all in the recess at the foot of the steps. "I shall be seeing the adjutant presently. It's all bloody rot having that relay post at Colincamps, in my opinion. The Brigade runners might easily come up here, and our runners go down to Courcelles. Wait a few minutes, and I'll see."

Bourne went in and sat by Weeper, who neither moved nor spoke to him; and after a few minutes the sergeant-major came in.

"You may go back, Bourne. There probably won't be anything but the report at midnight. Goodnight."

"Goodnight, sergeant-major," he said, and, taking up his rifle, climbed up the stairs into the rain and darkness again.

When he got back to the cellar, he found that Martlow had brought in a stray terrier. The dog was obviously suffering from shellshock, he was trembling in a piteous way, and Martlow said that when he had caught him, he had tried to bite. The only domestic animal which Bourne had met among these deserted ruins had been a gaunt and savage cat, which, on seeing him, had cursed the whole human race, and fled precipitately. They had supper, and some hot tea with their rum, persuaded the dog to eat a little bully, and then lay smoking on their beds. They heard trains of limbers passing through the village. Bourne and Martlow curled up to sleep, and Shem waited for the night report to take it back to Courcelles.

In the morning at seven o'clock, Fritz sent over his three shells, and the trench mortar battery barked out the same reply as on the previous night. Fritz's shells had fallen very close. Martlow went out first, and then put his head through the doorway to announce that the latrine had been blown up; where it had stood there was nothing but a large hole.

"Well, what do you want," said Shem; "a bloody bathroom?"

The dog had another fit of shivering when the shells came over but it recovered later, and Martlow took it outside for a short walk. Exploring the ruins a native instinct got the better of the dog's recently acquired caution, and it disappeared out of history in the pursuit of a cat.

"'E were a good dog, that," said Martlow, regretfully.

Chapter XIV

Between the acting of a fearful thing
And the first motion, all the interim is
Like a phantasma or a hideous dream. – SHAKESPEARE

After three days in the trenches, the battalion was relieved, and moved to Courcelles, where they were to remain for one night on their way to rest billets at Bus. The village had been heavily shelled from time to time, but had not been damaged to quite the same extent as Colincamps, which offered, on the crest of the hill, a more conspicuous target. Courcelles was uncovered at one end, but screened partially by rising ground on two sides. As Corporal Williams had said of Mailly-Maillet, it was simply lousy with guns. There was visible evidence on every side that the local farmers had reaped a bountiful harvest. Bourne, carrying messages between Colincamps and Courcelles, had noticed three haystacks in a picturesque group standing a little way back from the road. Then, one night, he saw a very faint gleam of light coming from inside one of them. It was a lucid explanation of the apparent fertility of the countryside. Monster guns, too, were secreted somehow in the courtyards of houses in the village itself. The Hun had his suspicions, and would explore the possibilities of the situation, rather too frequently, with high explosive.

Their own battalion did not line up or parade for meals. When breakfast or dinner was ready, a couple of orderly-men would carry a dixie or a tea-bucket from the cooker to some convenient place, and the men, coming promptly, but rather casually, for their share, took it away to eat in tents or billets. They came together and dispersed again in a moment. There was practically no crowding.

Battalion headquarters in Courcelles was in a small chateau, which stood, with its farm buildings, on a little hill practically encircled by a road. On their first morning there, Bourne and Shem, coming from the barn in which they had slept to get their breakfast from the dixie a few yards away, could see some little distance beyond the road the men of a

Scots battalion, which was brigaded with them, lined up with their mess tins waiting for breakfast. As Bourne and Shem were returning to their barn, leaving behind Martlow, who had followed them out, they heard a shell coming and, as they dived for cover, a terrific explosion. There was an instant's stillness, and then from across the road shouts and cries. Again a shell whined overhead, and exploded, and then a third. That was apparently the ration. The next moment Martlow, with a white face, appeared in the doorway.

"Them poor, bloody Jocks," he said in a slow, pitiful whisper.

What the casualties were they did not know, though various rumours gave precise, and different, details; one shell did all the damage, the others exploding in an empty field. The sympathy they felt with the Scotsmen was very real; the same thing might so easily have happened to themselves, and as they talked about it, the feeling turned gradually into resentment against an authority which regulated, so strictly, every detail of their daily lives. The shell falling where it did, at that particular time, would probably have caused a certain number of casualties, even if the men had been moving about freely, but this kind of discipline, excusable enough when men have to be kept under control, as with a carrying party lined up at a dump, was unnecessary on this occasion. After all, the place was liable to be shelled at any moment; and, for that reason alone, it was wiser to avoid assembling a large number of men at any one point. They remembered their own experience at Philosophe.

"Bloody swank. They don't care a fuck what 'appens to us'ns." They were angry and restive, as men are who expect that they may be ordered to make an attack at any time. That kind of feeling is not without value as a military asset, provided that behind the discipline, against which it is a natural reaction, there is sufficient intelligence and foresight to avoid mistakes. It does a man no harm to know that he may be sacrificed with some definite object in view; it was the kind of hazard which many Lewis-gunners faced continually, with great courage, but no man likes to think his life may be thrown away wantonly, through stupidity or mere incompetence. Officers and men alike grew careless as they became accustomed to danger, and then an incident of this kind, an event almost inevitable, filled them, with surprise.

Whether it were justified or not, however, the sense of being at the disposal of some inscrutable power, using them for its own ends, and

196

utterly indifferent to them as individuals, was perhaps the most tragic element in the men's present situation. It was not much use telling them that war was only the ultimate problem of all human life stated barely, and pressing for an immediate solution. When each individual conscience cried out for its freedom, that implacable thing said: "Peace, peace; your freedom is only in me!" Men recognised the truth intuitively, even with their reason checking at a fault. There was no man of them unaware of the mystery which encompassed him, for he was a part of it; he could neither separate himself entirely from it, nor identify himself with it completely. A man might rave against war; but war, from among its myriad faces, could always turn towards him one, which was his own. All this resentment against officers, against authority, meant very little, even to the men themselves. It fell away from them in words.

Later in the morning, Sergeant-Major Corbet, speaking to Captain Thompson outside battalion headquarters, saw Bourne crossing the yard. He called him up, and turning to the officer, said bluntly: "Captain Malet was going to send in this man's name for a commission, while he was with A Company, sir."

He looked at Bourne with a stern and critical eye while he spoke. Captain Thompson recognised Bourne as one of the three culprits who had been before him at Reclinghem, but gave no sign of remembering the incident. He asked him a few questions, spoke sympathetically about Captain Malet, and said he would look into the matter.

"If Captain Malet thought of recommending you, I have no doubt you will make a very good officer," he said.

That closed a brief and business-like interview. After it was over, Bourne confided in Shem, and saw at once that Martlow had kept his own counsel as to the chance words of Sergeant-Major Robinson at Vincly. Shem, however, was not surprised.

"I thought you would go sooner or later," he said in a matter-of-fact way.

They moved back to Bus in the afternoon, marching through fine, steady rain. Days passed, and the weather showed no signs of mending, and as they settled down to the routine of a battalion holding the line, the attack, without fading from their minds, no longer seemed an imminent trial, becoming only a vague probability of the future. It had certainly been delayed. The colours with which they had been so gaily bedecked became a little dingy.

Their life was now one unresting struggle against the encroaching mud, which threatened to engulf roads and trenches in liquid ruin. Daily, when out of the line, they were sent off with shovels and brooms to sweep it off the roadway, and shovel it up as a kind of embankment against the barns and stables bordering the road. What was too liquid to heap up, they trapped in sumps. A man pushing a broom through it would find two converging streams closing behind him. A train of limbers or lorries passing seemed to squeeze it up out of the road-metalling. Earth exuded mud. Most of it had the consistency of thin cream, and threatened, if it were neglected for a moment, to become tidal. They had to scrape it from their puttees and trousers with their jack-knives, and what was left hardened the serge to cardboard. When they became dry they were beaten against the corner of a hut, and the dust flew from them; but that was seldom. In the line there were trenches which could only be kept clear by pumping. Sometimes frost would congeal the mud, and then a quick thaw would cause part of a trench to slide in, and it had to be built up again: sand-bagged and revetted. They became almost indistinguishable from the mud in which they lived.

The weather grew colder too, and they wore their cardigans; then leather jerkins, lined with fleeces or thick serge, were issued to them, and in the resulting warmth the lice increased and multiplied beyond imagining. It was some weeks before they could get a bath, and then necessarily it was a makeshift. Half a company stood under trickling showers, while the other half-company pumped up water outside, and when the men were covered with a lather of soap the water invariably failed.

The strange thing was that the greater the hardships they had to endure, for wet and cold bring all kinds of attendant miseries in their train, the less they grumbled. They became a lot quieter and more reserved in themselves, and yet the estaminets would be swept by roaring storms of song. It may have been a merely subjective impression, but it seemed that once they were in the front line, men lost a great deal of their individuality; their characters, even their faces, seemed to become more uniform; they worked better, the work seeming to take some of the strain off their minds, the strain of waiting. It was perhaps that they withdrew more into themselves, and became a little more diffident in the matter of showing their feelings.

Actually, though the pressure of external circumstances seemed to wipe out individuality, leaving little if any distinction between man and man, in himself each man became conscious of his own personality as of something very hard, and sharply defined against a background of other men, who remained merely generalised as "the others". The mystery of his own being increased for him enormously, and he had to explore that doubtful darkness alone, finding a foothold here, a handhold there, grasping one support after another and relinquishing it when it yielded, crumbling; the sudden menace of ruin, as it slid into the unsubstantial past, calling forth another effort, to gain another precarious respite. If a man could not be certain of himself, he could be certain of nothing.

The problem which confronted them all equally, though some were unable or unwilling to define it, did not concern death so much as the affirmation of their own will in the face of death, and once the nature of the problem was clearly stated, they realised that its solution was continuous, and could never be final. Death set a limit to the continuance of one factor in the problem, and peace to that of another; but neither of them really affected the nature of the problem itself.

As neither Bourne, Shem nor Martlow were sufficiently trained to take over the duties of signallers, when they were in the line they were employed not only as runners, but sometimes on ordinary duties as well. Once, when he was on duty with his old company, Bourne went out on patrol with Mr Finch. Under cover, not of darkness, but of a thick fog, they crossed to the enemy wire, and had examined it for a considerable distance when they heard the movements of another party, and Mr Finch signalled desperately to them to keep still.

"Ach, so!" came in a low voice through the fog; and, moving diagonally away from them, roughly in the direction of their own trenches, they saw the vague silhouettes of a German patrol. Crouching, but ready with shot or steel, they watched the vague shadows moving away in the mist. The enemy were apparently at a disadvantage in the matter of light. They were on slightly higher ground, inclined away from them; and not giving a thought to the possibility of a party of Englishmen being actually between them and their own trenches, they were searching ahead of them in what seemed the only direction from which danger might be expected. Bourne thought that the mere breathing of his companions would be sufficient to give them away, and, while he restrained his own, he felt an insane desire to laugh.

The enemy patrol faded again into the fog, from which they had never completely emerged; and when, after listening intently, one ceased to hear them, Mr Finch, turning to them with a grin over his shoulder, beckoned for them to follow him. They continued for a little way along the wire, and then doubled back to their own trenches, passing over the vestiges of a ruined hovel. Apparently it had been one of those mud-walled affairs, with nothing very solid about it but a brick-built chimney, and already it was practically merged in earth again; though the smoke-blackened bricks, most of them not only broken but pulverised, still resisted utter dissolution, and rose in a crescent-shaped heap a few feet from the surface of the ground. At a very little distance it might be taken for a slight hump in the earth.

They were well pleased with themselves on their return, and still more pleased to hear, later, that a Hun patrol reconnoitring their wire in the mist had been fired on, and had withdrawn, with what casualties it was impossible to say. The one thing they professed to regret was that Mr Finch had restrained them from attacking the enemy patrol; but for him, they would have got the lot, they asserted; and if their dissatisfaction on that point ever reached the ears of Mr Finch, he probably smiled and said nothing, because he was quite pleased, too, and wise beyond his years.

The rain continued, broken only by intervals of mist or fog and spells of cold, which became more intense as the weeks drew on into November. The relay post at Colincamps was abandoned, and they took their messages direct from the trenches to Courcelles. During one tour in the trenches, Bourne was attached to Brigade, and took possession of a tent just outside Brigade headquarters. It contained one bed, of the wooden frame and rabbit-wire type, and Bourne placed his things on the bed, establishing a claim to it.

Presently a large Jock, who described himself later as a native of Pe'er'ead, as though it were a place of which everybody must have heard, came into the tent, and looked at Bourne's things on the bed with displeasure.

"A 'ad yon kip las' time a were 'ere," he said indignantly.

"Did you?" Bourne inquired with mild interest. "Well, you don't expect your luck to last forever, do you?"

A marked difference in their mode of speech seemed likely to increase the misunderstanding, and Bourne, rather ostentatiously drawing up his legs, and half reclining on the disputed piece of furniture, lit a cigarette, and waited for the situation to develop. The big Scotsman sat on the ground, and investigating the contents of his haversack, produced a lump of something wrapped in newspaper. It proved to be an extremely solid piece of plum cake: cutting it in two, he returned half to the newspaper, which he put back into the haversack, and, dividing the other portion in two, he held one piece out to Bourne.

"Thanks," said Bourne, taking it.

One insuperable bar to conversation with a Scotsman is that it is impossible to persuade him that an Englishman speaks English, but Bourne gave him a cigarette, and they smoked in what was at least an amiable silence. Then another Scotsman arrived, and Bourne's responsibility ended.

He met the man from Pe'er'ead in the line that night. They were both taking back a midnight report to Brigade, and, on leaving the trenches, made a short cut skirting the eastern side of Colincamps. They passed behind several batteries, each with its tiny glow-worm lamp suspended from an upright rod. Passing over the crest of the hill they continued a little way down the reverse slope, and then decided to rest and smoke a cigarette. There was a tree there, undamaged, and they sat with their backs against it. Then, when they had finished their cigarette, the big Scotsman rose.

"Let us no bide lang i' this place, laddie. They're aye shellin' this tree at ane o'clock."

Bourne laughed softly, glancing at his wristwatch, which said it was within a minute or so to one o'clock. They set off to strike the road. They were within a few yards of it when a big shell landed at the foot of the tree, and left nothing of it but some slivers. They looked at each other in blank wonderment and hurried down the road.

"Mon," said the Scotsman, after a long silence, "it were proveedential."

Bourne was always amazed by the superstition and the sentimentality of the ordinary man; he thought both forms of self-flattery.

"You evidently suffer from second-sight," he said, "and you don't know it."

He became very bored by the monotony of those frequent journeys to and from the trenches. The attack remained a probability of the future, they never seemed to get any closer to it. Rumours floated among the men: it had been fixed for the day after tomorrow; it had been postponed again; it had been abandoned. They ceased to be fresh troops, becoming indeed, under the influence of bad weather, constant fatigues, and the strain of uncertainty, rather jaded. Nothing had been gained by delay. One rumour said that Hun prisoners captured in a raid had admitted that the Germans knew all about the proposed attack, having extracted the information from two British prisoners they had taken some weeks earlier.

One day at Courcelles, having come out of trenches on the previous night, the men were paraded, and asked to volunteer for a raid, with the object of securing some prisoners for identification purposes. Men volunteered readily enough, but, at the same time, even some of the volunteers grumbled that they should be asked to make a raid the day after they had been relieved. Work was thrown at them that way, with an implied doubt as to their fighting qualities, and they accepted the challenge resentfully. A party of ten men with Sergeant Morgan, under Mr Barnes, reached the enemy trenches, bombed a dugout, but had to kill the men they encountered, as they resisted capture. They brought back some papers and other evidences of possible value. Perhaps, as they brought back no prisoner, it may have been an additional cause for blame that they had suffered no casualties.

The men were able to form opinions as to their prospects from their own experience. They knew that the Hun was prepared, and that they would meet the same Prussians or Bavarians whose fighting qualities they had tested before on the Somme in July and August, and, if they did not know the strength of the position held by the Hun, they knew at least the difficulties of the ground over which they would have to attack, and the enormous handicap of the mud. They were neither depressed nor confident; it would probably be more accurate to say they were determined and resigned. The worst feature of the business was the delay; it fretted them into impatience. A rumour would make them suddenly tense, and then, the strain relaxing again, they would fall back into the attitude of passive endurance. One cannot keep the bow bent indefinitely. The weather, which was the cause of it all, grew steadily worse.

Then they got their orders; and they knew it, even before they were officially told. Truth travels as mere rumour does, but has its own distinguishing quality of unexpectedness. It no longer mattered now whether the delay or the subsequent decision were right or wrong, a decision had been reached and was irrevocable. They were relieved, and went back to billets at Bus. There the orders were to be prepared to move off the next morning. Men shouted across the huts to each other that the attack had been washed-out, and were asked derisively what kind of bloody 'opes they'd got. We're on the move, anyway, they cried in chorus. Yes, where? Blighty, some humorist shouted.

"Yes, you'll go to Blighty in a fuckin' ambulance, if you've any luck," said Weeper in a more sardonic vein.

The first excitement subsided into a quieter but continuous murmur and movement, like the singing of tense strings. Swagger was there, but restrained; men tightened their belts, stuck out their chins, and threw a taunting challenge at fate. Their speech, though mainly in undertones, was quick and excited, even their movements seemed to have more speed, and their faces to grow sharper, as though whetted by that angry impatience which is a kind of anxiety. How much confidence they felt was the secret of their own hearts; they had enough courage to share with one another. The passion of their minds threw an unreal glamour over everything, making day, and earth, and the sordid villages in which they herded, seem brief and unsubstantial as though men held within themselves the mystery which makes everything mysterious.

On the march to Louvencourt they passed an Australian driving a horse-drawn lorry, with a heavy load whereon he sprawled, smoking a cigarette with an indolence which Bourne envied. The colonel wheeled his grey, and pursued him with a fire of invective practically the whole length of the column, to the man's obvious amazement, as he had never before been told off at such length, and with such fluent vigour, in language to which no lady would take exception. He sat up, and got rid of his cigarette, looking both innocent and perplexed. The men were delighted. It was quite time somebody was made to pay a little attention to their bloody mob.

In Louvencourt the signallers were billeted in a barn of a large farm, on the left-hand side at the corner where the road from Bus turned into the main street. The town itself had an inviting and civilised air compared to Bus, and seemed to promise some opportunities for pleasure.

"Let's have a spree tonight," said Bourne, "even if we never have another."

"No use talkin' like that," said Martlow, "we'll 'ave many a bloody good spree together yet, me lucky lads."

"Well, we'll have one tonight, anyway," said Shem.

As soon as they were free, they sauntered out to see what the possibilities were. They soon found that the amenities of Louvencourt had attracted quite a number of unnecessary brass hats, as well as military police with an exaggerated notion of the value of discipline. They saw only one estaminet, which was closed for the greater part of the day, and only supplied the sour, flat beer of the country when it was open. French beer is enough to make any reasonable man pro-German. Somewhat out of humour, Bourne continued along the street until he came to the expeditionary force canteen. The chaplain had cashed him a cheque for five pounds the night before, and the shop window was as rich in delicacies as any in London. Hams, cheeses, bottled fruits, olives, sardines, everything to make the place a paradisal vision for hungry men. Shem and Martlow continued down the street, and Bourne went inside and stood at the counter. He expected there might be some possible difficulty about wine, but he intended only to buy food, leaving the wine problem to be settled later. He wanted sweet things; macaroons, cake and crystallised fruit, all of which he had seen displayed, and when a shopman dignified by uniform came up to him, he began by asking for these things. The man merely asked him for a chit; and when Bourne replied that he had not got a chit, that he would pay cash, the other man turned away superciliously, saying that they only served officers. Bourne stood there immobile for a moment. Another attendant spoke to him in a friendly way, and told him he could get cocoa and biscuits at a shed in the yard.

"Money has been collected from the public to provide expeditionary force canteens for the men, and you say you only serve officers!" he said in a white heat.

"Well, it's not my fault," answered the other, in a deprecating tone. "Those are our orders. You can get cocoa and biscuits round at the back; and you'll only get into trouble if you stay in here."

Cocoa and biscuits. Bourne strode out of the shop in such a blind rage that he bumped into one of the lords of creation in the doorway, and didn't stop to apologise. He described him afterwards, while his temper was still hot, as "some bloody officer got up to look like Vesta Tilley," and it was a fair comparison, except in so far as the lady was concerned. The miracle of neatness turned a glance of offended dignity over his shoulder, hesitated, and then continued on his way, with an air of Christian forbearance under very trying provocation. Bourne strode off in the direction Shem and Martlow had taken, and almost collided with young Evans.

"What the 'ell's the matter wi' you?" inquired that cheerful individual, looking with an astonished grin at Bourne's congested face. Bourne grabbed his left arm.

"Look here, Evans; can you go into that bloody canteen and buy me anything I want, if I give you the cash?"

Evans caressed reflectively an unshaven chin.

"Well, I don't know as I could get you a bottle o' whisky," he said slowly; "tho' I 'ave faked a chit afore now to get some. I could get you most anythin' else."

"Oh, I can get whisky more easily another way, if I want it," said Bourne, truthfully; "but I want you--come in here, and have a glass of bad beer, while we talk--I want you to get me a couple of bottles of the best champagne they have got; they'll let you have that more easily than anything else, because they'll feel quite certain it's for some bloody officer or other..."

"What are you cribbin' the officers for?" exclaimed Evans with amusement. "Aren't you goin' in for a commission yourself?"

"If I were a colonel," said Bourne; "mind you, only a colonel, and a man like that bloody lance-jack, who has never even smelt a dead horse in South Africa, turned one of my men out of a canteen started for the benefit of the troops by public subscription, I would get the battalion together, and I would sack the whole bloody institution from basement to garret, even if I were to be broke for it."

"I'll get you all you want, without sackin' the bloody place," said Evans reasonably, though he could not stop laughing. "Look 'ere, I've only come down to get some cleanin' kit. I'll be down again later, an' I'll work what you want all right. Don't you worry."

Bourne gave him a list of things apart from the wine, and then handed him over some notes.

"I don't want you to chance your arm for nothing," he said; "you keep twenty-five francs for yourself, and if you can come along to our billet at about half-past eight tonight, you can have anything we've got. I don't see why we shouldn't have a good time, even if we're not a lot of bum-boys attached to the staff of some bloody general or other. There will only be Shem, Martlow, myself, and perhaps Corporal Hamley. He's not a bad chap, though he had a bit of a down on us at first. Are you going over the top?"

"Too bloody true I am. I'd as lief go as stay be'ind in fuckin' detail camp."

They finished the beer and went into the street, Bourne pointing out where his billet was.

"I'll bring them things along between 'alf-past one an' two o'clock," said Evans; "but I shan't be able to get down tonight. Look 'ere, there'll be a lot o' stuff to carry, wi' two bottles o' wine an' all. Couldn't you be outside the canteen at 'alf-past one?..."

"Shem and Martlow may go," said Bourne, with a return to heat. "I am not going near the bloody place again. If I see that lance-jack outside, I'll make his face so that he won't be able to smile for a week. I don't want to get into the mush for bashing him only once, but if I could have an uninterrupted three minutes..."

Evans turned away, laughing; he could not wait longer, as he was already a bit behind time. He met Shem and Martlow outside the expeditionary force canteen, and they asked him if he had seen Bourne.

"Seen 'im, yes, I've seen 'im. They 'oofed 'im out o' the canteen, an' 'e's gone completely off the 'andle about it. What I like about ol' Bourne is, that when 'e does get up the pole, 'e goes abso-bloodylutely fanti. 'E 'as been lookin' for you two. Where've you been?"

"We went round the back an' 'ad some cocoa and biscuits," said Martlow, innocently.

"For Gawd's sake don't mention cocoa an' biscuits to 'im," said Evans. "You'd better go an' take 'im back to billets, before 'e starts fightin' a policeman. Everybody seems to be in a bloody bad temper today. All got wind-up, I suppose. Meet me 'ere at 'alf-past one, 'e'll tell you about it. Just because they wouldn't serve 'im, 'e wants the best they've got. Well, see you later.'

"Let's find Bourne," said Martlow to Shem, as Evans went into the shop; "when 'e's like that, 'e'd quarrel with 'is own bloody shadder."

They found him at last in their own billets, talking to Corporal Hamley, who was in a silent humour. He had recovered, but you could see he was still sore from injustice. Trying to make cheerful conversation, Shem inadvertently mentioned the incident of the colonel and the Australian driver.

"You want a few thousand Australians in the British Army," said Bourne angrily. "They would put wind up some of these bloody details who think they own the earth."

"What are you talkin' about? What details?" inquired Corporal Hamley, who knew nothing about the matter.

"The whole bloody issue," said Bourne, comprehensively. "Officers, and other ranks. You can't put eight hundred fighting men into the line without having another eight hundred useless parasites behind them pinching the stores."

He gave them a rapid, and somewhat incoherent, account of the episode which had ruffled him; and they could not quite make up their minds, either from what Evans had said, or from his own account, how far the trouble in the canteen had gone. The arrival of the orderly-corporal perturbed them still more.

"Bourne 'ere?" he asked, and then seeing his man, added: "You're to go before Major Shadwell at two o'clock, at 'is billet, by the orderly-room. You'll take 'im up, corporal."

"What's the trouble about?" asked the corporal, alarmed at the possibility that one of his section might have disgraced himself.

"Oh, there's no trouble," said Bourne, with a weary impatience. "It is probably about my commission."

His interview with Major Shadwell did him a lot of good. It was a plain, matter-of-fact conversation. The second-in-command apparently knew all he needed to know about him, merely asking him a few questions and then explaining the procedure. At the same time, he managed to put into what was only a matter of routine, a touch of humanity. He was quiet, serious, yet approachable. He made only one reference to the attack, and that was indirectly, when he told Bourne that the colonel would see him after it was over. It seemed to reduce the attack to the right proportions, as being after all only a matter of routine too. As he walked back to billets with Corporal Hamley after the interview was over, the corporal turned to him.

"Anyway," he said, "Major Shadwell's the right kind of officer."

"Yes," said Bourne, a little preoccupied. "He's all right. He's in the cart with the rest of us."

They carried on with their routine training for the next hour, but the work seemed irrelevant, and they were preoccupied and dreamy. After Corporal Hamley told them they might pack up for the day, they wrote letters home, and during this laborious business the stable became extraordinarily quiet and pensive. Suddenly reality cut across the illusion. Weeper turned a lachrymose face from one to the other.

"What would our folks think," he said, "if they could see us poor buggers sittin' 'ere writin' all manner o' bloody lies to 'em?"

"I'm not writin' any bloody lies," said Madeley. "I'm tellin' 'em I'm in the pink, an' so I am. An' I'm tellin' 'em everythin' 's all right, an' so 't is, up to the present."

"What the 'ell are you tellin' 'em?" said Glazier, more brutally, turning on Weeper. "Nothin' but the bloody truth, eh? 'Dear Mother, by the time you get this I'll be dead.'"

"If you do write the truth they rub it out in th' orderly-room," said Martlow, "so you might just as well write cheerful. Me mother told me the first letters I sent 'ome was all rubbed out wi' indelible pencil, so as she couldn't read anythin' 'cept that it were rainin', an your lovin' son Babe: that's the silly name they give me when I were a kid."

"It's 'igh time they sent you 'ome again, now, to the bloody Veterans Corps," said Glazier, kindly enough.

Bourne wrote three brief notes, and then lounged back on his folded greatcoat and blankets. He could feel with his elbow the two bottles of wine and a tin of sausages in tomato sauce; the rest of the provisions had been distributed under Shem's or Martlow's kit. He was in much the same mood as the others were. One did not face the possibilities quite squarely until they were thrust on one, and yet one never lost completely the sense of them; whatever kind of hope or imagining held for a moment the restless mind, one heard behind it the inexorable voice: it must be, it must be; seeming to mark the dripping of time, drop by drop, out the leaky vessel of being. One by one they finished their letters and turned gradually to quiet conversation, the arrival of tea at last bringing with it, instantly, a general movement as much of relief as of appetite.

After tea, Bourne told Shem he was going to ask Sergeant Tozer to come to their supper, and he set off to A Company's billets. The sergeant was not there when he arrived, so he waited, talking to Pritchard and Minton. Conversation with them was inclined to become monosyllabic at the best of times, for, to them, speech was either an integral part of action, as it is to the dramatist for instance, or it was an imperfect means of ventilating their grievances. At the present moment, they were inactive, and they had no grievance, except against war, which had become too much a part of the natural order of things to be worth discussing. So Bourne leaned against the doorpost and waited. He saw Miller crossing the yard, and looked curiously at that degenerate face. It had in it a cunning which might or might not be insane. He gave Bourne a meaningless grin, and went into one of the stables. Minton and Pritchard glanced at him as he passed.

"They ought to 'ave shot that bugger," said Minton, indifferently. "E's either a bloody spy or a bloody coward, an' 'e's no good to us either way."

The indifference of this judgment was its remarkable feature. Bourne found himself contrasting Miller with Weeper Smart, for no one could have had a greater horror and dread of war than Weeper had. It was a continuous misery to him, and yet he endured it. Living with him, one felt instinctively that in any emergency he would not let one down, that he had in him, curiously enough, an heroic strain. Martlow, who had been brought up to read people's characters, said of him that he would be just as bloody miserable in peacetime, and perhaps he was right. Bourne, contrasting the two men, had almost decided that Weeper's defect lay in being too imaginative, when it flashed on his mind that while his imagination tortured him with apprehensions, it was actually his strength. Yes, it was Weeper's imagination, not his will, which kept him going. Bourne did not know whether Madeley's or Glazier's tenacity ought to be described as will, but he was quite certain they had more will than Weeper had. They had less imagination, though they were not devoid of it. Miller might be one of those people whose emotional instability was not far from madness. Perhaps he was not a coward at all, and the men may have been right in their earlier judgment that he was a spy; though it was possible that he might be an English, and not a German spy; and then, quite suddenly, from amusing his mind with the puzzle presented to it by Miller's character, Bourne found himself probing anxiously into his own. It was only for a moment. As soon as one touched the fringe of the mystery which is oneself, too many unknown possibilities confronted one, everything seemed insecure and unstable. He turned away from it, with a restless impatience. He would not wait for Sergeant Tozer any longer, and turning out of the yard he came face to face with him. He refused Bourne's invitation.

"I must stay in billets tonight and keep an eye on things," he said quietly. "There's a lot to do, one way an' another; an' I'll just 'ave a drink with Sergeant Gallion and the sergeant-major in the comp'ny office before turnin' in. 'Ow are you keepin', pretty fit?"

Bourne's assent was somewhat qualified, and the sergeant smiled quietly.

"Got the bloody wind-up, eh? Well, we all 'ave. You're goin' over the top wi' us again, ol' son, comin' back to the company for the show, the three o' you. Don't let on as I said anythin' about it to you, you know; but that's what I 'eard. It'll be all right. You know the comp'ny, an' it'll be a dam' sight better than messin' about with the runners or sigs as a spare man."

Bourne agreed, and his relief was quite apparent. Captain Malet had hit on one cause of weakness, when he said that Bourne looked at a question upside down and inside out, and then did exactly what the average man would do in similar circumstances. It did not, as a matter of fact, delay him in action; it was only that he experienced a quite futile anxiety as to whether he were doing the right thing, while he was doing the only possible thing at that particular moment, and it troubled him much more in the interval before action. He had worried for some time as to what his job would be in the attack, and, the moment he knew he would be with the company, his mind cleared.

"I 'eard you were puttin' in for a commission," the sergeant continued irrelevantly. "We'll 'ave a spree in Bus, after the show's over. I'm sorry I can't get down tonight."

They parted, and Bourne walked back to his billet in a quieter frame of mind. He was not very confident, or very cheerful, but for the moment at least he was free from doubt, and was not groping forward apprehensively into the future. He had noticed recently in himself an increasing tendency to fall into moods, not of abstraction or of rapture, but of blankness, and in a moment of solitude he seemed to become a part of it, his mind reflecting nothing but his immediate surroundings, as the little puddles in the road reflected whatever lees and dregs of light lingered in the sky.

But this mood was not dreaminess, he did not rouse himself out of it with any effort, or with a start, as one wakes again after lapsing into a moment's sleep. He was instantly aware of the presence of another in his neighbourhood, and always very keenly and definitely. After a few minutes, he met a couple of men in the twilit street. "Goodnight, chum," they called out to him, softly.

"Goodnight."

And they were gone again, the unknown shadows, gone almost as quickly and as inconspicuously as bats into the dusk, and they would all go like that ultimately, as they were gathering to go now, migrants with no abiding place, whirled up on the wind of some irresistible impulse. What would be left of them soon would be no more than a little flitting memory in some twilit mind.

He turned into their billets, and found them deserted except for Martlow, who told him that Shem and Corporal Hamley had gone off together for half an hour, leaving him behind to mount guard over the provisions. Bourne sprawled beside him in the dry dusty litter; it was hay, not straw, the fine stems of it just strong enough to prickle where it touched the skin.

Anyway, they would have some wine, some variation of food, and some quiet talk, before turning over to sleep. They were the masters of the moment at least, fate could not rob them of what they actually had now. Food and sleep they needed, in the interval remaining to them, as much of both as they could get. Once they went over the top, with the best of luck the world would be shattered for them, and what was left of

211

ould have to piece together again, into some crazy makeshift
it last their time. He could not believe that after the show was
would be sent back to Blighty, drilled as though he were a
recruit again, and, after he had been smartened up, dressed in a Bedford
cord suit and Sam Browne and sent back again, to take up an entirely
different position in regard to the men. He would have to forget a lot;
and, even while he was thinking how impossible it would be to forget,
Martlow looked up at him with a grin on his puckish face.

"D'you remember the night we pinched all them pertaters an' Swedes
out o' the fields at Reclinghem, an' made a stew wi' some bully in a
biscuit-tin? 'Twere real good, that stew."

Bourne laughed, a little absently, as one who is being beaten by
circumstances and must make the best of them. Men are bound together
more closely by the trivial experiences they have shared than by the most
sacred obligations, and already his memory was haunted by outstretched
hands seeking rescue from oblivion, and faces half-submerged to which
he could give no name. Martlow only grinned more broadly, thinking he
laughed at something funny in the episode itself.

"When I've got me bellyful, I don't care a fuck if it snows ink," he
continued. "The worst o' goin' over the top is that you get tired an' cold,
an' empty. It's that empty feeling in the pit o' the stomach what gets a
man down. You feel as though all your guts had dropped out."

They both looked up as the corporal and Shem came in, and Martlow
turned on them at once with his inevitable questioning, while Bourne
took out the bottles and tinned food from under the blankets.

"Oh, they're quite lively down the road," said the corporal. "It puts you
in quite a good skin to 'ear 'em all singin'. Shem an' I just went in an'
'ad a glass o' beer."

They each took a tin of sausages in tomato sauce, and after debating for
a moment whether it would not be better to heat them over the brazier,
decided, partly from idleness, and partly from appetite, to eat them cold.
Bourne uncorked a bottle of champagne, and was holding it over a mess-
tin into which bubbled the creaming foam, when they all turned towards
the doorway again, and Weeper Smart came in alone. He looked at them
in some embarrassment, and crossing to his own corner, to which the
glow from the brazier and the light from the hurricane lamp scarcely
penetrated, sat down dejectedly.

"Give us your mess-tin, Smart, and have a drink with us," said Bourne. Up went Weeper's flat hand.

"No, thank 'ee," he said abruptly. "Tha needst not think a come back 'ere just to scrounge on thee. If a'd known a would 'ave stayed out yon."

"Give me your tin," said Bourne. "You're welcome. It's share and share alike with us. Where's the sense of sitting alone by yourself, as though you think you are better than the next man?"

"A've never claimed to be better nor the next man," said Weeper, "an' a've got nowt to share."

Bourne, taking up his mess-tin without waiting for him to pass it, poured out a fair share of the wine; he felt ashamed, in some strange way, that it should be in his power to give this forlorn, ungainly creature anything. It was as though he were encroaching on the other man's independence.

"You don't mind taking a share of my tea in the morning," he said with a rather diffident attempt at humour.

"A've as much reet to that as tha 'ast," said Weeper sullenly. And then he was ashamed immediately of his surliness. He took up the mess-tin and drank a good draught before putting it down again, and breathing deeply with satisfaction.

"That's better nor any o' the stuff us poor buggers can get," he said with an attempt at gratitude, which could not quite extinguish his more natural envy, and he moved up closer to them, and to the warmth and light. The wine may have taken some of the edge off his bitterness, but if he felt less unfriendly, he remained rather aloof, only touching on the fringe of their conversation. They were very conscious of his presence there, but gave no sign of it, merely passing him some food from time to time, as though it were a matter of course. They had finished the wine, and thrown away the bottles, when the rest of the section began to come back, singly or in twos and threes, some of them a little drunk. Bourne handed round the rest of the macaroons, all that remained of their feast, and they made ready to sleep.

Chapter XV

He may show what outward courage he will; but I believe as cold
a night as 'tis, he could wish himself in Thames up to the neck;
and so I would he were, and I by him, at all adventures, so we
were quit here. – SHAKESPEARE

They moved back to Bus on the third day after their arrival at
Louvencourt, and were in their usual billets by about four o'clock in the
afternoon. They had taken off their packs, and leaned their rifles up
against the boarding of the hut, to rest awhile, when the post arrived, and
they all crowded in front of the hut which served as Headquarter
Company's office.

It was a large mail. Shem had gone off on his own somewhere, and one
of the first letters was for him, so Bourne took it; Martlow had a letter
and a parcel, but the remarkable feature of that particular post was that
there were fourteen letters and parcels for Bourne. There was no kind of
preliminary sorting, everything lay in a heap on the floor, and the post-
corporal dished them out himself that day. As a rule the orderly-corporal
brought the letters up from the post-corporal's billet, and the
quartermaster-sergeant called out the name of the man to whom anything
was addressed, and then flung it towards him with an indifferent aim. But
to get rid of the stuff early, and also because he wanted to talk to the
quarter-bloke, the post-corporal had brought it up to the company before
they had arrived back from Louvencourt, and there, the other N.C.O.'s
being busy, he dished it out himself, the quarter-bloke seated at his table,
taking only a perfunctory interest in the proceedings, while he continued
with some other work. It was remarkable that so many of his friends
should have shown their solicitude for Bourne's welfare about the same
time. After a couple of parcels and three letters had been thrown at him,
the repetition of his name was answered by groans from the crowd, and
even the post-corporal seemed to resent the fact that he should be
expected to deliver so many things to one man.

"Bourne!" he shouted impatiently, and shied another letter through the air like a kind of boomerang.

The pile gradually decreased, but Bourne's name was reiterated at intervals, to be met with a chorus of derisory complaint. "D'you want the whole bloody lot?" someone cried.

He was childishly delighted, and laughed at the kind of prestige which the incident brought to him. At last there were only a few letters left, and one rather large box of threeply wood, with a label tacked flat on it. One of the few remaining letters was tossed to him, and at last only the box remained. The post-corporal lifted it in both hands and read the label.

"Bourne; 'ere, take your bloody wreath," he cried disgustedly, and the sardonic witticism brought down the house. The box actually contained a large plum cake. When Bourne got back to his hut, he divided the contents of his parcels among the whole section, keeping only the cigarettes, cake, and a pork pie, which a farmer's wife of his acquaintance had sent him, for himself. Most of it was food, though there were a few woollen comforters and impossible socks, as well as a couple of books, with which one could not encumber oneself.

During their time in Louvencourt, they had not seen much of their officers, who had probably been receiving their final instructions, but now there was continual wind-up. A hot and exasperated officer would suddenly appear outside the huts, and the men were fallen in to receive his orders. The first was about overcoats. Each man was to go over the top with his overcoat, which was to be worn en banderole, and as most of the men did not know how to roll up their coats in this fashion, they had to learn the art from the few regular soldiers who did. It tried the patience of everybody concerned. When the overcoat had been rolled up into a tubular form, one end was inserted in the other and fastened there, and a man put his head and one arm through the kind of horse-collar which it formed, so that it rested on one shoulder and passed under the other arm. The first man to achieve this difficult feat of arms was an object of admiration to his fellows.

"Oo's the bloody shit 'oo invented this way o' doin' up a fuckin' overcoat?" shouted Glazier indignantly.

"It's a bloody wonder to me 'ow these buggers can think all this out.'Ow the 'ell am a to get at me gas mask?" asked Madeley.

"You put on your gas 'elmet afterwards, see," said Wilkins, an old regular who was explaining matters to them. "But it beats me 'ow you're goin' to manage. You'll lave your ordinary equipment, an' a couple of extra bandoliers, an' your gas bag, and then this bloody overcoat."

"A can tell thee," said Weeper, "the first thing a does when a goes over the bloody top is to dump it. What bloody chance would us'ns 'ave wi' a bay'net, when we can scarce move our arms."

"It's fair chokin' me," said Madeley.

"Fall in on parade," shouted Corporal Marshall, putting his head through the door, and divesting themselves for the moment of this latest encumbrance, they turned out into the twilight. This time it was Captain Thompson, with the R. S. M. in attendance, and he went through a list of the things the men would be expected to carry: two extra bandoliers of ammunition, two bombs, and either a pick or shovel. But at least there was one unusual piece of foresight: the men were ordered to go to the shoemaker's shop and have bars of leather fixed across the hob-nailed soles of their boots, to prevent them slithering in the mud, and, with the initial unreason which so often accompanied orders, they were forbidden to leave billets until this order had been executed. There were only three cobblers, who started on the work at once, and it was arranged almost immediately afterwards that the work should be carried out section by section, so that the men did not have to wait about indefinitely. It was characteristic that the men did not grumble at this latest order, as they saw at once its utility, and the precaution seemed to give them some confidence. It soon became equally clear that the order about overcoats worn in banderole was a matter for some misgivings with the officers themselves.

"This overcoat business will have to be washed out," said Captain Thompson to the regimental sergeant-major.

"They seem to think we're goin' straight through, sir," said the regimental with a short, hard laugh.

And the few men who overheard them spread abroad what had been said. The men were all quiet, alert and obedient. They had an almost pathetic anxiety to understand the significance of every order, and even in the matter of the banderole, which hampered the freedom of their movements considerably, after reflection they became ready to offset the disadvantages by the advantages of having an overcoat with them. Even the sharp impatience with which a harassed and overdriven officer spoke to them, or the curses of a sergeant bustled by the suddenly increasing pressure of his work, did not cause more than a slight and momentary resentment.

"They're all in it wi' us, now, an' one man's no better nor another," said Weeper, when Humphreys said something about Mr Rhys being a bit rattled. "They can do nowt wi'out us'ns, an', gentlefolk an' all, we all stan' the same chance now."

The thought of that equality seemed to console him. The change in him was perhaps more apparent than real; all his pessimism and melancholy remained, but now his determination emerged from it. Looking at that lean, ungainly, but extraordinarily powerful figure, with the abnormally long arms and huge hands, one realised that he might be a very useful man in a fight. And yet there was nothing of cruelty in him. The unbounded pity he felt for himself did, in spite of his envious and embittered nature, extend to others. Glazier was the kind of person who killed automatically, without either premeditation or remorse, but Weeper was a very different type. He dreaded the thought of killing, and was haunted by the memory of it; and yet there was a kind of fatalism in him now, as though he were the instrument of justice, prepared for any gruesome business confronting him. There was something in what Bourne, half in jest, had said to him, that he thought himself better than most men. He knew that the others, including perhaps Bourne himself, did not face the reality of war squarely. They refused to think of it, except when actually involved in battle, and such thought as they had then did not extend beyond the instant action, being scarcely more than a spontaneous and irreflective impulse; but most of them had made their decision once and for all, and were willing to abide by the consequences, without reviewing it. It was useless to contrast the first challenging enthusiasm that had swept them into the army with the long and bitter agony they endured afterwards. It was the unknown which they had challenged, and when the searching flames took hold of their very flesh, the test was whether or not they should flinch under them. The men knew it. We can stick it, they said, and they had to retrieve their own failures, to subdue their own doubts, to master their own pitiful human weaknesses, only too conscious for the most part, even when they broke

important quote

217

into complaints, that the struggle with their own nature was always inconclusive.)

Bourne, Shem and Martlow were ordered to report to Sergeant-Major Robinson and have their boots barred with the rest of A Company. The cobblers worked hurriedly, in a ring of light surrounded by a press of waiting men. As each man got his boots back, he showed them to Mr Sothern, who approved the work, rather perfunctorily, with a nod. When Bourne and his companions presented themselves to the sergeant-major, Mr Sothern wanted to know why they were there; and when the sergeant-major told him that they would rejoin the company on the following day until after the attack, the officer said they had better have their boots done at once, so as to get them out of the way. As soon as the job was finished, shouldering his way to the door, Bourne turned irritably to the other two.

"For God's sake, let's get out of this bloody confusion, and go somewhere where we can see life," he said, almost as though they were the cause of keeping him waiting about the camp. There was really very little confusion, in spite of the haste and strain.

"We'd better see the corporal first," answered Shem quietly.

He and Martlow both noticed the acerbity in Bourne's tone. "You can go out for 'alf an hour or so," said Corporal Hamley indifferently, "but you may be wanted later. There's a carryin' party goin' up the line."

It was not very welcome news, but they accepted the fact quietly and merely walked down to the estaminet for a drink, and returned. They were detailed for a carrying party sure enough and set off on limbers for Courcelles, continuing for the rest of the way on foot. It was very misty and cold, and under the moon, never clearly visible, the cloud and mist seemed curdled milkiness.

While they were drawn up waiting by the dump, they heard something ponderous coming towards them, and, looking sideways along the road, saw their first tank, nosing its way slowly through the stagnant fog. They drew in their breath, in their first excitement, wondering a little at the suggestion of power it gave them, for its uplifted snout seemed to imply a sense of direction and purpose, even though it was not, in bulk, as formidable as they had expected. A door opened in the side, and a gleam of light came from it, as a man inside questioned another in the road; there was a tired note even in their determined voices.

"If a can't be inside one o' them, a don't want to be anywhere near it," said Weeper, with absolute decision.

The carrying party moved off, just as the tank was being manoeuvred to change direction, and the men, their eyes searching the fog for it on their return, found it gone. They marched the whole way back to billets, and, tired after a long day, as soon as they had finished drinking some tea and rum slept heavily.

When Bourne woke early in the morning, he heard the guns drumming in the distance, a continued dull staccato, which had in it momentarily, from time to time, a kind of rhythm. He listened intently, and the bombardment seemed to increase in violence; and but for a vague reflection that the Hun must have wind up at the avalanche of shells assailing him, his mind was blank and empty. He moistened dry lips with a tongue scarcely less dry. The but smelt damp and frowsty. He saw Martlow's small face, pillowed on his pack beside him, the brows puckered slightly, and the lips parted, but breathing quietly in a dreamless sleep, and he looked at him in a kind of wonder for a moment. Sleep was the only blessing they had. Bourne drew his knees up, dropping his chin towards them, and sat clasping his feet with locked fingers, while he brooded over nothing. Shem stirred on the other side of him, cleared his throat, and then lifted himself to lean on one elbow, listening.

"D'you hear that?" he asked.

"Yes," said Bourne, with dry brevity, and Shem fell back again flat, his eyes contemplating the rafters. Bourne sat immobile for a moment or two, and then drew in a quick deep gasp of air, to exhale it again in a sigh. He remained still.

"What d'you do that for?" asked Shem.

"Do what?"

"Gasp like that. I had an aunt who used to do that, and she died o' heart."

"I don't think that I'm likely to die of heart," was Bourne's dry comment.

He lay down again, pulling the blanket up to his chin. It was only about half-past five, and in a few minutes they were both asleep again, while the rhythmic drumming of the guns continued.

After breakfast that morning, Bourne passed by the regimental's tent and saw his batman, who had just finished shaving, sitting on a box by the doorway. Bourne noticed that his boots had been barred.

"I didn't think you were going over the top with us, Barton," he said, his surprise giving his words the turn of a question.

"The regimental didn't want me to go," said Barton, blushing and smiling; "'E tried to work it so as I shouldn't go, but they wouldn't 'ave it."

He was smiling, even as he blushed, in a deprecating way.

"I don't know what 'e wanted to bother for," he said reasonably. "It's only right I should go with the rest, and I'd as lief go as stay. You think o' things sometimes as seem to 'old you back; but it's no worse for me than for the nex' man. I think I'd rather go."

The last words came from him with slow reluctance and difficulty; and yet the apparent effort he made to utter them, hurrying a little towards the end, did not imply that they were untrue, but only that he recognised a superior necessity, which had forced him to put aside other, only less valid, considerations. He was thinking of his wife and children, of the comparative security in which he had left them, and of what their fate might be in the worst event; but war is a jealous god, destroying ruthlessly his rivals.

"You're in B Company, aren't you?" Bourne asked him, trying to carry the conversation over these awkward reflections.

"Yes," said Barton cheerfully. "They're a nice lot in B Company; N. C. O.'s an' officers, they're a nice lot of men."

"Well, good luck, Barton,' said Bourne quietly, moving away as the only means of relief.

"Good luck, Bourne," said Barton, as though he did not believe in luck.

All day the business of preparation went on, with the same apparent confusion, haste and impatience, but with quite a painstaking method underlying all that superficial disorder. To some, who did not understand the negligent manner of British officers and men –even the most efficient–, the business may have seemed careless and perfunctory, when as a matter of fact all details were scrupulously checked, and all errors and deficiencies corrected. Bourne, Shem and Martlow paraded with A Company, though their kit and blankets remained in the signals section hut, and were glad to find themselves in Corporal Jakes's section, under

Sergeant Tozer. Jakes sometimes gave one the impression of being a stupid and stubborn fellow, but, as a matter of fact, he was a cool, level-headed fighting man, with plenty of determination, but with sufficient flexibility of mind to make the best of any circumstances in which he might find himself. Like most men of his county, he was short, broad and ruddy with plenty of stamina.

Mr Finch was more in evidence than Mr Sothern in the morning. He would take a parade, as when he inspected gas helmets, with the utmost seriousness and the most regimental precision, and the moment it was over, he would be laughing like a schoolboy, as though the excitement had gone to his head. Excitement was certainly increasing. In the intervals of that appearance of disorder, caused, mainly, by the haste with which parades and inspections succeeded one another, there was an apparent stillness, which was equally illusory. It might be broken by Mr Finch's high-pitched laughter, suddenly cut off again, or by an explosion of anger from some individual man, but between these interruptions there was a glassy quiet.

Men may conceal their emotion easily enough, but it is more difficult to hide the fact that they are concealing it. Many of them seemed oblivious of each other, as they sat, or waited about, with pondering brows, and one might pass a group of two or three hastening on their business, talking quickly together, and one caught a hint of something sinister and desperate in their faces. That was the oddest thing perhaps, the need for haste which obsessed them. Other men, recognising one, seemed to warp their faces into a nervous grin, showing their teeth as a dog might, and then it would be wiped out by a pathetic weariness. One only caught such glimpses of the tension beneath the surfaces momentarily, and at unawares; and while it was more or less apparent in each individual, the general temper of the men was quiet and grave.

Bourne sometimes wondered how far a battalion recruited mainly from London, or from one of the provincial cities, differed from his own, the men of which came from farms, and, in a lesser measure, from mining villages of no great importance. The simplicity of their outlook on life gave them a certain dignity because it was free from irrelevances. Certainly they had all the appetites of men, and, in the aggregate, probably embodied most of the vices to which flesh is prone; but they were not preoccupied with their vices and appetites, they could master them with rather a splendid indifference, and even sensuality has its aspect of tenderness. These apparently rude and brutal natures comforted, encouraged and reconciled each other to fate, with a tenderness and tact which was more moving than anything in life. They had nothing; not even their own bodies, which had become mere implements of warfare. They turned from the wreckage and misery of life to an empty heaven, and from an empty heaven to the silence of their own hearts. They had been brought to the last extremity of hope, and yet they put their hands on each other's shoulders and said with a passionate conviction that it would be all right, though they had faith in nothing but in themselves and in each other.

The succession of fatigues, parades and inspections barely distracted their thought, so much a habit obedience had become. In one of the intervals, Martlow and Shem were sent off on some small fatigue to the stores, and as Martlow leaned his rifle against the side of the hut, he said something to Bourne, and, turning, hurried after Shem. Mr Finch was standing only a few feet away, and he glanced at the boy talking to Bourne, looked after him as he turned and ran, and then turned to Bourne himself.

"Seems a bloody shame to send a kid like that into a show, doesn't it?" he said, in a kindly undertone.

"He was with us on the Somme in July and August, sir," was all Bourne's reply, though that he, too, thought it a bloody shame was sufficiently obvious.

"Was he?" exclaimed Mr Finch appreciatively. "Stout fellow. It's a bloody shame, all the same."

He struck at a clod of mud with his stick.

"Bloody awful weather to go over in, isn't it?" he said, almost as though he were only thinking aloud. "However, we can only do our best."

Some other men coming up, he moved off a few paces, and the drumming of the distant guns came to them. Bourne thought now that it did not sound so heavy as some of the bombardments on the Somme. Sergeant Tozer came on the scene, and when he went into the empty hut, Bourne followed him.

"What do you make of it, sergeant?" he asked.

"I don' know what to make of it. What the bloody hell do you make of it, yourself? After all, that's what matters. I suppose we'll come through all right; we've done it before, so we can do it again. Anyway, it can't be more of a bloody balls-up than some o' the other shows 'ave been. Give us over that entrenching tool handle; that bloody snob drove a nail through my boot."

He had unrolled one of his puttees, taken a boot off, and sat on the ground while he felt for the offending nail with his fingers, a look of exasperated patience on his face; having found it he tried to flatten, bend or break the point off with the metal-bound end of the handle.

"Fuck the bloody thing!" he said fiercely under his breath. Ultimately he succeeded in his object, and after feeling where the point had been, critically, with his fingers, he drew on his boot again.

"You don't want to get the fuckin' wind up, you know," he said kindly.

"Who's getting wind up?" replied Bourne, resentfully. "Don't you worry about me, sergeant. I can stick it all right. If I do get it in the neck, I'll be out of this bloody misery, anyway."

"That's all right," said the sergeant. "You needn't take me up the wrong way, you know. I'm not worryin' about you. I'm a bit windy myself. It'll be all right when we get started. We'll pull it off somehow or other."

He stood up, and then stooped to pull his trouser down over the top of his puttee, turning himself sideways with one arm outstretched, and glancing down, afterwards, to see that it hung straight and neat. Then he chucked out his chest, flinging his head back so that his chin seemed more aggressive, and swung out of the but into the mist.

"I'll lay our artillery is puttin' the bloody wind up them fuckin' Fritzes," he said to Bourne over his shoulder, so that he failed to see Mr Finch, who had returned. "If they haven't got a suspish already, they'll be wonderin'...I beg pardon, sir, I didn't see you was there."

"Shall we win, sergeant?" said Mr Finch, laughing.

"Oh, we'll win all right, sir," said Sergeant Tozer grimly, "but not yet."

"Sergeant, about those bombs," began Mr Finch, and Bourne, saluting, walked off to the signallers' hut again.

They didn't do much that night. Going into an estaminet early, they had a bottle of wine between them, and then strolled from one end of the town to the other. It was a long, straggling town, with a large civilian element, and chinks of light came between the blinds of the windows. On their way back to billets they turned into the Y.M.C.A. to get some cocoa. They did not feel like drinking bad wine or beer in a crowded and noisy estaminet, and argued that in any case they would have a rum ration that night.

The Y.M.C.A., however, was as noisy and as crowded as the estaminet; and there was a good deal of clowning. One man was singing "I Want to Go Home":

Oh, my! I don't want to die,

I want to go 'ome!

He was dancing as he sang with a kind of waltz step. At the next table, were three men smoking and talking, so close that above the murmuring din one heard snatches of their talk. Bourne ordered cocoa, and paid for it, and they talked a little to Weston, the attendant, who had been in the Westshires at one time. Then he left them, and they sat there, smoking. One of the men at the next table was talking to the other two.

"'What's the matter wi' the girl?' the officer asked 'im. 'I don' know, sir,' said Sid, 'she went into one o' them out'ouses wi' Johnson, an' the nex' thing I 'eard was that Johnson 'ad gone for the doctor. Said she'd 'ad a fit.' 'Oh," said the officer, 'bloody tight fit, I suppose.'"

They all laughed, and Bourne looked at their sneering faces, and turned away again. He wanted to get out of all this senseless clamour, and as his eyes turned away, he chanced to see over the door a red strip on which was printed in white letters: "AND UNDERNEATH ARE THE EVERLASTING ARMS." It struck him with an extraordinary vividness, that bare text sprawling across the wall above the clamour of those excited voices; and once again he knew that feeling of certitude in a peace so profound that all the turmoil of the earth was lost in it.

"Shall we go back?" he asked the others quietly, and they followed him out into the mist and mud.

After they had had their rum ration, they took off boots, puttees and tunic, and rolled themselves into their blankets, spreading their greatcoats over them as well because of the cold. Bourne felt quiet and was almost asleep, when suddenly full consciousness came to him again, and, opening his eyes, he could just see Martlow looking abstractedly into the dark.

"Are you all right, kid?" he whispered, and put out a hand to the boy's.

"Yes, I'm all right," said Martlow quietly. "You know, it don't matter what 'appens to us'ns, Bourne. It don't matter what 'appens; it'll be all right in the end."

He turned over and was soon sleeping quietly, long before Bourne was.

And the next day was the same, in all outward seeming. They got their tea, they washed, shaved, and had their breakfast, smoked, and fell in on parade, in the ordinary course of routine. The extra weight they were carrying was marked, but the overcoat worn banderole had been washed-out, a rumour among the men being that the colonel had sent a man up to Brigade, equipped as they had ordered, to show the absurdity of it. As he arrived in front of A Company's huts, Bourne, Shem and Martlow found groups of men talking among themselves.

"What's up?" he asked.

"Miller. 'E's 'opped it, again. I knew the bugger would. 'E's a bloody German spy, that's what 'e is. They should 'ave shot the bugger when they 'ad 'im! One o' them fuckin' square'eads, an' they let 'im off!"

There was an extraordinary exultation in their anger; as they spoke, a fierce contemptuous laughter mingled with speech.

"Yes, they let a bloody twat like 'im off; but if any o' us poor fuckers did it, we'd be for th' electric chair, we would. We've done our bit, we 'ave; but it wouldn't make any differ to us'ns."

The angry, bitter words were tossed about from one to another in derision. Bourne was more struck by the severity and pallor of Sergeant Tozer's face, when he saw him in the hut. He did not ask any questions; they just passed the time of day, and there was a pause broken by Bourne.

"You shouldn't blame yourself, sergeant," he said. "It's not your fault.'

"That's all right," said Sergeant Tozer. "I'm not blamin' meself. On'y if I saw the bugger in the road I'd put a bullet into 'im an' save 'em any bloody fuss with a court-martial."

The men fell in, and Captain Marsden, with Mr Sothern and Mr Finch, came on parade. The final inspection was a very careful one. Bourne noticed that Marsden, who often spoke with a dry humour, restricted himself to a minimum of words. He saw that one of Bourne's pouches didn't fasten properly, the catch being defective. He tried it himself, and then tried the clipped cartridges inside, satisfying himself apparently that they fitted into the pouch so tightly that they would not fall out until one clip had been removed. Anyway, he ignored it, and loosening Bourne's water bottle, shook it to see if it were full. Bourne stood like a dummy while this was going on, and all the time Captain Marsden looked at him closely, as though he were trying to look into his mind. It angered Bourne, but he kept his face as rigid as stone; in fact his only emotion now was a kind of stony anger. Some of the men had forgotten to fill their bottles, and were told what bloody nuisances they were. Eventually it was over, and they went off to their huts for what little time was left to them. One had a vague feeling that one was going away, without any notion of returning. One had finished with the place, and did not regret it, but a curious instability of mind accompanied the last moments; with a sense of actual relief that the inexorable hour was approaching, there was a growing anger becoming so intense that it seemed the heart would scarcely hold it. The skin seemed shinier and tighter on men's faces, and eyes burned with a hard brightness under the brims of their helmets. One felt every question as an interruption of some absorbing business of the mind. Occasionally Martlow would look up at Shem or Bourne as though he were about to speak, and then turn away in silence.

"We three had better try and keep together," said Shem evenly.

"Yes," answered the other two, as though they engaged themselves quietly.

And then, one by one, they realised that each must go alone, and that each of them already was alone with himself, helping the others perhaps, but looking at them with strange eyes, while the world became unreal and empty, and they moved in a mystery, where no help was.

"Fall in on the road!"

With a sigh of relinquishment, they took up their rifles and obeyed, sliding from the field into the road, which was about five feet lower, down a bank in which narrow steps had once been cut, though rain and many feet had obliterated them. The details crowded there, to see them go. They fell in, numbered off, formed fours, formed two deep, and stood at ease, waiting, all within a few moments. A few yards on either side, the men became shadows in the mist. Presently they stood to attention again, and the colonel passed along the ranks; and this time Bourne looked at him, looked into his eyes, not merely through and beyond him, and the severity of that clear-cut face seemed today to have something cheerful and kindly in it, without ceasing to be inscrutable. His grey horse had been led down the road a few minutes before, and presently the high clear voice rang through the mist. Then came the voices of the company commanders, one after the other, and the quick stamping as the men obeyed, the rustle as they turned; and their own turn came, the quick stamps, the swing half-right, and then something like a rippling murmur of movement, and the slurred rhythm of their trampling feet, seeming to beat out the seconds of time, while the liquid mud sucked and sucked at their boots, and they dropped into that swinging stride without speaking, and the houses of Bus slid away on either side, and the mist wavered and trembled about them in little eddies, and earth, and life, and time, were as if they had never been.

Chapter XVI

We see yonder the beginning of day, but I think we shall never see
the end of it...I am afeard there are few die well that die in a
battle. – SHAKESPEARE

The drumming of the guns continued, with bursts of great intensity. It
was as though a gale streamed overhead, piling up great waves of sound,
and hurrying them onward to crash in surf on the enemy entrenchments.
The windless air about them, by its very stillness, made that unearthly
music more terrible to hear. They cowered under it, as men seeking
shelter from a storm. Something rushed downward on them with a
scream of exultation, increasing to a roar before it blasted the air asunder
and sent splinters of steel shrieking over their heads, an eruption of mud
spattering down on the trench, and splashing in brimming shellholes. The
pressure among the men increased. Someone shouldering a way through
caused them to surge together, cursing, as they were thrown off their
balance to stumble against their neighbours.

"For Christ's sake walk on your own fuckin' feet an' not on mine!"
came from some angry man, and a ripple of idiot mirth spread outwards
from the centre of the disturbance. Bourne got a drink of tea, and though
it was no more than warm, it did him good; at least, it washed away the
gummy dryness of his mouth. He was shivering, and told himself it was
the cold.

Through the darkness the dripping mist moved slowly, touching them
with spectral fingers as it passed. Everything was clammy with it. It
condensed on their tin hats, clung to their rough serge, their eyelashes,
the down on their cheekbones. Even though it blinded everything beyond
the distance of a couple of yards, it seemed to be faintly luminous itself.
Its damp coldness enhanced the sense of smell. There was a reek of
mouldering rottenness in the air, and through it came the sour, stale
odour from the foul clothes of the men. Shells streamed overhead,
sighing, whining and whimpering for blood; the upper air fluttered with
them, but Fritz was not going to take it all quietly, and with its increasing

roar another shell leaped towards them, and they cowered under the wrath. There was the enormous grunt of its eruption, the sweeping of harp-strings, and part of the trench wall collapsed inwards, burying some men in the landslide. It was difficult to get them out, in the crowded conditions of the trench.

Bourne's fit of shakiness increased, until he set his teeth to prevent them chattering in his head; and after a deep, gasping breath, almost like a sob, he seemed to recover to some extent. Fear poisoned the very blood, but, when one recognised the symptoms, it became objective, and one seemed to escape partly from it that way. He heard men breathing irregularly beside him, as he breathed himself; he heard them licking their lips, trying to moisten their mouths; he heard them swallow, as though overcoming a difficulty in swallowing; and the sense that others suffered equally or more than himself, quietened him. Some men moaned, or even sobbed a little, but unconsciously, and as though they struggled to throw off an intolerable burden of oppression. His eyes met Shem's, and they both turned away at once from the dread and question which confronted them. More furtively, he glanced in Martlow's direction and saw him standing with bent head. Some instinctive wave of pity and affection swelled in him, until it broke into another shuddering sigh, and the boy looked up, showing the whites of his eyes under the brim of his helmet. They were perplexed, and his underlip shook a little. Behind him Bourne heard a voice almost pleading: "Stick it out, chum."

"A don't care a fuck," came the reply, with a bitter harshness rejecting sympathy.

"Are you all right, kid?" Bourne managed to ask in a fairly steady voice, and Martlow only gave a brief affirmative nod. Bourne shifted his weight onto his other foot, and felt the relaxed knee trembling. It was the cold. If only they had something to do, it might be better. It had been a help simply to place a ladder in position. Suspense seemed to turn one's mind to ice, and bind even time in its frozen stillness, but at an order it broke. It broke, and one became alert, relieved. They breathed heavily in one another's faces. They looked at each other more quietly, forcing themselves to face the question.

"We've stuck it before," said Shem.

They could help each other, at least up to that point where the irresistible thing swept aside their feeble efforts, and smashed them

229

beyond recovery. The noise of the shells increased to a hurricane fury. There was at last a sudden movement with some purpose behind it. The men began to fix bayonets. Someone thrust a mug into Shem's hands. "Three men. Don't spill the bloody stuff, you won't get no more."

Shem drank some of the rum and passed it to Bourne.

"Take all you want, kid," said Bourne to Martlow; "I don't care whether I have any or not."

"Don't want much," said Martlow, after drinking a good swig. "It makes you thirsty, but it warms you up a bit."

Bourne emptied the mug, and handed it back to Jakes to fill again and pass to another man. It had roused him a little.

"It'll soon be over, now," whispered Martlow.

Perhaps it was lighter, but the stagnant fog veiled everything. Only there was a sound of movement, a sudden alertness thrilled through them all with an anguish inextricably mingled with relief. They shook hands, the three among themselves and then with others near them.

Good luck, chum. Good luck. Good luck.

He felt his heart thumping at first. And then, almost surprised at the lack of effort which it needed, he moved towards the ladder. Martlow, because he was nearest, went first. Shem followed behind Bourne, who climbed out a little clumsily. Almost as soon as he was out, he slipped sideways and nearly fell. The slope downward, where others before he did had slipped, might have been greased with Vaseline, and immediately beyond it, one's boots sank up to the ankle in mud which sucked at one's feet as they were withdrawn from it, clogging them as in a nightmare. It would be worse when they reached the lower levels of this ill-drained marsh. The fear in him now was hard and icy, and yet apart from that momentary fumbling on the ladder, and the involuntary slide, he felt himself moving more freely, as though he had full control of himself.

They were drawn up in two lines, in artillery formation: C and D Companies in front, and A and B Companies in the rear. Another shell hurtled shrieking over them, to explode behind Dunmow with a roar of triumphant fury. The last effects of its blast reached them, whirling the mist into eddying spirals swaying fantastically; then he heard a low cry for stretcher-bearers. Some lucky bugger was out of it, either for good and all, or for the time being. He felt a kind of envy, and dread grew in proportion to the desire, but he could not turn away his thought: it clung desperately to the only possible solution. In this emotional crisis, where the limit of endurance was reached, all the degrees which separate opposed states of feeling vanished, and their extremities were indistinguishable from each other. One could not separate the desire from the dread which restrained it; the strength of one's hope strove to equal the despair which oppressed it; one's determination could only be measured by the terrors and difficulties which it overcame. All the mean, piddling standards of ordinary life vanished in the collision of these warring opposites. Between them one could only attempt to maintain an equilibrium which every instant disturbed and made unstable.

If it had been clear, there would have been some light by now, but darkness was prolonged by fog. He put up a hand, as though to wipe the filthy air from before his eyes, and he saw the stupid face of Jakes, by no means a stupid man, warped into a lopsided grin. Bloody fool, he thought, with unreasoning anger. It was as though Jakes walked on tiptoe, stealing away from the effects of some ghastly joke he had perpetrated.

"We're on the move," he said softly, and grinned with such a humour as skulls might have.

Then suddenly that hurricane of shelling increased terrifically, and in the thunder of its surf, as it broke over the German lines, all separate sounds were engulfed: it was one continuous fury, only varying as it seemed to come from one direction now, and now from another. And they moved. He didn't know whether they had heard any orders or not: he only knew they moved. It was treacherous walking over that greasy mud. They crossed Monk Trench, and a couple of other trenches, crowding together, and becoming confused. After Monk was behind them, the state of the ground became more and more difficult; one could not put a foot to the ground without skating and sliding. He saw Mr Finch at one crossing, looking anxious and determined, and Sergeant Tozer, but it was no more than a glimpse in the mist. A kind of maniacal rage filled him. Why were they so slow? And then it seemed that he himself was one of the slowest, and he pressed on. Suddenly the Hun barrage fell: the air was split and seared with shells. Fritz had been ready for them all right, and had only waited until their intentions had been made quite clear.

As they hurried, head downward, over their own front line, they met men, some broken and bleeding, but others whole and sound, breaking back in disorder. They jeered at them, and the others raved inarticulately, and disappeared into the fog again. Jakes and Sergeant Tozer held their own lot together, and carried them through this moment of demoralisation. Jakes roared and bellowed at them, and they only turned bewildered faces to him as they pressed forward, struggling through the mud like flies through treacle. What was all the bloody fuss about? they asked themselves, turning their faces, wide-eyed, in all directions to search the baffling fog. It shook, and twitched, and whirled about them; there seemed to be a dancing flicker before their eyes as shell after shell exploded, clanging, and the flying fragments hissed and shrieked through the air.

Bourne thought that every bloody gun in the German army was pointed at him. He avoided some shattered bodies of men too obviously dead for help. A man stumbled past him with an agonised and bleeding face. Then more men broke back in disorder, throwing them into some confusion, and they seemed to waver for a moment. One of the fugitives charged down on Jakes and that short but stocky fighter smashed the butt of his rifle to the man's jaw, and sent him sprawling. Bourne had a vision of Sergeant-Major Glasspool.

"You take your fuckin' orders from Fritz!" he shouted as a triumphant frenzy thrust him forward.

For a moment they might have broken and run themselves, and for a moment they might have fought men of their own blood, but they struggled on as Sergeant Tozer yelled at them to leave that bloody tripe alone and get on with it. Bourne, floundering in the viscous mud, was at once the most abject and the most exalted of God's creatures. The effort and rage in him, the sense that others had left them to it, made him pant and sob, but there was some strange intoxication of joy in it, and again all his mind seemed focused into one hard bright point of action. The extremities of pain and pleasure had met and coincided too.

He knew, they all did, that the barrage had moved too quickly for them, but they knew nothing of what was happening about them. In any attack, even under favourable conditions, the attackers are soon blinded, but here they had lost touch almost from the start. They paused for a brief moment, and Bourne saw that Mr Finch was with them, and Shem was not. Minton told him Shem had been hit in the foot. Bourne moved closer to Martlow. Their casualties, as far as he could judge, had not been heavy.

They got going again, and, almost before they saw it, were on the wire. The stakes had been uprooted, and it was smashed and tangled, but had not been well cut. Jakes ran along it a little way, there was some firing, and bombs were hurled at them from the almost obliterated trench, and they answered by lobbing a few bombs over, and then plunging desperately among the steel briars, which tore at their puttees and trousers. The last strand of it was cut or beaten down, some more bombs came at them, and in the last infuriated rush Bourne was knocked off his feet and went, practically headlong into the trench. Getting up, another man jumped on his shoulders, and they both fell together, yelling with rage at each other. They heard a few squeals of agony, and he saw a dead German, still kicking his heels on the broken boards of the trench at his feet. He yelled for the man who had knocked him down to come on, and followed the others. The trench was almost obliterated; it was nothing but a wreckage of boards and posts, piled confusedly in what had become a broad channel for the oozing mud. They heard some more bombing a few bays further on, and then were turned back. They met two prisoners, their hands up, and almost unable to stand from fear, while two of the men threatened them with a deliberate, slow cruelty.

"Give 'em a chance! Send 'em through their own bloody barrage!" Bourne shouted, and they were practically driven out of the trench and sent across no-man's-land.

On the other flank they found nothing; except for the handful of men they had encountered at first, the trench was empty. Where they had entered the trench, the three first lines converged rather closely, and they thought they were too far right. In spite of the party of Germans they had met, they assumed that the other waves of the assaulting troops were ahead of them, and decided to push on immediately, but with some misgivings. They were now about twenty-four men. In the light, the fog was coppery and charged with fumes. They heard in front of them the terrific battering of their own barrage and the drumming of the German guns. They had only moved a couple of yards from the trench when there was a crackle of musketry. Martlow was perhaps a couple of yards in front of Bourne, when he swayed a little, his knees collapsed under him, and he pitched forward on to his face, his feet kicking and his whole body convulsive for a moment. Bourne flung himself down beside him, and, putting his arms round his body, lifted him, calling him.

"Kid! You're all right, kid?" he cried eagerly.

He was all right. As Bourne lifted the limp body, the boy's hat came off, showing half the back of his skull shattered where the bullet had come through it; and a little blood welled out onto Bourne's sleeve and the knee of his trousers. He was all right, and Bourne let him settle to earth again, lifting himself up almost indifferently, unable to realise what had happened, filled with a kind of tenderness that ached in him, and yet extraordinarily still, extraordinarily cold.

He had to hurry, or he would be alone in the fog. Again he heard some rifle-fire, some bombing, and, stooping, he ran towards the sound, and was by Minton's side again, when three men ran towards them, holding their hands up and screaming. He lifted his rifle to his shoulder and fired, and the ache in him became a consuming hate that filled him with exultant cruelty, and he fired again, and again. The last man was closest to him, but as drunk and staggering with terror. He had scarcely fallen when Bourne came up to him and saw that his head was shattered, as he turned it over with his boot. Minton looking at him with a curious anxiety, saw Bourne's teeth clenched and bared, the lips snarling back from them in exultation.

"Come on. Get into it," Minton cried in his anxiety.

And Bourne struggled forward again, panting, and muttering in a suffocated voice.

"Kill the buggers! Kill the bloody fucking swine! Kill them!" All the filth and ordure he had ever heard came from his clenched teeth, but his speech was thick and difficult. In a scuffle immediately afterwards a Hun went for Minton, and Bourne got him with the bayonet, under the ribs near the liver, and then unable to wrench the bayonet out again, pulled the trigger, and it came away easily enough.

"Kill the buggers!" he muttered thickly.

He ran against Sergeant Tozer in the trench.

"Steady, of son! Steady. 'Ave you been 'it? You're all over blood."

"They killed the kid," said Bourne, speaking with sudden clearness, though his chest heaved enormously. "They killed him. I'll kill every bugger I see."

"Steady. You stay by me. I want you. Mr Finch 'as been 'it, see? You two come as well. Where's that bloody bomber?"

They searched about a hundred yards to the right, bombing a dugout from which no answer came, and again they collided with some small party of Huns, and, after some ineffective bombing, both sides drew away from each other. Jakes, with about ten men, had apparently got into the third line, and after similar bombing fights with small parties of Germans had come back again.

"Let's 'ave a dekko, sir," said Sergeant Tozer, taking Mr Finch's arm.

"It's all right," said the young man, infuriated; but the sergeant got his arm out of the sleeve, and bandaged a bullet wound near the shoulder. They were now convinced they could not go on by themselves. They decided to try and get into touch with any parties on the left. It was useless to go on, as apparently none of the other companies were ahead of them, and heavy machine-gun fire was coming from Serre. They worked up the trench to the left, and after some time, heard footsteps. The leading man held up a hand, and they were ready to bomb or bayonet, when a brave voice challenged them.

"Who are ye?"

"Westshires!" they shouted, and moved on, to meet a corporal and three men of the Gordons. They knew nothing of the rest of their battalion. They were lost, but they thought one of their companies had reached the front line. These four Gordons were four of the quickest and coolest men you could meet. There was some anxiety in the expression of their eyes, but it was only anxiety as to what they should do. Mr Finch ordered them to stay with him, and almost immediately they heard some egg-bombs. Some Huns were searching the trench. Sergeant Tozer, with the same party, went forward immediately. As soon as some egg-bombs had burst in the next bay, they rushed it, and flung into the next. They found and bayoneted a Hun, and pursued the others some little distance before they doubled back on their tracks again. Then Mr Finch took them back to the German front line, intending to stay there until he could link up with other parties. The fog was only a little less thick than the mud, but if it had been one of the principal causes of their failure, it helped them now. The Hun could not guess at their numbers; and there must have been several isolated parties playing the same game of hide-and-seek. The question for Mr Finch to decide was whether they should remain there. They searched the front line to the left, and found nothing but some dead, Huns and Gordons.

Bourne was with the Gordons who had joined them, and one of them, looking at the blood on his sleeve and hands, touched him on the shoulder.

"Mon, are ye hurt?" he whispered gently.

"No. I'm not hurt, chum," said Bourne, shaking his head slowly, and then he shuddered and was silent. His face became empty and expressionless.

Their own barrage had moved forward again, but they could not get into touch with any of their own parties. Then, to show how little he knew about what was happening, Fritz began to shell his own front line. They had some casualties immediately: a man called Adams was killed, and Minton was slightly wounded in the shoulder by a splinter. It was quite clear by this time that the other units had failed to penetrate even the first line. To remain where they were was useless, and to go forward was to invite destruction or capture.

"Sergeant," said Mr Finch, with a bitter resolution, "we shall go back."

Sergeant Tozer looked at him quietly. "You're wounded, sir," he said, kindly. "If you go back with Minton, I could hang on a bit longer, and then take the men back on my own responsibility."

"I'll be buggered if I go back with only a scratch, and leave you to stick it. You're a bloody sportsman, sergeant. You're the best bloody lot o' men..."

His words trailed off shakily into nothing for a moment. "That's all right, sir," said Sergeant Tozer, quietly, and then he added with an angry laugh, "We've done all we could. I don't care a fuck what the other bugger says."

"Get the men together, sergeant," said Mr Finch, huskily.

The sergeant went off and spoke to Jakes, and to the corporal of the Gordons. As he passed Bourne, who'd just put a dressing on Minton's wound, he paused.

"What 'appened to Shem?" he asked.

"Went back. Wounded in the foot."

"E were wounded early on, when Jerry dropped the barrage on us," explained Minton, stolidly precise as to facts.

"That bugger gets off everything with 'is feet," said Sergeant Tozer.

236

"E were gettin' off with 'is 'ands an' knees when I see'd 'im," said Minton, phlegmatically.

There was some delay as they prepared for their withdrawal. Bourne thought of poor old Shem, always plucky, and friendly, without sentiment, and quiet. Quite suddenly, as it were spontaneously, they climbed out of the trench and over the wire. The clangour of the shelling increased behind them. Fritz was completing the destruction of his own front line before launching a counterattack against empty air. They moved back very slowly and painfully, suffering a few casualties on the way, and they were already encumbered with wounded. One of the Gordons was hit, and his thigh broken. They carried him tenderly, soothing him with the gentleness of women. All the fire died out of them as they dragged themselves laboriously through the clinging mud. Presently they came to where the dead lay more thickly; they found some helplessly wounded, and helped them.

As they were approaching their own front line, a big shell, burying itself in the mud, exploded so close to Bourne that it blew him completely off his feet, and yet he was unhurt. He picked himself up, raving a little. The whole of their front and support trenches were being heavily shelled. Mr Finch was hit again in his already wounded arm. They broke up a bit, and those who were free ran for it to the trench. Men carrying or helping the wounded continued steadily enough. Bourne walked by Corporal Jakes, who had taken his place in carrying the wounded Gordon; he could not have hurried anyway, and once, unconsciously, he turned and looked back over his shoulder. Then they all slid into the wrecked trench.

Hearing that all their men had been ordered back to Dunmow, Mr Finch led the way down Blenau. His wounds had left him pallid and suffering, but he looked as though he would fight anything he met. He made a report to the adjutant, and went off with some other wounded to the dressing-station. The rest of them went on, crowded into a dugout, and huddled together without speaking, listening to the shells bumping above them. They got some tea, and wondered what the next move would be. Bourne was sitting next to the doorway when Jakes drew him out into a kind of recess, and handed him a mess-tin with some tea and rum in it.

"Robinson's gone down the line wounded, an' Sergeant Tozer's takin' over," he whispered.

Presently Sergeant Tozer joined them, and looked at Bourne, who sat there, drinking slowly and looking in front of him with fixed eyes. He spoke to Jakes about various matters of routine, and of further possibilities.

"There's some talk o' renewing the attack," he said shortly.

Jakes laughed with what seemed to be a cynical enjoyment. "O' course it's all our fuckin' fault, eh?' he asked grimly.

Sergeant Tozer didn't answer, but turned to Bourne.

"You don't want to think o' things," he said, with brutal kindness. "It's all past an' done wi', now."

Bourne looked at him in a dull acquiescence. Then he emptied the tin, replaced it on the bench, and, getting up, went to sit by the door again. He sat with his head flung back against the earth, his eyes closed, his arms relaxed, and hands idle in his lap, and he felt as though he were lifting a body in his arms, and looking at a small impish face, the brows puckered with a shadow of perplexity, bloody from a wound in the temple, the back of the head almost blown away; and yet the face was quiet, and unmoved by any trouble. He sat there for hours, immobile and indifferent, unaware that Sergeant Tozer glanced at him occasionally. The shelling gradually died away, and he did not know it. Then Sergeant Tozer got up angrily.

"Ere, Bourne. Want you for sentry. Time that other man were relieved."

He took up his rifle and climbed up, following the sergeant into the frosty night. Then he was alone, and the fog frothed and curdled about him. He became alert, intent again, his consciousness hardening in him. After about half an hour, he heard men coming along the trench; they came closer; they were by the corner.

"Stand!" he cried in a long, low note of warning.

"Westshire. Officer and rations."

He saw Mr White, to whom Captain Marsden came up and spoke. Some men passed him, details and oddments, carrying bags of rations. Suddenly he found in front of him the face of Snobby Hines, grinning excitedly.

"What was it like, Bourne?" he asked, in passing.

"Hell," said Bourne briefly.

Snobby moved on, and Bourne ignored the others completely. Bloody silly question, to ask a man what it was like. He looked up to the sky, and through the travelling mist saw the half-moon with a great halo round it. An extraordinary peace brooded over everything. It seemed only the more intense because an occasional shell sang through it.

Chapter XVII

...on their watch
In the dread east and middle of the night.
– SHAKESPEARE

All the following day they were heavily shelled, and their own guns developed a terrific intensity of fire.

"There's too much fuckin' artillery in this bloody war," said Jakes irritably, as though they had all failed to appreciate the fact. "You don't get no sleep."

He had slept placidly through every interval of duty. Towards evening it became quieter, and they were relieved, marching back to Bus. The village, with its chinks of light in the windows, seemed indifferent and unsympathetic. It had a hard, cold reality, and was as squalid and comfortless as truth.

Bourne was ordered to remain with A Company for the present, and he went across to the signallers' hut to get his pack and bedding. He saw Corporal Hamley, and faced the inevitable questions. He heard that Glazier had been killed in their own front line, and Madeley wounded, apparently by the same shell. Weeper, dumping the ridiculous flapper, had taken over Madeley's job; he was the only man close to the corporal's corner, and he listened without joining in the conversation. Then Bourne told them about Martlow. He spoke in level, almost indifferent tones. There was not a trace of emotion in his voice, and yet he seemed to see the boy objectively in front of him. Corporal Hamley showed much more feeling, and when Bourne began to tell him about Shem, he rose abruptly, and got Martlow's kit, which Bourne had tried not to see. There was one thing that Bourne did not want to do, and yet he knew he would have to do it, however strongly he might resist it. Corporal Hamley's fingers were holding a letter, and Bourne could see the address, and below it, to the left, the firm, rather business-like handwriting, flowing across the page: My darling Boy. He looked across the hut with an indifferent air, and the address seemed to be scrawled upon the darkness.

"Poor old Shem," he said softly. "I'm glad he got away with it."

"Some buggers 'ave all the bloody luck," said the corporal enviously.

And Bourne wondered why the dead should be a reproach to the living. They seemed so still, and so indifferent, the dead. Corporal Hamley went out of the but without speaking again, taking the boy's kit with him; the company office was only next door. Bourne collected his own things to go, and, as he was passing, Weeper Smart put out his hand.

"A'm real grieved," was all he said.

"Thanks. Goodnight, Smart," said Bourne, a little shakily, as their hands dropped again.

When he got back to A Company's hut, he found Sergeant-Major Tozer with a crown on his sleeve.

"Are you going out tonight, son?"

"I'm too tired, sergeant-major," he said, reluctantly. "I think I'll get down to it early tonight."

"That's all right," said the sergeant-major, approvingly. "But there's some buckshee rum in the company office, an' you'll sleep better wi' a bit of a skinful. You come along with me."

They found the regimental in A Company's office, talking to the quarter-bloke. The sorrow of men is often angry and recalcitrant.

"It was bloody hard luck," he was saying in a low, uneven voice. "I can tell you I'll go a long way before I find another man like Barton."

Still shaken and dazed, Bourne tried to realise that some shattered fragments of poor Barton lay out neglected in the engulfing mud, and these men were talking of him with kindly regretful voices, praising him for the qualities which he had really possessed, and then the unreasoning anger of the regimental broke out again.

"They might have given him a bloody chance."

"I suppose one man can't expect to have no more chance than another," said Quartermaster-Sergeant Hales quietly.

"I'm fed up with the bloody life," said the regimental, and Bourne knew by his voice that he was looking for trouble, but they all sat there for some time, drinking rum, and talking about dead men. They had not suffered very heavily in casualties. When Tozer got up to go, Bourne was glad to follow him, and then surprised to find himself walking a little unsteadily. That much of the stuff wouldn't have gone to his head six months ago. He undressed partly, and rolled himself up in his blanket, feeling friendless and miserable. Then he fell into sudden sleep. He became aware of himself walking through a fog, only less thick than the mud underneath; it became almost impossible to breathe in it, and then he felt the mud sucking him down, he could not extricate his feet from it, and shells burst all round him with jagged red lightnings, and then terrible hands, terrible dead hands came out of that living mud and fastened onto him, dragging him down inexorably, and the mud seemed full of rusty cruel wire, and men with exultant bestial faces rushed at him, and he fought, fought desperately.

"'Ere," said Corporal Jakes, "what's the bloody fuss about?"

Bourne woke to find himself trying to strangle the astonished man who slept next to him, and Jakes disengaging him from his victim.

"It's all right, kid. 'e's on'y dreamin'."

"Dreamin'! What's 'e want to go dreamin' all over the fuckin' 'ut for?" asked Bourne's exasperated victim.

Bourne muttered some unintelligible apologies as he rolled himself up in his blanket.

"If you don't use any bad language when you're awake, you make up for it in your sleep," observed Corporal Jakes, as he settled himself again to his disturbed slumbers.

In the morning, almost the first thing Bourne heard was that the regimental, after a quarrel with Reynolds, the orderly-room sergeant, had insisted on seeing the adjutant, in order to obtain an assurance of his own perfect sobriety. The adjutant had found the question too nice a one to be settled without medical advice; and the regimental was a prisoner awaiting a court-martial, as a result of the doctor's quite unqualified decision against him. Bourne found him in a bell-tent behind the huts, with the sergeant-major of D Company, whose prisoner he was. He was unrepentant, and full of contempt for life, talking to Bourne only of licentious nights in Milharbour. One could not help admiring the way he declined to share his troubles with anyone.

There was only one parade in the morning, rollcall, and Bourne had to give Captain Marsden details of Martlow's end, and of Adams's, and then to describe Minton's wound. Pritchard told about Shem's wound, and corroborated Bourne's evidence on some points about the others. It was a long, disconsolate business. In the afternoon they moved up to take over the new front line to the right of Blenau. They were all indifferent; it was a matter of routine.

A couple of days later, in the small hours of the morning, Bourne was on the fire-step, and Corporal Jakes was asleep in the same bay. The weather had become much clearer. After a time, Bourne seemed to forget his own existence; not that he was dreaming, or was unaware of the world about him, for every nerve was stretched to the limit of apprehension. Staring into the darkness, behind which menace lurked, equally vigilant and furtive, his consciousness had pushed out through it, to take possession, gradually, and foot by foot, of some forty or fifty yards of territory within which nothing moved or breathed without his knowledge of it. Beyond this was a more dubious obscurity, into which he could only grope without certainty. The effort of mere sense to exceed its normal function had ended for the moment at least, not only in obliterating his own identity and merging it with those objects of sense which he did actually perceive but in dissolving even their objective reality into something incredible and fantastic. He had become so accustomed to them that they had ceased to have any reality or significance for him.

The night was quiet. Puddles and flat wet surfaces reflected what was no more than a reminiscence of light. Against the skyline he could see strands of wire, and the uprights leaning awry and beyond them little waifs of diaphanous mist drifting into the darkness. The darkness itself changed continually, clearing at times to a curious transparency and then clouding again. The moon was behind a bank of cloud in the west, but the stars sparkled with the brilliance they gain from frost. At intervals the silence became so intense that he almost expected it to crack like ice. Then the whine of a shell would traverse it, or several in succession pass overhead, a pack in full cry; and there were dull explosions, or the sudden stutter of a machine-gun in the distance. The mind, so delicately sensitive to the least vibration from the outer world, no longer recorded it in the memory unless it had some special relevance. The sound for which he was waiting was that of a stumble in the dark, or of a shaken, creaking wire, and that for which his eyes sought, where darkness swallowed up the travelling wraiths of mist, was a crawling shadow advancing stealthily towards him.

It was such an unearthly stillness that he almost prayed for something to happen, so that he might kill, or be killed. Sooner or later it would come, out of the hostile night. He waited in motion less expectancy, his tin hat tilted forward slightly over his eyes and gleaming very faintly, as his waterproof groundsheet, worn capewise and tied at the neck with a bootlace through two of its eyelets gleamed also from the damp air which had condensed on it.

Corporal Jakes slept. Bourne could hear his breathing, but for that matter he could hear his own breathing, as though it came from a third man. Then, within that territory, which had become as it were his whole mind, something shifted, and he drew in his breath quickly, all his previously passive awareness concentrating itself purposively on one point. It was almost imperceptible, as though a clod of mud had shifted a little; but it continued, something separated itself from the mass, and the intaken breath escaped from him in a sigh of disgust, as a rat came hurrying, with a quick dainty movement of its twinkling feet, towards him. Seeing him, it stopped a few yards from the parapet, its muzzle twitching sensitively, sat up, sleek and well-fed, to stroke its whiskers with its forepaws; then, avoiding the puddles and shellholes, turned aside in a direction parallel to the trench, not taking a straight path, but picking its way delicately along the ridges, as though to keep its feet dry.

Rats nauseated him. He shifted his stand slightly, feeling cramped and cold. His mittens were caked with wet mud, and the stock of his rifle was greasy with moisture. A thin stalk of silver shot up into the sky, curved over, and flowered into a sphere of light, which expanded, pulsating, to flood the pocked earth beneath it; falling slowly, it dwindled, and was engulfed again abruptly in darkness. For those few seconds Private Bourne was motionless, and then he changed his position, moving towards the other corner of the bay. A machine-gun stammered angrily. The sleeper roused himself and sat up, pushing his tin hat back from his face.

"Is Fritz gettin' the fuckin' wind up?" he asked, sleepily.

"It's quiet enough," answered Bourne, carelessly, in little more than a whisper.

"Stand easy, and I'll take a spell. It's about time they relieved you."

He stood up on the step, and then they both swerved, ducking quickly as something ripped up the air between them, flicked a stone from the parados, and sang, like the vibration of a tense wire, into the air behind them. Bourne recovered from the instinctive movement first, slid his rifle into a new position, and, crouching a little closer to earth, waited.

"That bugger's too bloody personal," said Corporal Jakes with some appreciation.

Bourne said nothing. Now that the tension of his solitary watch had been relieved, he felt tired and irritable. The movements and whispers of the other man only exasperated his angry nerves. A sniper's bullet has too definite an aim and purpose to be dismissed from the mind as soon as it is spent, like the explosion of a more or less random shell. Even a machine-gun, searching for possibilities with a desultory spray, did not have quite the same intimate effect. So Bourne crouched a little lower over his rifle.

The Hun certainly had become suspicious of that brooding quiet. Lower down the line, on the left, another star-shell rose to spill its hoary light over that waterlogged desolation, and it had scarcely died when another took its place. Bourne was vainly trying to regain control over the narrow territory he had possessed so securely a little while ago. His impassive face was thrust forward, and the beaky nose between the feverishly bright eyes, the salient cheekbones above the drawn cheeks, the thin-lipped mouth, set, but too sensitive not to have a hint of weakness in it, and the obstinate jaw, had a curiously still alertness in its expression. He raised his head a few inches, to get a clearer view, and then, directly to his front, a third shell burst into spectral radiance. He was motionless, in the glare, but his eyes turned searchingly half-right, towards a heap of shattered rubble, something over a hundred yards away, the remains of some farm building. Jakes, too, confronted possibilities with a stolid indifference. Then the light died again, and Bourne turned to his companion.

"He hadn't spotted us," he said under his breath; "he just took a chance at the trench."

And Jakes looked at Bourne with a solemn face.

"Don't you trust the bastard," he said with pointed brevity.

Sergeant-Major Tozer with the relief came along the trench. They were a little overdue. When Jakes mentioned the sniper, the sergeant-major turned to Bourne.

"Where do you reckon he is?" he asked, quietly.

245

"In that building rubbish," answered Bourne, without conviction. "There's a heap of bricks left, where the chimney collapsed: that's where I think he is."

"You don't want to think," was Tozer's comment. "If Captain Marsden asks you anything about it, you want to be sure, see? They got Brigadier-General Bullock just about 'ere, an' that will give our chaps a kind of interest in the matter."

He spoke a few words to the men on the fire-step, and led the way towards the dugout, Jakes and Bourne following him.

"There's a chance you're right," said Tozer, without looking round, "an' if so, I want 'im shifted."

Stooping in turn, they felt for the steps with their feet. Two had given, from the wet, and had been converted into a muddy slide. A third of the way down, a blanket, frosty with damp, shut off the starlight from them. Groping in darkness they found at the bottom another blanket, muffling the light within. As Bourne entered, his nostrils dilated at the reek, as though some instinct of a beast survived in him. Each of the fluttering candles had a halo round it. The smoke from them, and tobacco, and acrid fumes from a brazier, could not mask the stale smell of unwashed men, and serges into which had soaked and dried the sweat of months. Some few men who were awake looked up as they entered, showing impassive faces, with hard, bright eyes. The majority slept, a little restlessly, and were scarcely more than shadows in the uncertain light.

About a third of the dugout, which had two entrances, had been screened off from the rest by blankets; and there the officers had their quarters.

"Captain Marsden wants to ask you something, corporal," said Tozer. "Bourne, you'd better come, too."

They passed behind the blankets, and Captain Marsden looked up, exactly as the men had done, and with the same impassive face and hard eyes, while Mr Sothern slept with the same frowning brows. They were all equally damned.

"Corporal Jakes, sir," said the sergeant-major, by way of introduction.

"Oh, yes," said Captain Marsden, a trace of anxiety vanishing from his face. "Corporal, when you were out on patrol with Mr Sothern, I hear that you saw a corporal dead in a shellhole. Is that right?"

"Yes, sir," answered Jakes, with no more than his usual solemnity; "'e were lyin' 'ead down in a shell'ole; with 'is feet on the rim. It were a fairly fresh 'ole, sir. Not much water in it."

"Ah," said Captain Marsden. "Did you know Corporal Evans, of D Company?"

"No, sir. I 'ad 'eard the name, sir, but I can't say I knew 'im, not personally; 'e 'ad only come to the battalion lately, sir."

"I see. If he had been Corporal Evans, who is missing, you could not have identified the body; but you are quite sure the body you saw was that of a corporal?"

"Yes, sir. I noticed 'e 'ad a couple o' stripes up. What I noticed was 'is overcoat. It were a good overcoat, nearly new; an' I've been lookin' out for a good overcoat a long while now, but I didn't lave time to get it. A few shells came over, an' Mr Sothern seemed in a 'urry..."

The officer looked with some severity at a face innocent of offence.

"You don't even know his regiment?" he continued, interrogatively. "No; of course, as you say, there was no time."

He spoke in a low even voice, almost as though preoccupied with other matters. Then he looked up again.

"But I suppose you can describe him to some extent, can't you, corporal? Was he a small man? How do you think he had been killed?"

"'E were a biggish man, sir, bigger'n I am; seemed tallish, lyin' there. 'E were lyin' on 'is face, an' I could only see the back of 'is 'ead. I thing 'e 'ad been shot."

"Corporal Evans was last seen the day we came up; but for all you know the man you saw might have been lyin' there for weeks, eh?"

"No, sir. 'E couldn't lave been dead long, because the rats 'adn't begun on 'im."

"Ah, I see. Rats are rather bad round here, corporal, eh? Well, that's all we shall ever know, I suppose. I am very sorry about Evans, they tell me he was a good man. What do you want, Bourne?"

As he turned to Bourne his manner became perceptibly colder.

"Beg pardon, sir," said Sergeant-Major Tozer. "Just before being relieved, Corporal Jakes and Bourne were fired on by a sniper. Bourne thinks he saw him."

Bourne was about to protest, but something in Captain Marsden's manner prevented him. Both men felt some embarrassment on such occasions as these, for although the conventions which separated officers from men were relaxed to some extent on active service, between men of roughly the same class they tended to become more rigid. Even when momentarily alone together, they recognised, tacitly, something a little ambiguous in the relation in which they stood to each other, and with a non-commissioned officer intervening, as in the present case, the difficulty became greater. Even before the lie which rounded off Sergeant-Major Tozer's statement so effectively had been uttered, Captain Marsden had taken up an indelible pencil from the ramshackle table, on which one of the versatile army blankets did duty as a cloth, and was contemplating the point with an air of judicial detachment.

"Oh," he said crisply. "Did you see anything, corporal?"

"No, sir," answered Jakes, "but I could swear that bullet came atween us.'

"Really the only thing you could swear is that a bullet came unpleasantly close to you," said Captain Marsden with a trace of sarcasm.

Sergeant-Major Tozer stiffened a little at his company officer's apparent indifference.

"I'm afraid, sir, I spoke a bit 'asty. Private Bourne didn't exactly see where the shot came from, but as 'e seemed pretty certain, I thought you might like to know about it. Sniping 'as been rather troublesome in this sector. It was only about twenty yards from where Bourne was standing that the brigadier was 'it, an' then there's this Corporal Evans, sir."

"Well, Bourne," said Captain Marsden, impatiently, "what have you got to say?"

"I think the shot came from that direction, sir. It is the sort of place in which I should post a sniper, if it were my job. It is difficult to judge from the sound, but I think the bullet came between us, and it certainly hit a stone behind us.'

"Well, I had better see for myself, I suppose. You needn't come, sergeant-major. Get a bit of rest before stand-to."

There was a touch of kindliness in his voice, and the sergeant-major, without attaching too much importance to it, felt less ruffled. He found it always a little difficult to guess what his company officer was thinking, or what effect any of his own suggestions might have on Captain Marsden's conduct of affairs.

Bourne followed his officer up the steps, and into the cold starlight, without speaking. After a few paces, Captain Marsden spoke.

"You know, Bourne," he said; "Sergeant-Major Tozer thinks I am likely to pay more attention to what you say, and of course to some extent that is right; but it doesn't do to allow that kind of impression to spread. Oh, I know the place you mean. I wondered why Jerry had not included it in his trench system."

Bourne did not see why Captain Marsden should take the trouble to explain to him. He felt rather resentful, but he had been strange in his behaviour since the attack.

"There's nothing there, sir," he said. "Nothing but the remains of the chimney; no cellars..."

"How do you know that?"

"I went out there once, with Mr Finch, sir, to look at their wire. Almost as soon as we got across we heard a Hun patrol coming towards us. We crouched down, we were in a dip in the ground, and could see them through the mist against the light. Mr Finch motioned us to keep quiet. I expected every second that someone would loose off a round. Six buck Huns and only the pull of a trigger between them and peace, perfect peace. It was too easy. They looked like shadows on a window-blind. They had crossed the line we had taken, and passed diagonally behind us, between us and our own wire. After they had passed us, we went on for quite a long way, and coming back we passed through those building remains. There was nothing to be seen but a few light tracks."

They were challenged by a low voice, and then Captain Marsden got up on the fire-step, but could not pick up the mound of rubble even with his glasses. It needed a star-shell behind it to make it clearly visible; even by daylight it was almost indistinguishable from its surroundings.

"Everything quiet?" he asked the boy beside him.

"Aye, sir, but sergeant-major, 'e said there were a sniper about. They send up a star-shell now and again, but not close. A can just see t' place, but th' art not used to t' light yet."

Captain Marsden searched the night again, but could not pick it up. He decided in his mind that as the boy had seen it under a starshell, he imagined he still saw it, an image remaining on the retina, after darkness had hidden the object again. Then a distant star-shell revealed it, exactly where the boy had said it was. Captain Marsden made the most of his opportunity, and stepped down again.

"You keep your eyes skinned, m' lad," he said, cheerfully. "You may see something interesting over there, yet. All right, Bourne. We shall go back. I suppose you'll get some tea, or something, and a smoke. I'm glad I came out, and glad you knew something about the place. I knew there were no cellars, but I was wondering how you had got to know. A good fellow, Finch; always knew how to concentrate on the job he was doing, and he did a lot of good work. Did very well in the attack, too, and got a nice blighty. I'm glad you're going to become one of us, Bourne. You should have gone for a commission long ago. Perhaps the colonel will see you after we are relieved."

He acknowledged Bourne's salute, and left him, Bourne going into the dugout by the other entrance. After duly slipping on the two damaged steps with the invariable surprise, and curses, Bourne found Sergeant-Major Tozer and Corporal Jakes in their corner.

"There's a drop o' tea still 'ot," said the sergeant-major, "an' your rum ration."

"What's 'e goin' to do about it?" inquired Jakes more directly.

"Well, he didn't let me into any secrets," said Bourne, "but I believe, corporal, he wants you to go out and bury that man you saw."

"It's a funny thing," said Jakes with the utmost seriousness; "but I'd like to think I'd be buried, that is, if I were scuppered, you know. What gets me with the captain is the way 'e talks to you, as though you weren't there. 'Ave you noticed that, sergeant?"

Sergeant-Major Tozer, on principle, disapproved of a corporal expressing any opinion about his company commander; but for once he condoned a fault.

"What gets me," he said, with even greater vehemence, "is the way 'e looks at you from be'ind 'is face."

"Orderly," came a voice from behind the blankets, and a runner emerged from stupor and answered in clumsy haste. Bourne lit a cigarette, after passing his tin to the other two, and then leaned back against the damp wall. He looked round cursorily on those faces, from which sleep had banished all expression save of hopeless weariness. Pritchard and himself, apart from Tozer of course, were the only two men left of the men composing their section on the Somme in July. The rest were all strangers to him.

Then he seemed to see Martlow in front of him: a freakish schoolboy, jealous, obstinate in all resentments, but full of generous impulses, distrusting the whole world, and yet open and impressionable when one had gained his confidence. He had come up to Shem and himself casually at Sandpits, after the last Guillemont show, and had sat with them ever since. It had been just a chance encounter. They had been three people without a single thing in common; and yet there was no bond stronger than that necessity which had bound them together. They had never encroached on each other's independence. If the necessity had been removed, they would have parted, keeping nothing of each other but a vague memory, grateful enough, though without substance. Shem was all right, he had gone his own way, but Martlow would go no farther, and Bourne would always see those puckered brows, and feel the weight of him. He closed his eyes.

The boy on the fire step watched his front intently. The expectation that he would see something move, or a sudden flash there, became almost desire. But nothing moved. The world grew more and more still; the dark became thinner; soon they would stand to. He could see the remains of the building now, almost clearly. There was nothing there, nothing, the world was empty, hushed, awaiting dawn. And then, as he watched it less keenly, something from the skies smote that heap of rubble, the shadowy landscape in front of him blurred and danced, and a solid pillar of darkness rose into the air even before he heard the explosion, spreading out thicker at the top like an evil fungus; spread, and dissolved again, and the heap of rubble was no longer there.

"Christ!" said the boy. "That were a good 'un."

Chapter XVIII

Fortune? O, most true; she is a strumpet. – SHAKESPEARE

After another tour in the trenches, their rest billets were changed, and they moved to huts in Bus wood. A court-martial reduced the regimental sergeant-major to the rank of a sergeant, and he was sent to A Company under Sergeant-Major Tozer. He took it very well, but became rather unapproachable, though Bourne sometimes succeeded in drawing him out of himself. Tozer handled him tactfully, never consulting him, and yet taking his opinion, when he offered it, very much as though they were of equal rank. He knew how to nurse a sorry man. The men, too, no longer bore him any ill-will, his punishment wiped out any score they may have had against him, but his manner did not change perceptibly, even though his conduct became more circumspect, he still faced matters in his own rather arrogant and scornful way.

Bourne himself had become rather melancholy and unsociable. Chance threw him fairly often in the way of Morgan, the bombing sergeant, and they would go out together from time to time, to a house in Bus where they could get rum and coffee, and talk in quiet. Morgan drank very little, and was seldom seen in an estaminet. He was a keen, dapper, confident little man. Sometimes a tall man with a gipsy face, one of the bombers, would join them. Bourne had first seen him at Reclinghem, when they had been billeted together; and, as he never seemed to get any letters or parcels, Bourne had asked him to share in his occasionally. They had become more or less friendly, and one day Bourne asked him what he had done in civil life.

"I was at school," he said, after a moment's hesitation.

Bourne looked at him in amazement, as he was at least thirty years old, and Whitfield explained quite simply that he had been serving a sentence in gaol. Apparently he was a burglar, but he made no attempt to justify his choice of a profession which was both hazardous and ill-paid; and Bourne, recovering from a momentary bewilderment, accepted his statement as confidential, and kept the matter to himself. He liked

Whitfield, who after all was a bomber, was labouring in his vocation, but though he kept the man's secret, he once turned to Sergeant Morgan and asked him what Whitfield had done before the war.

"E kept a bicycle repair shop," said Morgan. "'E's a bloody good man, you know, one of the best I've got. I've recommended 'im for a stripe once or twice, but they don't seem to take no notice. 'E doesn't mind, but I'll keep on recommending 'im. You ought to come out with me some night, when we're up in the tronshay. A lot o' the men don't see it, but it's a good game really. You're free to do very much as you please. O' course you get your orders, an' they make up some kind of a plan, but that's all eyewash.

You've got to forget all that as soon as you start, an' make your own arrangements as you go on. I've taken out quite a lot o' officers now, an' they're all the same, pretty decent chaps as a rule. They draw up a plan, an' then they just come to me an' ask me to take a glance at it, an' see if it's all right. It's all right, sir, I always say to 'em; you just bung it in at th' orderly-room, an' we'll do what's possible. On'y one officer ever gave me any trouble, a chap attached to us, no names no pack-drill, but 'e were a bastard, 'e were. Military Cross, an' bar; reg'lar pot-'unter; an' we lost one o' the best corporals we've ever 'ad through that bloody man. Wouldn't be told, 'e wouldn't."

Bourne knew something of the story, but he was not paying much attention. Very slowly, and less as a possibility than as a kind of dream, there woke in him a desire to see and explore a little of the Hun trenches again. The desire grew, fascinating him, and then faded again, as a dream might, for he knew the reality too well. They finished their rum and coffee, and walked back together to the huts.

"Where've you been?" said Sergeant-Major Tozer. "I don't seem to get much time these days, but I was lookin' for you tonight. Thought we might go out an' see what was doin' in this bloody 'ole."

"Sergeant-major," said Bourne, "we won't go out. I'll try and scrounge a bottle of whisky, and we'll have a spree tomorrow night in the company office, with Sergeant Hope and Corporal Jakes. Never mind how I'll get it. You're not supposed to know that; it's not in Infantry Training."

All the talk in the camp on the following morning was about Miller the deserter, who had been arrested near Calais, and had been brought back under escort.

"Wish they'd shot the bugger, an' saved us the trouble," was all Sergeant-Major Tozer said.

"He gave you the slip all right, sergeant-major," said Sergeant Hope, with a laugh that sounded a little supercilious.

"He gave me the slip all right," admitted Tozer, "but then he wasn't a prisoner."

A new regimental sergeant-major had come to them from another battalion some days earlier. Hope knew him a little, and said he was a pukka soldier, reserved and strict, but very reasonable. He came into A Company's hut and asked for Bourne at half-past five that afternoon, and when Bourne came to him at the double, he was told to make himself look smart, as he was to go before the commanding officer at six o'clock about his commission. For the moment Bourne felt an almost uncontrollable desire to draw back, if possible; then he accepted the situation, and went to brush up and wash. While he was rolling on his puttees again, Sergeant Hope came to him.

"D'you mind asking the regimental to come along tonight, too?" he asked.

"You ask him, sergeant," said Bourne characteristically.

"No bloody fear," said Hope. "I don't mind letting him know what's in the wind. He's a jolly good sport, is old Traill, though he does stand a bit on his dignity; it will be all right if you tell him it's just a kind of farewell drink together; but it wouldn't do for us to ask him. He would think we had put you up to getting it, but after you've seen the colonel you could ask him."

A little reluctantly Bourne agreed, but he felt awkward about it, because after all he did not know the regimental, and the whole business was, to say the least, irregular. As soon as he was dressed, the regimental looked him over.

"As you are ready," he said, "we may as well walk down. I want to have a talk to you."

They set off together, walking slowly, and even stopping; and he had his talk. He knew as much about Bourne as anybody in the battalion knew, evidently; and his remarks were very much to the point. Discipline was discipline, he said, though one allowed a certain latitude to the reasonable man.

"You're quite right to be friendly with everyone, so long as you behave yourself, and don't try to take advantage. All the same, you know, some of the men with whom you're friendly may be all right in their place, but you don't want to judge the whole army by them. You will have to forget a lot, and begin again; that is, you will have to take a different view. You know the men. But when you're an officer you won't know your men. You'll be lucky if you know your N.C.O.'s, and you'll have to leave a lot of it to them. You'll have to keep them up to the mark; but you'll have to trust them, and let them know it."

He went into the orderly-room, and presently resumed to take in Bourne. The colonel was sitting at his table, which was covered by the invariable blanket, and apparently Bourne's business was only one of many matters engaging his attention. He seemed thoughtful and preoccupied rather than tired, and he looked at Bourne with his inflexible blue-grey eyes, while he questioned him about himself and his life. His manner seemed to grow a little kindlier, without ceasing to be detached, as he proceeded. Then, without asking any more questions, he gave Bourne some advice which did not differ substantially from the regimental's.

"I shall make you a lance-corporal," he said in conclusion. "It may be some weeks before the matter goes through; and you will have to go before the brigadier-general for his approval. I think they're very lucky to get you, as I feel sure you will make a good officer."

Bourne thanked him, saluted, and left. Outside, he waited for the regimental in a curious state of pleasurable excitement. The colonel's praise and encouragement filled him with gratitude, but something warred against his elation; he felt through all his excitement some intractable regret, and could only say to himself what he had said through all the past months: one is bound to try, one is not bound to succeed. Then the regimental came out to him.

"Sir," said Bourne, "as I may be going away at any time now, I asked Sergeant-Major Tozer, and Sergeant Hope and Corporal Jakes to have a drink with me tonight; and I should be very glad of your company too. I have a bottle of Scotch whisky."

The regimental wondered how he had got it, and noticing Bourne's anxiety, he concealed a smile with a hand stroking his moustache.

"I suppose it's an exceptional occasion," he said, quietly. "I'll come along at eight. After all, a bottle of whisky will do less harm to five men than to four."

He walked into the dusk, and Bourne went to his hut.

"How did you get on with the C.O.?" said Sergeant Hope. "There's a letter there for you."

Bourne picked up the letter with a shock of surprise. It was a cheap, shiny envelope with a thin black edge to it, addressed in a woman's handwriting which was old-fashioned, precise, and easily recognised. He saw the postmark, Squelesby.

"Oh, all right," he said absently.

"Is the regimental coming in tonight?" Hope asked him.

"Yes," he answered, even forgetting to add the customary "sergeant".

Hope looked at him curiously, and said nothing more. Bourne, getting closer to the candle, opened the letter and read it. It was from Mrs Martlow.

He returned it to its envelope and buttoned it into his breast-pocket. Martlow had told his mother all about him, even that he would miss him when he went "to be made an officer"; and Bourne found himself remembering the walk back to Reclinghem from Vincly, and the old priest, hatless in the twilight, and the reproach in the boy's voice as he asked him whether what Sergeant-Major Robinson had said were true.

Presently he got up, and walked out between the trees for a little while. He felt restless. The extraordinary reserve and courage in this woman's letter, the painful way in which she reached out for Bourne, piecing him together out of her son's letters, as though he kept something of him which she had lost, that, too, seemed a reproach to him. He had heard nothing of Shem. Shem was in a hospital somewhere, recovering from his wound, but he had vanished completely, so completely that Bourne did not even expect to hear from him again. Men passed out of sight like that, and seemed to leave very little trace. Their term had been completed. Martlow, for some reason he could not grasp, persisted in his memory, seemed to be only out of sight, behind the hut, as it were, or even just on the point of coming through the doorway. Bourne went back and sat with Hope.

"You haven't had any bad news, have you?" Hope asked him.

"No, sergeant. Oh, you mean the letter. No, it was only an answer."

They went off together to the hut used as a company office and store; and found Corporal Jakes there with Sergeant-Major Tozer. Presently the regimental arrived, and, taking out his jack-knife, Bourne drew the cork slowly and softly, Jakes mimicking the sound of it with his tongue against the roof of his mouth, and immediately looking as though he had made a breach of good manners. Bourne paid more attention to the regimental and to Corporal Jakes than to the other two; because apparently the R.S.M. found it a little difficult to throw off a certain presidential air, and Jakes, feeling some constraint, looked rather as though his clothes were too tight. That awkwardness wore off. Some kind of warmth and excitement came into Bourne's blood as they laughed at his stories.

"You seem in a pretty good skin tonight," said Sergeant-Major Tozer.

"Well, I suppose you'll 'ave a lance stripe up tomorrow, an' then it'll be goodbye in no time. Funny thing, life. We just sit 'ere an' talk as though we'd sit 'ere for ever, an' when one or two ol' friends drop out, an' one or two new uns come along, it don't seem no different some'ow. All the same, I expect we'll remember you longer'n you'll remember us."

"Damn it," said the regimental, very reasonably, "you can't forget a man who finds a bottle o' Scotch in a place like this."

"Have some more, sir? Corporal?"

"Just a spot more. Merci blow-through," said the corporal.

"I mean we'll be still 'ere," explained Tozer; "an' you'll be out of it. It won't seem real to you any longer."

"You don't want to think about things," said Corporal Jakes. They all started talking in a desultory way about the war. The regimental was confident, but had no illusions. It could only end when Germany had been beaten, but the end seemed a long way off yet.

"I lost my elder boy," he said quietly.

Bourne looked at him, at once. Here was a man with a personal feeling against the Hun, and it was curious how seldom one thought of men except as soldiers. One forgot that they were husbands, or fathers, or sons; they were just a lot of anonymous men.

They talked and drank together quietly while the whisky lasted. It was a break; they became easy, comfortable, friendly with each other, and then they went their several ways to sleep.

Bourne was in orders for a stripe next day, and went to the tailors to get it sewn on his sleeve at once. He gave the tailors some money to wet it.

"I suppose you'll be goin' out on a bit of a spree wi' the S.M. an' Sergeant 'ope tonight," said Snobby Hines, approvingly.

"No, I'm going to kip," said Bourne. "Sergeant Hope's on guard tonight."

In the morning Miller, the deserter, had assumed heroic proportions. He was a prisoner in the police tent, right at the edge of a quarry, with three of the police sleeping there and a sentry outside. In the night he had crawled out under the skirt of the tent, and climbed down the quarry in the dark, then he had crept back into the camp and stolen one of the orderlies' bicycles.

"That bugger deserves to get off," said Sergeant-Major Tozer, but the unlucky Sergeant Hope, who was the person responsible, shoved a revolver into his pocket, took another bicycle, and scoured the country like a desperate man. Even when he returned, empty-handed, he could not say all he felt. In the afternoon they moved up to the front-line trenches.

Brigade had ordered them to make a raid to secure identifications, and the various companies were asked to provide volunteers. Weeper Smart, who had been down to the headquarters dugout to get something, had brought back the message. With Lance-Corporal Eames and a man called Jackson, he had been attached to A Company as signaller for that tour in the trenches. He handed the message to Sergeant-Major Tozer, who gave it to Captain Marsden; and they discussed the matter in a low tone of voice. The Hun had become a little troublesome in no-man's-land, and it was a mistake to let him have too much of his own way.

"Mr Cross will be in charge, with Sergeant Morgan and ten men."

Bourne had been out with a fatigue party, draining a low-lying bit of trench which needed the pump daily. The trenches were rotten with wet, and when the frost gave, the sides tended to collapse. He had brought his men back to the dugout by the time Captain Marsden and Sergeant-Major Tozer had digested the message, and Captain Marsden looked up and saw him, muddy up to the thighs.

"Lance-Corporal, we're to make a raid tonight. I believe you know something about the lie of the land up here. Do you wish to make one of the party? We're asking for volunteers."

"Lance-corporal Bourne is down for a commission, sir," interposed Sergeant-Major Tozer, "and per'aps..."

"I know all that," said Captain Marsden, shortly. "What do you say, lance-corporal?"

Bourne felt something in him dilate enormously, and then contract to nothing again.

"If you wish it, sir," he said, indifferently.

"It's not a question of my wishes," said Captain Marsden, coldly. "We are asking for volunteers. I think the experience may be useful to you."

"I am quite ready, sir," said Bourne, with equal coldness. There was silence for a couple of seconds; and suddenly Weeper stood up, the telephone receiver still on his head; and his eyes almost starting from their sockets.

"If tha go'st, a'm goin'," he said, solemnly.

Captain Marsden looked at him with a supercilious amazement.

"I don't know whether your duties will allow of you going," he said. "I shall put your name down provisionally."

A young man called Gaymer volunteered; no one else. They got some food, and sat in silence, smoking. After some time, Bourne, Smart and Gaymer were told to report themselves outside H.Q. dugout at once. The trenches by day were as forlorn and desolate as by night, but without the enveloping mystery. Everything was stark, bare and cold; one crept within the skeleton ribs of the earth. The party gradually came together, and the adjutant climbed out of the dugout, and spoke to each man individually. He seemed a little perplexed as to what he should say. He looked at Bourne rather doubtfully.

"Feel you ought to go, Bourne?" he inquired, and passed on without waiting for a reply.

Sergeant Morgan smiled at Bourne.

"It'll be all right," he whispered, "just take a peek at 'em, give 'em a bit of a surprise and come back."

Bourne saw Whitfield there, and felt as though he would like to hunt in couples with him. Otherwise he felt quiet, almost indifferent, except for the sense of adventure that thrilled in him occasionally; and then, with that perversity of mind characteristic of him, he laughed at himself for a fool, and, when that phase passed, found himself thinking of Captain Marsden with an obscure resentment. Anyway, he argued, probably none of our actions are quite voluntary; if compulsion is not explicit, it is perhaps always implied. Then he found himself wondering whether the determination, which became stronger and stronger in him, was not after all his real self, which only needed the pressure of circumstances to elicit it.

They moved off into an empty stretch of trench, and there the officer explained to them what they had to do, Sergeant Morgan intervening occasionally. They were shown a sketch-plan of the enemy trenches, the point where it was proposed to enter, the post which, if occupied, they intended to attack, and then men were told off for their several jobs. Bourne found himself paired off with Weeper, with orders to hold the trench at a point where it made a junction with a communication trench running back to the support line, and give warning of the approach of any hostile party moving along the trench.

They were told also that there might be a machine-gun post in their neighbourhood, but this was not clear. Their duty, in short, was to cover a flank and give protection to the raiders. If they were obliged to use their bombs, they were to retire immediately on the rest of the party, without ceasing to give what protection might be possible. If a signal were given by whistle, they were to go straight for the lane in the wire, and if unable to rejoin the others, they were to make their way back to their own trenches as best they could. They were cautioned as to the danger from their own sentries, and warned as to the necessity of answering a challenge promptly.

Mr Cross, when he was satisfied that the men understood the plan as a whole as well as their individual parts in it, turned to the sergeant, and asked him if he had forgotten anything. The sergeant seemed to be quite certain that he had not, but thought it as well to go over the whole plan again himself. He was less insistent than the officer on the value of teamwork, and seemed more inclined to stress the fact that while the whole affair was a single action, in which their separate parts were co-ordinated, each man was expected to rely on himself and use his own judgment.

"You want to get the ball out into the loose, an' keep it movin'," he said by way of metaphor; and they seemed to relish it, even if they didn't quite understand how it applied.

Then they went back to their several companies, with orders to assemble at nine o'clock by the junction of Delaunay and Monk trenches. Weeper and Bourne were alone together after a few paces. "What 'opes 'ave us poor buggers got!" exclaimed Weeper.

"Why did you come, Smart? I thought it awfully decent of you," said Bourne.

"When a see'd that fuckin' slave driver look at 'ee, a said to mysen, Am comin'. A'll always say this for thee, tha'lt share all th'ast got wi' us'ns, and tha' don't call a man by any foolish nicknames. Am comin'. 'T won't be the first bloody raid a've been out on, lad. An' 'twon 'a be t' last. Th'ast no cause to worry. A can look after mysen, aye, an' thee too, lad. You leave it to me."

He was always the same; determination only made him more desperate. Bourne thought for a moment, and then, lifting his head, turned to his companion.

"I don't suppose Captain Marsden meant to put things that way, you know, Smart. It's just his manner. He would always do what he thought right."

Weeper turned on him a fierce but pitying glance. "Th'ast a bloody fool," was all he said.

It was enough. Bourne laughed softly to himself. He had always felt some instinctive antipathy against his company commander.

"I'll show the bastard," he said to himself in his own mind, "if I get a chance."

Chance. They were all balanced, equally, on a dangerous chance. One was not free, and therefore there would be very little merit in anything they might do. He followed Weeper down into the dugout.

Sergeant-Major Tozer was at the foot of the stairs, with Corporal Jakes.

"You want to look after yourself, see?" Tozer said, seriously. "Captain 'ad no right sendin' you like that."

"E's no bloody bottle, anyway," said Jakes.

"You don't want to talk like that," said the sergeant-major, and then, turning to Bourne: "there's a drop of 'ot tea there, wi' a tot o' rum in it, you can 'ave if you like."

"No thanks, sergeant-major," said Bourne; "but keep my ration for when I get back. And don't worry about me. I'm all right. I want to go."

He knew that he did, then, very definitely. It was a part of his road, to whatever place it might lead; and he went to sit down by Weeper Smart. They talked together a little, not very much. They did not talk to anyone else, but, from time to time, one of the other men would look at them in a kind of disinterested speculation. The mist was luminous in the moonlight, but very variable, clouding and clearing, hurrying away on the wind, which was not strong enough to dissipate it entirely. One question was, would it last long enough? They had daubed their faces with mud. Starting at a walk, they dropped after a little while, and crawled slowly and cautiously forward. The mud had become moderately firm under the frost, which was not hard enough to coat the puddles with ice to crack under their weight with the sound of splintering glass.

There were a few pauses, when Sergeant Morgan whispered to the officer; and once again Bourne felt inclined to laugh, for some of the men breathed heavily, like oxen, in the night. At last there was a definite pause; and Whitfield wriggled forward with another man. They waited, listening intently. It was very silent now. Suddenly a machine-gun started to chatter, but it was only an admonition. Once they heard the vibration of a wire, and a rattle, and, listening intently, they ceased to breathe. Bourne and Weeper were next to a man with a mace, some of the men called it a kosher-stick, and Bourne looked at it curiously. He felt very cool, but it seemed a long time to wait there. At last Whitfield came back. Then he led the way forward again, the sergeant following immediately afterwards, then came Mr Cross, and the men with maces, and the rest of the party.

Bourne found himself crawling over a mat of wire, rusty in the mud; loose strands of it tore his trousers to tatters, and it was slow work getting through. He was mortally afraid of setting some of the strands singing along the line. Every sound he made seemed extraordinarily magnified. Every sense seemed to be stretched to an exquisite apprehension. He was through. He saw Whitfield and the other man slip into the trench, and out the other side. Sergeant Morgan gave him the direction with his hand. Weeper passed him, and he followed, trying to memorise the direction, so that he would be able to find his way back to the gap in the wire. They crossed almost together, Weeper taking his hand and pulling him up the other side without apparent effort. The man was as strong as an ape. Then they wormed their way forward again, until they found their position, where the communication trench formed a rather sharp angle with the fire-trench. The fire-trench itself still showed the effects of their bombardment; after passing the communication trench it changed its direction in a rather pronounced way, running forward as though to converge more closely on the British line. They were now in a shellhole, or rather two shellholes, which had formed one, Weeper looking down the communication trench and Bourne along the fire-trench.

The mist was very light now, it looked as though it might almost clear. Bourne shifted his position slightly, to get more comfortable. He already had a bomb ready, with his finger in the ring of the safety pin. As he moved, he saw, not ten yards away, a faint gleam of yellowish light, that had none of the spectral pallor of moonlight. He kicked Weeper, and pointed silently. The gleam came again. It came from a large shellhole curtained over, probably by a camouflaged tarpaulin; and something moving inside pressed against the slit by which men entered, displacing it almost imperceptibly, so that there came from it, every now and then, a winking gleam of light. He heard Weeper mutter something no louder than a sigh. Farther, much farther, away, a star-shell shot up into the sky.

Suddenly they heard a shout, a scream, faint sounds of struggle, and some muffled explosions from underground. Almost, immediately the machine-gun in front of them broke into stuttering barks; they could see the quick spurting flashes in front of it; and Bourne threw his bomb, which went straight for the crack in the curtain. Ducking, he had another ready and threw that, but Weeper had already thrown. The three explosions followed in rapid succession. They heard a whistle. The machine-gun was out of action, but Weeper, leaping towards its wreckage, gave them another, and rushed Bourne into the trench. They saw through the mist their own party already by the gap, and Weeper's parting bomb exploded.

The party under Mr Cross had made a slight encircling movement, and then, after creeping forward until within striking distance, rushed the trench. As the sentry turned, one of the maces crashed into his temple, and another man finished him with a bayonet. There were two other Huns in the same bay, and one had his arm broken with a mace, and screamed. Simultaneously the dugout was bombed, and a couple of men hurled themselves on the third Hun, a Prussian sergeant, who put up a fight, but was overmastered, and lifted, booted, hustled out of the trench. They killed any survivors in the dugout, and another Prussian had been killed in the next bay.

While they were forcing the sergeant and the man with the broken arm towards the wire, they heard Weeper and Bourne bombing the machine-gun post, and Mr Cross blow his whistle. Almost immediately a star-shell went up, and there was some blind desultory rifle fire. They had got their men through the wire. Suddenly the Hun sergeant, with a desperate effort, wrenched himself free, and faced them with lifted hand:

"Halte!' he shouted, and flung himself on Sergeant Morgan. They went down together. Mr Cross fired, and fortunately killed the Prussian.

"I hope you'll never do that again, sir!" said Sergeant Morgan, rising.

"Get his helmet off."

The chain was tight in the thick fat under the chin. Taking his bayonet, the sergeant tried to prise it off, and cut through all the soft part of the neck so that the head fell back. The helmet came away in the end, and they pushed on, with their other moaning prisoner. Weeper was ahead when he and Bourne reached the gap in the wire. Star-shell after star-shell was going up now, and the whole line had woken up. Machine-guns were talking, but there was one that would not talk. The rattle of musketry continued, but the mist was kindly to them, and had thickened again. As they got beyond the trammelling, clutching wire, Bourne saw Weeper a couple of paces ahead of him, and what he thought was the last of their party disappearing into the mist about twenty yards away. He was glad to be clear of the wire. Another star-shell went up, and they both froze into stillness under its glare. Then they moved again, hurrying for all they were worth. Bourne felt a sense of triumph and escape thrill in him. Anyway the Hun couldn't see them now. Something kicked him in the upper part of the chest, rending its way through him, and his agonised cry was scarcely audible in the rush of blood from his mouth, as he collapsed and fell.

Weeper turned his head over his shoulder, listened, stopped, and went back. He found Bourne trying to lift himself; and Bourne spoke, gasping, suffocating.

"Go on. I'm scuppered."

"A'll not leave thee," said Weeper.

He stooped and lifted the other in his huge, ungainly arms, carrying him as tenderly as though he were a child. Bourne struggled wearily to speak, and the blood, filling his mouth, prevented him. Sometimes his head fell on Weeper's shoulder. At last, barely articulate, a few words came.

"I'm finished. Le' me in peace, for God's sake. You can't..."

"A'll not leave thee," said Weeper in an infuriate rage.

He felt Bourne stretch himself in a convulsive shudder, and relax, becoming suddenly heavier in his arms. He struggled on, stumbling over the shell-ploughed ground through that fantastic mist, which moved like an army of wraiths, hurrying away from him. Then he stopped, and, taking the body by the waist with his left arm, flung it over his shoulder, steadying it with his right. He could see their wire now, and presently he was challenged, and replied. He found the way through the wire, and staggered into the trench with his burden. Then he turned down the short stretch of Delaunay to Monk Trench, and came on the rest of the party outside A Company's dugout.

"A've brought 'im back," he cried desperately, and collapsed with the body on the duck-boards. Picking himself up again, he told his story incoherently, mixed with raving curses.

"What are you gibbering about?" said Sergeant Morgan. "Aven't you ever seen a dead man before?"

Sergeant-Major Tozer, who was standing outside the dugout, looked at Morgan with a dangerous eye. Then he put a hand on Weeper's shoulder.

"Go down an' get some 'ot tea and rum, of man. That'll do you good. I'd like to 'ave a talk with you when you're feelin' better."

"We had better move on, sergeant," said Mr Cross, quietly.

"Very good, sir."

The party moved off, and for a moment Sergeant-Major Tozer was alone in the trench with Sergeant Morgan.

"I saw him this side of their wire, sergeant-major, and thought everything would be all right. 'Pon my word, I would 'ave gone back for 'im myself, if I'd known."

"It was hard luck," said Sergeant-Major Tozer with a quiet fatalism.

Sergeant Morgan left him, and the sergeant-major looked at the dead body propped against the side of the trench. He would have to have it moved; it wasn't a pleasant sight, and he bared his teeth in the pitiful repulsion with which it filled him. Bourne was sitting, his head back, his face plastered with mud, and blood drying thickly about his mouth and chin, while the glazed eyes stared up at the moon. Tozer moved away, with a quiet acceptance of the fact. It was finished. He was sorry about Bourne, he thought, more sorry than he could say. He was a queer chap, he said to himself, as he felt for the dugout steps. There was a bit of a mystery about him; but then, when you come to think of it, there's a bit of mystery about all of us. He pushed aside the blanket screening the entrance, and in the murky light he saw all the men lift their faces, and look at him with patient, almost animal eyes.

Then they all bowed over their own thoughts again, listening to the shells bumping heavily outside, as Fritz began to send a lot of stuff over in retaliation for the raid. They sat there silently, each man keeping his own secret.